Deeds and Words

Sarah Bell

This book is written in British English and therefore uses British spelling, punctuation and grammar.

Chapter One

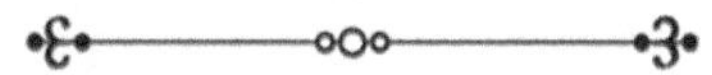

The Missing Maid

Leeds, West Riding of Yorkshire
June 1913

Something was burning. The acrid scent stung at the back of Ada's nostrils, and she froze with a hairpin halfway towards her head, her confusion reflected in the vanity table mirror.

Has Sophie burnt breakfast? A quick glance at the clock on the bedside cabinet confirmed it was half ten, far past when Louisa rose for the day. Ada's waking patterns and habits had been so unpredictable recently that Sophie never started cooking her breakfast till she was already downstairs in the dining room.

Letting her unpinned hair tumble back down into loose curls, Ada made her way downstairs to investigate. All she found in the sitting room, though, was the cat they had adopted in the winter months—or, more precisely, the cat who had adopted them. The tortoiseshell had snuck into their kitchen near Christmas, and no one had the heart to kick the skinny thing back out into the cold. Ada remained unconvinced they would've succeeded if they'd tried. Not if the glare currently aimed at her for having the audacity to wake the cat up was anything to judge by.

'Ey up, Gal. What's that smell, eh?' Ada scratched her behind her ears, and she settled into a slow purr, oblivious to the fact the house could be burning down around them. 'And where is everyone?' But Gal provided no answers, only stretched and settled back into her sunny spot on the pale lemon damask sofa.

The dining room was also empty, of both humans and cats, and so, following her nose more than anything, Ada headed down the servants' stairwell towards the kitchen. She pushed the door open to be greeted by a haze of smoke that stung her eyes and made her cough and a smell of burning so overwhelming, she pictured the kitchen aflame. From somewhere inside, a posh accent muttered a couple of mild curse words.

'Louisa?' Ada flapped at the smoke in front of her face, still coughing. 'What are you doing?'

The haze cleared to reveal the kitchen. The room was dominated by the sturdy black cast iron oven that had first enticed the cat into their home, and a dishevelled Louisa stood in front of it. Ada did a double take. A stained beige apron covered Louisa's moss green skirt and white blouse, the latter's sleeves rolled up to her elbows. Her usually serene oval face was bright red and framed with sweaty strands of flyaway light brown hair, fallen out of her wilting low pompadour.

'Oh, morning!' Louisa's voice came out an octave higher than usual. 'I did not hear you get up. And I am making breakfast.' She waved at a plate on the counter besides the oven, which contained two blackened lumps that may once have been bread.

Ada turned towards the plate and then back to Louisa, eyebrows raised.

'Or attempting to, anyway. I may have burnt the toast.'

'*May have*?' Ada said with a laugh, moving closer towards the counter to peer at the two sad charred squares.

'I have definitely burnt the toast.' Louisa attempted to blow a runaway strand of hair out of her face, but it flopped back.

'Here.' Ada stepped close and tucked the defiant strand behind Louisa's ear, vividly remembering all the times Louisa had done the same when Ada's curls refused to be controlled. 'Now, who has unruly hair?'

'At least most of mine is still in its pins.' Louisa replaced the ghost fingers of Ada's memories with a feather soft touch, twisting one of the loose ginger curls.

'Touche.' Which was a French word Louisa had taught her. 'Good morning, anyway.' She stood on her tiptoes to brush a light kiss against Louisa's lips. 'Now, I have to ask, why are you making—attempting to make, sorry—toast? Where's Sophie?' Ada stepped backwards from their embrace and looked around the kitchen, as if the maid might suddenly appear or at least pop out from within the pantry.

'I could not say. She was simply not here when I got up this morning.'

'What?' Ada jerked her head back round to look at Louisa.

'At first, I assumed she was unwell, but I have been up to her room, and she is not there. And I have found no note or anything.'

'What do you mean? 'ow can she not be 'ere?' In her surprise, her accent reverted to its more Yorkshire variant.

'I am sure there is an explanation. Sophie would not do something like this without good reason.'

Ada snorted. 'That's a lot more lenient than most employers would be.' Realising how that sounded, she rushed to add, 'Though that's no insult, mind you. Nevertheless, I've known enough people who work in service t' know you can't just...not be there. Shirking your work? Yes, fine, everyone does it and who can blame them. But you at least have to be there to look like you're working. You can't not show up. Plenty of servants get fired for less. Again—and I cannot stress this enough—not a suggestion. Not that I think you would fire Sophie.'

'I did not take it as one. Besides, you know it is a rather mutually beneficial arrangement.'

'Yes,' Ada agreed sarcastically. 'That's the only reason.'

'It is some of the reason.'

'And is this the rest of the reason?' Ada pointed at the black lumps of dubious toast. 'Have you ever even had to make your own breakfast before? Honestly, you fancy people, you'd be helpless without us.' As she spoke, Ada moved to the long counter across from the oven, where half a loaf of bread sat on a chopping board. The edge was uneven, evidence that someone unskilled with a bread knife—Louisa—had been attempting to cut a slice.

Louisa replied as Ada cut, 'You forget I lived alone for a while.' Ada did indeed try to forget that. The image of Louisa rattling around this big house alone always pulled at her heartstrings.

'Yeah, well, you're not alone anymore.' She turned and pointed at Louisa, who took a hasty step back. Only then did Ada factor in the knife still in her hand, and she rapidly put it down. 'You could've come and asked me for help.' She stepped towards Louisa and took one of her hands in both of her own, which admittedly was the more traditional way of comforting one's partner.

'I did not want to wake you.' But Louisa smiled.

'Well, I'm awake now.' She gave a soft squeeze to Louisa's hand, then turned her attention back to the bread and cut off three more slices, making a mess of crumbs as she did. She would have to tidy up before Sophie came back from wherever she was. Whatever was happening with her, the last thing she needed was them messing up her kitchen.

Worry gnawed at Ada's stomach as she placed the toast into the oven. Louisa was right to say Sophie would most likely have a sensible explanation, but Ada couldn't even begin to guess what it might be, for this was so unlike Sophie's usual behaviour. There was little to do but wait for her to return. Or not return.

No, don't think like that. How much trouble can Sophie, of all people, get into? Unless there's another pretty maid involved, of course. That last thought did little to ease her concern. But no, Sophie had learnt that lesson the hard way. Surely, she wouldn't repeat her mistakes.

She's still only a girl of seventeen. How many silly risks did Mabel and I take at that age? And a pretty girl is always going to be a pretty girl. Some mistakes are made to be repeated. Ada kept that line of thinking to herself, pushing aside the usual dull stab of pain that accompanied thoughts of Mabel. Her regrets for how it ended, her frustration at seeing her former lover stuck in gaol for the death of a man who got what was coming to him.

Once she had removed edible toast from the oven, with a flourish that earnt her a well-natured eye roll, they returned upstairs to the dining room. In the morning light, Ada's redecoration was even more obvious. Last year, Louisa had finally agreed to her stripping the room of its dark furniture and décor—except for the mahogany dresser that contained her late mother's China—and replace it with the light shades she had installed across the house.

Ada's head jerked round at the creaking open of the door from the hallway, but it was only the cat who plunked herself beside Louisa's chair, looking up hopefully.

Louisa reached down to stroke Gal's head, who turned to sniff her fingers instead. 'Sorry, Galapagos, nothing for you today.' The full name was Louisa's doing, obviously, for who else would name a tortoiseshell cat after an obscure tortoise fact?

Ada smiled despite herself. 'You are still banned from naming any and all future pets.' Gal might not be their missing maid, but she was a welcome distraction from the worry nonetheless.

'Well, that ruins my plans for our future menagerie.'

Ada chuckled, then took a bite of her toast. It wasn't half bad, if she did say so herself, though she shouldn't be proud of managing to cook toast; living with Louisa had turned her soft.

Louisa also took a bite and nodded approvingly. 'This is good. Much better than my attempt.'

'Louisa, Gal could have done better than you did.' She smiled to gild the insult. 'And don't change the subject. I want to hear more about these menagerie plans.'

Gal meowed at Louisa's feet in protest at the idea of having to share them with other animals. Or, more likely, in protest of the fact the humans had not deigned to share their food yet.

Louisa reached down to stroke her again. 'How is your painting of her coming along, anyhow?'

Now there was a topic that could keep Ada talking and distracted for a while, and she seized it gratefully. Once it was exhausted, she moved onto how she hoped to get out this morning to do some sketching since the weather was fine—hence her proper dress, half-unpinned hair aside, instead of her usual painting wear of a man's shirt and trousers. She spoke like it was still a possibility, as if whatever had happened to Sophie was something inconsequential that didn't affect their plans for the day. Louisa's half-hearted responses, a token effort at best, belied the truth it was not.

Ada had poured herself a second cup of tea and moved the conversation onto Louisa's latest read when the click and slam of the front door interrupted. Louisa's speech trailed off, and they both turned once more towards the door to the hallway.

Sophie jumped when she entered the dining room to find both her employer, her employer's companion, and their cat staring at the doorway, awaiting her arrival. Her eyes were red-rimmed, and Ada jumped out of her seat at the same time Louisa said, 'Sophie, what has happened? What is wrong?'

'I'm sorry, ma'am.' Sophie's words came out in a garbled rush. 'I didn't mean to be so late. It's just... it's just that...' She gasped, a small sobbing noise, and then cried in earnest, a hand pushed to her mouth, muting the apologies that continued to spill out of her. 'I'm sorry, I can't, I'm sorry, I'll stop, I...' She wiped at her eyes with shaking hands but could not stem the flood of tears.

Ada patted her dress, confirming this was one with pockets—Mum's sewing lessons coming in handy—and searched for a handkerchief, but found only two ha'pennies, a button, and a sticky sweet.

'Excuse me, ma'am, I should get t' work.' Sophie nearly tripped over the cat, now twisting round her feet, as she turned and fled through the open door, her footsteps echoing up the stairs. With a meow, Gal followed.

A brief silence fell as her footsteps receded and into it, Ada voiced her confusion. 'What was that about?'

Louisa stood with an unused handkerchief held out in her hand and her mouth open as though mid-sentence, staring at the door. 'I have no idea.'

'Should we...' Ada gestured in the vague direction of upstairs and the distressed maid.

Louisa nodded. 'Yes. I mean we cannot leave her in such a state.'

'Of course, but I'm not sure if she wants to talk. She did just run away from us.'

'Let us give her a moment then, but she will need to explain herself.' Louisa sat back down.

Ada rolled her eyes but joined her at the table. 'Oh, don't hide your concern behind snobby *I'm her employer* tactics.' In the early days they might have argued about that, but Ada knew Louisa too well now not to see the concern hidden behind the statement.

They were quiet as they finished the last of their tea. Ada no longer felt capable of keeping up a conversation and pretending nothing was wrong, and Louisa must have felt the same. Once they had drained their cups, they stood by silent mutual agreement and went upstairs. They found Sophie in their room; she sat on the bed with the cat standing in her lap, its head pressed against her face where tears still streamed. A litany of Louisa's dresses spread across the bed beside her implied she had begun some work prior to the scene before them.

She looked over at their entry and shifted as if to remove the cat and stand.

'It's fine.' Louisa motioned for her to remain seated. 'Stay where you are.'

'Can I help you, ma'am? I'm sorry about before. It won't happen again. And I'll catch up with everything I have to do.' Her voice shook as she spoke, and her hands worked their way into Gal's fur, who bore it with much greater patience than usual.

'That is not why I came to talk to you. Can you tell us what happened this morning? Where were you? Something has clearly caused you great distress.'

'It's nowt, ma'am.' She sighed, frustrated. 'Nothing. It will not happen again, I promise.'

Ada's impatience bubbled over. 'Sophie, we don't care about you not being here. We care 'cos you came in crying your eyes out.'

'I know,' Sophie muttered. She looked down at the cat, scratching her ears. 'But I don't know how to tell you.'

'Are you in trouble?' Louisa said softly, stepping forward. 'A similar sort of trouble to before?'

But why would Sophie hesitate to tell them that? If anyone wouldn't judge her for being caught kissing another girl, it was them. Unless she was ashamed of allowing herself to be caught again.

She gave the slightest shake of her head. 'No.' An amused smile curled at the corner of her lips. 'Definitely not. It's about a boy, you see.' And all traces of amusement fell from her face. 'They're going to hang 'im.' Sobs overtook her body then, shaking Gal, who jumped down with a distressed meow.

Ada sat beside Sophie and pulled her sideways into a hug as old memories of Mabel looped through her brain, real and imagined. How many times had she pictured Mabel's hanging? Her thin neck in a noose and the trapdoor slamming open beneath her feet. The unthinkable happenstance that, for a few months, had been such a crushing, haunting possibility.

Louisa, too, moved to sit beside her. Once Sophie's sobbing had rescinded, she asked, 'Who is he?', her voice still soft.

'His name's Artie, short for Arthur. He's my age, turned seventeen last month.'

Still old enough to hang then, even under the Children's Charter.

'And he goes to my church, here in Roundhay. You know I stopped going to my mum's church after, well, what happened.'

'So, he is from around here?'

'No, but he works in the park, as an apprentice gardener.'

Ada asked the more important question. 'Do you like him?' It came out more disbelieving than intended.

'I do.' Sophie didn't explain beyond that.

'You do?' Louisa repeated, bemused.

Ada shared her surprise. She'd never thought of the possibility of Sophie fancying boys, even though she knew it was possible to like both. Louisa should have, too, since it was her sexology texts that had taught Ada that fact. But Sophie had never mentioned an interest in boys before. Then again, she had never talked about her attractions with them, because why would she? It was not an appropriate conversation between maid and mistress.

Sophie nodded. 'I do. I know that might come as a surprise given, well, what happened, but I really do, ma'am. I've liked him ever since I first saw him, sat in the opposite pew, though I know I shouldn't be thinking about such things at church. And he's been so kind to me. I never thought I could enjoy being with someone so much. Not after...'

'How long have you been seeing this boy?' Louisa asked.

'A few months. We've been stepping out on our half-days or whenever we can. We went dancing last week when you gave me the night off. And you know I rarely enjoy dancing, but it was so much fun with him. Every time I got nervous, he said something to make me laugh, and I forgot. And we weren't very good, kept stepping on each other's toes, but I had such a great time. I think I finally understand why people enjoy dancing, even enough to rearrange the furniture.' Dawning horror creeped across the girl's face as she realised she had taken a dig at her employer, and she hurried quickly on, 'And we go 'round park after church. He was telling me about all the different flowers and plants. Oh! I never told you—he helped me figure out what that new flower is int' garden, the one I couldn't find in your books. It's a lady's slipper orchid. And—'

'He sounds lovely, Sophie.' And he did. And no one deserved a chance at love more than Sophie. Which meant Ada did not want to ask the follow up question.

'He does,' Louisa agreed. She hesitated, clearly also not wanting to ask. Ada prepared herself to speak into the silence and had opened her mouth to do so, when Louisa continued, 'So, can you tell us what has happened to him? He...has been arrested?'

Sophie stared at her, eyes wide, but no answer came.

'Sophie?' Ada prompted. *What has he done? This boy who she painted such a kind picture of. And who a sweet girl like Sophie has taken a shine to. Then again, Sophie also took a shine to the other maid at the Gotts' house, and she'd turned out to be a piece of work.*

'It's a mistake,' she said. 'It's not true. It can't be true.' She shook her head frantically as she spoke. 'It can't.'

'What's a mistake?' Ada asked.

'A man was shot.'

Foreboding snaked its way around her heart.

A man was stabbed. It had been Davey who told her. After the police took Mabel away and the whole neighbourhood was ablaze with gossip about what had happened at the mill, rumours and tall tales piling up on top of one and another, each more ludicrous than the last. He was the one to lay it bare before her, to tell her, in not so many words, that her entire life was about to be pulled apart.

'Do they think he did it?' Ada asked.

Louisa gasped, but Sophie nodded, her eyes on the floor. 'But he didn't. I swear he didn't. He'd never do owt like that.'

'She didn't do it. I won't believe it. It's not true.'

But Mabel did.

And maybe this Artie did, too.

She couldn't say that, but any words of comfort stuck in her throat. Her mum had told her so many times that everything would be alright in the end. But it wasn't alright. It never truly would be.

Over Sophie's head, Ada sent a pleading look to Louisa to fill the silence.

'Do you know anything else? Who was shot? Where?'

A tiny shake of her head. 'From what I've heard, it happened at a pub in town, but Artie doesn't drink much. And why would he go int' town? There are plenty of pubs up near mansion if he did want t' drink. It doesn't make sense, but I couldn't find owt else out. They wouldn't let me speak to 'im. He's down at Millgarth, and that awful police sergeant snapped at me, the one who was so mean last year, and none of the constables would tell me owt. I was gonna mention Miss Chapman, but...'

'I'm not exactly in their good books right now, either.' They had not requested her assistance as a sketch artist since last October. Inspector Lambert was still certain they had interfered further on the Pearce case and was fuming about being hoodwinked by two silly women. Davey, meanwhile, knew for sure they had, having helped cover it up; that added an awkwardness to their friendship which had never been there before.

'How did you find out?' Louisa asked. 'Who told you?'

'Mrs Yates, who works across street. She goes to our church, too, and she knew we were close. Said she'd heard it from someone who works up at mansion—that they'd arrested him and some suffragette. Some friend of his sister's, maybe? No one seemed to think it was his sister, at least, and I'd have thought they would've known if it was. You know how servants gossip. Or...maybe you don't.'

'Oh, I have an idea,' Ada said. 'The things I could tell you about some of Leeds' "leading families".'

'Ada.' Louisa turned to face her. The 'not now' went unsaid, which was fair enough. 'Do you think the police would be willing to speak to you?'

Ada considered it. 'Depends who's there. Davey, maybe. Smith, almost certainly; that boy'll take any chance to talk. Sergeant Potter, definitely not. It might be worth the attempt, though.' She had to try. For Sophie's sake. If they could do more than sit around and say 'it can't be true' and 'it'll be alright' then they had to take that chance.

'Will you, miss?' Sophie seemed to perk up at the idea, her gratefulness clear in every inch of her.

'Of course.' Ada squeezed Sophie's shoulder.

'Oh, thank you.'

'Do you want to come with us?' Louisa asked.

'Oh, um, maybe?' She frowned. 'Or maybe not. It might be better if I don't. I've already been told they don't need unbidden maids underfoot once today.'

'Yes, three women invading his police station at the same time may give Potter a...' Ada turned to Louisa. 'What's it called when a vein pops?'

'Do you mean an aneurysm?'

'Maybe. Probably. Anyway, he'll have one of those.'

Louisa snorted, an unladylike sound that never ceased to amuse Ada when she made it, and even Sophie hid a smile.

But then Louisa turned serious again. 'Perhaps it is best you stay home then.'

'Yes, and I should get back to work. I'm sorry again, ma'am.' Sophie stood from the bed and turned to face the spread of clothing, where Gal had nested herself into the centre 'Oh, kitty, you're not supposed t' be there, shoo!' But Sophie's scolding was half-heartened, and the cat did not move.

'There is no need to worry about work today,' Louisa said. 'And this is hardly the first time my clothes have been infected with cat hair in recent months.'

Sophie gave a watery smile. 'I am aware of that, ma'am. But no, I should work. It'll be good to have something to think about.' She said it brightly, but Ada was not sure who she was trying to convince, them or herself?

'Then we should be off,' Louisa also stood and turned to Ada. 'Though perhaps you should sort your hair out first. As much as I am a fan of your curls...'

Ada waved a hand at her head. 'This is not appropriate for leaving the house? Though, um, I'm not sure I'm the only one who needs to control my hair.'

Louisa frowned and turned to the mirror. She laughed at her reflection, hands trying to flatten her runaway strands. 'Fair point.'

'Miss Knight tried to make toast,' Ada said as an aside to Sophie.

'Oh no,' the maid muttered, her fluttering hands stilling on the dress she was trying to rescue from the pile on the bed.

'You'll be glad to know you still have a kitchen.'

Ada glanced over at Louisa's reflection in the mirror, who attempted to glare back at her but failed. Her eyes held far too much fondness, and a warmth spread through Ada.

Sophie rather wisely ignored the digs at her mistress' attempt at cooking. 'Do you need help with your hair, miss?'

'Please.'

Louisa moved aside so Ada could sit at the vanity table, her own hair already smoothed and pinned back into place.

'Show off,' Ada muttered, craning her head backwards to look up at Louisa, so her runaway curls flowed behind her. 'I'm going to get it all chopped off one day. Just you wait.'

Louisa bent and kissed her forehead, a soft lingering touch. 'Don't you dare.' She twisted a couple of curls through her fingers once more, and Ada nearly asked Sophie to leave them be, for there were other—better—uses for those long, elegant fingers.

But no. They needed to focus. There was a life at stake here. And Sophie's happiness. Now was not the time for frivolity.

'Are you going to let Sophie deal with this mop of mine or not?'

Louisa's hands fell, and she stepped back to let Sophie begin the arduous task of trying to tame Ada's unruly hair.

Ada considered their options as the maid set to work. They would need to come up with a plan, but it would be better to discuss that without Sophie present. Any plan would need to include the possibility this Artie boy was guilty.

But for now, Ada gave him the benefit of the doubt. They would have to see what information came to light. If any. There were no guarantees the police would tell them anything and every chance they could end up going up against the inspector and his constables again if the police had already decided they had found their suspects and didn't wish to be challenged.

With a final twist, Sophie finished pinning Ada's hair into two neat side swirls and fetched a light straw summer hat with a lemon-yellow ribbon that matched her dress to top it.

'Right then,' Louisa said. 'Shall we?' She had located and pinned her own hat—a dark green picture hat with minimal trimming, only a couple of feathers—into place during Ada's distraction.

'Thank you again, ma'am, miss.' Sophie's words were a whisper.

'Of course, Sophie,' Louisa said. 'But you understand we can make no promises?'

She nodded, her face grim.

Ada stood. Perhaps they could make no promises, but that didn't mean she couldn't hope for a happier ending this time.

Chapter Two

An Unexpected Ally

Millgarth Police Station was a squat, militant building, still as grey and miserable as the last time Louisa had been here. With determination, she strode towards it, careful to make no outward sign of the nerves pooling in the pit of her stomach. She would not allow herself to be intimidated by it or its officers.

At her side, Ada kept pace and gave her a quick, fleeting smile of encouragement, its message clear: we can do this; we are in this together. Louisa wanted to reach out and take her hand but resisted. Whilst their relationship might not be illegal, it was still playing with fire to walk into a police station clasping hands.

A vaguely familiar constable sat at the front desk; he must have been one she met during the Pearce case. He glanced over in their direction, bored, but surprise spread across his face as his gaze locked onto them. 'Huh.' A small, amused sound. 'Inspector was right. Wait there.' He stepped out from behind the desk and hurried through a door into the depths of the station without another word.

'It would appear our interference was expected.'

Ada frowned. 'Why do I suspect that's not a good thing?'

'What do you mean? Inspector Lambert loves it when we interfere with his cases,' Louisa deadpanned.

A short huff of laughter was Ada's only response.

'Do you think the inspector will at least let us meet this boy?' What sort of person was he, this boy Sophie cried over?

The sort who gets arrested for murder.

But Sophie had spoken so warmly of him.

Then again, Sophie did not have the best track record of whom she fell in love with.

'I couldn't say. I was rather hoping we'd be able to convince one of constables t' be 'onest with you.' Ada's accent slipped into its broader version, a sign of her agitation. Her eyes flickered across the station foyer as if its blue wallpaper and wood panelling would give her the answers they sought.

'This way.' The constable had returned, standing in the inner doorway. They hurried over, Ada leading the way. Once they reached him, he contemplated Ada. 'Actually, you don't need me to show you inspector's office, do you? It hasn't changed since you were last 'ere.'

'I don't know, Goodwin. That was a while back now.'

'Yes... well...' He tugged at the collar of his dark navy constable's jacket. 'We both know why that is, don't we?'

'I suppose we do.' Ada's voice was taut, her head jutting upwards, refusing to be cowered.

Louisa fought to stop herself from smiling at the sight of Ada staring down a clearly somewhat intimidated police officer.

He caved first, stepping aside and averting his gaze to nod towards the corridor beyond. 'Go on then.'

Ada stomped off down the corridor, and Louisa followed in what she hoped was a more sedate manner, though she had to rush a little to keep up.

How does someone with such short legs move so fast when she wants to?

The corridor remained as depressing as it had been a year ago, the same dull grey walls and carpet. 'Funny to think the last time I was here, I was under arrest.'

Ada slowed and turned back to face her with a smirk. 'In hindsight, it is kind of hilarious you got arrested.'

Louisa's lip quirked in response, but any amusement disappeared as Ada stopped outside a brown wooden door, and apprehension twisted up her spine. They had come here for Sophie, who waited at home, distraught, and to save her from the same fate a younger Ada had suffered. To prove a boy's innocence and spare his life. Or, if he was guilty, at least provide Sophie with the truth instead of leaving her to be eaten by doubt for the rest of her life.

Ada raised a fist to the door but paused mid-motion and glanced over her shoulder at Louisa, who nodded.

She knocked.

A few seconds later, the door clicked open, and Inspector Lambert filled the frame. He also had not changed since their arrest. A tall man of middling age, with a stern pale face undercut by ridiculous outdated sideburns.

'Ah.' He stepped inside to let them through. 'I knew I could rely on you two.'

'Sir?' Ada paused halfway across the room and turned to face him near the doorway.

Louisa moved a step or two further into the room, past Ada, her attention caught by his messy desk. Files lay open, their contents overflowing. Beside the chaos of paperwork stood a decanter half-full of an amber liquid – most likely whiskey – and a tumbler with a few drops remaining at the bottom.

It was the desk of a man in the midst of a professional crisis.

But why would a shooting at a public house throw a police inspector into such disarray? I doubt it is that common an occurrence, but also not a particular cause for concern. Except perhaps as an excuse for the newspapers to further decry the decaying morals of the labouring class. That last sarcastic part was Ada's opinions sneaking into her thoughts. It happened more and more nowadays.

She stepped closer, trying to read one of the papers. A report, by the looks of it; nothing out of the ordinary for a man like Inspector Lambert.

'Nosy as ever, I see, Miss Knight.'

She jumped and stepped back, heat rushing to her cheeks. She should have been subtler but had thought his attention caught by Ada.

'I never took you as a man to have such a disorganised desk.'

'He's not,' Ada chimed in before he could reply. She kept her focus on him as he shut the door behind them. 'Not usually.'

'Not usually,' he agreed. 'But today has been a most trying day, and it is not even noon yet.' He moved to his seat behind his desk and gestured to the chair opposite him.

Ada waved Louisa into it.

'Why?' Louisa asked. 'What has happened?'

'I assume your maid told you she was here earlier.'

Louisa nodded. She could not see Ada stood to her side, not without turning, but imagined she had done the same.

'And how her sweetheart is sitting in our cells? Though not for much longer.'

'You're letting him go?' Hope rang in Ada's voice, and, despite herself, Louisa's heart lifted. Could it really, truly, be this easy?

But Inspector Lambert shook his head, and her hopes crashed as quickly as they had soared. *Of course not.*

'Another inspector is taking over the case. Inspector Brenner from over at Kirkstall Road Station.'

'But town's not their jurisdiction. We've – you've – always had that *honour*.' Ada's emphasis made it obvious how much of an honour he considered it.

'It's been deemed there is a conflict of interest, so I cannot investigate the case.' He paused and stared over at Ada. 'But you can.'

A beat of silence followed that statement. Was this the same man who had lectured them – on two separate occasions – not to interfere with his cases? Who had warned of dire consequences and even arrested them to emphasise his threat?

The silence stretched on. Louisa waited for the outburst that was sure to come, but Ada remained quiet. Daring a glance to her right, Louisa took in her partner's blank face and how she'd bunched her hands into tight fists.

Perhaps it was wiser for Louisa to respond.

'You wish for us to investigate?'

'Why?' The question was a bullet shot from Ada's mouth before he could even begin to formulate an answer.

'We have a common goal. We're on the same side in this, Miss Chapman, so if you could please refrain from striking me, that would be greatly appreciated.' He glanced down at her curled fists. 'I would hate to have to arrest you for assaulting an officer.'

'Would you?'

'No one is assaulting anyone.' Louisa sent a glance in Ada's direction she hoped carried an obvious message. *We need his help.*

Ada's hands flexed, and she crossed her arms over her chest instead, scowling.

Fighting down the urge to reach out and soothe her anger, Louisa turned back to the inspector. 'You mentioned a common goal?'

'You want to know who killed Mr Richardson.' This must be their dead man. 'I want to know who killed Mr Richardson.'

'Why?' Again, Ada forced the word through her clenched teeth.

'Did your maid tell you about the woman we've arrested?'

Louisa tried to remember what woman Sophie had mentioned, but Ada got there first. 'The suffragette?'

'No,' he barked. 'She's not a real suffragette.'

'A fake suffragette?' Scepticism oozed from Ada.

But the penny dropped for Louisa. 'A spy. And on your payroll, I presume? Hence the conflict of interest.'

'You hired someone to spy on them?' Ada scoffed. 'You know, it'd be simpler to just let women vote.'

He sighed. 'I'm not here to debate the merits of the female vote with you. And as for why a spy was necessary, just open your newspapers, Miss Chapman. Three men dead in that arson attack in Bradford two days ago, and now one of yours dead soon enough.'

'One of ours? What sort of threat is that?'

But dread flooded through Louisa as Inspector Lambert shuffled through the mess of paper on his desk. What now? More letter bombs? Another fire? Or a bigger bomb, this time? Had one of the explosives not been found in time and carnage followed?

No, he said one of yours, meaning the suffragettes. One of them has gotten hurt.

Had playing with gunpowder finally backfired? Or the hunger strikes? Or had the police gone too far and a protest turned deadly?

'The newsboys,' Ada muttered, then looked over at Louisa. 'When we were walking through town, they were all shouting about the suffragettes.'

Louisa had paid them little attention at the time, trying to order her thoughts and figure out how best to help Sophie. However, if the other suspect had been spying on the suffragettes, perhaps it could be relevant after all.

What were they saying? Something about the King? Involving His Majesty would certainly be an escalation.

Finally, Inspector Lambert extracted a newspaper from the mess. He smoothed it out on top of all the other papers and tapped the leading headline.

Louisa leant forward to read it, and Ada stepped closer.

SENSATIONAL DERBY.

SUFFRAGIST'S MAD ACT.

Louisa was halfway through the article when Ada interrupted. 'She ran in front of an 'orse?'

'Not any horse. The King's horse. These meddlesome women have found a new way of causing us all trouble.'

The comment rankled. 'They are drawing attention to the plight of women in this country.'

He raised his eyebrows. 'I am not here to argue politics with you, Miss Knight. My point is merely that the suffragette's actions continue to escalate, so I would think the necessity of a spy is self-explanatory.'

'Still be easier t' just let us vote,' Ada muttered.

He ignored her. 'I'm giving the pair of you my permission to make a nuisance of yourselves – I thought you would jump at the chance.'

Ada snorted. 'By the sounds of it, it's not your permission to give.'

'Perhaps not. But if you came here to investigate, I'm offering you an unprecedented opportunity. The pair are still in our holding cells for now. I can take you to them without the new investigating officers being any the wiser.'

'Why?' The question – the one Ada kept asking with such anger – burst from Louisa before she could stop it. Reputed wisdom was to never look a gift horse in the mouth, but she suspected the horse was Trojan. She would not make the same mistake as that ancient civilisation and trust blindly.

'Miss Franklin is family.'

He sent his own family to spy on the suffragettes?

Ada gave a short huff of disbelief. 'And you're the one who got her into this mess. Your own flesh and blood.'

'My wife's, actually.' The much younger wife, as Ada always called her.

'What an excellent husband you are.' Sarcasm dripped from Ada's response.

'Emma knew the risks she was taking. She wanted to help.'

Did she?

Then again, there were plenty of women who hated the suffragettes as much as any man did.

And as a motive for his uncharacteristic behaviour, it made at least some sense, though it was still a large gamble to take for a relation by marriage. Or maybe that was just Louisa, having so little understanding about what it was to have a family.

'I am sure she did,' Louisa said before Ada made any more sarcastic remarks. 'Can I ask exactly how she is related to your wife?'

'Her niece.'

'The one who's lived with you since she was a young girl?' Ada asked, incredulous.

'Yes. That is the one.' He turned to Louisa. 'Emma's mother died when she was young. She has been a part of our household ever since.' More than a mere relation by marriage, then. A child he had helped raise.

Ada squinted at him. 'Didn't you marry–'

'That is enough, Miss Chapman.' His grave tone was an obvious warning. Ada was extremely close to pushing him over some invisible boundary. 'We do not need to dissect my family's entire history. Are the pair of you willing to help or not?'

'Yes,' Louisa said. Ada echoed her agreement and thankfully did not try to ask her question again. 'We will help if we can. Is there anything else you can tell us? Have you learnt anything about Mr Richardson – any reason someone would want him dead?'

Inspector Lambert picked up a paper from the top of a pile and read from it. 'Thirty-six years old. Recently widowed with one surviving child. Factory worker. Member of the MPU.' The Men's Political Union, the male counterpart to the radical Women's Social and Political Union, which only increased the chances Miss Franklin's spying for the suffragettes might indeed be relevant.

Inspector Lambert pushed the piece of paper aside. 'That was all the landlord at The Packhorse–'

'The pub off Briggate?' Ada interrupted.

He nodded. 'Yes. Mr Richardson was shot in the alleyway beside it. Anyway, as I was saying, that is all the landlord could tell us. We've questioned Mr Dixon's sister, as well, a young woman about your age, Miss Chapman, but she was of little use. She was too distressed to answer properly and kept asking after her brother. All we learnt from her is she was still inside the pub at the time the shot was heard.'

'And you believed her?' Ada said sceptically.

'Miss Dixon walks with a cane and appeared to be in a great deal of pain whilst she was with us. The landlord sent the two men – well, boy and man, really – out after some sort of altercation–'

'Altercation?' Both Louisa and Ada interrupted.

'No one has been very clear on the details of it so far.'

But any sort of altercation with the man shortly before his death makes Artie look guilty.

'Miss Dixon claims she asked Emma to follow them to prevent any further trouble.'

Ada snorted. 'That worked well.'

'Indeed,' he agreed wryly. 'But I do not find it implausible, given her affliction, that she could not go herself, and therefore she was witness to very little.'

We should still try to speak with her. She might have more she is willing to say to people who are also trying to save her brother rather than arrest him.

'Though, of course, it could all be part of an elaborate ruse.' He reached into his jacket pocket but hesitated.

'Is there something else you need to tell us?' Ada demanded.

With a sigh, he extracted a small, crumpled slip of paper. 'Someone with the suffragettes wants Emma dead. They pushed this through our letter box yesterday afternoon.'

He passed the paper to Ada. Louisa stepped closer to peer over her shoulder as she opened it. The handwriting had once been neat calligraphy – the type Louisa had learnt in grammar school – but the ink had smudged.

All traitors burn.

Ada read the words out loud and flipped the paper over to reveal a blank side. 'That's it? Nowt else?'

'No stamp and no address,' Louisa said. 'It must have been hand-delivered. And no name, so they could have intended for you or your wife to read it as much as your niece. Though the threat is implicitly towards her, assuming no one else in your household has carried out any betrayals recently.'

'We can assume that, yes, Miss Knight.' Inspector Lambert's dry reply was laced with derision, but she brushed it off, still engrossed in the note's mystery.

'Why burn, though? It has been some time since we executed women by burning them.'

'I think it might mean Hell, Louisa,' Ada said.

'Ah, yes, that is also a possibility.' She stepped away to address Inspector Lambert once more. 'Have you asked Miss Franklin if she knows what it might mean?'

In a quiet voice, he answered, 'She refuses to talk to us.'

'Why would your niece refuse to talk to you?' Ada asked. 'She's under arrest for murder, and her uncle's a copper. I'd be using that to get out of here if I was her.'

And she was a police spy. Why refuse to cooperate with them now?

'Well, thankfully, Miss Chapman, you are not my niece, so we do not have that particular problem. I am hopeful she might be more willing to speak with you.'

'Why would she–' Ada began, but he spoke over her.

'Speaking of which,' Inspector Lambert raised his wrist to check his watch. 'Inspector Brenner will be here soon. If you wish to speak to the pair of them, it will need to be now.' He stood without waiting for an answer and led the way out of his office. Ada did not move, and Louisa gave her hand an encouraging brush as she passed. A sigh and footsteps from behind told Louisa she was following.

He led them to yet another door, a steel contraption with a barred window all too familiar to Louisa from her brief imprisonment. 'Emma,' he called into the room but got no response.

Inching forward, Ada invaded the inspector's personal space to peer through the window, but Louisa hung back. There was no room for three, not comfortably, and she had no desire to stand that close to any man. Or any woman who was not Ada, if she was being honest.

Ada blocked her view of the inspector's hand, but a loud click announced the door being unlocked, and it swung open. The pair entered the room, and Louisa followed, curiosity compelling her forward. Who was this niece Inspector Lambert was willing to break all police procedures – and his own sense of superiority – to help.

Chapter Three

The Suffragette

Inside, a young woman sat on a wooden bench – the only furniture in the sparse holding cell – looking entirely out of place. She wore a neat, white cotton dress, all frills and lace, with a matching wide-brimmed hat, both decorated with pink ribbons. It was an outfit for strolling in the park, not being held prisoner in a police cell. The hair and face underneath the hat were pale, but her eyes were a bright blue. She would be beautiful if not for the expression marring her features; she glared at Inspector Lambert with such intensity Louisa wanted to step back on his behalf.

'You must be Miss Franklin,' Ada said.

'And who are you?' Miss Franklin spoke with an accent similar to Louisa's, and she, too, had mastered the art of using it to cut people down when desired. Her gaze stayed on Ada, lingering on her red hair and the birthmark on her cheek, then she threw back her head and laughed.

It was not the act of a woman under arrest for murder, nor that of a woman whose uncle was trying to save her life. Was Miss Franklin quite mad?

'Emma,' Inspector Lambert shouted over her laughter. 'I need you to speak to these two ladies. They might be able to help you.'

'Who said I want their help, Uncle?' She spat the familial term at him like an insult. 'I thought I made myself clear to you and your men, I have nothing to say.'

'Please, Emma.' He closed his eyes, and it made the plea almost a prayer.

She stared at him and said nothing.

In the awkward silence that followed, Louisa shared a look with Ada. *What do we do now?*

'Well,' Ada said to Miss Franklin. 'We're here now. You might as well let us try.'

'Oh, might I?' Quiet amusement laced Miss Franklin's response.

'I mean it, Emma, please.' With what looked like great effort, Inspector Lambert opened his eyes again. When his niece made no response, he turned to address Ada in a falsely matter-of-fact manner, 'I'll be back in a quarter of an hour.' And with that, he stepped out of the room and pulled the door shut. The lock clicked back into place.

'Wait!' Ada spun round to face the entrance. 'You can't just lock us in 'ere again.' She raced over and tugged at the handle, but it did not move.

Louisa took a deep breath, pushing away the memories of the last time she had sat in this cell.

A loud clang rang throughout the room as Ada whacked the door. The cursing that followed was much more inventive than anything Louisa had thought up earlier in the kitchen.

'Ada.' Louisa moved to stand next to her partner, using her body to block Miss Franklin's view of them, and gently clasped Ada's wrist. Her pulse raced like a stampede under Louisa's thumb. Bending down to her ear, Louisa whispered, 'He will be back. We are not in trouble this time. No one is going to hurt us. There is no need to fret.'

'Has anyone ever been soothed by being told there's no need to fret?' But a slight smile graced Ada's lips, and some of the tension leaked out of her stance. 'What next? Going t' tell me t' calm down?'

'I mean, I can if you want? Will it at least convince you not to hit any more metal doors? I am rather fond of these hands of yours, so please do not break them.'

'Oh, really?' Ada smirked, and it occurred to Louisa how very filthy her words could be interpreted.

'I did not...' Heat spread up her neck and across her cheeks. 'I meant...' Images flashed through her mind: their hands clasped together, a warm, solid reminder she was no longer alone; a paintbrush between Ada's fingers, bringing beauty from blankness; a gentle touch on her back, feather soft, as music played in the background and peace engulfed her. But how to put all that into words?

She sighed. 'Just try not to break your hands, please.'

'If you insist.' Ada stepped back from the door, and Louisa let go of her wrist. 'He still shouldn't 'ave locked us in, though. Not that he'll care, bloody sod.'

'Ha! What an accurate summary of my dear uncle.' Sneering contempt jolted Louisa back to the reality of the situation. She spun round to face Miss Franklin, who had been all but forgotten in her focus on Ada's distress and then her own embarrassment.

Sophie's blotchy, tear-stained face hovered in her mind. *We need to concentrate. This may be our best chance to learn what happened and save Sophie's sweetheart.*

'Indeed,' Ada agreed with Miss Franklin. 'Least he could have done is warned us, but why bother not further distressing the women you falsely arrested last year?'

Her strategy was obvious but clever – an affinity with this woman who had made no secret of her dislike for her uncle.

I might be best to let Ada do the talking for now. She probably has more of a chance of building a rapport with Miss Franklin.

'You think you can win me to your side by hating my uncle as well?'

Or maybe not.

'Is it working?' Ada asked.

'A little,' Miss Franklin admitted. 'You are Miss Chapman, are you not? The insubordinate female sketch artist.'

Ada frowned. 'Your uncle's words?'

'What gave it away?' Miss Franklin's tone was dry. 'But why would he let you in here? As you have already gathered, he has made no secret of his dislike for you. Aunt Madeline grew quite tired of his rants, and who can blame her? No wife wants their husband obsessing over another woman.'

Louisa stopped herself from pulling a disgusted face. That had to be the most uncomfortable way possible of interpreting Ada and Inspector Lambert's professional relationship. *And deliberately so, I suspect.*

Ada did not stop herself from pulling a disgusted face, scrunching up her nose. 'Your uncle isn't obsessed with me. And as for why we are here, he thinks we can help.'

'With all due respect, Miss Chapman, you are the last person I can imagine my uncle turning towards for help.'

Ada gave a little tilt of her head. 'An hour ago, I would have agreed with you.'

'Well, how very interesting.' A small, cruel smile curled on her lips, and Louisa wondered once again if she was bound for an asylum rather than a gaol.

Though one is much the same as the other for the women imprisoned inside.

Miss Franklin said no more, just kept smiling, and a brief glance at Ada and her bemused expression told Louisa she, too, was out of her depth.

What to make of this contradiction of a woman? The frivolous clothes, the twisted expression, the desolate police cell – none of it added up. 'Miss Franklin, do you understand why you are here?'

'Perfectly. I have been charged with murder. Do *you* understand why you are here? What possible reason do you have to help me? Or my uncle? He has not exactly been kind to either of you.'

Ada muttered something unintelligible under her breath.

'No, he has not,' Louisa agreed. 'But he told us just now we have a shared goal in this. Whatever the relationship between the two of you, your uncle does not believe you are guilty. And the boy arrested alongside you; he is important to someone who is important to us. And she swears he did not do it – that he is innocent.' Too late, Louisa remembered the words Mabel had cried when she was arrested. The ones Ada said still echoed through her mind. She risked another glance at Ada, whose right hand plucked at the left sleeve of her dress, distressed.

No doubt she noticed my slip then.

She should apologise, reach out and comfort her, but before she could do either, Ada crossed her arms behind her back and said to Miss Franklin, 'Did you do it?'

Louisa winced. It was far too blunt.

Miss Franklin stared at her and raised an eyebrow. 'What if I did?'

'Then you could confess and save us all a lot of trouble.'

She considered it for a moment. 'Uncle Oliver would not be happy with that.'

'Even better,' Ada said.

She considered a moment longer. 'What if the boy did it? What then? You have interfered before; I should know—I heard my uncle's ranting enough times. You let a guilty woman walk free. Will you hang a woman this time to let a guilty boy walk free?'

'No,' Louisa said and meant it. She may have strayed a long way from the little girl sitting cross-legged on her father's study floor, but that was still a step too far. She would not look the other way from cold-blooded murder.

What if he had a good reason? What if Mr Richardson was a cruel man like Mr Pearce?

'Did Artie kill him? Is that what you are trying to tell us?'

'No. He was not even supposed to be there; he followed his sister. She was not supposed to be there, either.' Her tone made her irritation at their presence clear.

'*There* being The Packhorse with Mr Richardson?' Ada asked.

She inclined her head. 'Indeed.'

When she said no more, Louisa followed up with, 'Why were you meeting him?'

She smiled. 'A drink with an old friend.'

'How much of a friend?'

She would never have thought to ask, but even Louisa could understand the implications of Ada's question.

Miss Franklin smirked and, in a sickly-sweet voice ladened with innuendo, said, 'Just a *friend.*'

'Then why was Miss Dixon there?' Louisa asked.

Her smirk widened.

'She wasn't supposed to be,' Ada said. 'That's what you said.'

'Clever girl,' Miss Franklin cooed.

If Ada did not hit her, Louisa might.

But Ada studied her instead. 'Why did you not speak to your uncle or his men earlier? You were his spy, and the suffragettes, or at least one of the suffragettes'—she held up the slip of paper from earlier, which she must have never given back—'wants you dead. If I were you, I'd be singing like a canary.'

The smile slid from her face, and she stared at the slip of paper in Ada's hand.

'Do you know who wrote it?' Louisa asked.

She shrugged. 'My uncle, I imagine. Some clever trick of his, to'—she put on a mocking voice—'"make me see sense."'

'He did a good job of disguising his handwriting then.' Ada held the paper out towards her. 'Will you at least look at it? Tell us if you recognise the handwriting.'

But Miss Franklin did not take the paper. 'I do not.'

'You didn't even look!' Ada punctuated her shout by jabbing the paper towards Miss Franklin.

Before an argument could break out, Louisa said, 'I cannot imagine the WSPU were too impressed to discover a spy in their midst.'

'Not when they are out there risking their lives.' Ada's eyes bored into the other woman. Her frigid posture told Louisa her temper was still simmering under the surface. 'A woman was trampled by a horse yesterday fighting for our rights – she is more than likely going to die for her beliefs. Meanwhile, there are women like yourself, willing to hand information over to the very men who have been brutalising our fellows.' She waved the note again. 'Who can blame the sender for their anger?'

Without leaving time for a response, Louisa asked, 'Was the shot meant for you, Miss Franklin?'

'No!' She jumped up from the bench, 'And I am not a spy! I was there for the cause. Which is more than either of you can say. And more than Miss Dixon and her brother can say, interrupting us, trying to lecture me on what I should and should not do, as if I cared what they thought, as if that didn't prove me right.'

'Prove you right about what?' Ada asked.

'That I believed more than they did. They were not willing to do what is necessary, but I am.'

'Ha!' Ada stared at Miss Franklin with something akin to pride. 'I knew it. You became a suffragette. For real.'

That delighted smile irked Louisa. 'And what exactly did you – as a real suffragette – deem necessary?'

Smashed windows and bombs, and three men dead in a fire in Bradford. Hunger strikes and broken bones, and a woman mangled under the hooves of the King's horse.

Miss Franklin glared at her. 'I do not have to tell you anything. You are the ones'—here she turned to Ada and repeated mockingly—'willing to hand information over to the very men who have been brutalising our fellows.'

Ada's hand twitched at her side.

Louisa hurried on. 'If you were fighting for the suffragettes' cause in truth, is it the police you betrayed? Is it them who threatened you?'

Though it is not the handwriting one would suspect of a police officer.

Miss Franklin let out a short huff of breath between a sigh and a laugh. 'So very inquisitive. So very clever. And if it is the police, Miss Knight? If one of my uncle's men wrote that note? What can you do about that?'

The only answer Louisa had was 'tell your uncle', and she suspected Miss Franklin would scoff at that. If that was the solution to her problems, she would have already done so herself.

Or not—given how much she appears to despise him.

'We can...' Ada said into her silence but stuttered to a stop, unable to finish the sentence.

'Exactly,' Miss Franklin laced her tone with condescension. 'I do not know who wrote that note. Nor do I care.'

'You do not care someone might have threatened to burn you alive?' Ada did not try to hide her disbelief, and Louisa could not fault her.

Miss Franklin tilted her head and put on a show of pondering. 'No.'

'What the f—' Ada cut herself off. 'Louisa, ask her some more bloody questions before I...' She stepped away from Miss Franklin, shaking both her head and hands, like she was trying to wave away Miss Franklin's disturbing behaviour.

A part of Louisa would have quite liked to have finished Ada's expletive, to yell and rave at Miss Franklin until she spoke sense, but she suspected it would yield no useful answers. Instead, she pushed down her disquiet and did as Ada suggested.

'Perhaps we should go back to Mr Richardson.'

She still has not given us a straight answer on whether she murdered him. Does she think we have not noticed?

'If we must.'

From where she now leaned against the wall, arms crossed, Ada scoffed.

'This meeting with him. It was more than a drink with an old friend. It was about the suffragettes' cause?'

'Could it not be both?' Miss Franklin smirked again, but it looked more forced this time.

'What was the altercation that happened?' Ada asked.

'Ah, Uncle Oliver is aware of that, then? It cannot look good for young... Is his name Albert?'

'Artie,' Louisa said. 'Short for Arthur.'

'Oh, I was close. Anyway, Miss Dixon started arguing with Mr Richardson. His response was cruel, and *Arthur* took offence and squared up to him, and never mind that he was two decades younger, five stone lighter, and destined for a lifetime of not reaching the top shelf. A mewling kitten, essentially. Mr Richardson laughed in his face.'

Now Miss Franklin appeared more willing to talk – and what had caused that? – Louisa reached inside her bag for her notebook and a pen, belatedly remembering she would be better off taking notes.

'Still, the landlord ordered them out, and Miss Dixon begged me to follow. She cannot move very fast, you understand, with her bad leg and her stick – and she wanted me to make sure Mr Richardson wouldn't really fight some puny seventeen-year-old.'

'Did he?' Ada asked.

Miss Franklin shook her head. 'Arthur was still trying to goad him. He is protective of his sister – it's only the two of them, no parents, no other siblings – and so he does not take insults against her lightly. But Mr Richardson pushed him aside and started walking down the alley. The boy did not follow, so perhaps there is some sense within that adolescent brain of his. That's when the shot rang out. It came from in front of Mr Richardson, though it was hard to tell; it was all such a blur. One second, he was standing, walking away, and the next, he was on the floor, in a pool of blood, clutching his gut.' She spread her hands across her stomach.

Louisa kept writing, the scratch of her pen filling the silence that followed.

Miss Franklin's head jerked round to face her. 'Are you writing this down? Fancy yourself a police constable?'

The scornful amusement stung, but Louisa refused to rise to the bait. 'What did you do next?'

'I ran towards him to see the wound, to see if I could help. What else was there to do? I tried to put pressure on the wound—I know a woman who is a nurse; that's what she says you should do—and told the boy to keep his hands there, whilst I went to find help, and, do you know, that's why they arrested us.' She held her hands out in front of her, spreading the fingers out, though they were clean now. 'It meant we were covered in blood when they found us. We tried to help, and it got us arrested. By my uncle's men, nonetheless. A constable on the beat had heard the shot, and he got there as I stepped away, at the same time as the first patrons came spilling out of the pub, clamouring to see what had happened. Miss Dixon screamed; I remember that.'

'Can you blame her?' Ada said. 'Her little brother in an alleyway, hands covered in blood and a corpse at his feet. I'd scream, too.' She clicked her tongue. 'And with Pete, it's not outside the realm of possibility.'

Miss Franklin frowned at that. No doubt wondering who Pete was.

Worryingly valid though Ada's observation was, their fifteen minutes must be drawing to an end, so Louisa brought the conversation back to its main topic. 'But blood on your hands is not definite proof.' *Though it does not look great.* 'And I am guessing these are not the clothes you were wearing last night.

'Yes, Aunt Madeline brought these; they needed to take the dress I was wearing for evidence. Aren't they terrible?' Miss Franklin tugged at her frilly neckline. 'She even said she chose them because she thought they'd help me look innocent. You know, sweet, unassuming.' Her voice turned cloying, 'Just another pretty little woman who could never possibly hurt a fly.' She tilted her head. 'Or a man.'

Ada laughed, but Louisa's unease grew. Miss Franklin's return to her strange manner unnerved her.

She tried to push past it, focusing on the facts. 'I assume neither of you was in possession of a gun at the time?'

'No, unless Miss Dixon's brother has more secrets than I can imagine from a quiet boy like him.'

'Let us say for now he does not. In which case, there is no solid evidence either of you fired that shot. Only that you were in the alleyway.' With a good defence lawyer, they might stand a chance. She would have to mention it next time she spoke to Mr Connolly, her lawyer and a friend of her late father's. Though, he would no doubt have questions about why she was once again involving herself in matters that were not her domain. He'd claim it was paternal concern, ignoring that she was the one paying him.

'Ah yes,' Miss Franklin said with a creeping smile. 'You're a lawyer's daughter, if I remember correctly. Didn't your father have one of the best prosecution records in the county? Was every person he helped charge guilty?'

No. All the hours she had spent in her father's study over the last year, decades' worth of case files spread out in front of her, trying to reach back into the past and decode her own father.

'Or do innocent people sometimes go to gaol and hang? Innocent women.' Miss Franklin's eyes cut across to Ada, whose hands curled up into fists again.

Louisa took a step closer to her. Just in case.

'Don't break my hands?' Ada muttered.

'Preferably,' Louisa replied in the same undertone.

'Oh, sorry. Have I upset you?' Miss Franklin did not sound sorry at all. Amused, more like.

Louisa turned back to face her but remained close to Ada, whose anger was still palatable. 'You know a lot about us.' An unnerving amount.

'As I said, you quite riled up Uncle Oliver last year. So, bravo for that, I suppose.'

Louisa ignored that and searched for a way to get the conversation back to where they needed it again. 'Tell us more about Mr Richardson.'

She shrugged. 'He...was a complicated man. But not an evil man, even if his final actions in this world were not his best moment.' She sniffed. 'No, he wasn't...' She looked away from them, down to where her hands fiddled with the fabric of her skirt. Even with her face hidden in the dull light of the cell, her misery was obvious.

Perhaps her talk of 'friends' had some grain of truth to it.

'I'm sorry for your loss,' Ada said.

Miss Franklin scoffed at that.

Louisa didn't know what else to say, so even though it felt heartless, she moved on. 'Do you know any reason someone would want him dead?'

She tilted her head, considering. 'I mean, some men hate other men who support female suffrage, but that leads to pub brawls and shouting matches, not an assassination.'

'Is that what this was?' Ada asked.

'It was targeted. Or we have a man who's shooting people down erratically in the streets and alleys of our city, which is hardly a comforting thought.'

Neither is someone assassinating suffragists.

There must be more they needed to know about the dead man or Miss Franklin, but Louisa drew a blank.

Ada spoke into the silence, 'What made you change your mind?'

'About what?'

'Women's suffrage. The WSPU. We quite offended your uncle when we called you a suffragette. If you were once a police spy, what changed your mind?'

'I listened to sense, Miss Chapman. To reason. Like all the women of this country should.'

Her scorn sparked a fresh flurry of anger in Louisa's chest. 'And reason compelled you to put bombs in people's letters?'

'Yes,' Miss Franklin replied. 'For otherwise, they will never listen to us, no matter how much you pretend. You're the closest to free a woman can be, Miss Knight, no man to answer to, and yet that makes you of little value to the world, to society. What could you be if the world—if men—would only let you?'

'I...' She could study. Go to university. Study the sciences or do her own sexology research. She had so many thoughts, so many arguments, so much she could reason if only someone would listen when she shared them.

'My uncle told me those women were dangerous. That's why I offered to help him, but the more I learn, the more I suspect he is the dangerous one.' She turned to Ada. 'And I think you know that. What will you do if this is another woman with a good reason?'

An excellent question, and Louisa had no answer. Ada's silence said neither did she.

The door swung open, and all three of them jumped. Inspector Lambert stood framed by the doorway. Had he heard his niece's words?

'Do you want to speak to young Mr. Dixon?' He spoke to the two of them as if his relation was not there.

'Please.' Louisa left the room at the slowest pace she could feasibly get away with, waiting for one of them to say something to the other. However, stubbornness must have run in the family, even if they were not blood relations.

As soon as the door shut behind them, Ada rounded on the inspector. 'You could have told us you were going to lock us in there.'

'Was that necessary?' Inspector Lambert replied. 'Emma is hardly a threat to you.'

She is a suspected murderess who approves of bombing people.

'That is...' Ada sighed but did not finish her sentence.

So, Louisa continued the conversation for her, 'It is still polite to warn people before you lock them in a police cell.'

'Duly noted.' It was sarcasm so crisp it could nip at her cheeks in the autumn. 'Shall we?' He led them the short distance to another locked door. This one was without a barred window. 'I've given Mr Dixon his own cell. We had some...*unsavoury* characters in the main male holding cell.' He moved to unlock the door.

'You know she hates you, right?' Ada said before he could complete the motion.

Ada, this will not help anyone. Louisa tried to send some kind of signal to her partner with her eyes, but Ada's focus was firmly on the inspector.

'Yes, Miss Chapman,' he whispered, a voice of defeat. 'I am aware.'

'Then why–'

He turned the key, and the loud clunk of the lock cut her off. His hand moved to the handle, but he paused. 'Oh, and I am going to lock this one behind you, too.'

Ada glared. 'Duly noted.'

He ignored her, and the door swung open.

Chapter Four

Sophie's Sweetheart

Artie Dixon gasped and jumped up from the bench as they stepped into the boxy room. He was a short, skinny reed of a lad with a face tanned from the sun and a mop of sandy curls in need of a cut, dressed in clothes that had seen better days. Miss Franklin's amusement at the idea of him squaring up to anyone was understandable. Far less understandable was what Sophie saw in him.

Though that is hardly my area of expertise.

'I want you to speak with these two ladies, Mr Dixon,' Inspector Lambert said. 'Miss Knight and Miss Chapman.'

The boy's mouth formed a little 'o'.

'You may recognise the names from your Miss Dawson.'

He nodded and, after a few seconds, added, 'Yes, sir.'

To them, Inspector Lambert said, 'Quarter of an hour again. Inspector Brenner will be here shortly after that.'

All three of them watched him leave. As soon as the door slammed shut behind him, the barrage of questions began. 'Did Sophie send you? Is she alright? Do you know what happened? Are you going t' investigate? Sophie says you've done that before.'

'That depends if there is something to investigate?' The words came out harsher than Louisa intended, still unable to figure out how she should react towards this boy and already left off-kilter by the strangeness of Miss Franklin's changing manner.

His forehead creased. 'What do you mean?' Entirely guileless. Impossible to imagine the confused, lost waif of a boy in front of her as a cold-blooded killer.

An impressive act, if it is one.

'The police already have two suspects in custody. Is there anything else that needs investigating?' She had to push him. No matter how innocent he looked, if he was lying, better to know now than lead Sophie on with days – maybe even weeks – of false hope.

'Yes. Yes. We didn't do this. You have t' find the man who did!'

'This mystery man who no one saw, who shot a man without ever entering the alley.'

'Yes, yes, that's the one.' His answer was earnest; her sarcasm ignored or unnoticed.

'And you expect anyone to believe that?' Apparently, she had chosen cruel bluntness as her interrogation method.

The boy stared at her, blinking, tears gathering in his lower lash line. 'It's the truth.'

'You didn't do it?' Ada spoke for the first time, her voice quiet, contemplating Artie Dixon intently.

Louisa fought the urge to reach out and take her hand. How truthful had Sophie been with this boy? Would it surprise him were she to do so?

'I didn't, miss. Please, I didn't. You have t' help. I can't hang. What'll happen to Hettie if I hang?'

'Hettie?'

'My sister, ma'am.'

Louisa bit back an inappropriate laugh at the title. Had he picked that habit up off Sophie somehow?

'I can't hang,' he repeated as if saying the words enough time could prevent it from happening. 'It'll break Hettie.

And what will she do to survive? We're barely making ends meet now. A gardener's wage ain't much, but it helps, it's still more than we had when I was younger, after...' His eyes glazed over, lost in some memory. It was distressingly easy to fill in what he left unsaid for two parentless siblings. There was always a before and an after when a parent died. Louisa knew that all too well.

'We were told your sister has some sort of injury,' Ada said.

He nodded. 'Burns.'

Ada's fingers tapped the birthmark on her cheek absentmindedly.

'Much worse than that, miss. There was a fire, a big one, it burnt our house down. We never knew why. It might've been a candle by a bedside or a stray spark from the fireplace.' He shrugged. 'Least, that's what the firemen said. Hettie got me out safe, shielded me, so she got the worst of it. Our dad didn't make it out.' He swiped at his face with a grubby hand. A pang of shock went through Louisa when she spotted the red stain still under one of his nails – a dead man's blood.

Was he trying to save his life or kill him for insults aimed at a beloved sister? A sister who might have saved his life at the cost of her own health.

'That's what Mr Richardson was throwing insults about?' Ada's hard tone implied she would have happily cussed the man out for herself, and Louisa was not inclined to stop her if she did.

'He called her a useless cripple. Was I supposed to sit there and let him say it? He deserved...' He cut off, eyes flickering between the two, no doubt aware whatever he was about to say was incriminating.

'A good thumping,' Ada finished for him.

'Maybe keep that part to yourself when you next talk to the police,' Louisa said.

'I know that. I'm not that silly.' Artie's petulant tone was reminiscent of Ada's troublesome brother, Peter. Perhaps it was a speciality of adolescent boys. 'But I don't think they'll believe me, anyway. If I tell truth, I mean. You were right, ma'am, about 'ow fake it sounds.'

'Then practise on us,' Ada said. 'Tell us what you're going to tell t' new police inspector when he gets here.'

Now, that's a clever way of getting information. And not one I would have thought to suggest.

Louisa focused on the notepad still in her hand as he talked, but there was little to add to her notes. The story he told matched up with Miss Franklin's. He had followed his sister to The Packhorse public house, where she had gone to interrupt Miss Franklin and Mr Richardson. He had no information on why the pair had met there.

'Hettie never said what it was. I'd gone to visit and caught her on the way out door, and she didn't explain. She kept telling me I didn't have to come, like I was gonna leave her to go to a pub on her own. And I never got to find out what it was before he...said what he said.'

'And then you argued...' Ada said. Which was definitely 'prompting the witness' as Father would have said, but Louisa left her to it.

'We argued. It got heated. I think he'd had a few already. And I... I'm not a fool. I knew I wouldn't win in a fight against him, but I couldn't just back down. Not after what he said. I hoped he would. That he'd realise fighting me made 'im look like a cad, but it didn't happen.'

'So, you go to alley...' Ada was prompting again.

'We go. I'm trying to figure out how to get out with my face in one piece.'

'Miss Franklin said you encouraged him to fight you.'

He winced at Louisa's comment. 'I did. I shouldn't have. I'm not proud of it. It's just... he said we're cowards, me and Hettie, as if 'e has any damned – sorry, ma'am – as if he has any idea what we've survived. So yes, I got mad when I shouldn't. I'm not usually like that, ma'am. I promise. Ask anyone up at mansion. They'll say I've got good character.'

And the people at Gotts Manor would say Sophie has bad character.

'I'm sure they would,' Ada agreed. 'But tell us about the alleyway. You were mad? You tried to get him to fight you?'

He ran a hand through his runaway curls, making them more array. 'Yes, miss. I shouldn't have been, but I was. That's when Miss Franklin stepped out. She told him t' leave me alone, and I thought he would then. Who fights in front of a woman? But he didn't. He just kept muttering insults. I really do think he was more blotto than I thought. He took a couple of swings at me, easy to dodge – he wasn't at all stable on his feet – and that's when he finally turned around, grumbling under his breath, and started walking away. I didn't even have time to be glad he was leaving before, well, bang.' He said the last word lamely, like a firework that fizzled instead of exploding.

'Where did the shot come from?' Louisa asked.

'Lands Lane, I'd guess, ma'am.'

'And was Mr Richardson walking towards or away from Lands Lane?'

'Away, towards Briggate. It hit him int' back.'

'His back? You are sure?'

He nodded. 'I saw the hole. The bullet hole, I mean. When Miss Franklin told me t' try and stem the blood.'

'And before that, when he was shot, you were looking towards him and Briggate?'

He frowned, no doubt thinking she was rather labouring the point, but nodded. 'Yes, ma'am.'

'And Miss Franklin watched him leave?'

'I think so, but, well, I was looking at him not her. Sorry, ma'am, that sounded rude, didn't it? But it wasn't supposed t' be.'

'It is fine. I did not find it rude.' She waved away his apology. 'Did you see anything else? No matter how small a detail, it might help.'

'No, sorry, ma'am. I was looking at Mr Richardson. I didn't understand what happened at first. Like my mind wasn't catching up t' what I was watching, what I'd heard.'

'Understandable,' Louisa said softly. But she forged onwards, regardless, because they did not have the time to be kind. 'Tell us what happened next, after the shot.'

'You ran to body?' Ada added.

He nodded. 'I didn't know what else to do. It was so... sudden. What do you do when someone gets shot out of nowhere?'

'I... I don't know,' Ada answered.

Run for the police. For a doctor. Do not get your hands covered in their blood. Louisa's gaze flickered back to his hands, to that blood-encrusted nail, disgust rising in her throat.

But it was much easier to say that afterwards, as someone who was not there in the moment, and pointing it out would help no one now. Better to stay on track.

'Do you know anyone with a reason to want Mr Richardson dead?'

He shook his head. 'No. Unless...'

'Go on,' Ada said.

'Anything you can tell us might help,' Louisa added.

'The WSPU has lost a lot of money, Hettie told me. Stolen. They're all looking at each other funny, wondering who took it. Which isn't great when you're taunting police about how they haven't found your money yet.'

'Yes, we read Mrs Cohen's speech in the *Mercury*,' Louisa said. The *Leeds Mercury* was not a paper she usually took in, but Ada had bought a copy last month. She'd wanted to know more about the procession the WSPU had done to Woodhouse Moor, including Mrs Cohen's rather incendiary speech.

He scoffed. 'I wouldn't believe a word of that, ma'am. I went with Hettie to listen t' speeches – it was my half day, you see. Coppers lied about what she said.'

'So, she did not taunt them about £15,000 worth of suffragette funding still being undiscovered then?'

'Well, alright, maybe that part was true. But some of it was lies. They made it sound worse than it was. It's why they had to let her go in the end. She's a clever one, our Mrs Cohen, and that husband of hers, too.'

'Having made their acquaintance on several occasions, I am inclined to agree. But you were telling us about missing money?'

He nodded. 'Someone's been stealing it. And Mr Richardson was seen hanging around their headquarters. He claimed he was waiting for Mrs Jennings – she's another suffragette, she's living at headquarters 'cos her husband kicked her out. And her daughter, too, who's a bit of a hellion. Apparently, they were heard arguing – Mrs Jennings and Mr Richardson, that is.'

Louisa made a note.

'So, people think he stole it?' Ada asked.

He shrugged. 'I guess so. You'd be better asking Hettie. She told me all this.'

Louisa nodded. 'Could you give us an address for your sister?'

He reeled off a street in New Wortley, and Ada wrinkled her nose.

'Aye, it's not best, but it's what we can afford. Wouldn't even be able to afford that without Miss Jain.'

'Miss Jain?' Ada asked. 'The actress?'

'She's not an actress no more – her partner left. Are you a fan of the music halls, miss?'

'I like a good show now and then. But I've actually met Miss Jain before. Briefly.'

Louisa turned her attention fully to Ada, combing her memory for mention of the other woman.

'Her acting partner was Miss Armstrong,' Ada explained to her.

'Ah.' That explained it. Yes, Ada had mentioned Miss Armstrong's protective friend and colleague.

'She's a suffragette now, as well. You should speak to them both – they can tell you about Mr Richardson, and the money, and Miss Franklin, too. Do you know what's going on with Miss Franklin? The constables were treating her very strangely.'

''Cos she's their boss' niece,' Ada told him.

'What? Nah, she can't be. For real? But she hates police. Said all kinds of horrible things 'bout 'em. She wanted to...'

'Wanted to...' Ada prompted when he didn't continue. 'What did she want to do t' police?'

'Nothing good, I suspect,' Louisa muttered.

'No, ma'am. Nothing good. But anyway,' he did a funny little cough, 'I wouldn't have thought her a peeler's niece. And a head copper, too?'

'It is a strained relationship, I gather,' Louisa said.

Both Artie and Ada snorted.

'Will he let her go?'

Louisa shook her head. 'That is why you are being transferred to a different police station – a conflict of interest.' She checked her wristwatch – their time was nearly up. 'Is there anything else you can tell us, Mr Dixon?'

'I've told you everything I know. I only met Mr Richardson tonight. It's my sister who's involved with the suffragettes. Don't get me wrong, I support them, but I can't risk my job by getting caught up in it. I'm sure my boss would think it was bad enough if he knew about my sister.'

Ada muttered something under her breath that Louisa assumed was a curse word.

Approaching footsteps echoed in the corridor outside.

Horror washed across the boy's face. 'They're coming for me, aren't they? Please, ma'am.' He seized the cuff of her dress like a child who did not want to let go of his mother. 'Tell me you'll look into it. Tell me you can prove me innocent. Please, please, I can't die. I can't leave Hettie alone. I don't want t' leave Sophie behind. Please.' A large sob broke from him, tears streaming down his face.

'I promise we will look into it. We will do all we can.'

But I cannot promise you will be found innocent. I cannot promise to save you from a noose.

He nodded, still sobbing. At the click of the lock, his grip only tightened, and a desire to protect him from whatever was coming overpowered Louisa.

It was only Inspector Lambert, as she should have known it would be. The boy's fear was infecting her. The inspector's gaze fell on her wrist, and she gave it the slightest shake. Artie loosened his grip, a blush blooming across his face.

'Inspector Brenner is here. Goodwin's distracted him with a cup of tea and the incident report, but you need to leave now.'

Louisa patted Artie's shoulder. 'Keep your head up. We will...' *Figure this out. No, I cannot promise that either.*

'Get you out of here.' Ada made the exact promise Louisa had been trying to avoid, and her stomach dropped.

Oh, Ada, my love, you should not have said that.

But, of course, she had. For all she had faced, for all she had lost, Ada was an optimist.

He nodded, smiling up at her with hope shining from his eyes, which only twisted the knife into Louisa's gut further.

'You have to go,' Inspector Lambert repeated, and they made their way through the door he held open. He locked it behind them with a clunk.

'I have to say it's rather strange,' Ada said as the group made its way back down the corridor. 'Having you help impede a police investigation.'

'I am not impeding; I am assisting.' He quickened his stride to walk ahead of them, and Ada's mouth closed on whatever sarcastic reply she was going to give. Instead, she turned to give Louisa a look that screamed the words she had swallowed.

'Come on,' Louisa said. 'I do not want to explain ourselves to this other inspector.' She hid her notebook and pen back inside her bag.

'It's fine. We're *assisting*, don't you know?'

Louisa rolled her eyes, but a grin tugged at her lips. Ada so often managed to get that reaction from her.

They stepped into the foyer at the same time as a short, squat man in a bowler hat came from behind the front counter.

'Ah, Lambert, there you are.' He did a slight double-take at the pair of them. 'And who are your fine lady friends?'

'Inspector Brenner, this is Miss Chapman and Miss Knight. Miss Chapman does sketch work for us occasionally.'

Though not recently.

'A lady sketch artist?'

Louisa braced for Ada's response, but she only forced a smile.

'We were just leaving, sir,' Louisa said. 'We would not wish to interrupt further. Good day, inspectors.'

'Good day,' they both responded. Inspector Brenner launched into discussing what he called the Richardson case, unconcerned that they were still firmly within earshot. Louisa longed to stick around and listen, but there was no way to do so without it being obvious. Inspector Lambert, at least, would realise what she was about.

Though he should, nominally, support our snooping for once.

Still, better not to risk it. The last thing they needed was Inspector Brenner's ire.

The second the entrance door closed behind them, Ada said, 'Well, what do you make of all that then?'

'At this point, I could not say. And you? How are you?'

'I am...' She sighed. 'I have been better.' She hurried around the corner and down the street away from the police station, coming to pause in the opening of an alleyway. Above them, laundry was strung between the houses, swaying in the light summer breeze.

Ada pulled the slip of paper from her pocket and studied it again, though the three threatening words could not have changed. 'This must have been written by a suffragette. None of the officers write this neatly, and Inspector Lambert has an eye for that kind of thing. Davey used to grumble about it – he'd rush a report and then pretend he didn't know who wrote it, but Inspector could always tell from his handwriting.'

'So, if one of his men wrote this, he would know?'

Ada nodded. 'And they would know that. Besides, who hand delivers a threatening note to their governor's house?'

'Rather awkward if one is caught in the act, I would imagine. So that leaves the suffragettes. Perhaps they were unconvinced by Miss Franklin's change of heart, but why threaten to burn her? It could be allegorical, like you suggested.'

'I did?'

'A reference to Hell.'

Ada shrugged. 'Oh, well, what else can it be? They surely can't mean to literally burn her.'

'Because the suffragettes have never been known to set fires,' Louisa said drily.

'There's a difference between a warehouse that wasn't as empty as they thought and deliberately setting fire to someone.'

'True enough,' Louisa conceded.

Ada peered at the note once more. 'It sounds like something from a history lesson. Didn't they burn witches?'

Louisa's mind filled with the image of terrified women tied to stakes, screaming, surrounded by a mob calling for their execution until her heartbeat accelerated, even though she remained safe in the twentieth century. The singed air from her earlier disaster in the kitchen hung over her mind's conjuring.

She forced herself back to the present. 'Sometimes,' she answered Ada. 'Though witches were more commonly hung. It was for treason,' she pointed at the note, 'for being traitors, that most women were executed at the stake, for betraying their masters, whether that was monarch or husband.'

'Charming.'

'Indeed. There was a letter in *The Times* a few weeks back, in which the writer called the suffragettes "traitors to the Empire".'

Ada huffed in frustration. 'It was never going t' be simple, was it? I need a cig.' She reached into her pockets and, after a few moments of searching, she pulled out her cigarette case and lighter with a triumphant flourish. 'I deserve this, and you know it.'

'I was not going to say a word.'

She raised an eyebrow.

'You are right; you do deserve it. I half wish I had an unhealthy-but-nerve-soothing habit I could indulge in.'

'You could take up drinking. Or snuff – do people still take snuff nowadays? Ooh, what about, is it cocaine the detective uses in those stories you love so much? Maybe it'll help us solve this mess of a case.' Ada lit a cigarette and took a drag, turning her face to blow the smoke away from Louisa.

'Cocaine, yes, but I do not think acquiring a drug addiction will be of much use.' She could never stand to be so out of control of her body and mind. 'Besides, in the Sherlock Holmes stories, his cocaine usage filled the quiet time when there was not a case. If anything, I have too much to think about right now.'

A male suffragist shot in an alleyway. A police spy turned true suffragette who someone wanted dead. A seventeen-year-old boy, still not quite a man, but who felt an older brotherly urge to protect his sister, no matter the realities of their ages. And Sophie, who may or may not love him but had told herself she did.

'Humph, that's true, I suppose,' Ada agreed. 'I guess that leaves smoking, then.' She sent Louisa a cheeky smirk and held out the burning cigarette towards her, which Louisa only answered with *a look*. Ada laughed and placed it back to her lips, taking another drag.

'I am not sure the people who own these houses will appreciate you making their fresh laundry smell like smoke.'

'Rent.'

'Hmm?'

'No one who owns houses like these lives in them.'

'Oh, right, of course.'

'Plus, it's not out of the norm to bring your sheets in with them smelling like smoke.' She gestured around her, a motion meant to encompass the entirety of their industrial city with its mills and factories and steelworks and railways, all belching out smoke.

Still, Ada took a step out of the alleyway before she took another drag on her cigarette. 'But we're getting off-topic. The real important question is, do you think they did it?'

'I...' Their whole story was as flaky as a freshly bought cheese pasty. The discrepancy in where the gunshot had come from and where he was shot. That neither of them had seen any sign of this mystery gunman. Louisa was not wrong in thinking a good defence lawyer might save them, yet she also suspected a good prosecutor could just as easily doom them. Father would have seen them sent to gaol. Yet, Artie's phantom fingers tugged at her sleeve cuff, pleading. An innocent boy? Or a guilty one, terrified of what he'd done and what it meant? His entire future disappearing down the drain like rainwater after a storm, a prospect too terrifying to face, so instead, he denied the truth of what had happened. *Like Mabel.* No doubt Ada had seen the similarities, too.

'I am not sure what to think.' Which was the truth, if a simplified version. 'Do you think they did it?'

Ada sighed, throwing her head back, smoke rising from her mouth as if she were a steam train. 'I don't know, to be honest. I was kind of hoping you would have some clever insight.' She threw her cigarette butt down onto the dirty cobbles and stubbed it out under the heel of her shoe. 'But we're going to look into it, aren't we? I mean, we have to, surely?'

Louisa nodded, even as nerves churned in her stomach. 'We do.' It was their only available course of action. They could not simply walk away from this, at least not with their heads held high. 'I think Artie's–'

Ada tilted her head, expression puzzled.

'What is it?'

'You called him "Artie". You, who steadfastly refuses to drop the letter r from Pete's name.'

'Well, he already annoys me less.'

Ada grinned. 'That's so delightfully petty, and I love you for it.'

Louisa ignored that comment. '*Anyway,* his sister is our best starting point. Then we need to find out all we can about Mr Richardson. We know he was widowed. Were there any other women? Was Miss Franklin just mocking us with her talk of *friends?* Does he have any other family? Inspector Lambert said he was a factory worker – what factory? How long had he been a part of the suffrage movement? Does he have any connections to any other WSPU members, like that woman... I can't remember her name.'

'Good job you wrote it down, then.' Ada smiled at her.

Louisa couldn't bring herself to return the smile. These were all questions she should have asked in there, but her mind had been too scrambled by the unexpected turn of events the morning had taken. She pulled her notebook and a pen from her handbag, flipping to the page with the woman's name – Mrs Jennings. In sloppy, rushed handwriting, she wrote down all the questions she could think of whilst she could remember them.

'And then there's the money,' Ada said as she wrote. 'The missing money Artie mentioned. Do you think that is a part of it? Maybe Mr Richardson stole it.'

Louisa added a note about the money to her list. 'Or maybe there is a rot in the WSPU they do not want to admit to.'

'Miss Franklin went to them a spy and came out a suffragette.'

'Or she is the one who stole the money and killed a man, and this is all a careful, deliberate act. Or Artie killed him for insulting his sister.' The words felt treasonous even as she said them. 'Or someone else entirely. But you are right – it will be worth looking into if we can.' She made another note in her notebook. 'And we cannot write off the possibility the bullet was meant for Miss Franklin. We will need to learn about her, too.'

'But who are we even best asking?' Ada frowned, deep in thought. 'You would think the obvious answer is Inspector Lambert and his wife, but if that display earlier is owt t' go by, I don't think either of them knows their niece as well as they would like.'

Which reminded Louisa, 'What were you going to ask him earlier? About his marriage.'

'It's only a rumour, and I heard it from Bertie Smith, so who knows if it's true – half what comes out of that boy's mouth is nonsense. He claims the reason Inspector has such a young wife is he really loved her older sister, who was married to another man.'

'That seems like a poor reason to marry someone.' Her heart twinged with a pang of sympathy for Mrs Lambert.

'That's precisely what I said.'

'Was the older sister Miss Franklin's mother?'

'I think so. From what I've heard, she went to live with her aunt after an illness took both her parents. She was only young, Rosie's age maybe.' Eight or nine, then. Another pang of sympathy tugged at her heart. Whatever she now was and whatever she might have done, Miss Franklin had once been a little girl suddenly a lot more alone in the world. Had her aunt and uncle welcomed her with open arms and raised her like her own? Was that why as an adult, she had been willing to help her uncle in his crusade against her own gender? Or had she been an unwelcome strain on an ill-fated marriage? Had living with that resentment led her to lie and trick and betray a man who had not done right by her or her mother or her aunt?

I cannot imagine either the inspector or Mrs Lambert will answer such questions. And it was unlikely they would get another chance to speak to Miss Franklin, and even less likely she would deign to answer.

'The inspector must truly think she's innocent,' Louisa said. 'Or he would never have invited us to investigate, not when it could lead us so deeply into his personal life.'

'Or it's all just Bertie's usual claptrap.'

'That is also an option,' Louisa conceded with a slight smile. She glanced down at her notes. 'I suppose the suffragettes might be our best chance for answers on Miss Franklin, too.'

'Shall we start with Miss Dixon? Artie said she didn't work, so she might be at home.'

'Let us go find out then.' Louisa turned to the page where she had written her address. 'You recognised it?'

Ada nodded. 'New Wortley. We can take the number nineteen or sixteen.'

Louisa put her notebook back in her bag. Her hands longed to reach for Ada's, but she held back. Two women walking hand-in-hand would not be too shocking a sight – nothing compared to two men – but it still skirted too close to the truth for in public.

What could you do? Miss Franklin's question came back to her unbidden. At the time, she had not even thought about what she wanted more than anything else in the world – to be truthful about her relationship with Ada – because it was too far outside the realm of possibility. The vote could not give her that. Better pay for women workers and acceptance of women in political positions and academia could not give her that. But if the world could change that much, could it change on this, too? It was a hypothetical far beyond her ability to imagine.

'Louisa?' Ada watched her, head tilted, concern pouring out of her. Was she, too, wanting to reach out? Wanting to comfort or be comforted?

Louisa shook her head as if to shake her thoughts loose from it. 'Sorry. Shall we go?'

'Yes. Let's.' But Ada did not move, her gaze still locked on Louisa with a million questions contained within it.

'Come on,' Louisa began to walk again. 'We have a murder to solve.'

That, at least, got a shadow of a smile from Ada. 'Yes, we do.' She looped her arm through Louisa's without hesitation, and they set off down the street and back towards town.

Miss Dixon wasn't home, or so the softly-spoken Black girl who opened the door told them. She could not have been older than twelve and failed to look them in the eye the entire time she spoke until she slammed the door in their faces with great haste.

'Do you get the sense she didn't want us here?' Ada stared at the closed door.

'Very much so. What are we going to do now?'

Ada thought for a second, then she turned to Louisa with a smirk. 'Want to join the suffragettes?'

Chapter Five

The WSPU

The room they entered was all abuzz. There was an energy to the women who crowded the space, a shiver of excitement, of anticipation, action yet to come and decisions in the making. A scene Ada would paint in fast, bold brushstrokes and still never capture properly. It was something that could not be contained, bottled down, not by her paintbrush and certainly not by the men who lined the green benches of the Palace of Westminster.

Looking closer, a few men and children were dotted amongst the women. Though men couldn't officially join the WSPU, some supported their wives in their cause. If Inspector Lambert's information was correct, Mr Richardson had been one of them, even as a widower.

The news of the derby and Emily Davison's bravery was on everyone's lips – news Ada had nearly forgotten in the havoc of their morning. Would it be a turning point in the WSPU's campaign? And if parliament ignored it, would it only lead to an increase in the suffragettes' more violent tactics? Louisa would disapprove, but a small thrill shivered through Ada. It would be more chaos, but maybe chaos was what the world needed to change.

In the centre of the room, a petite blonde woman stood on a chair, a metal badge – in the suffragette colours of white, green and purple – glinted on her chest, pinned to a lilac day dress that had seen better days. Heads swivelled round to her as she gave an impromptu speech, waving around bandaged hands. 'Now more than ever, it's time for action. Miss Davison's brave sacrifice shows we must be willing to take more risks.' Her eyes scanned the crowd and stayed for a few moments on a woman standing in an office doorway, who frowned. Her pallor suggested she spent all her time inside that office, and she stared back from behind thick glasses that enlarged her dark brown eyes. The speaker didn't break the eye contact as she continued,

'There are those who say some of our sisters have gone too far, but how can there be a limit on what action we must take for the sake of our freedom and our very ability to live and survive?' She turned to address the crowd at large once more. 'Will factories not be safer if we have a voice in who decides the laws that govern them? How many women die or have their limbs mangled in machinery every year? We all know at least one.' She paused, head bowed, and a hush fell at her words.

Ethel Long. Ada had not thought of the woman in years, a young mother of two who kept her head down and did her work and barely ever spoke. She couldn't picture Mrs Long's face anymore, but Ada could still hear her bloodcurdling scream and see the gory mess of what had once been an arm. She touched the scar on her wrist, a whisper of the fear that had overtaken her then fluttering through her body once more. The terror of a caught sleeve and the promise of the pain to follow. She had been lucky; many were not.

The woman continued her speech, pulling Ada from her memories, and she suspected she was not the only one lost in the past for a moment then. 'But the newspapers don't decry the factory owners as murderers. No, that's reserved for us alone, though the machinery of this country has killed more people than we ever will, no matter how many bombing campaigns we undertake. Better laws could have saved them, but saving the lives of poor women will never be our politicians' priority, not unless we make it so. I'm not fool enough to believe it is the priority of everyone in this union either, but here in Leeds, it should be. Equal wages. Safer working conditions. Better protections. But for that to happen, we have to make them listen. And it's becoming more and more clear we must deliver that message with a bang! We must assure there is no peace in this country until this country at least hears the voice of all its citizens, whether they be the great lords of this land or simple mill girls.'

A few people cheered. The loudest were a group to their left, young women dressed in plain day dresses and straw hats. If they were the mill girls mentioned, they must have hurried over after finishing their shifts; the average working day had only ended an hour earlier. Ada, too, applauded, the thrash of the loom loud in her ears. The fear had always bubbled below the surface every time she went to work at the mill, an anxiety she learnt to ignore, to tell herself it would never be her, even though it was an obvious lie. She flexed both her hands, a reminder they were still there, despite several clumsy near-misses. She had told Mabel once how she feared nothing more than losing her right hand, her ability to draw and paint.

And never mind my anger that Karl from across the road got three times my wage, despite us being the same age and him being the most useless person to ever grace a loom.

Not everyone approved of the speaker's fierce words nor the raucous cheering. A couple of women on the other side of the room – wearing dresses that would have cost the mill girls over a month's wage – frowned in the direction of both.

'She speaks well,' Louisa said in a quiet undertone to Ada.

Ada turned, trying to decipher if any more meaning lay behind those words – discussing the morality of the bombing campaigns was well-trodden ground for them. Recently, there had been weeks where each day brought a new headline with their breakfast – a bomb either exploded or discovered just in time. In theatres and train stations and post offices and churches and art galleries and hotels and sport pavilions and even lighthouses.

Ada tried to blink away the images that conjured – explosions and fires and screams – and with it, her savage anger. The part of her that said to burn the world down until it gave them at least a few crumbs, even if she couldn't revel in the thought of so much death.

'We should be taking a leaf out of Adele Pankhurst's book,' a woman in the crowd shouted. 'I don't usually give credit t' Bradford,' this neighbourly insult caused a smattering of laughter, 'but she has the right idea over there.' This was greeted with a cheer and more applause, particularly from the original speaker. Ada did not join in this time.

Three already dead in Bradford last month. Is that what she wanted? Fires in the city's warehouses? What if it was the warehouse where John, her eldest brother, worked? How could she ever support that, no matter how frustrated she was with the world?

'Today is not the day to make any decisions,' A voice Ada recognised interrupted – the accent Leeds through and through. The speaker stepped forward, a short woman with dark chestnut hair and a gentle face. Leonora Cohen, an acquaintance of theirs and secretary of the Leeds branch of the WSPU. Her husband and young son stood behind her and all three of their faces were serious. 'Emotions are running high. This could be a crucial turning point for our cause—let us not squander it with rash choices.'

'Is running under a horse not a rash choice?' A woman nearby muttered to her friend, who scolded her for the distasteful comment.

'This is not rash.' The speech giver stared down Mrs Cohen. 'This has been a long time coming.'

There is tension in their ranks. I doubt Miss Franklin's presence helped with that – either as a spy or a true suffragette.

'We can speak more on this later. For now, let us await further information from London regarding Miss Davison.'

The other woman gave a tight nod. 'Later, then,' and the crowd broke off into separate conversations.

At her side, Louisa nudged Ada. 'We should try speak to Mrs Cohen. She is our most likely source of information.'

Mrs Cohen must have felt their eyes on her, for she turned and did a small double-take when she noticed them. Beside her, Mr Cohen followed his wife's gaze and sent them a puzzled look. His wife muttered something to him and gently touched his forearm, then headed in their direction.

'Well, I must say, this is a surprise in a day already full of 'em. How are you both?'

'Fine, thank you,' Ada said. 'But we, too, are having a strange day. Could we talk to you?'

'About women's suffrage?' She spoke in a satirical manner that implied she knew it was not.

'To a certain extent,' Louisa said. 'But we need to speak with you about a woman by the name of Emma Franklin.'

'Miss Franklin? Is she alright? Where is she? I was expecting her to be here already.'

'Do you not know?' Ada asked. Surely, someone in the WSPU had heard talk of what happened. Or had they all been too distracted by the newspapers and Miss Davison and the future of their cause?

'Know what?' Mrs Cohen replied.

'Is there somewhere we can speak in private?' Louisa asked.

Mrs Cohen nodded and led them to a small office crammed with a desk, a few chairs, and a filing cabinet. There was barely room to manoeuvre inside.

'What has happened to Miss Franklin?' she asked as soon as the door closed.

'She's been arrested,' Ada said – might as well be straight to the point.

Mrs Cohen gasped. 'Where? Where was it?'

Which was not the question Ada expected. 'Here,' she said uncertainly. 'In town.'

'In town? We haven't 'eard... ah... it didn't go off then.'

It took Ada a few seconds to figure out what she meant.

'You assume she planted a bomb?' Louisa asked.

Mrs Cohen frowned. 'Is that not it?'

'No, they suspect her of killing a man. That her and a boy – Artie Dixon, brother to another one of your members – shot him in the alley beside a public house called The Packhorse.'

'What?' Her brow furrowed. 'That doesn't make any sense. Who? What man?'

'Mr Richardson. He's a member of the local men's suffrage group, I believe. You might know him?'

'Yes, I've met Mr Richardson. Henry – Mr Cohen – has had a pint with him before, once or twice, though not recently. I wouldn't call them friends, but...we knew him. And his daughter. She's been here before; when her mother was alive, she played with my son.' Her eyes glanced back towards the main room. 'What will happen t' her? His daughter?'

'Hard to say,' Louisa replied. 'It will depend on what other family she has.' Her voice softened. 'How old is she?'

'A little younger than Reggie, about eight or nine, maybe.'

'Right, of course, you said they played together.' Louisa sounded distracted, and Ada could guess why. The loss of Louisa's father was a messy tangle of guilt and love and relief, one Ada would never fully understand. When her father passed on – hopefully, long in the future – she could mourn him as a good man who loved his family and worked hard to provide for them, nothing more, nothing less.

'I can't believe he's dead.' Mrs Cohen moved to a chair and sat down with a heavy thump. Ada nearly offered her tea but had no idea where the kitchen facilities were or even if there were any. 'And the police think Emma did it? And Hettie's brother?' Her eyes snapped over to Ada. 'And you still work for police? This is how you know all this?' The scorn was hard to miss, but it barely prickled, not as it once had.

'Not anymore,' Ada said. 'I'm rather out of favour.' It hardly hurt to say it anymore. And this was not the time for despairing over her career prospects.

'Is that so?'

Ada ignored the obvious further question. There was no need to get into the messy details of what had happened. 'But this is where the situation becomes more complicated.' She glanced over at Louisa, who gave a tiny tilt of her head agreeing she should continue. 'Did you know Miss Franklin's uncle is a police inspector?'

On the way here, they had discussed the best way to approach the topic – Louisa dismissing outright Ada's half-joking suggestion about pretending to join – and agreed that forthright was their best option. If nothing else, it would take the suffragettes by surprise and, therefore, perhaps make them more honest. And if it didn't, that itself was revealing. Besides, whilst Louisa could be subtle when needed, it had never been a strong point of Ada's.

Mrs Cohen frowned. 'No. She spoke of...' She shook her head. 'When Miss Franklin came to us, she was a quiet, unassuming woman, but the longer she stayed, the more militant she became. In recent weeks, she has been one of our more outspoken members. Her and Mrs Green, who you may have just heard speaking.' She nodded towards the door, an exasperation to her voice, the familiar tone of a long-running issue.

'What counts as outspoken, amongst the "radical women of the WSPU"?' Ada said the last part with heavy sarcasm. 'Did she share beliefs similar to Mrs Green's?'

Mrs Cohen nodded. 'She wanted t' go further than some of us were comfortable with. We are a relatively peaceful branch. Yes, Miss Knight–'

Ada turned to Louisa, but whatever expression had crossed her face, she'd already hidden it away.

'Perhaps peaceful is not quite the right word, but I did say relatively.'

'Thrown stones and letter bombs, not warehouse fires and exploding train carriages,' Ada supplied.

'Indeed. Though, as you have just heard, that may soon change.' She spoke with a tone of grim acceptance. 'Mrs Green and Miss Franklin were not alone in their beliefs.'

'And you?' Louisa asked with an urgency Ada was not sure the situation warranted. 'What do you believe, Mrs Cohen?'

'We will never get the vote by merely asking. That has been proven time and time again – by Asquith.' Her voice hardened on the Prime Minister's name, like most suffragettes she hated him for his broken promises two years ago. 'By parliament, by all those posters depicting us as unlovable old shrews.'

Ada laughed, but Louisa didn't. She had once admitted they hit a little too close to home, that she could never be what society thought she should be, and Ada had been insistent that did not make her ugly or unloved, the very opposite in fact.

'But I 'ave always been of the opinion,' Mrs Cohen continued, 'that we should be attacking property not people. I still stand by that.'

Louisa nodded, her left hand tapping against her right wrist, her arms loosely crossed in front of her. A gesture she did without realising it when she was deep in thought.

'Hence smashing that cabinet down in London,' Ada said. Back in February, Mrs Cohen had made headlines by breaking into the Tower of London jewel house and smashing a cabinet with a crowbar adorned with the message 'This is my protest against the Government's treachery to the working women of Great Britain.' This act had earned her the nickname The Tower Suffragette, and a second visit to Armley Gaol, cut short by a hunger strike.

Mrs Cohen smiled. 'I must confess I was rather proud of that one.'

'And so you should be.'

'Thank you. Unfortunately, not everyone agrees with you, including Miss Franklin.'

Ada scoffed. 'Who cares for her opinions? She came here to spy on you, after all.'

'Spy?'

'Ah... yes.'

Mrs Cohen sighed. 'I mean, it's not too much of a surprise to learn the police are spying on us, but I wouldn't have guessed Miss Franklin as the one doing so.' She frowned. 'Except the police themselves have arrested her now? It feels silly to even say this, but since we are dealing with spies now, is it possible this is all some elaborate cover-up?'

Ada considered a moment, remembering Inspector Lambert's grief, Miss Franklin's anger, Artie's terror. 'If it is, everyone involved should try and make a career in the picture halls. I would say Miss Franklin came to you a spy; she did not remain one.'

'Huh, should we take that as a compliment?' Her tone was aiming for dry, but the slightest hint of hysteria snuck in. 'But if what you say is true, and this is not a part of her spying, I can think of no reason why Miss Franklin would want Mr Richardson dead. I wasn't even aware they'd ever spoken.'

'So, it's unlikely to have been an affair gone wrong?' Ada was almost certain Miss Franklin had been putting on an act in that regards, at least, but it was still worth asking.

Mrs Cohen stared at her for a moment. 'No. I can't imagine that. Mr Richardson was a widower, you see, but...I don't think it was a particularly *passionate* marriage. He's had a roommate living with him in recent years, even back when his wife was alive, to help cover the rent, *supposedly*.'

'Ah,' Ada said. So, Mr Richardson had potentially been like them. Could that be why he was dead? Fear crawled up her spine. *There will always be those who want us dead.*

But no, true as that may be, if someone had wanted him dead because of that, surely it was easier to go to the police and let them and the state do the dirty work. No one had hung for so-called "gross indecency" for decades, but the hard labour sentences handed out could just as easily kill a man.

The thought did little to ease the taste of terror on her tongue.

She glanced over at Louisa, who remained quiet, though her fingers were tapping faster now.

'Why do they think Hettie's brother is involved?' Mrs Cohen asked.

'He was there,' Ada answered. 'So was Miss Dixon. There was a bit of an altercation. Mr Richardson made some insults about his sister's burns.'

'No,' Mrs Cohen shook her head. 'No. I can't imagine him doing that. It would be quite out of character.'

'Both Miss Franklin and Artie say he did.'

Mrs Cohen frowned. 'Don't get me wrong, I only knew the man a little, but he never struck me as cruel. Henry would never have the time of day for a cruel man.' She thought for a moment and added, 'Yet why would Miss Franklin and Miss Dixon's brother lie?'

'Is Miss Dixon here?' Ada asked. 'She would know the truth of it.'

'No, but her friend, Miss Jain, is. You could try to speak to her if you wish, though I can't guarantee she will agree.' Which sounded about right, judging from Ada's brief introduction to Miss Jain last year. 'And you never have explained why you are here? What does any of this have to do with the pair of you?'

'Our maid, Sophie, is a friend of Mr Dixon's.'

'Friend?' She smiled slightly. 'I had hoped you were here to join our cause.'

'There's still time,' Ada said. It was only half a jest.

'And you, Miss Knight? Do you not want the right to vote?'

Louisa startled. Her mind must have been far away. 'Excuse me, sorry, I missed what you said.' A soft blush stole through her cheeks.

She had not been herself since they arrived at the WSPU. Worry sunk its claws into Ada.

Mrs Cohen stood, waving her apology away. 'It does not matter. I'll fetch Miss Jain, so you can talk to her in private. Whatever differences we have in our approaches to women's suffrage, it is clear we all want to get to the bottom of this. I imagine even Miss Franklin's police uncle is on our side.'

'Strange bedfellows, eh?' Ada said.

'Indeed.' Mrs Cohen flinched and turned the movement into a roll of her shoulders. 'The police have not been...*kind* bedfellows these last few years.' Her brow furrowed, and her eyes seemed to stare at her hands without seeing them. What was she seeing? There had been plenty of reports of extreme force. Rumours abounded that the reality of what was happening on the streets far exceeded what was reported in the press – stories of rough treatment and hands straying where they shouldn't.

Mrs Cohen cleared her throat. 'Sorry, where was I?'

'Miss Jain,' Ada prompted. She wanted to ask if she was alright but doubted Mrs Cohen would appreciate attention being brought to her discomfort.

'Ah yes, excuse me.' She bustled out of the room. As the door opened, shouting from outside could be heard. A call to action, by the sound of it, greeted by a roar of cheers.

'I suspect the more militant side may have won out by the time the day is over,' Ada said.

Louisa made no reply, stepping away from Ada and staring out the window.

Ada followed, though there was little to see. Just a busy city centre street full of carts, trams, motorcars and people going about their work.

'What would you say,' Louisa whispered, eyes never leaving the scene outside, 'if I said I do not know how to feel about that?'

Shock jolted through Ada, jerking her head sideways to stare at her partner. Was that Louisa admitting she was coming round to the suffragettes' way of seeing things? That she could no longer condemn their violence?

It should have been a victory. They had taken different stances on this for so long, and Louisa was finally seeing it from Ada's viewpoint, but it only left her disconcerted. This wasn't right. Louisa was supposed to disagree and say this wasn't necessary. She was supposed to be the logical calm to Ada's fierce wind.

Instead, it was Ada who felt like she'd had all the air knocked out of her.

She was spared from conjuring up an answer by the opening of the door. They both spun round to find a woman watching them. It was indeed the Miss Jain that Ada had briefly met during the Pearce case, a short woman – though still a couple of inches taller than Ada – with tawny skin and black hair rolled into a high pompadour, currently topped with a large navy picture hat sporting a riot of blue and white flowers. She wore a navy dress to match, its cuffs and hems neatly embroidered with a looping white pattern. An expensive outfit for a woman who had recently lost her job.

Though the same could be said for me.

Did Miss Jain have her own Louisa keeping her afloat? Though Ada hated to consider her relationship in such terms, it was the truth of where they were.

It is more likely a man. Though I, of all people, should know not to entirely discount another woman. It would be silly to believe we are the only women like us.

'Ada Chapman.' Miss Jain tilted her head to survey her. 'We have met before, briefly, Miss Chapman. Do you remember?' Her accent had a lilt to it that Ada – having never left the county of Yorkshire, never mind the country – did not recognise, a much subtler version of the over-the-top "exotic" voice she had used on stage.

'I remember. I wasn't sure you would. Has Mrs Cohen told you why we are here?'

'She said it was to do with Hettie and her brother. Artie's been arrested, apparently?'

Ada filled her in on the basics of what had happened. The pub. The alleyway. The arrests.

'Shit!' she muttered under her breath. 'I thought Hettie must be ill.' She swore again. 'I need to go home. I need to speak with her. I need to–'

'She isn't home. We went there first. We were hoping you would know where she is.'

Miss Jain thought for a moment. 'I have no idea where she could be. I am not her keeper. What is all this to you, anyway?' She stopped and stared at them. Ada could practically hear the cogs whirring in her mind. 'You're investigating again. Like you did with Eliza.' Her eyes cut across to Louisa. 'And I don't believe we've met?'

'Louisa Knight. It is a pleasure to meet you, even under these less-than-stellar circumstances.'

She frowned. 'How do you two know each other?'

'We're friends,' Ada said at the same time as Louisa said, 'Ada is my companion.'

Damn. I forgot about the companion lie.

'I need a cup of tea.' Which wasn't the response Ada expected. 'Has anyone shown you the kitchen, Miss Chapman?'

'No, not yet.' She knew a pretext when she heard one. If Miss Jain didn't want to speak in front of Louisa, better to lean into that. She sent her partner an apologetic glance as she left and received a nod of understanding in return.

Miss Jain led her into a tidy kitchen where a kettle sat on the counter beside some tea and sugar caddies, several teapots, and a collection of cups and saucers.

As soon as the door closed behind them, Miss Jain turned to Ada and said, 'You don't believe Miss Franklin or Hettie's brother killed that man, even if the police do.'

'No, I don't.' She hesitated for a second. 'Nor do all the police. Or, at least, her uncle doesn't.'

That threw Miss Jain off-stride, as intended. 'Her uncle?'

'Detective Inspector Oliver Lambert. My boss... former boss.'

'Her uncle's a copper?'

Ada nodded and pointed at a teapot. 'Are we having that tea or not?' Her throat was parched. She hadn't had anything to eat or drink since breakfast, and she'd barely had any food then, thanks to Louisa's culinary disaster.

Miss Jain filled the kettle with water. 'I remember him. He came asking questions about...*that man*.' She plugged the kettle in.

Electric. Fancy. The WSPU's headquarters were not lacking. They had only got electricity across the entirety of their house earlier this year, at considerable expense to Louisa.

'Yes, he's the one Miss Armstrong told about my supposed affair with...*that man*.'

'Supposed?' Miss Jain said, but the amusement in her voice was obvious.

'Supposed,' Ada replied lightly. 'Or have you not heard from Miss Armstrong?'

'A few letters.' She spooned tea leaves into the teapot. 'She's doing well. Or so she says. I'm not sure she'd tell me if she wasn't.' Miss Jain gave a quiet tut and faced Ada again. 'But anyway, it's the same copper?'

'Yes.'

'And he's Emma's uncle?'

Ada nodded.

'She never told us she had a copper for an uncle. Though why would she?'

'Why would she indeed?' As with Mrs Cohen, the decision came lightning fast. 'Miss Franklin was spying for him.'

'What?' Miss Jain laughed, though her amusement quickly faded when Ada didn't join in. 'No? No! That's not possible. She wanted us to bomb a police station, for crying out loud.'

'She wanted to do what?' Ada exclaimed, reeling. That was what Miss Franklin had planned?

Would she truly have gone through with it?

'Yes. She thought it'd send them a message.'

'Was it Millgarth?' *Was she planning to blow up her own uncle's police station?*

'Yes, how did you... is that where her uncle works?'

'Yes.' *And Davey, too.* The realisation hit her chest like a punch. The realisation of her own hypocrisy – once again – followed seconds afterwards for a second blow. *Bring on the chaos. But only if those I love aren't caught up in it.*

But Miss Jain was still talking, and she didn't have time to linger in the spiral of her own thoughts.

'Maybe she didn't mean a word of it. If she's a spy. If she was pretending all along.' Miss Jain scoffed. 'She seemed so genuine. God, she was trying to convince me to help with the bombing campaigns. To start a campaign here in Leeds – her and Lydia. Was that an attempt to trip me up? To get me to commit a crime so she could run back to her detective uncle and get me arrested? Fuck! The bloody bitch! How could she? How could she?' Miss Jain's hand tightened into fists, her eyes cast around the room as if searching for something she could punch, and Ada took a step backwards, out of range.

Behind Miss Jain, the kettle whistled, but she paid it no heed. 'She said it to Hettie, too, even though we'd agreed Hettie shouldn't do anything too violent, nothing that could get her imprisoned, not with her leg, not when they could take her stick away if they wanted to be cruel and leave her unable to walk, like they did with that woman in the chair on Black Friday. She knew that!' Miss Jain flung her arms out for emphasis, which was better than her hitting anything, at least. 'Miss Franklin knew that, and still, she tried to convince Hettie she had to do her part. That we all did, and never mind that women like me and Hettie – women who are already marked out as different – will be eaten alive by the system and spat out in pieces.'

The kettle was now screeching a high-pitched whistle, and Ada stepped around Miss Jain to unplug it. 'If it helps, I think she was genuine in the end. When we spoke to her at the station, she was full of contempt for her uncle.'

'Enough contempt to want him dead? Far be it for me to defend a police officer, but being murdered by their own relative is not a fate I would wish on anyone.' Ada had been too stuck on the thought of Davey's dying to consider the further implications of Miss Franklin's plans, but she had to concede Miss Jain was right. Even Inspector Lambert deserved better than that.

Miss Jain fell silent as she fetched three porcelain cups and gave them a quick rinse in the sink, only breaking it to ask 'Milk? Sugar?'

'Two sugars and milk in mine, please. None in Louisa's.'

As Miss Jain poured the tea, she asked, 'How was Artie? You say you saw him?'

She nodded. 'He's scared. Understandably so. I remember how terrifying it was to sit in a police cell accused of murder.'

'Still not quite forgiven Eliza, eh?' She stirred one of the teas, spoon clunking against the side.

'No, I...' She sighed, 'I didn't mean it like that.' Ada picked up the other two teacups. 'Shall we head back?' This conversation would be easier with Louisa there to interject with clever questions.

Though, she's done little of that since we got here. Being amongst the suffragettes has really disorientated her.

Her earlier concern pooled in her stomach again, but there was little she could say or do now, even as she followed Miss Jain back to where Louisa waited.

Concentrate. I need to think of my own clever questions.

She still needed to ask about the missing money.

Back in the small office, Louisa took the cup with a grateful smile.

'We do have something else we need to ask,' Ada said.

'Then ask away.'

'Artie mentioned missing money.'

'Ah, I've heard the rumours. Is it possibly related?' She frowned. 'Could Mr Richardson have stolen it? He was lurking around headquarters the other day. He was quite rude when I tried to ask why.'

'It's a possibility. Similarly, Miss Franklin could you be your thief.'

'Or Artie?' Miss Jain added.

'A rather bold move to tell us if that was the case,' Louisa said, finally speaking up to Ada's relief. 'I cannot say he struck me as a criminal mastermind.'

Miss Jain laughed. 'No. Not quite.'

'Can you think of anyone else who could have taken it?'

'I mean, I guess Miss Langwith would be best placed – she's treasurer for branch – but I can't say I see her doing it. Too straight-laced. Though the quietest amongst us can always be surprising.'

'Tell me about it,' Ada muttered, with a glance in Louisa's direction, who seemed determined not to look at her.

'Do you know a woman by the name of Mrs Jennings?' Louisa asked. 'Artie mentioned Mr Richardson looking for her and a possible argument.'

'Mrs Jennings? I mean, she's scary enough to have someone killed – certainly, not a woman I would cross. I can't imagine her as a thief, though.'

'Can you imagine any of the women here as thieves?' Louisa asked.

'No, I can't say I do. But clearly, someone is. Unless it was Mr Richardson, but how? I would like to think more care was being taken with our donations.'

'So would I,' Ada agreed.

Miss Jain raised her eyebrows. 'Have you donated, Miss Chapman?'

'Just a little.' They'd been collecting last winter, and she had given them five shillings. It was all she could afford, with barely any personal income.

'And you, Miss Knight?'

'I have donated to the suffrage movement.' A subterfuge that didn't fool Miss Jain for a moment, judging by the amused expression on her face. Louisa had donated to the more peaceful National Union of Women's Suffrage Societies. Ada had teased her on more than one occasion about whether she was sure she had donated to the right one – the names were so similar.

'As for your missing money and where it was kept,' Louisa moved the conversation on, 'I suppose we would need to speak to this Miss Langwith regarding it.'

'Good luck,' Miss Jain said. 'She isn't the most talkative. Though,' her eyes scanned Louisa, 'I suppose she might be more likely to speak to you.'

'Why is that?' Louisa asked.

'You are of a...similar breed.'

'A similar breed?' Louisa repeated back, tone biting.

'We may as well try and speak with her,' Ada cut in. 'In case this missing money is related somehow. If Mr Richardson did steal it.' *Or Miss Franklin. Or – sorry, Sophie – Artie himself.*

'Or if he found out who stole it,' Miss Jain added. 'That could be a secret worth killing over.'

'Indeed,' Louisa agreed, her tone much more amenable. She always had been better at tamping down her anger, burying it.

'Is she here today?' Ada asked.

'In her office. I'll show you.' Miss Jain led them out of the office and back into the main room, which still surged with people. They were halfway across when Ada stopped, all thoughts of Miss Langwith and missing money flying out of her head. For there was an adolescent boy in this sea of women, and it was the last boy Ada would ever have imagined she'd see there.

'Pete?' Her exclamation cut across the crowd, and her

brother's head shot up. So, too, did the head of the woman sitting next to him.

She hurried over to where he sat at a table piled high with pamphlets and envelopes.

'You finally did it, then?' He stood, reminding her how tall her little brother was nowadays. He was past Louisa now, and if he kept growing, he would catch up to their dad and eldest brother, John, soon enough, leaving only their second oldest brother, Walter, as the short man in the family.

'Did what?'

'Joined the suffragettes. It was only a matter of time.' He turned to Louisa. 'Surprised to see you 'ere though, miss. Though I suppose plenty of bored, rich women get involved elsewhere, why not 'ere in Leeds?'

'I am not here through boredom, Peter.'

Ada turned a laugh into a cough. Even after their conversation earlier, Louisa was continuing with her absolute refusal to shorten his name. It was an ongoing fight over who could be more stubborn that Ada suspected would never have a winner.

'What are you doing here?' Ada demanded.

'Blame Kitty.' He waved a hand at his companion, an adolescent girl around his age, though her clothes made her look older from a distance. She wore a full-length burgundy dress, tucked in at the waist in a manner that had been highly fashionable last decade, its neckline and sleeve hems embroidered with red, white and silver beads. Sitting atop a pompadour of dark brown hair, swept the highest Ada had ever seen, was a matching Merry Widow hat with a wide brim and a pair of white feathers. Both items showed signs of wear and tear; quite a few of the beads were missing from the embroidery, and up-close dirt marks could be seen in the bow.

Second-hand, most likely. Or third-hand. The ostentatious clothing clashed with a child-like freckled face that betrayed her youth.

'You must be Ada. I've heard all about you.'

'Oh? I can't say Pete has been as forthcoming with me.'

'Huh?' Kitty wrinkled her nose.

'That's a fancy way of saying she didn't know about you.'

'Do Mum and Dad?'

'What do you think?'

'What about John? Or Walter?' The last was more of a joke. If John had a friendly nature that made Pete confiding in him not completely unfeasible, the notion of Pete telling the uptight Walter anything was hilarious. The pair hadn't seen eye to eye since Pete first learnt how to talk.

'No! Bloody 'ell, of course not.' He scoffed. 'I'd rather ask your advice on women.'

'Pete!' Ada hissed.

He rolled his eyes. 'What? Like everyone doesn't already know. Is it supposed t' be some big secret?'

'What do you mean?' Louisa's fear was clear to all.

Pete smirked. 'Just what I said, miss.'

'Why wouldn't he ask you?' Kitty said. 'Who better to ask than a woman?'

'That's what I meant. Obviously.' All faux innocence, though his smile was still more of a smirk.

Being tall won't stop me from kicking you int' shins.

'Obviously,' Ada agreed drily. She turned to Kitty. 'So, you're a member here then?'

'Mum is. We're living here. Dad kicked us out. Well, he kicked her out. He tried to make me stay with my younger siblings, but I didn't want none of that. I ran away.' She said the last part with a proud smile. 'Came here. Found my mum.

Convinced her to let me stay.' With a gesture at the crowded room, she sang, in a passable key, the first line of a song popular in the music halls. 'Home, home, sweet, sweet home.' She rolled her eyes. 'My dad used to sing that when he came in from pub.'

Ada smiled. 'Mine, too.' Though her dad was never a big drinker, and he had always been a merry drunk when he did. The scrunch of Kitty's forehead suggested perhaps her memories were less nostalgic, and Ada's smile drooped.

'You are living here at headquarters?' Louisa asked.

'That's what I said.'

But Ada caught up with Louisa's line of thinking. *Like the woman Artie mentioned – the one he saw arguing with Mr Richardson. Is this her daughter then?*

As if summoned by Ada's thoughts, an older woman approached the group at a trot. As she neared, the family resemblance between the two became obvious. Her dress and hat were simpler than her daughter's, but they still had the same out-of-fashion look of those bought second-hand and cheap. She wore a similar metal badge to Mrs Green, and up-close Ada could read the slogan engraved upon it, DEEDS NOT WORDS, the suffragettes' infamous call to action. Her face curdled when she caught sight of Pete. 'What are you doing here?' It was a haughtiness the grandest of dowager duchesses would have been proud of.

A jolt of annoyance shot through Ada. Yes, she had asked pretty much the same, but *she* could talk to her brother like that. Who was this woman to do so?

'Have you met Pete's sister?' Kitty entirely ignored the question.

'*Pete.*' The way she sneered his name gave Ada a sudden urge to place herself between this woman and her little brother. 'Shouldn't even be here. It's the *Women's* Political and Social Union. Go join the MPU if you want to be of use.'

'Oh, my dear Mrs Jennings, why would I do that? They aren't ever going to give either of us the vote.'

Mrs Jennings. This is the woman Artie mentioned. One of our potential suspects.

Wait, did Pete say we're never gonna get the vote?

'Oi! Don't say that!' She whacked him on his shoulder and immediately regretted it. His lanky frame was all bone.

'Get out!' Mrs Jennings ordered. 'Out!' Her shout became a screech.

'He doesn't have t' go anywhere,' Kitty insisted.

They were gathering an audience. The women of the WSPU watched, curious.

'I think I'll stay right 'ere.' Pete sat back down and grinned at her.

Mrs Jennings fumed, her face red.

'Come on, Pete,' Ada said, all protective instincts squashed. 'There's no need for this.'

'No need for what? I'm helping.' He gestured to the flyers in front of him.

'For a cause you just proclaimed your disbelief for?' Though he deserved Louisa's scorn, it was not going to help the situation.

Mrs Cohen had made her way through to their little group, her husband behind her. 'I do think you should leave now.'

'I'm quite happy where I am, thank you.'

'Pete, get up,' Ada snapped. For a moment, she thought he would keep arguing, but then with a roll of his eyes he stood, took a peaked cap off the table and jammed it on his head. He slouched out the room, one hand in his trouser pocket, the other resting on his hip. He was trying hard to appear unbothered.

Ada followed him, Louisa behind her.

'What was that?' she demanded from him as soon as they were out of the headquarters.

'Kitty's mum doesn't like me, that's all.' He shrugged and started heading down the staircase.

'And I wonder why.' Ada dogged his steps. 'Sat in the middle of WSPU headquarters saying women'll never get a vote.'

'I said either of us.' His voice was a petulant whine. 'I couldn't have more clearly been including myself.'

'You truly believe our country cannot change for the better?' Louisa's voice held none of the expected scorn. She was wistful, and not for the first time, Ada wished she could read her mind and see what was happening behind that serene surface.

Pete scoffed but came to a stop on the mid-landing to face her. 'Has it ever?'

A cloud of despair fell over Ada. 'You're too young to be this jaded.'

'I call it sensible. Isn't that what you and Mum and Dad and John and Walter all want me to be? A sensible young man?'

'Yes, but we also want you to be happy.'

'Happy?' He scoffed. 'Are you happy, Ada?'

She wanted to say yes, but the answer stuck in her throat.

As happy as I can be. She had Louisa. She had a roof over her head and food on the table, all whilst escaping from the dangerous work of the mills and factories. It was more than many had. It was less than she wanted.

He gave her a grim nod in response. 'This country – its king and its great, grand Empire – will never give us owt. You have t' take what you can.' He patted the object under his jacket.

'Peter? What do you have under there?' The caution with which Louisa asked the question filled Ada with trepidation.

He grinned at her, full of malice, and opened the flap of his jacket to reveal the butt of a gun sticking out from the waistband of his trousers.

Chapter Six

A Good Kick in the Shins

Ada's blood froze. She wanted to grab the gun and toss it in the nearest bin, as far away from her little brother as possible. Then hit him again as hard as her tiny frame could muster.

What in God's name had Pete gotten himself into? Was he planning to shoot someone? Or was he at risk of getting shot himself?

Or has he already shot someone?

No, Pete had no reason to want Mr Richardson dead. No connection to this crime.

Except a gun and a connection to the daughter of the woman a dead man was seen arguing with.

No.

Or maybe he's a fourteen-year-old boy trying to act like a man. Nothing more.

It was a cold comfort. Even if it was posturing, it didn't change the fact that guns escalated everything. They could lead a silly boy trying to act tough all the way to murder and the noose. Poor, scared Artie Dixon was proof enough of that, even if he claimed not to be the one holding the gun.

The snap of the trapdoor and the creak of the rope. She flinched at the well-known and well-despised echoes in her head. Had she imagined a hanging so many times she had made it inevitable she would lose someone to the rope? If only she could convince Pete to visit Mabel, she'd set him bloody straight in no time.

'What the fuck are you doing with that thing?' The curse word came out unbidden, and she couldn't bring herself to care.

'It's just protection.'

'From who exactly? The suffragette movement isn't targeting idiotic young boys, so you should be safe there.'

'Peter,' Louisa interrupted. 'Has someone threatened you?'

'Your concern's touching, miss.' He said it as a sneer, and the desire to smack him round the head returned full force. The light touch of Louisa's hand on her wrist said her partner knew exactly what she wanted to do, and it would be better if she didn't. 'But not needed. Like I said, I can take care of myself.'

'And that requires *a gun*?'

He answered calmly. 'You never know when you might need one.'

Ada's reply was not calm. 'Why would you—'

'Pete,' a voice interrupted. He quickly moved his jacket to cover the gun as Kitty came down the stairs after them. 'Wait up! Did you really think I'd let Mum kick you out and not come after you?' She grinned at him, flashing the gap in her front teeth, and the smile only made her look younger. Ada wanted to yank this girl away from her brother and his secrets and his gun. 'Like I want to stick around once you've got Mum all riled up like that.'

'Don't take much. Not my fault she believes in a load of old cobblers.'

She should kick him. Louisa couldn't hold onto her ankle, at least not without causing a scene.

Kitty giggled, a shrill sound. 'You shouldn't say that, Pete.'

She turned to Ada. 'He's terrible, isn't he?' She said it like a compliment.

That wasn't Ada's current choice of words. A bloody blighter. A damned idiot. A fucking no-good fool.

A boy trying to make his way in a cruel world. But that would not do. She did not want to sympathise with him. He would not be the one who had to tell Mum if he wound up dead.

An old memory flickered across her mind – her mum hanging over Pete's crib, listening to him breathe, worry taut on her face, and even Ada, young as she had been, knew why. Her other little brother, George, had been put in his crib one night and never woke up.

'Shall we go?' Pete asked Kitty, yanking Ada out of her remembrance. He was not that baby anymore.

It won't hurt Mum any less.

Kitty nodded. 'Where to?'

'You wanted to go to that dress shop?'

She grinned and clapped her hands excitedly. 'Can we?'

'Course we can.' He said it in a proud tone he probably thought sounded suave.

Ada rolled her eyes. 'We ain't done talking.'

'I've got nowt else to say.' He pushed his way past Ada, Kitty's arm looped through his, and the two continued downstairs.

Ada stared after them, rage still simmering within. 'Tell me I can't chase after my brother and give him a good kick int' shins.'

'If you are relying on me to hold you back, you are going to be sorely disappointed.'

'You're supposed to tell me that,' She put on a poor mimicry of Louisa's posh accent, 'You could not possibly do such a thing.'

'Only if you tell me the same when I say I might be considering picking up that cocaine habit after all. I mean, doctors prescribe it to babies in cough medicine—how dangerous can it be, really?'

Ada laughed. It was a statement so ridiculous she had no choice but to do so.

'Speaking of bad habits.' She reached into her bag and pulled out her cigarette case and lighter, settling herself on the stairs. Would the WSPU approve of her smoking in their rented hallway? Probably not, but there was currently no one here to judge her, so she couldn't bring herself to care.

She took a long drag, hoping to calm her jittery nerves, but her mind kept coming back to that sinister metal glinting against Pete's off-white shirt.

'Pete's going to get himself killed if he keeps going on like this. Lord only knows who 'e's s got himself mixed up wit' that means he's 'ad to start carrying a gun.' But Ada had worked for the police – she did, unfortunately, know the names of some of the local gangs who preyed on young boys, either for their desperation or their greed.

Receiving no response, she turned her attention to Louisa, who stood staring down at her. 'This is the part where you tell me I'm wrong.'

Their gazes locked. 'I wish I could.'

'Huh, white lies really aren't your speciality, are they?' But she had already known that. If she wanted meaningless placating words, she had asked the wrong person.

Louisa moved to sit next to her, so they blocked the entire stairwell and placed a hand on her knee. Ada instantly moved her spare hand to cover it. She needed something to hold on to in a day that had moved far, far too quick.

'There is a chance this is all nothing more than posturing.

Just a boy trying to impress a girl,' Louisa said. 'I mean, people do go to weird lengths to impress those they are attracted to, right? That is something normal people do?'

Ada laughed. 'I bet you're glad to avoid all that. And who would ever want to be *normal?*'

Louisa smiled back, but it did not reach her eyes. 'Are you finished? We should probably head back upstairs. We still need to try to learn what we can about this missing money and talk to Mrs Jennings – at least we have an easier opening there now.'

'Oh yes, "Good day, ma'am, sorry about my brother being a..."' Ada didn't finish the sentence, instead taking a final pull from her cigarette.

'Shall I use my imagination for how that sentence should end?'

'Louisa, my love, I doubt you know the words to do it justice.'

She smiled. 'I have spent two years living with you now; I am sure I could give it a good go.'

'I would like to hear that.' Ada stumped the cigarette out on the handrail, which she probably shouldn't have done, but decided to at least wait until she found a bin to throw the stub away. No need to make life harder for whoever had the job of cleaning this place.

They stood and returned to the assembly rooms. Asking after Mrs Jennings, they were pointed towards a small adjoining room where several small mattresses and blankets were pushed against the wall. Was this her living quarters?

She turned towards them as they approached.

'Miss Chapman. Miss... I don't believe I caught your name.'

'Knight.'

'How can I help?'

'I wanted to apologise for my brother. He's...' She had no way to finish that sentence, at least not in polite company.

'Yes,' Mrs Jennings said with a slight smile. 'He certainly is.'

'Drives my mother barmy.'

'Now that is a feeling I know well.' Her face dropped. 'Not that I have seen my sons in recent months.'

'They are still with their father?' Ada asked, remembering what Kitty said about her siblings.

Mrs Jennings nodded.

'I'm sorry,' Ada said. 'It is...unfair.' That seemed too tame a word for the situation, though it was true enough.

Mrs Jennings shrugged. 'It is what it is. There is little can be done about it now, though I hope one day we can ensure future women are spared such pain. But that is not why you are here. Mrs Cohen tells me Miss Franklin has gone and got herself in trouble, as we always knew she would. Though, apparently, she was also a police spy, which came as more of a surprise, I will tell you.'

'She claims a change in heart,' Ada said.

'But then why kill Adam Richardson? The man was a pest, but he didn't have to die.'

'You knew him?' Louisa asked.

'A little.'

When it became clear she would say no more, Ada added, 'Artie Dixon says he saw the two of you arguing.'

'Well, Artie Dixon should mind his own business,' she snapped. 'Maybe if he had, he wouldn't be in this mess.'

'What do you mean?' Ada asked.

'Well, just what was he doing in an alleyway with Miss Franklin and Mr Richardson?'

Fair question.

'We never mentioned the alleyway?' Louisa said in a faux confused voice.

Oh shit. She's right.

'Maybe you didn't. You think you are the only people talking about this?'

'Who else is?' Ada asked.

'You're very nosy. For newcomers. Especially a newcomer whose brother makes a mockery of our cause.' She glared at Ada.

'I'm hardly responsible for Pete's actions.'

'Maybe someone in your family should take responsibility. Or are your parents idle layabouts, unable to control their son?'

'Excuse me?' Ada's question rang with warning, anger seizing her chest.

'You heard me. Now excuse me. Some of us have responsibilities to attend to.'

The abrupt dismissal only stoked her anger, as did the unfair characterisation of her parents. 'Like what? Attending to your daughter? Oh, where is she again?' She sneered. 'Maybe my parents aren't only ones who are *idle layabouts.* At least Dad always kept a roof over our 'eads and food ont' table. *We* never relied on charity.' There had been lean years, especially the winter when she was seven, and the factory Dad had been working at shut down, but this woman didn't need to know that. Her parents had always done the best they could – her father working hard his entire life, her mother working, too, when necessary, as well as keeping the house and caring for her and her siblings through all the years of pregnancy, childbirth and miscarriages.

Mrs Jennings coloured.

'Ada,' Louisa said softly. 'Maybe we should go.' She tugged at Ada's arm, and after a few stubborn seconds, Ada conceded.

'No charity, perhaps,' Mrs Jennings said coolly as they turned away. 'But you spend your life at the mercy of the whims of a rich woman.'

Ada whipped back around, uncertain what she would say but not willing to let that comment slide. The gentle pressure of Louisa's hand on her arm stilled her.

'No one is at the mercy of anyone's whims, Mrs Jennings.' Louisa used the voice Ada hated. The placating, calming-you-down one. She imagined Mrs Jennings would be no less impressed. 'Except perhaps all of us gathered here, at the mercy of parliament and our country's laws.'

Mrs Jennings scoffed. 'Isn't that the truth?' She turned back to Ada. 'What your friend is trying to say – in a roundabout way – is we shouldn't fight amongst ourselves.'

'Indeed,' Louisa agreed quickly before Ada could say another word. 'Thank you for your time, Mrs Jennings.'

Ada's anger still boiled, but she allowed herself to be led away. 'Well, that went according t' plan,' she muttered as they re-entered the main assembly room. It was emptier now, though; only a few women remained, talking amongst themselves. One group, Mr and Mrs Cohen amongst them, had gathered around a piece of paper, scrawled with rushed handwriting. The group appeared to be arguing over the wording of something. Miss Jain was nowhere to be seen.

Louisa replied in a low voice. 'She should not have spoken about your parents in that manner. Anyone who knows them – myself included – knows what she said could not be further from the truth.'

'Then why are you stopping me from arguing with her?'

'What good will arguing do? We do not wish to alienate the suffragettes.'

Ada paused for a second, but she had no retort, so she sighed instead. 'You're annoying when you're right.'

'I am aware. You keep telling me.'

Ada's response was cut across by raised voices. They came from the office where the bespectacled lady had stood in the doorway earlier. She turned, intrigued. 'It seems we're not the only ones causing arguments.'

A loud slam and a posh voice exclaimed. 'Why does it always come back to that with you?'

'Oh, they're at it again,' someone exclaimed from across the room. Turning, Ada found the group of mill girls from earlier.

'Who?' Ada asked the speaker and moved towards their group. She doubted it was relevant to their investigation, but it was not entirely impossible. Besides, she was curious.

'Miss Langwith and Mrs Green,' she answered. 'They've done nowt but argue this last fortnight.'

Ada tried to listen in again, but their voices had dropped, indistinguishable from the general chatter of the room.

'Daisy!' another of the girls snapped. 'Don't tell *her* anything.' She stared Ada down, hatred oozing from her gaze.

'Excuse me?' All her barely cooled anger ignited again. She had no idea what the girl meant but understanding flashed across Daisy's face.

'We have nowt t' say to you.' She crossed her arms.

'Maybe you should run off back t' police.'

Wait, do they believe I'm a spy? It made sense with her former job, but it didn't make it any less ironic. She would not take the fall for Miss Franklin's poor choices.

'Huh, you have the wro—'

'Ada,' Louisa interrupted, grabbing her arm. 'Perhaps we should go.' She was pulled away again before she even had a chance to process it was happening, as Louisa whispered, 'Let's not announce to the entire WSPU that Miss Franklin was a spy.'

'Fine,' Ada huffed. She did not repeat her earlier statement that Louisa was annoying when right. It would probably come out less like a tease this time.

'And we are probably best leaving Miss Langwith be for today.' Louisa turned to the office door, from which muffled voices could still be heard. 'Let us head home, we have learnt all we can here for now.'

By the time they had made it back on to the busy street below, Ada had forced down her frustration, reminding herself Louisa had done nothing wrong.

They discussed their next steps as they walked. 'We need to speak to Miss Dixon,' Louisa said. 'And Mr Richardson's *roommate*, but we would need an address first. I suppose the police may have one.' She checked her watch. 'But I doubt Inspector Lambert is still at work, and there is no guarantee any of the constables will help us.'

When they made it to Lowerhead Row, Ada pointed across the road, further down Briggate. 'Packhorse's down that way. Is it worth us trying to take a look? In the alleyway?'

'The police will have already been, so it is probably roped off. If anything, we would be better off trying to speak with the landlord, but...'

'He's probably not gonna react well to two unknown women alone in his pub asking him questions. I think, and this is something I never thought I'd say, but I think we need a man.'

Louisa raised an eyebrow. 'And where, exactly, does one find one of them?'

'Well...' The answer was obvious, and Ada hated herself for it. 'I have an idea. I might have to cash-in a debt, though.'

Louisa's brow furrowed. 'What kind of debt?'

'One that's eighteen years old.'

'Ah.' Understanding flooded both Louisa's voice and face. 'That is not going to go well, is it?'

Ada grimaced. 'Almost certainly not.'

Chapter Seven

From Playgrounds to Public Houses

Mrs Wilkinson beamed when she opened the door. 'Ada! It's been a long time since you were round. Does this mean you and Davey are done with your little tiff?' She turned to shout into the house. 'David! Get down 'ere! Ada's here t' see you.'

'It's good to see you, too, ma'am.' Mrs Wilkinson had been a maid, a mill girl, and then, as a married woman, taken in set pieces to sew until her hands grew stiff and Davey – her only son – began to bring in a semi-decent wage as a police constable to bolster his father's factory pay packet. The idea of anyone outside their neighbourhood calling her 'ma'am' would be laughable, but Ada had been taught to respect her peers' parents.

'Come in, come in. Your friend, too. Aren't you going to introduce us?'

'This is Miss Knight.' To Louisa, she said, 'This is Davey's mother, Mrs Wilkinson.'

'It is lovely to meet you, ma'am,' Louisa's voice was as posh as ever, but there was no hint of satire, and Ada loved her a little bit more for it.

Davey thundered down the stairs as they stepped inside, ducking his head to fit under the door frame. He took one look at them and said, 'Whatever this is, I want no part in it.'

'David!' Mrs Wilkinson scolded.

'And hello to you, too,' Ada said sarcastically.

Once, he would have laughed at that or rolled his eyes, but now the unhappiness etched onto his face didn't change.

'Could you give us a minute, please, Mum?'

'Of course.' She paused for a moment in front of him, and though her back was mostly towards Ada, her hand was just visible, pointing at Davey. Ada would have bet all the savings hidden in her old, battered cocoa jar – which admittedly was not a lot – that his mother had mouthed the words 'be nice' at him.

As soon as Mrs Wilkinson's footsteps faded upstairs, Ada said without preamble. 'How would you like the chance to help us interfere in a police case with your boss' permission?'

This, at least, got a reaction from him. 'Inspector gave you permission t' interfere with a case?'

'I didn't believe it either.'

'Why would he... oh, Richardson case, and his niece, right?'

'Right,' Ada said.

'I haven't been involved with that one. I don't know owt except station gossip.'

'Actually, we just need you to come down t' pub with us.'

'The pub Adam Richardson was shot outside, I assume? Why are you doing this, Ada? What do you care if Inspector's niece is guilty or not? You can't save every guilty woman in the country; no amount of interfering is ever going to change the fact that...' *That Mabel is in gaol.*

The unsaid words fell into the silent chasm that stretched between them. Silence had always been rare around Davey before, one or the other always having something to say, but that was when they had the easy air of long-term friends. Not now.

It was Louisa who spoke first. 'We do not know Miss Franklin is guilty yet. And the boy – Artie – is a friend of a friend.'

He turned to her. 'A friend?'

Ada answered. 'Sophie.'

'Your maid?' He was staring at Louisa, disbelieving. 'She's not your friend.'

'Whatever term you wish to use, I do care about her wellbeing.'

'Will you come with us or not?'

'If I say no?'

She stared at him for a moment before saying in a deadly serious voice, eyes never faltering from his. 'You made a promise.'

'Really? Exactly how long are you going to hold me accountable for a promise I made when I was six?' They had met on the playground in her first week at school, when he had made some joke about her birthmark, some childish insult she no longer remembered. What she did remember was rage compelling her across the playground, her fist smacking into this boy who, even then, was taller and broader than her. He had still tumbled to the ground, more due to surprise than anything. She could have made a lifelong enemy that day, but Davey being Davey had been awed by this whirl of ginger curls and tiny fists and decided there and then he wanted to be her friend, even if she was a girl. She hadn't been so keen on the idea for obvious reasons. But then he had promised to never say anything mean about her again and that they would be good friends, who stood up for each other and helped each other out, and she had desperately wanted to make a friend.

And he had kept that promise all through their childhoods. Even as an adult, he had still kept it, though he never stated it as such. He had helped her get her old job as a sketch artist, stood up for her with the other constables and took their teasing, and even during the Pearce case, he'd risked his job by not passing on the information they had been seen at the train station, potentially helping Mrs Pearce and Miss Armstrong escape. The only expectation was Mabel's arrest – he had not been able to help then, no matter how much she pleaded.

She wasn't so sure she had kept her side of the deal. But once again, lives were on the line, and their friendship was the price to be paid.

'Constable, we are asking you to come to a public house with us, not to commit treason.'

All traitors burn. Clearly, that letter was still on Louisa's mind.

'Treason?' Despite his best efforts, his amusement snuck through. Davey had never been able to stay mad for long – their current disagreement might be the longest he had ever managed. He sighed. 'If I say no, are you going to walk into a crowded pub, int' middle of town, full of rowdy drunk working men, with little care for your own wellbeing or reputation, or the fact one of you sounds like every inch the upper-middle-class lawyer's daughter she is?'

'Yes, obviously,' Ada answered cheerfully, and she knew she had him.

Still, he put on a show of protest. 'I could just let you go.'

'Well, fair enough. Can't say I didn't try.' She turned to Louisa. 'Shall we head off?'

He let out another sigh, exasperated enough she knew he was putting it on somewhat. 'Let me get my jacket and tell Mum I'm heading out.' He stomped back up the staircase.

'Thank you,' Ada called to his retreating back.

'You do know there was no way you would have actually convinced me to go inside a public house on our own?' Louisa said as a quiet aside.

'Yes, obviously,' Ada repeated in the same chirpy tone of voice.

Louisa covered her mouth to smother her laughter.

When Davey came back downstairs, he had put on a brown jacket but looked as unhappy about the situation as ever. 'Shall we go?'

'Lead the way, Constable.' This time there was definite satire in Louisa's voice.

Like his mother before him, Davey's back was now to Ada, yet she would just as willingly stake her tiny fortune he had rolled his eyes.

Let's hope we find something that makes this all worthwhile.

When they got off the tram at Briggate, Ada started to head up the street, but Davey called, 'That entrance is roped off. He was shot right int' passageway. We'll have to go t' Lands Lane.'

As they followed him, Ada said to Louisa, 'Maybe let us do the talking?'

'Unless you can do a passable working accent?' Davey turned to add.

'She cannot,' Ada replied for her. She held up a finger at Louisa's inevitable response. 'May I remind you of the one time you tried?' It had been in response to a jest and had been so terrible Ada had laughed for a solid ten minutes. How anyone could live in this city their entire life and fail so miserably at the local accent was beyond her.

'Now, that I would like to hear.' He smirked at her, walking backwards to keep facing them.

'Do be careful, Constable Wilkinson, you are about to walk into the road and that horse.'

Davey jerked around just in time to stop himself from falling down the kerb and into the path of a passing cart.

'Ha! Nearly went the same way as Emily Davison.'

'That's not funny,' Ada hissed.

'Oh, come on, Ada! It was kinda funny.' He strode up Lands Lane as if he could outrun his embarrassment.

'A woman is in hospital, Constable, gravely injured.'

'Keep making jokes about it, and maybe you will be, too,' Ada added.

He turned around just long enough that she saw him roll his eyes this time. 'You spend one afternoon with suffragettes, and suddenly you have no sense of humour.' He turned right down a narrow, cobbled alleyway. It was dimly lit, despite the sun still in the summer sky, tall buildings on either side casting it into shadow. At the end, it tapered into an arched passageway that led underneath the rooms above and onto the main street of Briggate. Rope stretched across both archways, blocking entry. Ada walked towards it, peering over the rope, but the enclosed passageway was even darker.

'Let's get this over with, shall we?' Davey moved to the pub's entrance.

'On that, we are in agreement.' Louisa followed him, and Ada – with some reluctance to leave whatever could be hidden in the gloom of the passageway – copied them.

A miasma of beer, smoke and sweat rolled over her. The pub was busy. Its patrons, as expected, were mostly men – with a few women dotted around – and a couple of their eyes lingered a little too long on the pair of them. One man glanced away guiltily when he caught Davey's eye, and Ada was hit with the frustrating knowledge he would have reacted entirely differently if it was her eye he had caught.

'Shall I get a table?' Louisa whispered. 'And you go speak to the man behind the bar.'

'Will you be alright?'

She gave a smile that was anything but convincing. 'Of course.'

Ada didn't buy it for a second, but Louisa was trying. She had come far outside of her usual habitat, for Sophie's sake. Ada wanted to take her hand or squeeze her arm, anything to offer comfort and offer thanks, but it was hardly the right location, so she nodded. 'We'll be as quick as we can.'

Davey and Ada headed towards the bar, weaving around chairs and people. A few patrons waited there, leaning against it, and they slotted into an empty space.

It took a few minutes before the barman approached them and took their order of a pint and two sherries. 'We heard you 'ad some hassle last night,' Ada said as he pulled the pint. Her voice was light, dismissive, like this was mere idle chatter.

He grunted.

'I hear the woman who did it was one of that suffragette lot. The man, too.'

The barman placed the pint on the bar. 'Adam Richardson's as much a suffragette as your friend there,' he pointed a thumb at Davey, 'isn't a copper.'

'Excuse me?' Davey said.

'Oh please, you think I can't spot a copper hiding in plain clothes? Though bringing two women with you is a new tactic, I'll give you that. Tell your friends down at station I'm not opposed to it.' He leered at Ada, who fought the urge to step away from the bar and place Davey's tall form between herself and him. 'Still, what can I help you with? I've already had your lot hanging around all day, asking questions. I've got nowt else t' say to you.'

'You wouldn't humour a lady?' Ada asked with what she hoped was a winning smile. She should have touched up her powder and rouge before she came in here.

He looked her up and down, and her skin crawled, even though she had been the one to instigate it. 'Are you a lady?'

But she could play this game. She could. She had to. 'When I want to be.'

He gave her one last appraising look and said, 'Go on then, ask your questions, and tell your police sweetheart here t' stop glaring at me.' Ada bit down the instinctive correction – it would do no harm for this lecherous man to consider her already another man's property.

Davey's thoughts must have been in line with her own because he kept quiet. If anything, he glared more.

'Was Adam Richardson 'ere often?'

He shrugged. 'Now and again. He used t' come with a few pals he worked with. Hard work to hear them tell it. Dangerous, too. He works – worked – at an arms factory. Papers may talk of alliances in Europe, with French of all people, but our army still wants all guns it can get.' He thought for a second. 'And then there was that roommate of his, but 'e only came once—bit of a pansy that one. Stuck out like a sore thumb. Bit like your friend over there.' He nodded to Louisa, who sat ramrod straight in her chair, eyes wide as the patrons at the next table got into a blazing row. Ada fought down the urge to go join her. The barman was providing potentially useful information – like the fact the man who had almost certainly been selling illicit items to the not-so-fake suffragette worked at an arms factory, and no one had thought to tell them. Inspector Lambert had said 'a factory worker'.

If Ada could ask, Louisa would tell her to stay here and get as much information as possible.

'But Adam Richardson fit in?'

'I mean, some of the lads didn't like the suffrage stuff back when he was on that.' The barman turned to a shelf behind the bar and fetched the bottle of sherry. 'Half of 'em don't even realise it affects them, too. Wouldn't know what t' do with a vote if they got it.' He sat two glasses on the bar and started pouring. 'They think it's just women getting ideas.'

Heaven forbid. She bit her tongue—hard—to keep the sarcastic response in her head only and winced at the pain.

'You alright?' the barman asked.

'Fine.'

'I thought you were about to tell me all about how women deserve to vote.'

'I'll spare my breath.' This time the sarcasm was out too quickly for her to stop it.

'Huh, smart girl.' Ada bristled at the supposed compliment. 'Is this all you wanted to know? I've already told all this t' his lot.' He jerked his head in Davey's direction. 'And I've got customers to serve.'

'Aye, hurry up,' shouted a man to Ada's right. 'What's all this about anyway? Thought you might 'ave stopped letting women in after all that hullaballoo last night.'

'Silly bugger had it coming,' called a voice from across the room. 'Going on and on about his big payday. Guess the suffragettes came for what was there's.'

'The suffragettes?' Another voice called back. 'We should shove the whole lot of them under 'orses far as I'm concerned.'

A man across the pub held his pint up. 'Three cheers t' Emily Davison, the silly old cow.'

Ada bit down on her tongue harder, the better not to cuss out an entire pub of men who were either drunk or on their way there.

'See what you've done now, miss,' the barman said. 'Might be best you get out 'ere. I don't want two murders in as many days.'

'Brown over there is right; Richardson got what was coming to him.' This from the man to Ada's left. He was older than her by about a decade, she would guess, age and work starting to weather an oval face with glinting blue eyes.

Schemer's eyes.

His gaze was so cold she had to suppress a shiver and told herself she was being fantastical. He was just a tipsy man in a pub, and she was letting her artistic tendencies run away from her.

'What do you mean? You sound like you know a lot about it.' She tried to pitch her voice so she sounded so *very, very* interested in what he, in particular, had to say. Should she flutter her eyelashes? Or was that something only done on music hall stages and picture hall screens? How did other women live their entire lives catering to what men desired? It was exhausting.

'I do. I can tell you all about it. Over a pint.'

'Another pint, please.' She slapped an extra thruppence on the bar.

'Your funeral,' the barman muttered before moving to the beer pump.

'Let's go sit with my friend,' Ada said once he had his beer, and they moved to the table, Louisa visibly sagging in relief when they did. Davey pulled a spare chair over for the man, cramming them too close round the table. With her eyes, Ada tried to tell him to take the other spare seat next to

Louisa instead of by her. She could cope with the man's closeness better than her partner. Not that Louisa would be particularly happy with Davey being too close either, but it was the better of the two options by far. Thankfully, he got the message.

'So, you want to know about Adam Richardson, eh?' the man said.

'You said he got what was coming t' him?

'Aye, what's that saying? You reap what you sow? My grandad was a farmer out Selby way before the houses went up, and that's what he always used to say. Never understood it when I was a kid.'

'What did Mr Richardson sow?' Louisa asked, and the man's head whipped around to stare at her.

'You're a posh one, aren't you?'

'What did 'e do?' Ada took a larger gulp of her sherry than advisable and winced.

'He wanted to hurt people. All these bombs and fires we're seeing, from those hell-raising women, he wanted a part of that. What he wanted t' sow was chaos, and he wanted to sell it, too, and, well, look 'ow that ended for him.'

'Sell it?' Davey asked.

'Well, that's just a rumour. I couldn't possibly comment further, officer.'

'How...' Davey threw up his hands in frustration.

'And this big payday that was mentioned earlier?' Louisa said.

'A week or so ago. He...had a few too many, shall we say? Started talking about he was going to get his fortune, leave, never come back. And he said he was going t' take it from – and this is exactly what he said, ma'am – "that fake suffragette."'

Emma Franklin. Who was buying something off him. Guns? Arms? Would that be the 'chaos' he was selling? Was she intending to turn the WSPU into an army?

Or is this how she intended to attack her uncle's police station?

'Well, guess she found out and killed 'im. Shame about that boy, like. There was no need for Richardson t' be saying the things he said that night. He should have kept the boy and 'is crippled sister out of it. And that's all I know. Thanks for pint.' He downed what was left and stood, but his gaze lingered on Ada a second longer. 'You could be a pretty girl,' he muttered, whether to himself or her, she couldn't tell, 'Shame about that mark.'

Ada's hand drifted to her cheek, too taken back to speak, even as Davey shouted, 'Oi! watch it!', his hand straying to his hip, where a truncheon would usually rest.

'She's perfectly pretty as she is.' Louisa's voice was cutting. 'Perhaps you just have poor taste.'

But the man had already walked away, oblivious to the insult he had caused, crossing the room to a table where a few men sardonically cheered at his return.

The many obscenities she should have said to him rattled through her mind, but it was too late.

Under the table, Louisa squeezed her knee. A brief touch, all she would dare to do in this crowded public space, but its message was still clear.

'Maybe we should take the barman up on his suggestion now,' Davey said, glancing around.

'What suggestion?' Louisa asked.

'That we get the hell out of 'ere.'

Their drinks were only half-drunk, Louisa must have taken two sips at most, but still, Ada stood and followed Davey out. Outside, a gust of wind blew up the alleyway, ruffling her skirts and hat, and causing the rope over the archways to creak, which stopped her in her tracks.

It's not a noose. It's only the wind. She took a deep breath and tried to steady her heartbeat.

Davey was already at the end of the alleyway near Lands Lane. Louisa had paused halfway between them and sent a querying look back at Ada.

She gave a tight nod in response. She would not think of Mabel hanging from a noose. Nor Artie. Nor Pete.

'Ada?' Davey, too, had turned round.

She had no desire to explain. But her excuse was easy and not even a true lie. 'Since everyone in that pub has already clocked you for a copper, no one's going to stop us from looking in that passageway.' She strode towards the rope, ducking underneath before either of them could protest.

She closed her eyes and took a step forward, casting herself into the role of Adam Richardson, walking away from an argument he should never have started, and not knowing his life was about to end in a dingy alleyway, his blood on the cobbles, and coating Emma Franklin and Artie Dixon's hands. Why had he been here? What had he been selling to Miss Franklin, the suffragette spy turned true believer? Guns? Explosives? And why had he picked a fight with Miss Dixon? Would he really have hit some scrawny seventeen-year-old? Why did someone want him dead?

'Ada?' Louisa broke her reverie. She, too, had passed the police rope, as had Davey. Though, he, at least, was allowed to do so.

'I'm trying to picture it. He's walking away.' She took another step forward and pointed back out the passageway, towards the door. 'If we believe them, Miss Franklin and Artie were still back there. He has his back to them.' The blood stain was easy to spot, halfway between the archways, and she walked towards it. Footsteps behind her said the other two were following. 'And is shot. Here.' She pointed at the stain, taking care with where she placed her feet, though the blood was long dried. 'And the shot came from, well, that depends who you believe.'

'He was shot in the back, according to the coroner. Inspector got him t' share his finding, despite us no longer being officially on the case,' Davey said. 'So, if he was walking away, facing this direction,' he looked out to Briggate, then turned around and pointed in the opposite direction, towards Lane Lane, 'the shot came from out there.'

Which matches what Artie says.

'Miss Franklin lied,' Ada said.

'Did she?' Davey asked, a little too interested. For the first time, it occurred to Ada that everything they had learnt would be in the ears of Inspector Lambert come tomorrow morning,

But what does that matter? We are not on opposing sides in this. We would have had to tell him anyway, eventually.

'She said the shot came from in front,' Ada explained. 'As they were watching him leave. And that he was shot in the gut.'

'More than she said to us,' Davey muttered.

'Would you prefer for your governor's insane niece to have lied to you, as well?'

He gave her the lop-sided smile she would never admit she missed. 'Well, when you word it like that... So, insane? Is that your measure of her?'

'That or she is putting on one hell of a show.'

'It honestly could be both.' Louisa crouched down beside the blood stain.

'Either way, governor won't be happy to learn his niece

said otherwise. It's not looking good for 'er. Or the boy, if he's covering for 'hr.'

'Artie told the truth,' Louisa said stiffly.

'Not if she was the one holding the gun,' Davey countered. 'Unless he told a very different story to you than he did to us. The whole story could be a lie, and they did a good job of correlating it except that one detail.'

'Perhaps.' Louisa didn't sound convinced. She paused, thinking. 'I assume the local residents have been questioned.'

Davey nodded. 'Many of them heard the shot, but by the time they got t' windows or doors, there was nowt t' see. Our suspect must have already fled.' He grimaced. 'Or remained in the alleyway and joined the pandemonium once the pub's clientele spilled out. We haven't found a single soul who saw a gunman.'

Ada cursed.

Davey chuckled drily. 'Yes, that about sums up the situation.'

She glanced around at the alley, its broken cobbles, its overflowing gutters. Did Miss Franklin or Artie throw a gun in there?

'Neither of them had a gun on them when they were arrested,' she said. 'Or at least I'm presuming we would have been told if they had.' She moved to peer closer at the gutters.

'We already searched them,' Davey said. 'Not a pleasant task, let me tell you.'

'And found nowt, I presume?'

He nodded. 'It's probably the strongest thing in their favour.'

'And brings us back to our potential mystery killer,' Louisa muttered. 'Who shot a man in, if not broad daylight than summer twilight, and disappeared without a trace.'

'That's about the long and short of it, yes, miss. Irritating, isn't it?' A shadow of his old grin crossed his face. 'But there is little more we can do here. Come, I'll walk the pair of you to your tram stop.' He held up the police rope for them to duck under.

A few passersby sent them curious glances. 'You shouldn't be in there,' a man in a cheap clerk's suit scolded them. He quickly deflated when Davey fetched his warrant card out of his pocket.

The three walked in quiet contemplation to the tram stop, where Louisa checked the timetable. 'One due in five minutes.'

Davey nodded. 'I can wait.'

Silence fell again, dragging on until Ada wanted to scream to break it.

'Who do you think did it?' she asked instead.

He thought for a second. 'Miss Franklin. Though I won't be telling governor that.'

'Probably a wise move.' Ada contemplated her next words for a few seconds before throwing caution to the wind. He had a right to know, after all, surely. 'She wanted t' blow up Millgarth.'

'She what?' Davey's shout startled a passing old couple.

'It makes sense, in a twisted kind of way.' Ada remembered Mrs Cohen's flinch, the rumours of police manhandling from Black Friday and other suffragette protests, the stories of mistreatment in the prisons, and the less-than-sympathetic enforcement of the Cat and Mouse Act.

'How exactly does me getting blown up make sense, Ada?' When he spoke in such a stern tone of voice to her, it was hard to imagine they had shared hundreds of jokes throughout the years.

'Not you, precisely.' That hypocrisy again. It was alright for the suffragettes to plant bombs, as long as it was not the people she loved in the firing line, even when they might have good cause to hate said person. 'Have you ever arrested them? The suffragettes?'

He paused, frowning, before answering. 'Once or twice. That business at the Coliseum a few years back, that protest in Armley last year.'

'Did you hurt them?' The question was out before she could stop it.

Beside her, Louisa froze.

'No! At least not intentionally. No more than necessary. I'm not Potter.' He said the last with a smile, a joke, like he expected her to laugh. She would have done once.

Ada rubbed her wrist where the odious sergeant's fingers had once dug into her skin. They'd left bruises, four stripes of purple that faded to yellow in the days after they'd left Mrs Pearce and Miss Armstrong on Liverpool's dockside.

'I have t' do my job, Ada.'

'Do you?'

'As I'm quite fond of my family having somewhere to live and food to eat, yes.' There was no humour in his voice now. 'Or have you forgotten so quickly that my dad is sick? Would you have my mum down mill age sixty – not that any of them would hire her, mind – or breaking her back taking in laundry?'

'I... No...' In her mind, Mrs Cohen flinched, and Mabel screamed as she was taken away, and Sergeant Potter's hand clamped down hard on her wrist. 'You could get a job not with police.'

'It's a bit late for that. Do you happen t' know anywhere that'll hire a former constable who got sacked? And everyone'll think I got sacked, won't they? That I was either incompetent or crooked.' He scoffed. 'So yeah, I'm sure places will be lining up t' hire me.'

'That's not...' She couldn't finish the sentence. It was true, and they both knew it.

But Davey was not done. 'It's easy to judge when you're safe and comfortable and living off the profits of all the people Benjamin Knight helped put behind bars.'

'I am not my father,' Louisa said, voice harsh.

Davey nodded. 'Do not mistake that for judgement, miss. Your father did his job, as I do mine. And no doubt many of the people he helped prosecute belonged in gaol. All I ask is for the same consideration.'

'Of course.' Louisa turned to peer down the street. Relief flickered in her eyes, and Ada followed her gaze to the approaching number three tram. 'Goodbye, Constable. Thank you for your help.' She stuck her arm out to signal to the tram.

Davey nodded his goodbye in return, a small, tight gesture, and strode away from them.

All Ada's words caught in her throat. She could do nothing but turn away, towards the road and the oncoming tram, and away from her oldest friend.

'I thought you wished to make peace with him?' Louisa watched Davey's retreating figure.

'Mrs Cohen flinched when we mentioned police.' Which was not an answer.

'Yes,' Louisa agreed softly. 'I noticed that, too.'

The tram came to a stop, and they boarded, leaving a lot unsaid and yet understood.

Chapter Eight

Speculations and Confirmations

Sophie was gone. Again. They searched every room in the house and only found Galapagos, lounging on top of one of Louisa's bookshelves. She showed no interest in coming down, so they left her in peace.

Ada led the way back downstairs. 'I suppose we shouldn't have expected her to just stay home and clean all day.'

That is what I pay her to do. Louisa kept her sarcasm to herself, trying to force down her irritation. Ada was right. Had she really expected Sophie to stay in the house and finish her work as usual?

I guess I did.

Was it not what any employer would demand? Most people would consider it a reasonable request.

Her rationale did little to stop the guilt twisting in her stomach.

'Did I ever tell you 'ow I nearly lost my arm the day after Mabel was arrested?' That drew Louisa's attention back to Ada, who turned at the bottom of the stairs.

'Excuse me?'

'I had to go t' work next day, and I was so distracted I got my sleeve caught int' loom.'

'That scar on your arm.' Louisa had asked what had happened once, several years ago. Something indiscernible had flickered across Ada's face, but then she laughed and said it was an accident when she was younger. Louisa, treading carefully back in those early days, had accepted the vagueness without questioning further.

Now, Ada pushed her sleeve up, revealing the thin white line. 'I got lucky. Fabric of my dress ripped, and I got my arm out in time. And the foreman – well, the man acting as foreman since our actual foreman was...'

Murdered. No, killed. It was not intentional.

'Anyway, he told me t' go home. I should never 'ave been there to begin with.' Her fingers traced the scar.

Louisa closed the distance and gently lifted the hand away from Ada's wrist and into hers. It was the only comfort she had to provide, for what words were there to say? Ada did not need to be told how terrible the experience had been. Nor would she appreciate pity.

Ada squeezed her hand in reply. 'But that was a long time ago now. Here in the present, it looks like I'm cooking tonight, doesn't it?'

'You do not have to. I can cook. Or, at least, I never gave myself food poisoning.' Looking back, she was uncertain how she had kept herself fed during those lonely months, but she had not starved to death, so she must have managed.

'Louisa, you burnt toast.'

'Joint effort?'

Ada raised her eyebrows.

'Where we leave you in charge of the timings?' Louisa conceded.

Her reward was Ada throwing her head back and laughing. The last of her grief washed away, or at least hidden from view. But what more could be done? What was past was past.

Unless Mr Connolly found something.

She still needed to speak with him when she had the

chance, check if he was getting anywhere with Mabel's case, and ask about Artie's representation, too.

But for now, it was time to prove she could be part-competent in the kitchen.

Dinner was not an entire disaster. At least it was not burnt. If the chicken was a little overcooked, well, Louisa did not mention it to Ada. It was, perhaps, slightly embarrassing that the two of them – at twenty-six and twenty-four – could not do a better job than one seventeen-year-old girl.

After dinner, they retired back to the sitting room. Louisa with her notebook, trying to order her thoughts, and Ada with her pencils and sketchbook.

Once she had read the same sentence three times without a single word sinking in, she gave up on the endeavour. Sophie's teary face from earlier forced itself to the forefront of Louisa's mind. What might she have done in her misery?

She ended up watching Ada sketching instead until she let out a little scream of frustration, screwed up the picture of Miss Franklin, and tossed it onto the coals of the unlit fire.

'I did not think it was that bad.'

'I don't understand her!' Ada exclaimed, jumping up from the sofa.

'You are not alone in that.' Louisa glanced at her book. Her clinical notes had captured what Miss Franklin said but gave no sense of her strange energy, her pouring hatred, her sudden willingness to talk. Louisa did not have the words to describe that.

'And where the hell is Sophie?' Ada paced in front of the coffee table, and it made Louisa tired watching her.

'She will be alright.' Louisa snagged Ada's arm as she passed, halting her frantic movement. 'Perhaps she will even have useful information. Come,' she tugged at Ada's arm, 'sit with me. Help me decipher these notes.' She smiled self-deprecatingly.

'I'm not sure how much help I can be.' But Ada acquiesced, returning to her seat and leaning in close, a hand resting on Louisa's lower back. 'But tell me, what is on your mind?'

'Why did Miss Franklin lie? About the gunshot, the position of the wound. The obvious answer is to cover up that she shot him from behind, but she must know it is an easy lie to be caught out in. And if she did not shoot him, then why lie at all?'

'She's covering for someone else?' Ada suggested. 'Though that doesn't change the fact it's a lie that's easily found out. But not everyone is as logical as you, darling.' She shot her a cheeky grin, and Louisa laughed despite herself. 'Especially not when they just witnessed – or committed – a murder. It's even possible she misremembered; the moments after the shot would have been chaotic, and we are reading guilt where there is none to be found.' Ada paused. 'And none of that helps, does it? It has cut down our options by precisely naught.'

'It was well-reasoned, though,' Louisa said. 'And Artie telling the truth to both us and the police is another strike in his favour. The lack of a gun helps, too, for them both. Though, that is another thing I do not understand. If Miss Franklin was buying something – guns or explosives – from Mr Richardson, where are they now? Inspector Lambert never mentioned...' She trailed off at the distant look on Ada's face. She doubted she had heard anything since Louisa mentioned the gun. Ada's argument with Peter felt like a long time ago, though it had only been a few hours.

'You are thinking of your brother?' She moved her hand

to rest on Ada's arm, using her thumb to caress it through the light cotton of her dress.

'He has a gun.' Ada's voice was small. 'And a link to the suffragettes.'

'But no motive.' It was the most reassuring argument Louisa had.

'Unless Miss Jennings is involved. It's her mother Mr Richardson argued with.'

'According to Artie. And we do not even know if this missing money relates to the murder. It might be a complete red herring.'

Ada's nose wrinkled in confusion. 'What do fish 'ave to do with owt?'

Louisa smiled. 'It is a literary device. It means a distraction from the main issue.'

'But why a herring...' Ada sighed. 'Never mind. That's hardly the key question here. And red fish or not, Mr Richardson's "big suffragette pay-out" could link t' missing money as much as t' whatever Miss Franklin was buying.'

'Or they could be one and the same. We do not know yet, either way. What we do know is there is no evidence so far to say Peter was involved.'

Ada scoffed. 'A missing gun and a gun in my brother's waistband – it's a hell of a coincidence. What will I do if it's Pete? I said I'd never cover for him – not for a crime like this – but that was always if they caught him. I never thought I'd be the one who leads police t' him. I can't do that. I won't. But if it is 'im and I don't...'

'Others take the fall in his place if you do not.' It was not a comforting addition. 'Whatever happens, we will face it together.' It was all she had to offer. A hand to hold and a shoulder to cry into.

Please let it not be Peter. Or Artie.

She was not sure who she was asking – the God she did not believe in? The universe cared little for anyone's pleas, and all the hoping in the world would not change facts.

Still, she hoped.

The opening of the front door interrupted her thoughts, followed by hushed footsteps.

'Meow!'

A gasp and a whispered, 'Oh, kitty, you scared me. I was trying to be quiet.'

But Ada was already up and out of her seat, opening the door to the hallway and announcing, 'Well, no need for that now, but where the hell have you been?' before Louisa had even gathered her wits and risen from the sofa.

Sophie ignored the question. 'Is Miss Knight in there, too?'

At Ada's nod, Sophie hurried past her, Galapagos at her heels. When she reached Louisa, she blurted out, 'She wanted to make bombs. The suffragette. The one they arrested. Emma Franklin, her name is. She was buying explosive powder for bombs.'

Which they had already suspected, but Louisa did not have the heart to take the victory of the discovery away from the girl. Besides, it helped to have it confirmed.

'T' blow up a police station,' Ada muttered.

'What?' Sophie's face creased with confusion. Wherever she had gained her information from, it had not included that little nugget. 'Surely, they'll—*we'll*—never get the vote if they blow up a police station.'

'It does rather feel orchestrated to generate negative attention,' Louisa agreed. 'If I had not met Miss Franklin, I would question if it was a police ploy.'

Sophie frowned at that, no doubt many questions firing in her mind, but she stayed quiet.

'Sophie, please, sit down.' She waved the maid into the seat next to her. Galapagos had already claimed the armchair, and though Ada could have sat on Sophie's other side, she plopped herself down at Louisa's feet instead, leaning against her legs. One of Louisa's hands strayed to her shoulder, but her attention remained on Sophie. 'How did you know about the powder?'

'I went to speak to Miss Dixon. I thought she might be more willing to talk to me.'

'You went to her lodgings?'

Sophie nodded.

So, she was in then.

Ada said it out loud. 'Huh, when we went, we were told she was not home. So, it would appear you were right on that score.'

'I wouldn't take it personally, miss. She wasn't up for many visitors, not after the previous night. She only let me in because Artie had told her about me. She even said she'd been hoping to meet me, though in better circumstances. We'd been talking about it before – me and Artie. He was looking forward to it.' Sophie's face lit up with a smile at the memory and just as quickly dimmed. 'He's going to be upset he missed it. If he gets out, I mean.'

'*When* he gets out,' Ada corrected.

Sophie gave her a thankful smile, but Louisa's earlier anxiety returned. It was still a promise they might not be able to keep, same as it had been when she made it to Artie.

But we have found nothing to imply his guilt so far. Nothing more than a few insults shared between him and a dead man.

And if Miss Franklin was guilty, would Inspector Lambert accept that truth and pass it on to his colleagues at Kirkstall Road Station? Or did Artie's freedom rely on Miss Franklin's innocence as well as his own?

Yet what reason did Miss Franklin have to want Mr Richardson dead? What they had learnt of their arrangement so far appeared ideal for them both. He got paid, and she got her powder for the cause. *Unless she never intended to pay him. Where had she gotten the money? An inheritance? The WSPU's missing money? But would the loyal suffragette she became have stolen from them? Or did she justify it with righteousness? That all she did, she did to help women secure the vote. Well, at least she was trying. Who am I to judge her? What have I done for a cause I supposedly believe in?*

'Inspector Lambert never mentioned any powder being found in Miss Franklin's possession. Wait, is that what you were trying to tell me earlier?' Ada's words dragged her from her spiralling thoughts.

'Yes, she did not have it on her at the time of her arrest. Or Inspector Lambert failed to inform us.'

'I don't think he knows,' Sophie said. 'Miss Dixon has it. She promised to watch the bag with it in, even though she disagreed, if Miss Franklin hurried after Artie and Mr Richardson and stopped the fight. Afterwards, she kept it, and the coppers didn't search her. No one views the young woman with a bad leg as a threat.' Scorn laced Sophie's usually placid voice.

'Of course not.' Ada rolled her eyes.

'Does Miss Franklin know she has it?' Louisa asked.

'I don't know. I didn't think to ask. Sorry, ma'am.'

'She must,' Ada said. 'If only because no one has questioned her about it.'

'And no need to apologise, Sophie. This is all helpful information. We suspected Miss Franklin was buying something from him, but this confirms it.'

'And makes her our most likely thief of the suffragette's missing money.'

Louisa was not so convinced, but if believing that helped assuage Ada's fears for her brother, she would keep her opinion to herself.

'Oh, could that be related?' Sophie asked. 'Artie mentioned it last week. Said his sister had told him.' Something about how casually she said it struck Louisa. A reminder that this boy had become an everyday part of Sophie's life, and they had been none the wiser. She had never told them.

I never asked. Why would she tell me? Unless she intended to marry and leave service.

And what would Louisa and Ada do then? How would they find a maid who could keep their secrets? And if today had proven anything, it was that Louisa was useless without a maid. Had she been too lost in her grief the first time round to notice?

I am quite possibly going to find myself in need of a gardener.

But that was getting rather ahead of matters.

'It could be related, it could not be. We simply don't know yet,' Ada answered Sophie's question.

'But it could be?' Sophie repeated. 'It could be all about this money, and Artie was just in the wrong place at the wrong time?' Her hopefulness coloured her voice. This was the solution she wanted.

And the solution most likely to involve Peter Chapman.

'It is possible,' Louisa hedged. It felt more and more like

there were no good answers to this mystery they had taken upon themselves. At the downcast expression on Sophie's face, she hastened to add, 'We will certainly investigate it, though.'

'Thank you.' With a grateful smile, Sophie stood from the sofa. 'But I am sure I've work to catch up on. And I am sorry for disappearing again, ma'am. Do you need anything? Tea perhaps? Or have you had any proper tea, I mean, dinner?'

'We have eaten.'

'I cooked, don't worry,' Ada interjected.

Sophie kept her face admirably blank.

Louisa, too, ignored that. 'A cup of tea would be lovely, thank you.'

Sophie bobbed a courtesy and left.

Ada's hands played with the skirts around Louisa's legs. 'You know anyone else would've fired her for this?'

'And who would I hire to replace her? Where I can do this,' she stroked a finger down Ada's cheek, 'and not worry about the maid walking in.' Remembering her thoughts earlier, she added, 'If this all works out well, I may have two members of staff soon.'

'Really?' Ada tilted her face upwards to look at Louisa. At such an angle, her expression was harder to read, but her surprise was still clear.

'If Sophie wants to marry.' And if Louisa could afford it. She needed to review her finances. She had her parents' inheritance and should never want for anything as long as she remained sensible. But hiring a second member of staff purely to cover up her relationship hardly counted as sensible. And that was on top of paying for two people's living expenses, especially now Ada's police sketch work had stopped.

But one problem at a time.

Ada leant her head against Louisa's leg. 'Sophie's rather young for us to be already talking about marriage, so I doubt you need to decide any time soon.' The fact there would be nothing to decide if Artie Dixon was executed hung between them, unspoken. 'And besides, we still need to talk to her about that. About, well…'

'Taking a fancy to a boy?' Louisa finished for her. 'It is possible.'

'I know. I've read your books and your pamphlets.' Ada said she had done so because she wanted to better understand Louisa's own lack of attraction. The memory warmed her heart. 'And is it not possible she enjoys this boy's company without…desiring him? I mean, you enjoy my company.' She tipped her head backwards again, grinning upwards, looking ludicrous.

Louisa rolled her eyes. 'For some reason. But yes, attraction and love and feelings and…' She stuttered over the word 'sex'. Strange to consider Sophie in such a context, though she was over the age of consent by a year. 'And, well, all that,' she finished lamely.

'All that?' Ada repeated with a laugh.

'My point,' Louisa said forcefully over her, 'is that it is complicated.'

'All the more reason for us to talk to her.'

'Yes. But…'

What to say? There was no script for this. If Louisa had wanted to ban her from having gentleman callers, there would be a precedent, orders to give, words well known to generations of both mistresses and maids. But for discussing the intricacies of her maid's sexuality? There was no status quo for that.

Perhaps because it is none of my business. Yet she did not want Sophie to get hurt or make a mistake because she wanted to deny the truth of herself.

She had been Louisa's first lifeline back to humanity after her father's death.

If her grief had clouded how inept she was at taking care of herself and her home, what state had the house been in when Sophie first came to work here? Louisa had apologised because there was extra work to do, a bit of extra clutter and dust, but when she tried to recall how bad it had been, her mind failed her. Whatever the answer, Sophie had taken it in her stride.

I can have one excruciating conversation for the sake of her well-being.

'We can do it together,' Ada murmured into Louisa's skirt.

'Please.'

'I guess if we're giving this talk, I should probably move. It's not a conversation to have sat on the floor.'

Which was such a risible notion Louisa had no choice but to laugh as Ada moved to sit beside her.

She sobered when Sophie re-entered the room and placed the tea tray on the coffee table with a slight rattle.

'Sophie, before you go, we do have one more topic we need to discuss.'

'Yes, ma'am?' Only the slightest of grooves on her forehead gave away her trepidation.

'Nowt bad,' Ada hastened to add. 'Just about Artie...and your relationship.'

'What do you wish to know, miss?'

'Well...' Here Ada tailed off.

'It is just...' Louisa did not get much further.

'He's a boy?' Sophie said it more like a question herself. 'Some people like men and women. I've read about it. Remember that time I was cleaning your study, ma'am, and you said I was welcome to read any of your books if I wished in my downtime?'

'Yes.' Louisa had thought Sophie might want a book to read before she went to sleep, but it was unlikely she had got that particular piece of information from a novel. 'Have you been reading my sexology texts?'

Red bloomed across her cheeks. 'I hope that's alright, ma'am? I didn't know what to think when I first met Artie. I was so confused, and I had seen them on your shelves before and thought they might help.'

'And they did?' Louisa asked.

Sophie nodded, and Ada chuckled. 'It appears we've prepared ourselves to have a very important conversation, and you are well ahead of us and have already done the research.'

Louisa, too, had to bite back a laugh, born more of relief rather than humour. Relief that Sophie's affection seemed genuine and also that she had not had to be the one to explain it.

'Is that all, ma'am, miss?'

'Yes, that is all. Thank you, Sophie.'

The maid retreated from the room a little quicker than usual.

I am not the only one relieved that was relatively painless.

'Well, that at least was easy,' Ada said with a grin. 'Why do I suspect it may be the only part of all this that is?'

'You should not tempt fate like that, Ada.'

She sent Louisa an incredulous look. 'Since when do you believe in fate?'

A fair point, and Louisa gave a slight tilt of her head to acknowledge it. Yet it was a fortunate happenstance that had brought Sophie into her life. She was transported back to that lonely, grieving woman in a dusty mausoleum of a house and the shy, kind girl – still overcoming her own trauma – who had helped her pick up the pieces of her life.

'We cannot let Artie Dixon die.'

The comment held little context for Ada, somewhat of a change of mood from their previous conversation, but she nodded. 'No. We cannot.'

Chapter Nine

A Nightmare

The cat would sleep in the kitchen – that was the rule Louisa had decreed when they let her stay.

The cat never slept in the kitchen. Her favourite spots included Louisa and Ada's bed, the sitting room armchair, and a cushion on Louisa's desk that she steadfastly denied leaving there on purpose. Tonight, Gal was curled up on the spare bed in Ada's painting room, relegating various half-finished canvases to the floor. Ada envied her slumber. She'd gone to bed at a sensible time with Louisa, but she'd given up on sleep after tossing and turning for hours.

She found no relaxation in her art tonight either, though that was her fault for her choice of subject. She'd covered the canvas in pencil lines, an attempt to sketch the scene at the Epsom Derby yesterday, hampered by the fact she had not been there, nor had she ever been to any horse derby. With a sigh, she reached for a rubber and scrubbed the markings away, accepting this was beyond her talents.

Still, she wanted to draw something to depict the suffragettes. Their struggle. Their fight.

Draw Millgarth going up in flames. Draw a widower shot to death in an alleyway. Draw a scared young man hanging from a noose.

She threw the pencil in frustration, straight into one of the stray water jars Louisa hated so much, splashing grey water onto the carpet. The clatter woke the cat, who meowed sleepily.

'Sorry, Gal.' She moved to crouch beside the bed and stroked the cat's head in apology. 'I just don't know what to...'

Paint. Do. Believe.

A noise in the hallway broke through Ada's self-loathing, and she stood from beside the cat as the door swung open.

'Ada?' There was a manic edge to Louisa's voice, her eyes scanning the dimly lit room.

'Louisa? I'm here. What's the—' But she could not finish her question. Louisa had pulled her into a tight hug, squashing Ada's face into her shoulder, and she was muttering a whispered litany of prayers to a God she swore she didn't believe in.

When Louisa's arms slackened, Ada stepped away.

She didn't need to ask out loud.

'I...' Louisa scrubbed a hand across her face. 'Sorry, I must have had a bad dream.'

When Ada took Louisa's hand, there was a slight tremor. 'Must have been one hell of a nightmare.'

'You could say that.'

Ada waited, tongue between her teeth to prevent any sarcasm.

'You ran in front of a horse.'

'Ah.'

'And a part of me wants to tell you to never do that, to beg and plead, and make you promise to never take a risk like that.'

Ada's chest seized, and her voice shook when she asked, 'And the other part?'

'Wishes to unleash you on the world until you force them to listen.'

'We haven't talked about what you said earlier at the WSPU.'

'Can we keep it that way?' It was a jest, though. They both knew that wasn't an option.

'Let's go downstairs, shall we? I'll make tea.'

Louisa smiled. 'You truly are your mother's daughter.'

'I should hope so. There are questions to be asked if I am not. Are you not supposed to be the scientist?'

Louisa ignored that last tease. 'Tea sounds good.' She moved towards the door and grimaced, hopping backwards. One of the water jars lay on its side, the grey liquid seeping into the carpet where Louisa's bare foot had been. She must have knocked it over during her volatile entrance.

'You may have a point about the jars.'

Louisa chuckled. 'If only I had known a nightmare would get you to admit that, I might have tried it sooner. Do you have something to clean it up?'

Ada pulled a cloth out of a basket of supplies and knelt to mop up the spill.

'I would have—'

'I know,' Ada said. She gave it a final scrub – it would have to do for now. Standing up, she retook Louisa's hand, and they made their way downstairs. A muffled bang on the floor announced Gal was coming, too.

Ada ushered Louisa into the sitting room, turning down her offer to help. 'I'm not aware of anyone ever burning tea, but I'd rather not risk it.'

'You are not letting me forget that anytime soon, are you?' But Louisa sat, and Gal jumped up to claim the spot on her lap.

'No. Never.' Ada grinned and left for the kitchen.

As she went through the routine motions of preparing the

water and tea leaves, her mind wandered to the conversation to come. What was she going to say? She imagined Louisa chained to gates, manhandled by police, starving in prison, crushed under a horse's hooves, and all her partner's fears over the last year made more sense. She had never had to worry Louisa would be the one to endanger herself, and she didn't appreciate the role reversal. Yet all Ada's arguments applied to Louisa as well. Could this now be something they did together, similar to the Cohens? How many times had Mr Cohen watched his wife risk her health and her freedom for their cause? And there must be other women in equivalent situations. They could not be the only Sapphic couple in the entire WSPU.

Some of the boiling water from the kettle splashed down the teapot as she poured, and she told herself to concentrate. She wouldn't make a fool of herself in the kitchen so soon after mocking Louisa's earlier mishaps. Then she would be the one to never live it down.

As she made her way back up the servants' staircase, the rattle of the crockery on the tea tray sounded too loud in the night's quiet. She half-expected Sophie to appear full of questions, but she must be used to sleeping through Ada's strange nocturnal habits.

'So.' Ada entered the sitting room. 'Tell me, what's going on in that great clever mind of yours?'

'Is the right to vote worth dying for?' Louisa kept her gaze on Gal in her lap, watching her hands stroke the cat's fur. 'Worth murdering for?'

Ada blinked. 'Oh wow, we're starting with the big questions, I see.'

'Sorry, I have just been...thinking.'

'Me too.' Ada placed the strainer over one cup and poured. 'But I don't have an answer. There needs to be change, of that I have no doubt.' She touched her arm, the scar from her near amputation. 'But I keep imagining Miss Franklin blowing up Millgarth. And I know the police have done terrible things. And yet...' She wasn't sure how to finish that sentence, 'and yet, and yet, and yet...'

'Nothing may ever change, not until the hands that hold the reins are forced to do so.' Louisa tried to reach for a teacup, constrained by Gal. Ada passed it to her, and she smiled gratefully. She took a sip and continued, 'But violence has achieved no progress either, or so I tell myself.' She sighed, leaning her head back against the sofa, not meeting Ada's eyes. 'Perhaps I am just a coward.'

'Why on Earth would you say that?' Ada paused halfway through dumping an extra spoonful of sugar into her drink, heaped teaspoon hovering in the air.

'I convince myself peace will prevail. Logic will prevail. All my life – with a few notable exceptions – I have believed in the law and justice and righteousness.' She spat the last like a curse. 'Did I let myself believe that because it was the simple choice? The path of least resistance.'

'No, I don't think so.'

Louisa smiled weakly. 'You have to say that, my love.'

'Your father taught you to believe all that. It is no simple task to unlearn everything you have been told is right, to sort out what you truly believe underneath all the opinions you were given as a child.' She paused for a second, but if Louisa could be this honest and vulnerable, so could she. 'Am I a coward?'

It was Louisa's turn to sputter out a shocked 'What?'

'The last few years, I've justified why I haven't got involved in the suffrage campaign – why I haven't done a single damn thing – with us, with you, and now I suspect I might not have that excuse any longer, and it terrifies me. I've been a coward before – no, please, don't argue, we both know who and what I'm referring to – but I did not think I would in this, given the chance.'

'It is only natural to be scared.' Louisa's brow furrowed. 'Do you think she was scared?'

It took Ada's tired brain a few seconds to realise who she meant. *Emily Davison.* 'I would imagine so. How can you make a choice like that and not be?'

'A choice,' Louisa muttered. 'Did she choose to die?'

Ada shrugged. 'Only she knows that. And she's not dead yet.'

'No, but...' Louisa sighed. 'I cannot imagine her chances are high.'

'No,' Ada agreed softly. 'But we're not talking about running in front of horses. We're talking protests, prison, hunger strikes—'

'Bombs?' The word vibrated in the air between them.

'Yes. Maybe. Empty buildings and warning notes. Not seeking to kill, like Miss Franklin.'

'Ah, yes, Miss Franklin. Perhaps all of this should wait until we have solved this case we promised to solve. Or is that more cowardice?'

'No. It's... what's that word you're so fond of using?'

Louisa raised an eyebrow. 'I am going to need more information than that.'

'When you're being *logical* and *sensible.*'

'Pragmatism?'

'Yes.' Ada clicked her fingers. 'Let's be honest, the question of women's suffrage is not going away anytime soon, but Artie and Miss Franklin are in a police cell as we speak.'

Louisa smiled softly. 'Now who is being *logical* and *sensible?*'

Ada wrinkled her nose, deliberately exaggerated. 'Ew. You rescind that.'

'So, solve a mystery and then cycle back to our collective crisis of confidence?'

'Surely, it's a collective crisis of cowardice?'

Louisa laughed. Loud and genuine and a little more than the joke had warranted, but it still warmed Ada's heart, and soon she was laughing, too. She tried to silence it, her mind drifting to Sophie upstairs, alone in her heartbreak.

Thankfully, Louisa's mirth had dried up, too. 'Sorry, I do not know what came over me. Your joke was not that funny.'

'Rude. True. But rude.'

'But you are correct. We need to focus on solving this. I allowed myself to be distracted. No more.' Louisa looked at her wrist, but it was bare.

Ada glanced at the mantelpiece clock. 'It's half two.'

'Will you come to bed? I sleep better when you are beside me.'

And how could Ada say no to that? She stood, feeling at peace, even though they had only delayed any decision that had to be made.

But at least we are on the same page.

Louisa held Gal in her arms. It would appear the cat would be sleeping with them, too, rule or not, and Ada smiled to herself as they made their way upstairs. Maybe between the two of them, they could ensure Louisa had a good night's sleep. No more nightmares. No more visions of Ada under a horse.

And placing bombs in a train carriage? Burning warehouses down?

Three dead in Bradford. Even if the suffragettes were not aiming to kill, their actions still had and would again.

And how many more women die because the mills are unsafe, and they are not lucky and do not get their arm free in time? Because a man presumed he had a right to her body, and she fought back? Can we ever live safely in a country where the laws are not written to protect or benefit us?

The decision was solidifying in her mind.

But first, Artie Dixon had to be free. That was one life they could save, and Sophie was at least one woman whose grief they could prevent.

Chapter Ten

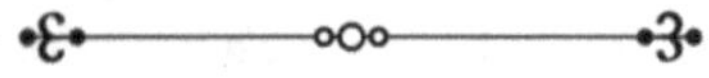

Money Matters

Several large stacks of banknotes sat on the desk between Ada and Inspector Lambert. They were in neatly tied bundles – over a few hundred pounds worth, she estimated. Ada resisted the temptation to ask if he was offering her a pay rise. The entire scene could have been transported onto a stage – the police inspector waiting for his final reveal to the audience.

What on God's green earth is this about?

The phone call she received this morning had requested her presence for a sketch. And she had indeed drawn a sketch for a befuddled witness who had mentioned her gender five times before Constable Goodwin told him to drop the matter. Afterwards, Goodwin sent her straight to Inspector Lambert's office, confirming her suspicions her newly re-hired status was a ruse.

'What have you discovered, then?'

Your niece wants to blow up a police station—probably your police station. Oh, and my brother carries a gun. And the suffragettes are missing money, and I suspect I might have just found it.

She couldn't help herself. 'What's with all the money?'

'All in due time, Miss Chapman, now, what have you found?'

It appeared the quickest way to get answers would be to give those of her own. She had discussed with Louisa what to tell him before she came. 'We went to the WSPU headquarters. There are no obvious suspects amongst them.'

'I find that hard to believe. Those women are prone to violence.'

'They want to smash windows and cause mild panic with letter bombs.' An understatement, but she would not encourage his censure of the suffragettes. 'Not shoot a man who supported their cause. Besides, if anything, they're less violent than some of the other branches of the WSPU. Maybe you should thank them.'

He scowled at her. 'You do say the strangest things, Miss Chapman. And you did learn one thing. Wilkinson says you went to the Packhorse, where Mr Richardson was seen bragging about a potential payday from the suffragettes.'

Ada nodded. 'Speaking of money...' She gestured at the notes again.

'What do you know about the WSPU's financial operations?'

'Um, not a lot. They receive money mostly from donations or the pockets of wealthy members. You lot weren't thrilled with Mrs Cohen's bragging about how much they had raised when she did that speech up on Woodhouse Moor last month, but you couldn't get the charges to stick.'

'We arrested her for inciting violence.'

'From what I heard, the police twisted her words. That's why she's not in Armley Gaol as we speak.'

His scowl deepened. Which, to be fair, had been her intention. 'What if they lied about the donations and their money was illicitly gained?'

Ada frowned. 'You think they what... stole it?'

'Forged it.' He gestured at the bundles on his desk.

'You sure?' she blurted.

He raised a sardonic eyebrow at her. 'Yes, we are. The bank confirmed it.'

'And that's suffragette money? How did you even get your hands on it? Wait, did the police steal the missing money? Is that not hypocritical?'

He didn't answer immediately, fingers tapping against his desk, his gaze flickering away from her and back, like he had to force himself to look at her. 'I found it in Emma's room, hidden beneath the floorboards. There were similar notes found on Mr Richardson's person when he died, though those are now in the evidence room at Kirkstall Road.' His gaze stilled, then sharpened, drilling into her. 'And missing money, Miss Chapman? What missing money?'

Shit.

There was nothing for it but to be honest. Mostly. 'There's a rumour the WSPU had money stolen. By your niece, by the looks of it.'

'She could have taken it as evidence of their crimes.' Even he did not sound convinced.

He is trying desperately to believe she still has some loyalty to him. The strangest swell of sympathy washed over her.

But he wouldn't appreciate her opinions or her empathy, so instead, she asked, 'What crimes?'

He tapped his desk again. 'Forging money. It always did seem unlikely so many people were willing to donate to such a renegade cause.'

The wave of her sympathy broke. Now back on more familiar territory, it took every inch of self-restraint she possessed to not roll her eyes.

'What's the sentence for forgery?' she asked instead, dreading the answer.

'A lot more than for chaining yourself to the rails of Buckingham Palace. It's a felony. Parliament is in the midst of debating a new law that would introduce a fourteen-year imprisonment.'

Ada gasped. It would be a tidy way for Leeds Constabulary to deal with the city's suffragettes. And she would have no part in it. 'I won't investigate this for you.' The fierceness of her voice surprised even her. 'I won't help you throw brave women in gaol for over a decade. Many of them have children – they'd be adults by the time their mothers got out!'

'Miss Chapman, I understand you might sympathise with the suffragette cause. Perhaps you believe their proclamations of freedom, but if they are forging money, they are in a world of trouble. Do you understand? Do not think your interference could save them. This is far above the head of a floundering artist from Leeds.'

'And also, far above the head of a deluded police inspector from Leeds?' Ada countered. The "floundering" stung.

She had hit the mark, though, and he looked away again. Ada would have bet – in non-forged money – whatever higher-ups he was supposed to inform remained ignorant about the forgeries in his niece's bedroom. He wanted Ada to investigate and find proof of her innocence before he did so.

And once I have done that – if Miss Franklin walks away – will he give the order for his men to round up the rest of the WSPU?

'I saw no evidence of forged money. And let me be clear, *I will not.*'

'You would stand by scoundrels and forgers?'

'You would arrest innocent women?'

'If they forged this money, they are not innocent. And whatever you may think, Miss Chapman, it's my duty to the law and my king and my country to ensure justice is done. And yours, too.'

'My duty to a country that won't even give me a vote?'

He sighed. 'I have arrested you once for perverting the course of justice. Do you want me to have to do it again?'

Ada glared. 'May I remind you, you asked for our help?'

'And you still want to save your maid's sweetheart, yes?'

'Yes,' Ada ground out.

'And if you're so certain he wasn't involved, then uncover the truth for me. This money may be a part of that truth.'

'And what if you don't like the truth?' There she said it.

'Why would I not like the truth? You are certain Arthur Dixon is not involved; I am just as certain Emma is not involved. My hands are tied by police protocols, but you can help find who did this. The WSPU is to blame, I am sure. Perhaps Mr Richardson had learnt the truth of their crimes.' Was she imagining the order in that sentence? The implication that, if she wanted to save Artie Dixon's life, she should find a rowdy no-good suffragette to pin it on.

Is this why he came to us instead of trusting his fellow officers? If they wanted to pin it on a suffragette, Emma Franklin was already there.

Did he really expect her to agree? That she would help him find some innocent woman to hang in Emma Franklin's place?

Anger roaring in her veins, she threw her last weapon at him. 'Do you know she wanted t' blow up a police station? Possibly 'ere, Millgarth. She was buying the powder t' do it – that's why she was int' pub that night, why Mr Richardson had some of that money on 'im when he died.'

His face sagged. 'That's a lie. A suffragette lie. If they do that, I'll hang the whole bloody lot of them.' He banged a fist against his desk, sending a bundle of cash toppling from atop its stack.

'You'd be dead. Can't hang anyone if you're dead, Inspector. But you're safe for now, as long as you keep an eye on your niece if she gets released. It was her idea. Even the other suffragettes said it was too extreme. You said it yourself; she hates you. So why go t' all this effort t' protect her? Tell me, if I come back here and say she's guilty, if I bring you the evidence to prove it, what will you do with it? Will it be you who's perverting the course of justice?'

'That's quite an accusation, Miss Chapman.' His voice was ice, slicing through her.

'You didn't say no.' And she shouldn't be enjoying goading him. But had he not done the same last year? Was he not still threatening her now?

And Artie. It's Artie's life that hangs in the balance.

'Do not make me regret asking for your help.'

'I want to find the guilty party to help Artie. That is all. I'm not investigating forgery. I won't help you set the WSPU up for that.'

'And if it is Mr Dixon?'

'Then I will tell you.' A lie. She had not decided – did not want to face that possibility. 'And if it is Miss Franklin?'

'Then she must face the consequences.'

She nodded. A beat of silence passed as the ramification of the conversation danced between them. 'I should be going.' She stood and walked towards the door.

'Oh, and Miss Chapman.' His voice brought her to a stop before the door. What now? What blow or threat was about to come?

She turned round, and he pointed at a pile of forged banknotes. 'Take one of these. It might help you, should you need to compare it to anything you find.'

'I am not investigating forged money.'

'No,' he agreed. 'But we still found similar notes on Mr Richardson's body. They could be relevant.'

Ada picked up a note gingerly. 'You're going t' let me walk out of here with evidence?'

'You still have the note that was delivered to my house, do you not? And besides, it would not be the first time you've taken something from my desk when my back was turned.'

'Your back isn't turned, though.'

His only answer was a wry smile, which unnerved her further. She slipped the banknote into her bag and said her goodbyes, hurrying out of the office wanting nothing more than to distance herself from the bizarre interaction that had taken place. She was at the exit when she remembered she was supposed to ask for Mr Richardson's address.

Luckily, Constable Goodwin was back at the front desk, so she did not have to return to the inspector's office. He was not impressed by her request, she could see every instinct he had telling him to deny her, but eventually, he caved and disappeared back into the station to retrieve the relevant file.

Which left Ada alone with her thoughts, trying to decipher what had just happened and what the next best move would be.

What is Louisa going to think of all this?

Ada barely knew what she thought of it all.

***

As agreed, Louisa waited in Victoria Arcade, peering at a display of hats in the milliner's window.

'That colour would suit you.'

Louisa jumped and tried to turn the motion into a smoothing down of her navy walking dress. Her sleepless night was plain on her face, even though she had borrowed some of Ada's powder.

'How did it go with the inspector?'

'He thinks his niece stole hundreds of pounds in forged money from the WSPU.'

Confusion, quite rightly, washed across Louisa's face.

'He insists she kept it as evidence of a suffragette crime. That Mr Richardson had some of it on his person when he died, however, implies she used it to buy powder to bomb her uncle's police station. He didn't particularly like it when I made that suggestion.'

'I thought we had agreed not to share that information?' She frowned. 'Did you tell him about the missing money?'

'Ummm...' She held a hand up before Louisa could respond. 'In my defence, he had piles of banknotes on his desk. It was disconcerting, and we didn't factor that into our decision.'

'I guess that is fair,' Louisa agreed with a slight smile. 'He just had the money piled on his desk?' She tsked. 'What cheap novels has he been reading?'

'Probably the same ones as you.' Ada grinned. Louisa's responding glare had no fire in it, and Ada tucked her arm through hers with a laugh, and they set off walking. 'But do you think I've got the right of it? That Emma Franklin was using forged money to buy illicit powder to blow up her uncle's police station?'

Louisa considered for a second. 'It is...unfortunately plausible.'

'But where did she get the forgeries from? Inspector Lambert is convinced they must have come from the WSPU.'

'That makes little sense, though. It would be out of character for the WSPU's actions – a strange choice for civil disobedience. Too quiet, for one thing.'

'Can buy a lot of firelighters, though.' That had been a part of Mrs Cohen's taunting speech to the police last month.

'And powder, as Miss Franklin proved. But would anyone in the WSPU even know how to forge money?'

'Someone might work at a printers' shop,' Ada suggested. 'Maybe one of the posh women has a husband who works in a bank.'

'Would that be enough to get the knowledge and equipment needed for a successful forgery operation?' She dropped her voice as they entered Briggate and a group of working men walked past, metal lunch boxes swinging. 'You said hundreds of pounds?'

Ada shrugged. 'It was a guess. From what I could see, they were only one and two pound notes.'

'Which makes sense, for a forgery operation, anything higher would be subject to further scrutiny.'

'Are you sure you are not involved? You seem very knowledgeable.'

'Alas, that is the extent of my knowledge,' Louisa deadpanned. 'Did you tell the inspector we would investigate this?'

Ada snorted. 'No. I made it clear I would not, in fact.'

'Good.' The reaction was so far from the law-abiding, strait-laced upstanding citizen Louisa once prided herself on being. 'Do not look at me like that. I thought you would approve.'

'I do. Still going to need an explanation, though.'

'Parliament is passing a new law. I have no desire to see any of the suffragettes imprisoned for that long.'

'Inspector mentioned it. My reaction was fairly similar. It didn't stop him from hoping I would investigate anyway. As if he could send me to do his dirty work because he no longer has a spy amongst the WSPU. Huh, I don't think so. What's he going t' do? Arrest us again?'

'He could make it difficult for us to free Artie.'

'No. He promised if we found evidence of Miss Franklin's guilt, he would see Artie freed.'

Louisa stopped and turned to study her. 'And you believed him?'

She had not considered the option that he had lied. That he would not let Artie go if they proved him innocent. For all he had tricked her last year, and she, in turn, had tricked him, so Mrs Pearce could walk free, some naïve part of her still clung to her faith in people.

'I did,' she admitted quietly. 'Now I wonder if that was foolish.'

'Or maybe I am being melodramatic. All those detective novels.' It was a weak attempt at a joke, but Ada appreciated it, nonetheless. 'For now, let us forget forgeries. Did you get Mr Richardson's address?'

'I did. He lives not far from the river; we can walk it.'

'Good, then let us stick with our original plan for the day. We will speak with Mr Richardson's roommate. And then I will go to the library, look up what I can about the arms factory, whilst you visit the gaol.' She said the last part so casually, Ada's visit to Mabel just a part of their lives now. 'Once we're home, Sophie should hopefully have got Miss Dixon to agree to see us. Then, once we know more, we can decide whether possible WSPU forging is relevant.' She gave Ada's arm a subtle squeeze. 'Come, let us go in search of answers.'

'How very melodramatic of you. Maybe you *are* reading too many detective novels.'

Louisa swatted her arm, and a laugh burst from Ada.

'If this ends with me faking my death, a la the Reichenbach Falls, let it be known you are the one who wished it into existence.'

'Come now, Louisa. I doubt Mr Richardson's roommate will be that bad.'

They crossed the bridge over the river, nearing the address they had been given.

'I hope not. I hope even more that he has answers for us.'

Chapter Eleven

Friends, Companions and Roommates

Mr Richardson had lived in a back-to-back house near the River Aire, in a row of houses stained black by soot, the original colour of the bricks a mystery lost to time. The reason for the discolourment was obvious. It sat opposite a large steelworks factory, its chimney belching out smoke, and the acrid scent mixed with the foul smell emitting from the river in the heat. If it would not have made her look like a total priss, Louisa would have fetched her handkerchief to cover her nose.

They were halfway down the street when a door burst open, and a crying girl stumbled out. 'I don't want to go. I don't want to go. I want to stay 'ere with Jacob. I want to go to Paris like Daddy promised. I WANT MY DADDY! I WANT MY DADDY! WHERE'S MY DADDY?'

An elderly couple followed her out, neatly dressed in plain clothes with no embellishments. The man gave the girl an ineffectual smack to the head.

Louisa counted the numbers down the street to confirm her suspicions. *That must be Mr Richardson's daughter.*

A glance towards Ada confirmed she, too, had figured this out. She hurried her steps, and Louisa matched her pace.

'Is everything quite alright?' They arrived as the elderly couple was trying to wrestle the girl towards a horse and cart with an impatient driver. In the doorway of Mr Richardson's house, a middle-aged man watched the unfolding event but made no move to help or ease the girl's distress.

'Fine,' the elderly gentleman said to them. 'My granddaughter is just a little upset, even though she should know such behaviour isn't acceptable.'

'Are you Adam Richardson's father?' Ada said.

'Not as far as I'm concerned,' he muttered.

The woman leant down and whispered in the girl's ear.

The girl shook her head, making her plaits swing wildly, and refused to move.

'What did your son do for you to disown him?' Louisa asked.

'Not my son,' the old man replied with venom. 'Just the man my daughter was foolish enough to marry. And who exactly are you?'

'We're old friends,' Ada lied.

The man did not look like he believed a word they said. 'Well, I am sorry for your loss, then, but we must be on our way. Come along, Cecilia.'

His granddaughter crossed her arms and planted her feet.

'You need t' go with your grandparents,' the man in the doorway said.

His gentle words knocked all the defiance out of the girl. She slumped and allowed herself to be pulled onto the waiting cart, sending a betrayed look at the man as she did.

Only after the clop of the horse's hooves and the rattle of the cart disappeared round the corner did the man speak to them. 'So, who are you? You are not old friends of Adam's – of Mr Richardson's.'

Louisa focused her attention on him. He was a plain-looking man: his face, his clothes, and his entire demeanour. His eyes did a similar sweep. What must he make of them? Two young women, dressed too finely for the area, showing up and claiming a friendship with his recently murdered roommate.

In his shoes, she would certainly find them suspicious.

His gaze lingered a second too long on Ada's birthmark, and he did the quick eye flicker of a man who did not want to be caught staring.

If Ada noticed, she did not react, but she had plenty of practice. She answered his question readily enough. 'No, we're not friends of Mr Richardson's, but we need to speak to you. You're his roommate, I assume?'

'Aye, that's me, Jacob Taylor, but I can't help you. I've already told everything I know t' coppers, and I ain't talking t' press. Tell your editor I'm impressed by his forward-thinking, sending lady reporters, but I still want none of it.' He moved to shut the door, but Ada placed her foot on the step.

'We are not press, Mr Taylor, nor police. We are just...people with an interest in seeing this crime solved. He was your friend, was he not? You must want justice for him.' She spoke kindly, a natural empathy Louisa envied.

Mr Taylor nodded slowly and sniffed. Tears were gathering in his eyes, which he ignored as if that alone could hide them. 'He was my friend, and now he's dead, and I have nothing more to say.' He moved to close the door again, but Ada's foot did not move.

'We're trying to solve his murder,' she said.

'Is that not what police are for?'

'Do you know who they have arrested for it?' Louisa asked.

'Some suffragette.'

'And a seventeen-year-old boy,' she added. 'Whose only crime might have been being in the wrong place at the wrong time. He's only just turned seventeen, not even a man yet, but still old enough to hang for a crime he did not commit. Would your friend have wanted an innocent child to go to his death for his sake?'

Mr Taylor opened his mouth and closed it again. He stared at them, struck silent by some unseen force.

'Would he have?' When Louisa had asked, she had said it as a rhetorical question, but Ada was being sincere now.

Mr Taylor's answer when it came was haunted. 'Is it terrible I don't know?'

'You don't know?' Ada was incredulous. 'What kind of company do you keep?'

'I thought I knew him, once upon a time, but...' He sighed. 'Why am I telling you this? This is none of your business.'

'Well, that's where we disagree,' Ada scoffed.

'Please,' Louisa said in a placating tone. 'If you can help make sure your friend receives justice, will you not do it?'

He paused, contemplating, and Louisa had visions of Ada's foot squashed in a doorway, but with another sigh, he stepped back.

The living room they stepped into was similar to the one in Ada's family's house, if in much more disarray. Mrs Chapman would have never left her floor in such obvious need of a sweep or allowed the mess of letters and newspapers that covered the small dining table. He waved them towards a grey sofa with fraying arms. They sunk into the fabric. If there had once been springs in its cushions, they had long since gone on strike.

He dragged a chair over from the table and faced them. 'So, how can I help?'

'Can you tell us about your friend? Anything that might be of use.'

'My friend,' he repeated bitterly.

'Yes.'

Louisa jumped a little when Ada took her hand.

'Your *friend.*'

His gaze fell to their interlocked hands, and Louisa's heart sped up. It was only a rumour he was like them. Was he about to throw them out in disgust?

'My *friend*. My *roommate*. As you are *friends.*'

'Gentlewoman and *companion*, actually.' Ada said the word 'companion' in her primmest accent.

'That rumour has travelled then. He wanted t' get us out of the country. He talked of going across Channel t' France or even further east, where the laws are not as strict, supposedly. Cece – Cecilia – wanted to go to America, but I believe it's as bad – if not worse – over there.'

'So, Mr Richardson wanted to take his family out of the country and start a new life elsewhere?' Louisa said.

'But for that, you need money,' Ada added.

Mr Taylor ran a hand through his greying hair with a sigh. 'Yes. It became an obsession after Petunia's death. He got it in his head that if we'd only left earlier, she might have survived. Somewhere away from the damp of England and this poky house.'

'Petunia being Mrs Richardson?'

'Wait, she was supposed to go with you?' Ada did not bother to hide her surprise.

'Of course.' Mr Taylor's response was curt.

'The three of you? You, your lover, and his wife?'

'That surprises you.' His voice turned sharp. 'Did you think we were sneaking behind her back? Just waiting for her to die. Adam loved Petunia, and I...' He swallowed. 'Well, whatever we were hardly matters now.'

Wait, is he saying they both loved her? And each other?

Louisa liked to consider herself more progressive than she once had been and that there was little left that could shock her. Yet it still took her back.

'Adam is dead. Petunia is dead. Cecelia is gone. Whatever strange version of a family we had is over, and whatever dreams for our future Adam harboured, they died with him.'

There was such open grief in his voice, Louisa was struck quiet. Here was a man who had lost everything – everyone – and if her own experience with grief was any barometer, she did not know how he was even still standing, talking, functioning.

'I am sorry,' Ada said. 'For your loss and for your grief. I wish we were not here, but the boy we mentioned... There is a girl who loves him, as you loved Adam and Petunia.'

He nodded stiffly. 'Ask what you need to ask.'

Louisa forced herself to focus, dredging the questions she had to ask from the back of her mind. 'What do you know about Emma Franklin?'

'She's one of the suffragettes? Petunia went to a few of their meetings, but it was a little...too much for her. She was a kind woman. The brightest person once you got to know her, but shy to those who didn't. The WSPU intimidated her a little. She never really understood the importance of the vote, not for her, but she understood the violence of smashed windows and bombs and rough police hands, and it scared her.'

He had not answered the question, but Louisa bit back her impatience. He spoke of the late Mrs Richardson with a quiet admiration that reminded her he grieved for two people.

'Adam was a suffragist, though, right?' Ada asked. 'Or is it suffragette? Can you call men suffragettes?'

Mr Taylor gave a weak chuckle. 'There was a time when Adam would have delighted in being called a suffragette, but that was before Petunia's death. After that, nowt else mattered but getting money t' get us out of old rainy Blighty.'

'And that's why he was meeting with Miss Franklin? He was selling her something?' Louisa asked. They already knew the answer, but it did not hurt to get it confirmed.

Mr Taylor nodded. 'I'd assume so. By Adam's account, she was one of the wild ones – I imagine she'd have been willing to give him money in exchange for goods stolen from his work.'

'So he stole goods from work?'

Mr Taylor hesitated but whispered, 'Yes. Powder. I found it hidden amongst the linen of all places.'

'Perfect for bomb-making.'

'Indeed.'

But then why is he dead? They both got what they wanted.

'Mr Taylor,' Ada started hesitantly. 'Was Mr Richardson ever...cruel?'

'Cruel?'

'Have you ever met Hettie Dixon?'

'Petunia mentioned her, said she was nice.'

'Did she mention her burns?'

'Yes... but what does any of this have to do with Adam being cruel?'

Ada opened her mouth to reply, but nothing came. Louisa, too, struggled to form the words. How to tell this mourning man what some of his lover's last words alive had been?

'Oh...' Mr Taylor's face fell. He must have correctly interpreted their silence. 'The man I fell in love with was never cruel. He laughed easily, but then...' He sighed. 'I didn't recognise the man he became these last few months. The anger, the grief... it changed him. Into this desperate man I barely recognised, scheming and throwing insults and threats, blackmailing people.'

'Blackmail?' Both Louisa and Ada exclaimed.

Mr Taylor winced. 'I suppose there is no use in lying to you now. It was one of the suffragettes. He never told me whom, just that they had a traitor in their midst.'

All traitors burn.

Louisa forced herself to keep her focus on Mr Taylor. If she and Ada were to trade glances, he would catch the significance in their gaze.

Emma Franklin. It has to be. How many traitors do the suffragettes have? Not another police spy, at least not one placed there by Inspector Lambert. He was too stubborn a man to have asked for their help unless it was a last resort.

'Is that who killed Adam?' Mr Taylor asked.

'It seems the most likely option,' Louisa said. 'Did he tell you anything else about this traitor?'

'No, sorry.'

'Could it have been Emma Franklin?' Ada asked.

He frowned, deep in thought. 'The last time I saw him, over breakfast, he said it was all coming together. That this time next month, the three of us would be aboard a ship t' France with enough money we would never have t' step foot in a factory again. The very last words I heard him say were a promise to Cecilia that he would take her t' top of that tower of theirs in Paris. That is all to say, the profit of stolen goods would not have been enough to live without working, but blackmail... that might have paid well enough to allow it. And it was Miss Franklin he went to see that evening, having been in such good spirits in the morning and sure of our future.'

'She refused to pay,' Ada muttered, and Louisa turned to her. 'He only had a little bit of money on his b—' She glanced over at Mr Taylor. 'When he was found. And that explains his foul mood, his comments to Miss Dixon.'

'Oh, Adam,' Mr Taylor sobbed. 'I told you it would all end in ruin.'

There was little else to ask him and even less they could say to ease his grief, so Louisa stood. 'Thank you for your time, Mr Taylor.'

He nodded, hands swiping at his eyes. 'Will you tell me? Once you know who did this? If it was Miss Franklin.'

'Of course,' Ada said.

Louisa pulled out her notebook and wrote their address and their telephone number on a page and carefully tore it. 'And here. If you need to be in touch.'

'Thank you.' He smiled at that, or at least a sad upturn of his mouth that mimicked a smile. They shook hands, and the pair of them stepped out into the humid, smoke-choked air.

'So, Miss Franklin did it, right?' Ada said as soon as the door shut behind them.

Louisa hurried them along the street, not at all convinced at how soundproof Mr Taylor's windows and front door were.

Ada kept talking. 'So, he was blackmailing her for being a police spy, and she shot him, and Inspector Lambert doesn't want to accept his niece is a murderer as well as willing to blow him to smithereens?'

'Maybe.'

'Maybe? It seems pretty clear from where I'm standing. The only question is how we convince inspector it's true.'

'And where's the gun?' She still kept coming back to that. 'And why did Artie lie for her?'

'The police could have hidden the gun. I honestly don't think the inspector's above tampering with evidence at this point. That forged money is on his desk and not int' evidence room in Kirkstall Road.'

'But he didn't have to ask for our help,' Louisa countered. 'If he knew Miss Franklin was guilty and wanted to cover it up, why drag us into it? Why give us access to his suspects and show us that threatening note and give you a forged bank note?'

'Are you just trying to be contrary at this point?'

'No.' The corner of Louisa's lips quirked for a moment, but when she continued, her tone was serious. 'We need to be certain – beyond all doubt – before we say Miss Franklin is guilty.'

Ada halted to a stop. 'Of course. You're right. We will not send an innocent woman t' gaol or t' noose. *We can't.*' There was a desperate plea in those last two words, and Louisa understood them all too well.

'We will not.' The street was empty, so she took Ada's hand. 'We will not.'

Ada clutched her hand a little tighter for a few seconds but then dropped it. 'We should be going.'

They had made it a few steps down the pavement when, with a loud 'Oh!', Ada reached into her pocket and turned on her heel. She was knocking on Mr Taylor's door again before Louisa could comprehend her action.

Mr Taylor opened the door with a puzzled expression that mirrored Louisa's confusion.

'I'm sorry to disturb you again, sir. But do you have owt with Mr Richardson's writing on it?'

'His writing?' Mr Taylor remained confused, but understanding flooded Louisa.

She wants to compare it to the note.

'If possible,' Ada said.

'I can look for something. May I ask why?'

Ada stretched out her hand to reveal the crumpled-up piece of paper Miss Franklin had given her, now even worse for wear.

Maybe leaving it in Ada's care was not the safest of plans.

He lifted it from her palm gingerly, and his eyebrows shot up when he read the words.

'All traitors burn. You think Adam wrote this?'

'He was—'

'Blackmailing someone.' Mr Taylor's voice was bleak. 'But this isn't his handwriting, I can assure you of that. It's far too neat. Adam could barely read most of the time. He was literate, but only just. He left school early. His family... well... I'm rambling, sorry. I'll see if I can find some of his writing like you asked.' He disappeared into the house.

Ada whispered, 'You were right. There goes our answer.'

'It does not entirely rule out that he was blackmailing Miss Franklin – maybe he had someone else write the notes. Or disguised his handwriting. But it makes it a lot less likely.'

Mr Taylor returned, a slip of paper in his hand that he passed to Ada carefully, who took it from him with equal care.

Louisa pressed in close to peer over her shoulder. It was a note written in a barely legible scrawl:

Gone out. Home before Cece's bedtime.

The simple domesticity of it hit Louisa hard. Had he written this the night he died? Set off with every intention of being home to put his daughter to bed?

Good night, little one. Father had made a habit of always being there at bedtime, even when he was busy for the rest of the day. One of the small ways a cold man showed his affection for his daughter. For all his austerity, she had never doubted he loved her.

The door closing dragged her back to the present, no longer that little girl.

But a woman Father could not love. Or maybe I do him a misjustice. Could he have loved me if he knew what I truly was?

'Louisa?' Ada's hand gently touched her arm.

'Sorry, I...' They had promised to talk to each other. Ada had shared so much of what she had gone through with Mabel. Did Louisa not owe her the same honesty? 'I was thinking of my father.'

'He was there every night he could be when you were a girl, to tuck you into bed and... not read you bedtime stories, I suppose. Sorry, that was...'

'True,' Louisa finished for her. Fiction was frivolous to her father, but he had still read to her – books on science, history, the natural world. 'I have told you that before?'

Of course, she had spoken to Ada about her father before, but she didn't remember sharing that exact detail.

Ada nodded. 'A while back – I don't remember how it came up in conversation.' She hesitated before adding, 'Are you questioning whether we should do this?'

'No.' One dedicated fatherly act did not make him right in all other things, even if telling herself that did not make the sense of betrayal go away. 'No. We need to do this.'

'Are you still going to the library, then?' And Ada to Armley Gaol went unsaid. 'And we will need to return to the WSPU soon. If anywhere is likely to have answers, it is there.'

'We should speak to Miss Dixon first, though, if Sophie has got her to agree. She is the suffragette most likely to help us.'

'Regroup at home then?' Ada said.

Louisa nodded. 'I shall see you later.'

Chapter Twelve

A Gaol Visit

Mabel was in high spirits today. She sat opposite Ada in the small, crowded visiting room, surrounded by other women and their families. The chatter of children filled the room, punctuated by the occasional shout from a husband or guard.

She appeared a lot healthier than when Ada had first visited eleven months ago. The shapeless grey dress was the same, but she had lost some of the hardness to her face and eyes and taken care with her hair, tying it into a neat plait. Ada never commented on these changes, never acknowledged her guilt out loud, for she could not help but attribute them to her starting to visit again, which made the broken woman Mabel had been last year her fault.

'Still hard to imagine little Pete grew up to be such a shit,' Mabel said. 'He used to follow me around like a lost puppy dog, remember? Telling me how pretty I was?'

Ada laughed, but then her smile fell. The little baby brother she once adored was now an adolescent boy with a gun down the waist of his trousers. The memories were only six years apart, a reminder that Pete was still so young. A boy out of his depth and refusing to be saved. Would she be visiting him here? Or would that gun one day lead him down the path to the noose?

Snap. Creak.

Was Ada doomed to spend her whole life worried about the people she loved being executed?

He's too young for that. For now. Thank heavens for the Children's Charter.

'Hey, none of that.' It was a light scold, not intended as a scold in truth. 'He's a silly boy; he'll outgrow this.'

'What if he doesn't get to?' The words were out before Ada could stop them.

Mabel opened her mouth, but no reply followed. What could she say, after all? Sat there as the perfect example of how one mistake could ruin an entire life, and an understandable mistake at that.

'Sorry,' Ada muttered. 'I'm being miserable. It's the last thing you need.'

'Well, tell me some good news then. What are you working on?'

Mabel asked the question every visit. Where once conversation had flowed so easily between them, it was now often stilted.

'Nowt much.' Which was the truth. Her artistic career had stalled before it ever truly began.

'Oh, come on, you must be working on something. You are always working on something. Don't tell me it's another picture of that cat of yours? The one wit' silly name.'

'It's not a silly name.' Ada insisted on this every time Gal was brought up, some stubborn defence of Louisa. It would have felt like a betrayal to agree, even though she had told Louisa countless times how ridiculous she found Gal's full name.

'Come on, you must have been up t' something interesting? Some of us have to live... What's the word? Re— ... Rec—... Vi—...?'

'Vicariously?' Ada guessed.

Mabel clicked her fingers. 'That's the one. That posh friend of yours is doing you some good.'

It hurt to hear her call Louisa a friend, even though it had to be done in such a public space. It wasn't a jape, not viciously meant.

'Anyway, I have to live vi-ca-ri-ous-ly,' Mabel sounded each syllable, 'through you. So, I need you to find something interesting to do.'

'I might end up joining you in here soon. Is that interesting enough?' The words came out blasé as if it was an ordinary thing to be saying when really, she had not decided to tell Mabel until the words were already on their way out of her mouth.

'You, what?' Any trace of amusement had disappeared from Mabel's voice. She leaned forward and whispered urgently. 'Ada, what have you done? Is this t' do with Pete? I know he's your brother, but don't you dare take any sort of fall for him. If you end up sharing a prison cell with me because of your moronic little brother, I'll kill you myself. And I'm a murderess, so you know I mean it.' If the last was meant to be a joke, it came out a little too serious sounding. 'And I may have never met her, but from all you've told me, I'm confident Louisa would agree with me on this, so that's two of us you'll have disappointed.'

'You didn't murder anyone, Mabel.' The words were rote – she'd said them many times in the last year. She wasn't even going to touch upon the comment on Louisa. If their conversation last night was any measure, even Louisa didn't know how she would react.

'Don't try and distract me with the difference between murder and manslaughter. Tell me what you've done.'

'It's what I might do.'

'Then just don't do it! That isn't complicated.'

'We're investigating the suffragettes.'

This baffled Mabel. 'And?' She only waited a second for an answer before adding, 'Also, why?'

The words spilled from Ada, all her wayward thoughts pouring out in a frantic, incoherent rush. 'A man was murdered, and Inspector Lambert's niece is a spy who turned out t' be an actual suffragette who wants t' blow up Millgarth, and Sophie's took a fancy t' a boy who might hang, and Louisa doesn't want me to die under a horse, but also doesn't want to stop me, and I don't know if I want t' be stopped or not, but if I'm not stopped then maybe I'll blow up Millgarth and end up 'ere. I mean, maybe not Millgarth—Davey is there—but there'll be something, somewhere, and I'll be 'ere. With you. Just like my worst fear, and I can't face it, I can't be trapped.' The ghost of metal handcuffs dug into her skin, the walls closing in. 'But I also can't be a coward. I won't be a coward. Not again. I won't.' She stuttered to a stop.

Mabel stared at her for a few moments, even more baffled than she had been a minute ago. 'Ada, not a single part of that made sense. Tell me why you might go t' prison.' It was a demand, not a request.

And Ada complied. 'Because once the investigation is over, I'm considering joining the suffragettes, and that will mean taking drastic action, which will result in me being imprisoned.'

'No.' Mabel crossed her arms and stared Ada down.

'Excuse me?'

'No. I won't let you, Ada.'

'You won't let me?' Ada stood from her seat, anger fizzling through her veins.

Across the room, one of the guards snapped to attention, watching her closely.

'Sit down and let me explain before you get thrown out of a prison visiting room.'

Ada sat. Mabel always had been a force to be reckoned with.

'I see them sometimes, you know, the suffragettes. They come in screaming about their rights and 'ow they're political prisoners and should be treated as such. And then they scream whilst 'ere, too, when they're strapped t' a chair and doctors are shoving tubes down their throats.'

'They've stopped that now. There's a new law.'

'Is there? I suppose there hasn't been any real commotion—no screams, at least—these last few months. But I still watch them leave. And maybe they put on a show for the outside world, for their organisation and their sisters and their cause, but I've seen the haunted look in their eyes. Some experiences can't be unlived.'

She twisted the end of her plait in her hands, her gaze over Ada's shoulder and far away. 'This isn't a kind place, Ada. I have learnt t' keep my 'ead down and my mouth shut. To swallow my pride and not look the wardens in their eyes, man or woman. To do my work,' she held out calloused hands, 'and never complain.' She put on a deferential voice, '"Yes, ma'am", "no, sir", "sorry, ma'am", "as you say, sir". You,' she pointed at Ada, 'hated how we had to grovel t' foremen and bosses at mill. And from what you've told me, you've gotten worse, you're now in the habit of talking back t' police inspectors.'

'Just one police inspector.'

Mabel shot her a glare that clearly stated the number of police inspectors was not the point, but it was the only thing

Ada could think to say, the rest of her taken back by Mabel's words. Of course, she knew Mabel was imprisoned, and prisons were not kind or gentle places, but to have it so starkly laid out before her was a different matter.

She stared at the woman before her and tried to see the high-spirited girl she had once been. *You used to stick your tongue out behind Mr Bentley's back. Look at me and pull a face during his visits. Mr Shaw caught you once and docked your wages, but we laughed about it afterwards, mocking him and his oily manner.*

Until Mr Shaw's slimy attention went too far, and Mabel had to kill him to make him stop.

Ada half-reached a hand across the table, filled with an uncontrollable urge to grab Mabel and run. Get her far away from here. Go to Roundhay, pick up Louisa and Sophie, and the four of them keep running until they were somewhere safe.

Is anywhere safe?

Mabel met her hand halfway, gently laying hers on top. 'This place breaks you, Ada. It broke me. I try my best, I look forward to your visits, and I put on my best smile, and sometimes it's genuine because, for a few brief moments, I get to feel like myself again. But that still doesn't change the person I have to be for the rest of my life. It breaks those suffragettes, much as they might lie to themselves on t'other side. If they're fool enough to come back, to be broken again and again and again... well, perhaps they'd be better off in bedlam than a voting booth. And it will break you, too. Nowt is worth that, and certainly nowt as meaningless as a vote. Most suffragettes that come in here think themselves better than me. That I belong here, and given a vote, they'd probably vote for me to stay here.'

'That's not true. Not if they knew what happened.'

Mabel smiled sadly. 'I think his wife knew. Knew what he was, what he did. Do you remember her crying at the trial? Do you think she would ever say I don't belong 'ere? Give her a vote, give her a say, and 'ere I remain.'

'Well, that's...'

'Go home, Ada. To your comfortable life and...' she dropped her voice, 'a woman who loves you. I still love you enough to want that for you over this.'

Ada was robbed of speech and thought. Mabel's words had carved into her chest and scooped her heart out.

But Mabel wasn't done. 'Do you still love me enough to do that?'

It was emotional manipulation, plain and simple. And Mabel wouldn't do that if this wasn't important to her.

'Yes,' Ada said.

Mabel closed her eyes and pulled her hand back. 'Thank you. I think you should go now.'

And senselessly, mindlessly, her mind still recoiling, Ada did.

Chapter Thirteen

Sisterly Love

Ada remained quiet as they walked, and Louisa, disconcerted, kept sending concerned glances her way, even though they were of no help. It had been the opposite when Ada got home from visiting Mabel yesterday. She had been agitated, too animated, as she told Louisa about her conversation with her former lover and the promise extracted from her. Louisa had still not decided how she felt about that – other than a general twist of anxiety every time she considered it. A year ago, she would have celebrated having the other woman as an ally, relieved their opinions were so aligned and that they would not be pulling Ada in different directions.

Now, maybe I will be the one pulling her in a different direction.

And yet she could not fault Mabel Spencer's reasoning. The idea of gaol was enough to once more keep Louisa up at night.

She yawned even as the thought passed through her mind.

Ada turned and gave her the slightest of smiles. 'This is what happens when you stay up to watch your lover paint still lifes.' They both knew Louisa had not been there simply for the love of art nor had Ada stayed up painting a vase of flowers for love of her craft. Watching her had been relaxing and quiet and a break from the voice in her head – full of questions with no answers – that would not let her sleep.

They turned onto Miss Dixon's street – Sophie had gotten her agreement to help them. This time when Louisa knocked, the same girl as before opened the door and let them in. She led them down a hallway with peeling yellow wallpaper, stopping at the bottom of a stairway to yell for Miss Dixon. It was Miss Jain who appeared, however, looking dishevelled, her long black hair plaited at the side, strands escaping. The dress she wore was a faded white, with a blotchy brown stain on one of its chest frills, startling after how smartly dressed she had been two days ago.

'Oh, it's you. Hettie said you'd be round. Come on, then. She's waiting upstairs.'

They followed her up the stairs – uncarpeted and unpainted – and along a dismal hallway to a room crowded with clutter. Every room inside a house had been forced into one space, including two beds, a dresser with its door open to reveal a hob, cutlery and crockery, and a washbasin and soap.

A woman sitting on one of the beds looked up at their entrance – Hettie Dixon. She shared the same sandy curls and soft brown eyes as her brother. A wooden cane sat propped against the wall beside her. From the discussions about her burns, Louisa had expected the scars to be quite dramatic. All that was visible, though, was a line of shiny, puckered pink skin that followed the curve of her face from her ear down past her chin and disappeared into her high neckline. It was only slightly more noticeable than Ada's birthmark. Trying not to stare – how many times had she judged others when their eyes lingered on Ada's cheek – Louisa took in the rest of the woman's appearance. She wore a faded brown day dress, fraying at the sleeves and hem, and a mostly eaten bowl of porridge balanced precariously on her lap.

'Oh, sorry,' Louisa said. 'We did not mean to disturb your breakfast.' Though it was late for breakfast. Even with their joint lack of sleep, Louisa only woke up an hour later than usual. Surprisingly, Ada, who had previously risen at noon on various occasions, was not far behind her. Miss Dixon, too, had experienced a most stressful couple of days. Perhaps she was also not sleeping well.

'My understanding is you want t' help my brother; that's worth a disturbed breakfast. I'm rather late eating, anyway.' Her spoon scraped against the bowl with a screech, and Louisa cringed as she shovelled the last few spoonfuls into her mouth.

Miss Jain took the empty bowl from her. 'Please, sit,' she said to them, using the hand holding the bowl to point at the bed opposite.

'How can I help?' Miss Dixon asked once they sat on the hard mattress.

'Can you tell us what happened that night from your perspective?' Louisa asked. Best to start with the basics and discover how her story lined up with Artie and Miss Franklin's. 'Firstly, how did you know about the meeting?'

'Kitty Jennings told me.'

'Miss Jennings is an excellent source of gossip.' Miss Jain sent a knowing look in Ada's direction, whose perplexed expression said she understood the double meaning as much as Louisa did.

'She said she heard Miss Franklin talking with Mrs Green. She was also due t' be there. You might have seen her; Aisha said she gave quite the speech at headquarters on Thursday.'

'She did indeed, and much though I'm loathed to confess it, she made several valid points.'

The woman with the bandaged hands who spoke of the horrors of the mills and factories.

'But Mrs Green did not show?' Ada asked.

'No. Miss Franklin was quite put out – though at least some of her concern was regarding whether Mrs Green had gone to cause havoc without her.'

If this Mrs Green had reason to want Mr Richardson dead, she would have known where he would be.

The rest of Miss Dixon's version of events aligned closely with Miss Franklin and Artie's. As she reached the end of her story, she paused and then added, 'I suppose Sophie told you I picked up Miss Franklin's package of powder. There was only one copper there at that point, and he was rather distracted by the dead man's body. By the time more arrived, it was already in my bag, and not even one of them considered searching me. I even took it t' police station for all the good that did me. They wouldn't let me see Artie, and no one would tell me owt. Kicked me out in the end. Sophie said they did the same to her when she got there a couple of hours later.'

'She also said you were quite ill by the time you got back,' Ada said.

She nodded. 'The barman at Packhorse, he was kind enough to pay for a cab to Millgarth, but I had to get tram home. That much walking, on top of standing around int' police station foyer, because I wasn't going to sit in their waiting room out of sight and forgotten—'

Miss Jain tsked at this.

'Aisha is about to give me one of her patented "you need to take better care of yourself" lectures.'

'Well, you do.' But Miss Jain's scolding sounded fond, like how Louisa teased Ada.

'Perhaps you are right, but this is hardly the time for it. I've already been of little use for these past two days. My brother's in a police cell, and I've been here asleep, dosed up on Winslow's.' Dr Winslow's, Louisa presumed, a well-known painkiller containing a potent mix of aspirin and heroin. It was their local pharmacist's solution to all ailments. 'But I'm awake now, and the pain is manageable. What is our next step, Miss Knight?'

They had agreed to be honest—within reason—with Miss Dixon. Her last question and her use of the word 'our' made it clear she would not tolerate being left out of the investigation or patronised with half-truths.

'Mr Richardson was blackmailing someone in the WSPU,' Louisa said. 'We need to find out who.'

Miss Jain's eyebrows shot up, and Miss Dixon frowned. 'Miss Franklin?'

'About her being a spy?' There was a hard edge to Miss Jain's words.

'We thought that, too,' Ada said. 'Someone certainly threatened her. Oh!' She reached into her pocket and removed the now familiar scrap of paper. 'Do either of you recognise this handwriting?'

Both examined the words, Miss Dixon mouthing them to herself, but answered in the negative.

'All traitors burn,' Miss Jain read out loud. 'So, someone knew she was a spy.'

'But not Mr Richardson, or at least we have reason to suspect he did not write this note.'

'Someone else could have written the note for him,' Miss Dixon said.

'True,' Ada said. 'But who?' She gasped, 'Bloody hell. I'm a fool.'

'You are nothing of the sort,' Louisa said. 'Now tell me what you just realised.'

'We never asked to see Mr Taylor's handwriting. He could easily have written the note on Mr Richardson's behalf.'

Miss Jain and Miss Dixon asked after Mr Taylor's identity, and Ada provided the watered-down roommate explanation, which gained a disbelieving snort from Miss Jain.

'We would still do well to consider who else it might have been,' Miss Dixon said. 'Mr Richardson's blackmail target, that is.'

'Artie told us that money has been disappearing – the WSPU's money. It could also potentially be linked if he knew the identity of the thief.' *And it is not also Emma Franklin and her piles of forged money hidden beneath her floorboards.*

Miss Dixon nodded. 'There's been rumours, some finger pointing.'

'And your fingers?' Ada asked. 'Where are they pointing?'

'I couldn't say,' Miss Dixon said.

At the same time, Miss Jain said, 'I already told you. Miss Langwith'

Louisa combed her memory until she reached the sound of raised voices behind a closed office door. 'Ah yes, the treasurer. We still need to speak with her.'

'Is there anything more you can tell us about her,' Ada said.

'Nothing much to say.' Miss Jain shrugged. 'She keeps herself to herself. She's never even talked to us, and she doesn't say much in union meetings, the odd comment on the budget, but that's about it.'

'Does she have any friends? Anyone she is close to?'

Both women paused to think.

'She talks to Mrs Jennings sometimes,' Miss Dixon said.

The woman who was seen arguing with Mr Richardson. Pete's sweetheart's mother. 'And the Cohens. I guess she gets along with Miss Gawthorpe, who stayed with her for a bit after getting out of Holloway. Have you ever read *The Freewoman?* Mary helps edit it.'

'I think the pair of you would like it,' Miss Jain interjected. 'She writes about all kinds of radical ideas.'

Louisa sensed there was a tease there – perhaps the idea of someone such as her, upper-middle-class and privileged, enjoying radical ideas.

'But we are getting off-topic,' Miss Dixon said with a glance towards Miss Jain.

'Right. Where were we?'

'Mrs Langwith and her associates,' Louisa said.

'Ah yes, and there's Mrs Green, too, who failed to show up for Miss Franklin. At least those two made unfortunate sense as friends. Green and Langwith, though, they were an odd pair, never made a lick of sense, them two being friends.'

'Aisha,' Miss Dixon said her friend's name in a tone Louisa knew all too well – fond exasperation.

'They were arguing,' Louisa said.

'They've done a lot of that recently,' Miss Jain said. 'Miss Langwith is a treasurer, not a bomb maker. Mrs Green, meanwhile, thinks we should all be willing to sacrifice ourselves for the cause,' Miss Jain said. 'Sometimes I would have quite liked to push her under a horse, see if she felt quite so self-sacrificing then.'

Both Louisa and Ada gasped whilst Miss Dixon hissed, 'Aisha!'

'Oh, there is no need to act like that. I'm not casting aspersions on Miss Davison's bravery, though I admit I may have done her a disservice in the comparison. Hopefully, she didn't share Mrs Green's tendency for self-congratulatory sacrifice, and God help the members of her branch if she did. I know I do not appreciate being lectured, and Mrs Green loves a lecture.' She turned to Ada. 'So did Miss Franklin near the end, I told you that. It was Mrs Green who was giving her ideas.'

'That's one way of wording it,' Miss Dixon said.

At the same time, Ada snorted, 'Ideas.'

'Glad we are all on the same page there,' Miss Jain said and turned to Louisa. 'So, what is *our* next move?' She was not nearly as subtle as Miss Dixon and Louisa suspected that was deliberate – in case they had not received the hint.

'We will need to go to the WSPU again,' Louisa said. 'I am convinced the answer to our mystery lies there, with whomever Mr Richardson was blackmailing.'

'And we need t' go back t' Mr Taylor again,' Ada said, sounding as unhappy at the prospect as Louisa was. There was no subtle way to show up on a man's doorstep and demand proof he had not written a threatening note.

'You do that first,' Miss Dixon said. 'And we will go t' headquarters. They know us. They trust us. If anyone has any rumours about Miss Franklin or the missing money, they'll be more likely to share with us.' She reached for the cane and stood with a wince.

'Also, neither of us are secretly married to police officers, which rather helps when trying to gain the trust of suffragettes.' Miss Jain smirked at Ada.

The words rattled around Louisa's mind, making less sense at every turn.

'Sorry, what did you just say?' Ada's voice went up several octaves.

'Or so your brother claims.'

Oh no.

Ada's reaction was as predictable as it was inevitable. 'I'm gonna kill 'im! I'm actually gonna kill 'im this time. After all this, I'll be one who hangs for murder, and isn't that bloody ironic?' A hysterical snort of laughter escaped from her lips.

'That's not funny.' Miss Dixon's words were harsh, her posture stiff, her knuckles white where she grasped her cane.

Ada's face fell. 'No,' she agreed. 'You're right. It's not funny. Sorry,' she added hastily. 'I'm sorry. I'm...'

'Not secretly married to a police officer?' Miss Jain finished for her, amusement laced in every word, though the glance she shot in Miss Dixon's direction was concerned.

'No,' Ada said through gritted teeth.

Maybe I will be the one to kill Peter Chapman. And that really will be ironic. Louisa, at least, had the good sense not to say it out loud.

Instead, she stood. 'Shall we go? It seems we have discussed all we need to.'

'Yes,' Miss Jain agreed. 'Though I have to be back for six,' she said to her friend.

'Ah, of course,' Miss Dixon agreed.

'What's at six?' Ada asked.

'I have an appointment. An important one. And no, I will not be expanding on that. Nothing to do with your investigation, I assure you. Now, if you would excuse us, we need to change into more suitable attire.' She waved at the door. 'There's a parlour downstairs where you can wait.'

'If you can call it that,' Miss Dixon muttered.

'There's a miserable little room our landlady insists on calling a parlour,' Miss Jain corrected.

Louisa moved towards the door, but Ada hesitated, still sitting on the bed. After a moment passed, she followed, and Miss Jain shut the door behind them.

'Oh, don't act like you weren't intrigued, too,' Ada whispered as they made their way downstairs.

'Miss Jain is not our mystery to solve... but yes, it is curious, is it not?'

'Very curious, though not enough to distract me from my plans to *murder Pete*.'

They found a door with a dull brass sign attached that said 'parlour' and entered the room. Miss Jain had not been lying when she called it miserable. With one look at the tattered chairs within, Louisa decided she would remain standing.

'You will not murder him, Ada,' she said lightly. 'How would you ever tell your mother?'

A strange flash of *something* crossed her face, gone before Louisa could even begin to interpret it. Then she rolled her eyes. 'Can I at least kick him in the shins? Hard.'

'I suppose I cannot argue against that, all matters considered.'

That at least teased a smile from her. 'How generous of you.' She rubbed at her forehead like she had a headache. 'Why would he tell the suffragettes I'm married to Davey?' Her exuberant gestures, hands raised questioningly, showed where her powder had stained the fingertips of her white lace gloves.

'Because he's a prick?' Louisa forced the curse word from her mouth.

As always, Ada delighted in hearing her swear, throwing her head back and laughing. 'That he is. At least none of this ridiculousness is likely to relate t' Miss Franklin. Speaking of which...' Her expression turned serious. 'We're off back to suffragettes.'

The unasked question after her nightmare. *'How do you feel about it?'*

Louisa shrugged. 'It was rather inevitable.' Which was a reply, if not an answer. She could process her emotions further once Artie Dixon was free. 'And to Mr Taylor's again first. Though I doubt he wrote that note.'

'No,' Ada agreed. 'Which leaves both blackmailer and blackmailee a mystery still.'

'Good job the pair of you are experts at solving mysteries then.' They both jumped at Miss Dixon's voice from behind, having not heard her come downstairs. 'Or so Aisha tells me.' She turned to smile at her friend beside her

'I would not say experts,' Louisa said. 'We solved one case.'

'Still did a better job than peelers from what I heard,' Miss Jain said. She carried a leather bag on her shoulder and when she noticed Louisa's eyes on it, she smirked. 'Ask me no questions, Miss Knight, and I will tell you no lies.'

But Ada started to ask anyway. 'Has that got—'

'That goes for you, too, Miss Chapman.'

It would appear the WSPU will receive Miss Franklin's gift in the end. The familiar squirm of anxiety wriggled in Louisa's stomach, joined by another emotion she could not place. Relief? Was she happy the WSPU would get their ill-gotten gunpowder?

'After all,' Miss Jain continued with a grin at Ada. 'I would not want you telling your hus—'

'Don't!' Ada held up a finger to cut her off. 'I'm...' She glanced at Miss Dixon. 'I'm going to tell my brother I love him and then have a very stern conversation with him.'

And also kick him in the shins, I imagine.

Miss Dixon smiled sadly. 'Me too.'

The ghost of Artie Dixon's fingers tugged at Louisa's sleeve, sweeping all other concerns aside. 'Shall we make a move then?'

Chapter Fourteen

The Treasurer

As planned, they arrived at the WSPU headquarters a few hours later, following on from their conversation with Mr Taylor. Louisa had let Ada take the lead, and though it had still been awkward, he provided proof of his own handwriting, confirming he was not the writer of their note.

The assembly rooms were quieter than last time. A few women were gathered in a small group when they entered the main room, Miss Jain and Miss Dixon amongst them. The sharp tang of paint lingered in the air, and Ada headed in their direction like it had lured her in, so Louisa followed.

Miss Jain clapped her hands in faux delight when she spotted them. 'Oh, Miss Chapman, you are an artist, are you not? We need an artist. We usually rely on Miss Acker, but she is currently indisposed.' *Imprisoned*, Louisa assumed that meant.

As the women moved to make room, the source of the smell became apparent – a half-painted banner lay spread out on the table. The paint was the signature green, white and purple of the WSPU, declaring FREEDOM FOR WOMEN. Stencilled figures were drawn on either side of the words, though Louisa could not decipher what they were supposed to be.

'Yes,' Miss Jennings said with a beaming smile. Louisa had not recognised her, for she had forgone her previous ostentatious outfit for a paint-splattered frock of indeterminable colour. 'We are certainly in need of an artist.' She glanced down at the poorly drawn figures.

Ada installed herself in front of the banner, pencil in hand, and the surrounding women resumed their conversation, leaving Louisa with little choice but to hover where she was and listen. They spoke about a woman named Lilian, imprisoned in Armley Gaol, and debated how long it would be until she was released.

They must mean Lilian Lenton. Louisa had read about her in the newspaper. Her near death in Holloway Gaol earlier in the year – and the Home Secretary's attempts to lie about it – had caused outrage and played a key part in the introduction of the Cat and Mouse act and the ending of the force-feedings. She had been in the newspapers again this week, following arson charges in Doncaster, and was, based on the conversation happening around Louisa, on another hunger strike, this time nearby in Armley Gaol.

Brave woman.

Mabel Spencer, listening to Miss Lenton's suffering from her nearby prison cell, might not agree with that assessment.

But for me to hide behind Ada's promises as an excuse truly would be cowardice.

'Miss Knight,' Miss Dixon broke through her self-deprecation. 'Since you are here, perhaps you could find a way to help, like Miss Chapman. I believe you mentioned being good with figures,' Louisa had mentioned no such thing, 'so may I suggest you would be best served speaking with Miss Langwith? Find out if there is any way in which you can assist her.'

It was not subtle, but it worked. 'What an excellent idea. Thank you.'

'She's with Leonora,' Miss Jennings called across.

'Oh, I'm sure Mrs Cohen won't mind. You two are friends, are you not?'

Acquaintances, perhaps. Ada might classify her as a friend.

'I will go ask.' Louisa strode away from the conversation before anyone else could interject.

She knocked on the office door and waited a few seconds before being called inside.

'Ah, Miss Knight,' Mrs Cohen said. 'I must confess, I am surprised to see you again so soon. This will be about Miss Franklin, then? Come in.' She shut the door behind Louisa as she stepped inside the office. 'Have you met Miss Langwith yet?' She gestured to the studious-looking woman, her dark blonde hair pulled back in a severe bun and thin oval spectacles perched on her nose. Her outfit was similar to one Louisa often favoured, a white blouse and a navy skirt.

'I have not. Pleased to meet you, Miss Langwith. In fact, I am here as it was suggested I ask if you need any help. My friend has embroiled herself in banner painting, but I am much more at home in front of an account book.'

Mrs Cohen peered at her. 'That implies you are here as members of the WSPU, not to investigate a murder. And we cannot have anyone but members see the accounts.'

'Ah. Of course.' Louisa was not sure what to say next, her ruse so quickly foiled.

'Though you already know about our missing money, I suppose.'

'The entire branch knows about the missing money,' Miss Langwith muttered bitterly.

'If it helps, we think Miss Franklin stole it.' This was not confirmed, but Louisa wanted to see Miss Langwith's reaction.

She gasped. 'Miss Franklin? How?'

'I do not know, but her uncle found hundreds of pounds hidden in her room.' She turned to Mrs Cohen. 'So, it turns out the police can find your money, after all.' She was baiting the other woman and was not happy about it. Whatever else, she had a lot of respect for Mrs Cohen: her determination, her bravery, her leadership.

'And you are certain that money is ours?' Mrs Cohen said.

'I am not, no, but he—Inspector Lambert, I mean—is.' Louisa paused. When they discussed their strategy over breakfast, neither she nor Ada had decided how much to tell the suffragettes about the suspected forgeries.

'We shall have to decide as we go,' Ada said, which was easy for her to say. Deciding as she went was not Louisa's speciality; she much preferred having a plan.

But now was the time to decide. Would telling them help or hinder their investigation?

If they are forging money, it gives them an opportunity to hide the evidence before Inspector Lambert arrives with a warrant.

The thought took her by surprise, but she could not shake it. It would pain her to see the WSPU thrown into further disrepute, and the prison sentences for forgery would certainly do that. Louisa had always wanted them to succeed, even if she did not always agree with their methods.

'Miss Knight?' Mrs Cohen prompted. 'Is there something else you wish to tell us?'

Moment of truth time. 'It's forged.' The words left her mouth in a hurry. 'The money Inspector Lambert found— it's forged. He thinks you produced it and asked Ada to look for the evidence to prove it, though she made her opinion on that idea quite clear.'

'It is not forged,' Miss Langwith said.

'Of course not, but now you know his suspicions. Do with them what you will.'

'It is not forged,' Miss Langwith insisted.

'At least not to the best of our knowledge,' Mrs Cohen added.

'If that is true—'

'It is,' Miss Langwith said between gritted teeth.

Louisa gave a concessional nod. 'Then Miss Franklin did not steal your money. Or someone stole it and replaced it with forgeries, and she unwittingly stole the forgeries. Either way, you still have a thief in your ranks as well as a former spy. Or someone who could be trying to set you up for a crime with a much longer custodial sentence than a few smashed windows.'

'And no suspects, still,' Mrs Cohen said.

'Unless you count me.' Miss Langwith smiled tightly. 'I am sure I am the prime suspect to some.' Her accent was cut-glass, which only made the sarcasm sharper, as Louisa herself well knew and had put to good effect on more than one occasion.

'You are certainly the obvious suspect, but that alone does not make you guilty.'

Miss Langwith inclined her head. Whether it was agreement or mere acknowledgement was hard to tell.

'I would ask you to keep this to yourself,' Mrs Cohen said, 'but I sense it is a pointless request the way rumours spread amongst us.'

'The missing money is a well-known rumour. The threat of being arrested for forgery, I would guess less so.'

'Then I would appreciate your discretion.' Mrs Cohen sighed. 'What a mess. I was due to go down south at the

Parkhursts' request, but it is seeming less and less likely that will happen.'

'So, you sent Lydia in your stead.' There was an edge to Miss Langwith's words, and Louisa tried to recall who Lydia was.

'She is well suited to the task required for her, you must admit. May I remind you she came to me and made the request?'

Miss Langwith deflated. 'Yes, I am aware.'

Louisa kept quiet. Lost though she was, she dared not remind them of her presence lest they clam up. However, another distraction came from a loud bang outside.

'What now?' Mrs Cohen stood and opened the office door, and Louisa moved to better see outside.

Miss Jennings glared at her mother from the middle of the room, arms crossed, every inch the petulant adolescent. 'You just don't care,' she spat. Folded across her arms was a dress that looked like Ada's, light green cotton, its buttons a colour Ada insisted on calling *forest green*, now marred with smears of purple and white paint.

Suffragette colours. In keeping with the theme, at least.

'That's not true,' Mrs Jennings told her daughter. 'If I didn't care, I wouldn't be trying to save you from your own foolishness.'

Which was an apt description of Peter Chapman. For she assumed he was the focus of this argument. He had a tendency to do that, cause arguments in his wake, as this morning only proved. Miss Jennings slammed something down onto the table and walked away from her mother in high dudgeon, leaving the door rattling in her wake. All eyes in the room turned to her mother. 'She's just being difficult again. Pay her no heed.'

A low murmur of voices replaced the silence hanging in the air. Ada chose that moment to cross the room and join them, greeting the other two women cheerily. She was definitely wearing a different dress than she had this morning; the yellow cotton drowned her lithe figure.

'Painting accident?'

'Maybe,' Ada replied with a smile, 'I let Miss Jennings keep my dress. She intended to try to salvage it for one of her sewing projects.'

'Miss Jennings is a wonder with a needle,' Mrs Cohen said. 'Speaking as the daughter of a talented seamstress, she will excel in that line of work, and hopefully, we can secure her better wages than my mother ever had.' Her voice hardened on those last words, and Louisa realised she knew little about Mrs Cohen outside her work for the suffragettes. Ada had once mentioned her marriage had been an upset for both families because of their differing religions. But beyond that, Louisa did not even know what line of work Mr Cohen was in or if Mrs Cohen had worked before her marriage.

'But, for now, you'll have to excuse me. I should go speak with Mrs Jennings.'

All three murmured assent, and Mrs Cohen left.

'I suppose you will wish to ask more questions,' Miss Langwith said. 'But I shall fetch tea first. I fear this will take some time.'

'That'd be lovely, thank you,' Ada said. As soon as the door shut behind Miss Langwith, she moved to the desk and started searching through the neat piles of paper.

'Ada, what are you doing?'

'This is the perfect opportunity. When else will we be alone in this room without suspicion?' She pointed at the papers. 'Take the drawers. Look for anything that might relate to the missing money. Any proof of who might have taken it.'

'What would that even look like?'

Ada's silence answered for her. She did not know.

'This is a terrible idea.' But Louisa moved next to her. 'But not the worst one you have ever had.' She bent down to try each desk drawer. The first one did not open, and she spotted a small bronze lock in the centre of the panel, but the next three slid forward to reveal more neat stacks of paper. 'We will not have time to search them all.'

'Then we should definitely start with whatever is in that locked drawer.'

Sound logic, but with one obvious flaw. 'We do not have the key.'

'Who needs a key?' Ada crouched down, studying the lock. 'Listen out for anyone approaching. I'll have it open in no time.'

'So much for plausible deniability?'

'Do you want to uncover the truth about the suffragettes' missing money or not? This could be the key to finding our blackmailee and, with that, our murderer.'

Louisa had changed her mind. Of all the terrible ideas Ada had ever had, this one was, in fact, the worst. If Miss Langwith returned, there was no sensible explanation they could give. Their access to the WSPU would be over, and so would any hope of Artie's freedom.

Still, she moved closer to the door and strained to hear any sound from the other side.

'Do you even know how to pick a lock?' she asked Ada.

'Yes, all you need is a hairpin.' Ada plucked one from her hair, causing several curls to fall loose.

'Should I ask how you know that?'

Ada bent down and inserted the pin into the lock on Miss Langwith's drawer. 'My granddad made John this wonderful hand-carved wooden box one Christmas. It had the most beautiful carving of a horse on it. At first, I just wanted to study the carving, the artistry of it. Then it rattled, and I realised he was hiding sweets in it. Looking back, I'm certain he must have stolen them from Mr Pallet's shop.' She interrupted herself to swear at the lock.

'Are you the only one of your siblings who has not committed a crime?'

'I'm fairly certain Walter is straight as an arrow. Also, have you forgotten we helped cover up a murder last year?'

'Ada!' Louisa hissed, glancing at the doorway as if it was going to swing open to reveal Inspector Lambert at the keyhole, listening in and primed to arrest them.

But Ada only laughed. 'Well, we did.'

She was not wrong, but for her to state it so bluntly, so nonchalantly, caused a shiver of fear to creep up Louisa's spine.

But Ada was not listening. With a triumphant 'aha', she jerked the drawer open to reveal stacks of envelopes. She lifted one from the top of the pile and gasped.

'What have you found?' Louisa moved to peer over her shoulder. Miss Langwith's name was written in neat calligraphy.

'It's the same handwriting.' Ada pulled the crumpled note out of her pocket and laid them next to each other. She was right. The writing looked similar – same loops, same lines, the same lean on the 't'.

'So, who is our mysterious writer...' Ada slid her finger into the clean cut at the top of the envelope and pulled out a folded sheet of paper. She opened it to reveal cramped, slanted handwriting, much more hastily written than that on the outside. Louisa leaned a little closer to read.

My dearest Aster,

I dreamt of you again last night and found it most cruel to be reminded of the truth by dawn's early light. There will come a day when it is you I awaken beside, when I see your beautiful body bathed in sunlight and have the time to drink my fill. Every morning will be spent making sure you are roused by the thrill of knowing one is alive and loved and adored.

And you would return the favour, of course. I can think of little else as I sit here, bereft, but your fingers inside me, your lips on my quim, the pleasure you bring me.

One day, we shall have that whenever we wish it. Until that day, I will dream of you at night and yearn for you on lonely mornings when there is only my own hand. It will be your name on the tip of my tongue, even as I wish said tongue could be put to much more gratifying purposes.

A thousand kisses upon your person,
Orchid.

Ada let out a low whistle and turned to Louisa with a grin and a cheeky sparkle in her eyes. 'Written by another woman, wouldn't you say?'

Louisa nodded absentmindedly, her mind still re-running through what she had just read. 'It means... that is, it's talking about... well, what...you like.' Heat flooded her cheeks. Of course, they had discussed these topics before, but it was different to do it outside their bedroom, as if a sanctity had been broken.

'I certainly do.' With a smirk, Ada closed the gap between them, her body the tiniest of hand movements away.

'I know.' Louisa's voice remained calm, even as her mind recalled Ada's gasps and moans and pleas. It had surprised her at first. That Ada's pleasure, her reaction, had been so clearly genuine, and even more surprising was that she was the one to bring forth such a reaction. There had been a time when she had believed every woman faked her interest – in sex, in marriage, in men.

Ada's breath tickled Louisa's neck. Louisa could have pulled her close and kissed her hard. Perhaps, if Louisa was a different person, this was where she would have lifted Ada onto the desk, skirts rucked up, and knelt to remind her how much she enjoyed what Louisa's lips and tongue could do.

But she was not that person. Especially not when they were still in the middle of conducting a clandestine search of someone's desk. A person who had probably finished making tea by now.

She nodded at the open drawer. 'What else is in there?'

The side of Ada's mouth curled upwards with wry amusement, but she turned away, stepping back towards the desk. Louisa mourned the loss of closeness whilst also being relieved by it.

How contrary of me.

But now was not the time to contemplate the complexities of her love life and her attitude towards sex.

Ada opened another letter and scanned it. 'More of the same. It would appear there was a secret rendezvous in a park where they were nearly caught. Who could have seen Miss Langwith as such a maverick?'

Not Louisa, that was sure. The other woman had appeared to be somewhat of a kindred spirit, but perhaps not. Would it always come as a surprise to her? To learn of other people's inclinations? It should not – she knew how most of the world thought. There was enough evidence of it once you stopped to consider it, and yet, she still found herself blindsided by what was so ordinary for other people.

'Who do you think wrote them?'

'Could be anyone. Close *friends* would be the obvious starting point. If only she had a *companion*, that would make it easy.'

Louisa's mouth quirked. 'And you are sure whoever wrote these letters is the same person who wrote that note to Miss Franklin?'

Ada nodded. 'Whoever addressed them, anyway? Fancy writing.' She waved the envelope.

Louisa was not convinced. 'Just because they were both written in calligraphy does not necessarily mean they are the same.'

'We could compare them. Steal one from the bottom of the pile to give us the time to do it properly.'

Footsteps made them both jump, and Ada slammed the drawer shut. They both turned as the door opened, and Louisa prayed Ada had hidden the letter in time.

Miss Langwith did not appear to spot anything amiss as she placed the tea tray on the desk. When Louisa dared a glance at Ada, both her hands were empty, though she appeared to be struggling not to smile.

'Miss Chapman, are you quite alright?' Miss Langwith's stern gaze across the top of her glasses reminded Louisa of her school mistress. It was hard to imagine her in a secret park rendezvous or with her tongue between another woman's thighs.

Though people would say the same about me. They were both spinsters, divorced from Society's notions of romance and sex.

'Fine,' Ada said, then coughed to smother a laugh.

Perhaps I will have to kick her in the shin.

Miss Langwith frowned.

'So, what more can you tell us about this missing money?' Louisa asked in a desperate attempt at distraction.

It worked, nonetheless. Miss Langwith passed them both cups of tea as she explained how she had noticed small amounts missing over the last six months, then a large sum last month. 'At least a few hundred pounds.'

The same as what Ada estimated Miss Franklin had in forged money.

'Who has access to the money?' Ada asked, her face and voice finally neutral.

'Just me and Mrs Cohen. And no, I will not be telling you where we keep it. And no, I do not think Leonora Cohen would steal from the organisation and cause she has dedicated the last four years of her life to serving.'

Louisa was inclined to agree. The one thing she did know about Mrs Cohen was her dedication to the fight for women's suffrage.

'Something amusing, Miss Chapman?' Miss Langwith's words were cutting.

Ada shook her head, but she was fighting a smile again.

It was perhaps best to beat a hasty retreat before Ada's composure fled altogether.

Louisa drained the last of her tea and stood. 'Thank you for your help, Miss Langwith.'

She frowned. 'I thought you might have more questions?'

'No, no, thank you, you have been a great help.' Louisa inclined her head and hurried out of the room, Ada on her heels. They made it out of the office and through the assembly room, to the entrance hall and its thankfully empty desk, before Ada let out a loud laugh.

'Are you going to explain the joke?'

'Those last answers she gave us. She certainly has spirit; I'll give her that. I should have learnt by now'—she gave Louisa a significant glance—'that there can be more to people than you expect.' She extracted an envelope from her pocket and brandished it with a flourish, but then frowned. 'Do you think she knows she is in love with a blackmailer?'

'It is possible. Mr Taylor knew; it did not stop him from loving Mr Richardson. Or, equally, she could be clueless. And we do not know that it was blackmail if Mr Richardson was not involved. It could be that whoever wrote it was simply infuriated to learn of her spying. A threat but not necessarily blackmail. We need to figure out who wrote that to figure out their intentions.'

'I guess the place to start is the woman Miss Langwith argued with. That suggests both a temper and a potentially volatile relationship.'

'Mrs Green?'

Ada nodded. 'Was she not also the one who encouraged Miss Franklin to violence? Who was supposed to be at the meeting?'

'And might have been deeply offended to learn her new protégé was a spy.'

'Offended enough to threaten her, possibly blackmail her. Maybe even try to kill her at the meeting she helped set up.'

'And if Miss Langwith learnt of that, it certainly is good cause for an argument.'

'We need to learn everything we can about Mrs Green.' Ada waved the envelope, and they both turned towards the door they had left through.

Miss Langwith's earlier irritation with Mrs Cohen flashed into Louisa's mind. 'Starting with whether her name is Lydia.'

Chapter Fifteen

A Family Meeting

Queen Victoria wore suffragette colours. The image was so arresting, Ada paused mid-sentence to stare. Her speculating on whether Lydia Green—for they had learnt back at the WSPU headquarters that was her name—was their murderer died on her tongue. The statue had sat proudly outside Leeds Town Hall for the last eight years, the late Queen surveying the city, enthroned up high on her plinth. Some daring soul had managed to climb up there and drape a purple, white and green striped banner across her chest, a mimicry of the suffragettes' sashes. A tribute to the dying Miss Davison, perhaps?

'Do you mind if we stop?' Ada was already reaching inside her bag for her sketchbook. It was too good an image not to capture on paper. Perhaps the WSPU could find a use for the picture? Or it could be part of the portfolio she showed to Frank Rutter, should such a meeting truly come about.

'Oh, I just remembered! I have something to tell you. How could I have forgotten?'

'Well, a little light larceny can be distracting.' Louisa pitched her voice low enough no passersby would hear.

Ada was too excited to give the equally sarcastic response it deserved. 'Did you know Frank Rutter supports the WSPU?'

Louisa paused for a moment. 'The curator? Who founded that fund?'

'The Leeds Art Fund, and yes. When I was working on the banner earlier, one of the women said I should speak to him.' She grinned.

'About what?' Louisa gasped, 'Wait, about displaying at the Art Gallery? Ada, that's always been your dream!'

'Well, yes, I know that.' Her glee ruined her attempt at a droll reply.

'That's amazing.' Louisa clasped her hands together, a joyful smile spreading across her face. The one Ada loved, that she wore when she dropped her armour against the world and was just herself. 'Which pictures are you going to show him? What kind of art does he want? Oh, what about that one from last winter when the lake froze over? You did such a great job of showing the cold desolation of that scene – it makes me shiver to look at it. Or will that be too miserable? If he prefers something cheery, what about the one of Galapagos by the flowers you did back in Spring? It's so cute, and you really captured how darn cheeky that cat is. Or would he prefer portraits? Please don't use one of me, but you could—'

'Louisa!' With a laugh, Ada cut her off. 'You're getting a little ahead of things here. I might get a chance to speak to the man, and if I do and he seems interested, then I'll find out what he might want to display.'

'Right, yes.' Louisa's smile dropped, and her posture stiffened. 'That makes a lot more sense.'

'I appreciate the enthusiasm, though.' She lay a hand on Louisa's arm. A gentle touch. It would look like nothing more than one friend comforting another to anyone who walked past.

She got a brief smile in return, softer, fleeting, but it still warmed her. 'Still, your work in the Art Gallery.'

'I know.' Ada's grin returned.

'I suppose you best get on with it, then.' Louisa stepped away with a brief nod at the statue. 'It will make a good painting. Gloriana in her new regalia.'

Ada scrunched her face up. 'I don't understand what those words mean, and you know it.' She held a finger up to stop the inevitable explanation that was about to follow and paused a moment to scrutinise the statue.

'I take it that means you would prefer to return to our previous conversation.'

'We've exhausted that topic for now, don't you think?'

Louisa retrieved a small notebook and pen from her bag. She had written all the facts they—with considerable assistance from Miss Jain and Miss Dixon—had learnt about Lydia Green in there. Married, but not happily. No children of her own but at least one stepson. Rumours abounded that she was a bastard, the illegitimate daughter of a rich businessman, though no one could agree on who her supposed father was, and she had not benefited financially. Her mention of the factories and their degradations was based on experience. Miss Langwith and Miss Franklin were both close friends, which made her the main candidate to be the writer of both love letters and potential blackmail notes. Though she had no known motive to want Mr Richardson dead, she did have a potential motive to either try to kill Miss Franklin or set her up for murder. And she was currently down south for unspecified reasons, though most believed it was so she could get involved in a bombing campaign, as she desired. *Or to get her out of Leeds whilst there's a murder investigation ongoing.*

But that was, as Louisa had said, speculation, not proof.

Ada left Louisa to her writing and focused on the blank page, sketching in the initial shape of the statue. Her mind, however, was determined to stray. 'I should go visit my family this evening.'

Louisa's pen stilled. 'Ah yes, your brother and his rumours.'

'Rumours,' she scoffed and then cursed as she drew a line a little too thick and slightly left of where she wanted it to be. Art had always been the one thing she excelled at. She sure as hell would not let that slip away from her, and certainly not because of her bloody brother. 'It makes little sense. Personally, if I was up to my neck in illegal activity and at some point in the future going to be reliant on my sister and her police constable friend to bail me out, I wouldn't be spreading rumours about them.'

'Unless he thinks it is true.'

Ada's hand jerked across the page, destroying Queen Victoria's noble face. 'What?'

'I am not saying it is true.' Louisa spoke in her most soothing tone, the one Ada hated. 'I do not believe you and Constable Wilkinson have been secretly married all these years.' Her lip quirked ever so slightly. 'But what if – for whatever reason – he thinks it is true? Perhaps he overheard something as a child and misunderstood.'

'Maybe he's just a blighter who likes to cause trouble.' Ada flicked to a clean page with a little more force than necessary. There was no rescuing the Queen's face.

'That does feel like the more likely case,' Louisa conceded. 'I am merely considering all options.'

Or maybe he is trying to discredit me because I am investigating the death of the man he shot with that gun in his waistband. Her pencil lines were far too heavy. She nearly ripped through the new page, and she readjusted her grip before continuing.

No motive. He has no motive.

Unless Pete's criminality now involved forged money.

A loud tear dragged her attention back to her sketchbook, her new drawing ruined by a large rip. She slammed the book shut with a sigh. 'Will you come with me? I need someone to stop me from throttling my little brother.'

But Louisa shook her head. 'I have my meeting with Mr Connolly soon.' She had telephoned this morning to make an appointment about Artie's case. 'I am not sure how long it will last. He tends to start reminiscing about his best cases and those of my father.' She grimaced, and Ada reached out to squeeze her shoulder. Louisa had never fully explained why she had spent so much of the autumn and winter engrossed in her father's old case files, but it was not hard to fill in the gaps.

'Wish me luck then,' Ada said.

'Good luck. I think you are going to need it.'

Ada laughed and then stuck her tongue out. 'Enjoy your tales of past glories.'

Louisa glared at her – the glare with no heat that Ada always considered more loving than angry – and how she wished she could kiss her goodbye. Instead, she nodded and said, 'I'll see you at home.'

Ada opened the front door to be greeted with a cloud of cigarette smoke that cleared to reveal four guilty faces – her parents and her older brothers, John and Walter.

'Oh, Ada, it's you,' John announced unnecessarily, and then some of the tense atmosphere in the room dissolved. Tall like their father, with the same dark brown hair and wiry face, he leant beside the fireplace, his elbow propped up on the mantelpiece and his jacket discarded so his shirt and suspenders were visible.

In contrast, Walter sat ramrod straight on a dining chair, every yard of his clothing ironed within an inch of its life. He looked like he had never been relaxed in his life. Or happy. He stared at her from under furrowed brows, his hair several shades lighter than John, nearly blending into his pale face. It always irritated Ada's artistic tendencies that Walter – the moodiest and severest of them all – had the lightest complexion. Both her brothers had a cigarette burning in their hands, as did their dad. Judging by the more than half-full ashtray on the table, it was not their first.

If Mum is letting them smoke in the house, whatever they are discussing must be bad.

Ada was certain by the time this conversation was over, she would wish she had the nerve to smoke in front of Mum. It was so much easier for her brothers, though.

She fought down the desire to fetch her own cigarettes or to at least take a large inhale for a second-hand hit and steeled her nerves for whatever was to come.

'Nice to see you, too, Johnny,' she replied to his less-than-stellar greeting with an equal tone. 'Were you expecting someone else?'

'We just weren't expecting you,' Dad said from the sofa. Beside him, Mum frowned. 'You by yourself?'

'Yes.' She glanced between them all. 'What is going on?' A moment of realisation. 'Oh God, what has Pete done?'

'Don't take the Lord's name in vain, Ada,' both her mum and Walter said at the same time.

It took all the willpower Ada possessed not to catch John's eyes and roll her own.

'How'd you know Pete's done something?' John flicked his cigarette stub into the ashtray. A few stray motes of ash fell to the floor as he did.

Mum took a deep breath but kept quiet. Serious indeed, then.

'Lucky guess,' Ada replied. *And an easy one.*

Dad stood and placed his own cigarette stub in the ashtray. 'He hasn't been home all week.'

'What? But he was at WSPU yesterday.'

Her statement was followed by a short, stunned silence and then an explosion of sound as everyone clamoured to ask questions at once.

'Enough.' Dad smacked the arm of the sofa as he sat down again, then turned to Ada. 'Pete was with the suffragettes yesterday?'

As Ada nodded, he was already reaching into his cigarette case – the fancy enamelled one Mum had saved up to buy him a few Christmases ago – for another. He offered it to both his sons, then hesitated, his eyes on Ada.

'Please.' She reached over and claimed her prize before he changed his mind.

He then offered it to Mum, who sighed and took one.

Ada dared a glance at her brothers, and, by silent collective agreement, they decided not to mention it.

There was a conversation lull as everyone reached for lighters or across to the fire.

Unfortunately, it was Walter who broke it. 'Why were you with the suffragettes, Ada?'

'I went to tell them to stop embarrassing womankind and to return t' their homes and husbands.'

Walter blinked at her.

Ada scoffed. 'Why do you think, Walter?'

'So once again, you're embarrassing this family.'

'I'm... *I'm* embarrassing the family?' She gestured with her cigarette towards Walter, her erratic movement sending more ash to the floor. Mum winced. 'Pete's possibly shot someone, and *I'm* embarrassing the family? For what? Believing women deserve a say in how this country is run, in our own lives and our livelihoods?'

'Shot someone?' Her mother had gone very pale, hands frozen halfway to her mouth, and Ada realised what she had said.

'I... I mean... I don't know that for sure.'

'Then why would you say it?' Though Dad's tone was gruff, the hand he placed on Mum's arm was a gentle touch.

'He had a gun, when I saw him. And someone was shot. Someone connected to WSPU.'

'And you just assumed the shooter was your brother?'

'Yes, well... he's been telling people me and Davey are married!'

John snorted, and Walter frowned. If both her older brothers had always suspected the truth of what she was, they had differing opinions on it.

'I always thought—' Mum began, and Ada immediately regretted ever mentioning Davey and marriage in front of her.

'I don't think now's time, Grace,' Dad interrupted. 'And annoying as that might be for you, Ada, it doesn't mean 'e shot someone. Irritating your older sister is not a crime.'

'I didn't mean...'

The look on her mother's face shut her up. Why was she making the case to their family that her brother was a killer?

She sighed. 'I shouldn't have said it, never mind. I'm sorry. But what's this about him not being at home for a week?' She went to take a long drag on her cigarette, hoping it would calm the gnawing in the pit of her stomach.

'We haven't seen hair nor hide of him since last Tuesday,' Dad said.

'He was with WSPU?' Mum was still wrapping her mind around that particular fact. Ada didn't blame her.

'He's not exactly befriending them.' She took one final drag and then leant over to the ashtray to deposit the stub. Dad and Walter copied her action, and Ada waited to see if the cigarette case would make another appearance, but it did not.

'But why is he there?' Walter asked. 'If he's not befriending them, as you say. Do you think whatever mess he has clearly got himself entangled in relates to suffragettes? He could be working with them, helping sow violence. You mentioned a gun. Heaven help us all if the Pankhursts start arming women.'

Ada snorted. 'If they do, I'll shoot you first.'

'Not if I beat you to it!' This high-pitched, gleeful shout came from behind the door leading to the staircase. Which was cracked open, just a slither, enough that it was unnoticeable until someone went looking for the gap.

'Rosie!' all the adults shouted.

The door swung open, and Ada's younger sister emerged with not an ounce of shame on her round child's face.

'No one is shooting anyone!' Mum attempted to glare in three different directions at once, which lessened its potency.

'Charming as always, little sisters.' John was even more amused than earlier.

Walter stared at them with unchecked disgust.

It might be best to move the conversation on. 'His sweetheart lives there – at their headquarters. Her father kicked her and her mother out.'

'His sweetheart?' The various shouts all mingled together again, though Ada could take a good guess at who was shocked and who was disgusted.

'Yes, I meet her, too. Seems like a sweet girl.'

'Far too good for Pete then,' John said before she could.

'So, he can visit his sweetheart but not let his mother know he's alive.' Mum crossed her arms over her chest.

The fury on her parents' faces ignited some childhood instinct to make herself scarce. It took a lot of force of will to remind herself she was an adult and to remain where she sat.

If the longing look Rosie gave the door was any indication, she was not the only one; her hands fiddled with a necklace, silver flashing. It wouldn't be genuine silver, but still, their parents had not trusted Ada to own a piece of jewellery until she was twelve.

It was churlish to point that out, though, no matter how irrationally angry she was, that *Rosie* had been deemed more trustworthy.

And if I lost that bracelet only three months after getting it, that is beside the point.

'Ada,' her father's stern tone brought her back from that long-ago devastation. 'If you see Pete again, tell him he needs to come home. Drag him by the ear if need be.'

Oh sure, I'll just drag the boy with the gun.

But she agreed.

'Well, that is that then, I suppose.' Walter stood from his chair.

'Oh, are you all not going to stay for tea?' Mum said it with such hope Ada immediately hurried to reassure her she could. Louisa would understand.

'Well, I think...' Walter began but then gave a tentative half-smile under Mum's earnest gaze. 'Sure. Tabitha and the children will be fine without me for one meal.' Considering his wife was of a similar stern disposition, Ada doubted that was true, but it was a well-intended lie.

Walter can be not entirely terrible. On occasion.

John smiled. 'Course, Mum. Wouldn't want to miss a chance to eat best cooking on right side of Pennines.'

Mum beamed at the compliment.

Rosie mimed throwing up.

'I'll tell Abigail you said that,' Ada joked as their mum went into the kitchen, still smiling.

'You do that, Ada.' Given John's wife also shared his more laid-back character, it wasn't much of a threat.

'Well, I would if I ever got an invite round. Those nieces and nephews of mine will forget what their Auntie Ada looks like. That goes for you, too, Walter.'

'You're one who disappeared up to Roundhay to play at *lady's companion.*' The way Walter said it came with about fifteen different unsaid insults. Any warm feelings she'd had towards her brother vanished.

She tried to keep her answer light. 'By which you mean I have a roof over my head, three meals a day provided for me, an *actual maid* who does the housework, and time to work on my art?'

'Can we not bicker, please?' Dad interrupted, voice stern.

'I'll go see if Mum needs any help.' How she had hated being relegated to the kitchen as a girl, but the distraction would stop her from shouting the truth of her relationship in front of her entire family. Well, her entire family except for Pete, but he had already made it clear on more than one occasion that he knew.

As do John and Walter, I suspect. Not Mum and Dad, though. They never asked, and she never said, and that was the way it would stay. The safest way. If they never acknowledged the truth, then there never had to be any repercussions.

She gave her mum a hollow smile as she walked into the kitchen and offered her help. Reality squeezed her heart in its grip, that if she told the truth, her mum might turn her away. She didn't want to be like Sophie, estranged from her family.

If we get Artie free, will her relationship with him help heal the rift with her family?

The thought irritated Ada. Sophie shouldn't have to date a boy – even if it was a boy she genuinely liked – for her family to accept her back.

That's the way of the world. It won't change anytime soon, not when people still quake at the mere thought of women voting.

'Is everything alright with you, Ada? We've talked about your brother, but I haven't asked how you are.'

Ada forced another smile. 'I'm fine. Things are still going great with Miss Knight.' *I love her. I wish I could tell you that. I wish you could accept that. Or even be happy for me.* The vice had not lessened its grip.

'Well, that's good. And you still have time to work on your paintings?'

'Yes. I might have an excellent opportunity coming up soon, actually.'

'Oh, what good news! Tell me all about it.' And Mum's enthusiasm was so genuine that some of Ada's former excitement returned, and the pain in her chest lessened. They settled into an old rhythm in the cramped kitchen. Ada told her mum about her chance to meet with one of the directors of Leeds Art Gallery, though the WSPU became 'friends of hers' in the retelling.

Once everything was chopped and prepped and cooking, her mother leant against the counter and said, 'Tell me about this man who was shot. You mentioned him earlier. The one whose death you think Pete might be involved in.'

'I shouldn't have said that. There really is no evidence.'

Except a gun at his waist, but how many people in this city have guns at their waists while I am simply ignorant of it?

'I want t' know, Ada. If there owt I can do t' help my son. Whatever he has done, I can't lose him. Do you understand?'

She had once promised Pete she wouldn't come to his aid when he inevitably got himself in trouble with the law. Did Mum remember that argument?

Mum reached for her hand. 'Do you understand? I cannot lose my son to a gaol.'

'It would be a borstal, not a gaol.' Ada didn't mention the Children's Charter. It wouldn't lessen her mother's fears. Like many working women she saw it as a threat, the possibility of the government taking her children away, even though in this case it could help save her son's life.

'Same difference. What is a borstal but a gaol for children? I still lose my son to misery and high walls and barred windows. And I can't. I won't.' She shook her head. 'Do you remember... Maybe you don't. You were only little for so much of it...' She turned back to the hob, stirring a pan of peas unnecessarily.

Little, yes, but Ada had been eleven when Pete was born. Old enough to understand the significance. Old enough to have some knowledge about the miscarriages and stillbirths that had happened between her birth and his. To remember the last baby, George, two years previous, and the month he had lived for.

The words 'you have a little brother' and the unbidden question that even then she knew not to say out loud, 'for how long?'

'I remember enough.'

Whatever Pete was up to, however much she wanted to kill him herself on occasion, she would not allow the answer to that question to be fourteen years.

She squeezed her mum's arm.

'Tell me. Tell me about this murdered man.'

So, Ada did.

And afterwards, she made her mother a promise.

Chapter Sixteen

What We Are

A large white porcelain bathtub, stood on four curved gilt feet, dominated the bathroom. Ada lay within, her head resting against the back of the tub, eyes closed, her ginger curls falling down her front to float in the water. The bathtub was dangerously full, and she was not going to get out without causing a flood. However, since Ada had been so excited about having a bathroom and an inside water closet when she first moved in, Louisa was more than willing to let her have this indulgence unquestioned.

Her slim pale body was partially obscured by the purple tint of the water, caused by the lavender bath salts she favoured, their scent infusing the room.

If only I were the one who could paint, this would make a sublime picture.

Ada's beauty struck her at the strangest times but never accompanied by the pull that was supposed to come with it. The one which would tell her to undress and clamber into the bath, too, floorboards be damned.

Would Ada like it if I did?

She tried to push the thought away, but the follow-up question still came. *Would Mabel do that if it was her stood here?*

Ada's eyes fluttered open. 'What's going on in that clever brain of yours? You're thinking so loud I can hear the cogs whirring.'

'Nothing all that clever,' Louisa admitted with a rueful smile as she sat on the floor beside the bathtub.

Ada arched an eyebrow.

'I was wishing I could draw because you would make for a fine picture.'

Ada let out a sound that was half a laugh and half a snort. 'I would quite like to see you exhibit that.'

'Yes, because the art world has never seen a painting of a naked woman before.'

Ada's raucous laughter caused the water to lap over the side of the bathtub and onto the floor and Louisa's dress. 'I might have over-filled the tub again.'

'Might?' Louisa leant forward and splashed some of the water in Ada's direction.

'I'll mop it up once I'm done. One day I will draw a bath with the right amount of water.'

'I shall not hold my breath.'

'I'm rather fond of you alive, so I have to agree with you on that.'

'Well, that is reassuring to know.' Louisa splashed a little more water in Ada's direction, and in return, Ada shook her wet hands at her face, sprinkling it with droplets of water.

Was this not enough? Two women in love teasing each other.

Louisa forced her thoughts to less dangerous territory. 'What did your brother have to say for himself?'

'Not a lot. No one in my family has seen him since last Tuesday.'

'Well, that is not good.'

'And that is an understatement.' She gave a brief, sad smile. 'How about you? Did you have a more successful afternoon?'

'Yes.' Louisa tapped her fingernails against the bathtub's rim, the noise echoing in the small room.

'And?' Ada stared at her expectantly.

'He said he would represent Artie if necessary.'

'And?' Ada continued to stare at her. 'I sense there's more...'

And a woman you once loved more than anything else in the world might soon be free if she can stomach retelling the worst moment of her life to a panel of potentially unsympathetic men.

Both parts unsettled Louisa, but it was her unease at the former that disgusted her, especially compared to the latter.

'And...' The words still did not come. She had yet to tell Ada that she had tasked Mr Connolly with examining Mabel's case, fearing it might get her hopes up too soon.

'Are you still thinking about the suffragettes?' Louisa heard the unsaid *about your nightmare?*

She nodded because she had been, even if it was not true at this exact moment in time. 'I am going round in circles in my mind, full of doubts that anything will ever change, violence or no violence.'

'You, Louisa Knight, overthinking? I am shocked at the mere suggestion.' Ada shot her a teasing smile.

'At least, *I* think before I act.' But Louisa's answering smile was just as teasing.

Ada splashed her and Louisa squealed in surprise, causing Ada to laugh, her head thrown back, eyes shining with merriment. She was a miracle for a woman who believed in neither God nor miracles, and Louisa leant down to kiss her because it was the only possible option at that moment. It was a joyous kiss. The sort of kiss you want to do again and again because it was all that was right with the world.

Louisa could jump into the bath with her and keep kissing her. The sort of kissing that led to more, the type of more that left Ada screaming her name. Never mind the soaked floor or the sort of woman she was. Why could she not be this kind of woman?

Before she could second guess herself, she broke off the kiss and scrambled off the floor. 'Room for one more?' But she was already stripping. She could do this. It would be fun. Different. Exactly what Ada deserved.

Ada's laughter turned raucous once more. 'I will not say no. Physics might.'

'Bugger physics.' Louisa pulled her stockings off with less grace than she would have preferred. Usually, she was not the one undressing for these encounters.

'Louisa Knight! What has gotten into you today?'

To even Louisa's surprise, the crude answer sprung to the forefront of her mind. 'You, hopefully.' She finished unbuttoning her blouse and shrugged it to the ground.

Ada laughed again, eyes grazing over Louisa's semi-naked body appreciatively, and then her smile drooped. 'This isn't our agreement.'

'Agreements can change.' She reached for her corset strings, but she was wearing a corset that tied at the back. She cursed mentally. Ada would need to undo it, and that would take time. Time for her to rethink. Time for whatever was currently possessing her to abandon her.

Ada still did not look convinced. 'But something must have changed for that to happen?'

But Louisa did not want to stop and talk about this, not whilst with every passing second her resolve might crumble. 'Does there have to be a reason for me to want to make love to the woman I adore?' And without giving Ada a chance to respond, she clambered into the bath, corset and all, causing water to splosh over the sides and join the increasing puddle on the floor.

'Louisa!' Ada's arms reached out to grab her as she tried to lean down.

It was a big bath, but there was still nowhere near room for two. Louisa's body pressed against Ada's, their arms and legs tangled together, the soaked fabric of Louisa's corset and chemise against Ada's breasts.

Was she supposed to glory in this? Feel her skin set alight? All she had was increasing regret that this was the worst idea of her life.

But too late to go back now. She cupped Ada's face and tried to lean in for a kiss, but Ada moved away, trying to sit up straighter.

'Louisa! Stop! What is going on?'

The word 'stop' vibrated through her mind. This was wrong. This was terribly wrong. Whatever nonsense ideas she had gotten into her head, she needed to banish them.

'Sorry! Sorry! Sorry!' She tried to scramble out of the bath, but her limbs kept slipping. Finally, she made it out, barely managing to stay upright on the wet tiled floor. 'I'm sorry!' And then she ran out of the room, leaving a trail of water. She slammed her study door shut and locked it behind her.

Why did I do that? Why did I do that?

But she knew the answer. The thoughts that had churned through her mind all the way home.

Mabel could be free someday soon. And why would Ada choose me and all I cannot give her?

All Louisa had to offer was material things and a love that could never be enough. She trusted Ada to know she would never stay for the former alone. Her frustration at the loss of her sketch work and her recent struggles with selling her art was proof of that.

Plus, if her meeting with Mr Rutter comes to fruition, she could be about to have her big break as an artist, and then she will not even need me for that, either.

She needed to do something. She should go back and explain. If she could not face that yet, she should at least go to their room and get out of these wet clothes. That would involve fetching Sophie to help with her corset, though, which was nearly as excruciating an idea as talking to Ada.

Instead, she slid down the closed study door till she was on the floor, hugging her knees to her, tears streaming unchecked down her face.

She did not know how long she had stayed there, her thoughts spiralling, when the handle jerked down, and the locked door rattled in its frame.

'Louisa? Can you open the door? I've brought hot cocoa. And a dressing gown.'

Hot cocoa. And a dressing gown. Such a simple, kind gesture, and it nearly caused Louisa to sob afresh.

But instead, she took a deep breath, wiped her face with her hands as best she could, stood, and unlocked the door. Ada stood there in her nightgown, a tidemark round its neck and shoulders showed where her dripping wet hair had soaked the material. In her hand, she held a tray with two cups, and over her arm was Louisa's favourite dressing gown. The one with the bird pattern Ada had chosen at Kirkgate Market last year.

Louisa stepped aside. 'Come in.' The words sounded ridiculously formal the second she said them.

Ada placed the tray on her desk and held out the dressing gown. 'Here.'

For the first time, Louisa noticed how cold and clammy her chest was from her wet corset and chemise, and she shivered. 'Thanks.' She wrapped it round herself and sat at her desk, reaching for a cup.

'What the fuck was that? I'm sorry, I was going to word that better, but...' Ada spread her hands in a questioning gesture.

Louisa sighed. 'It was...not my finest moment.'

Ada raised her eyebrows, still waiting for more of an explanation.

'Do you ever think it would be easier if I was not...' She paused—she had never found a word she liked.

'The way you are?' Ada finished for her.

Louisa nodded stiffly.

Ada did not answer immediately, and Louisa's hands tightened on her cup as she waited, clutching its warmth to her cold stomach.

'I could lie and say it wouldn't make a difference, but we would both know that for a lie, so I shall not waste my breath. But,' Ada chewed her lip, 'what do you always say about my birthmark?' She tapped a finger against the red blotches on her cheek.

That was not what Louisa expected her to say as a follow-up. 'What has your birthmark got to do with anything?'

'You always tell me it's a part of me, one of the things that makes me, well, me. Your sexuality is the same, surely? Yes, our lives – and our relationship – might be easier if it was different, but then you wouldn't be you, and we wouldn't be us, and why would I ever want that?'

Louisa let the words sink in, so plainly spoken, so clearly honest, and exactly what she had needed to hear.

'Does that make sense?' Ada asked, her top teeth chewing

at her bottom lip, finger still tapping her cheek, waiting for the response Louisa was yet to give.

She nodded and tried to reply but instead found herself fighting back tears once more. She should have expected nothing else, and yet it was such a relief, such glorious relief. This was Ada. Her wonderful, loving Ada. How silly to think she would walk away. She reached out to take Ada's hand within her own, linking them across the desk. Her tears won their battle, and she tried to brush them away with her spare hand.

'Should I have brought a handkerchief as well?'

'I have one.' Louisa opened one of her desk drawers, where she had several clean spares, and then dabbed at her eyes.

'Show off.'

She gave a watery smile at that, but when she was done with the handkerchief, Ada watched her with serious eyes. 'You still have not explained what brought this on.'

And this was the moment she would have to tell the truth. 'I asked Mr Connolly to examine the details of Mabel's case.'

Ada stared blankly at her. 'I don't understand. What is there to examine?'

'He thinks she may have a chance at parole. If she is willing to give an honest account of what happened that day. He could spin it as a woman forced to defend herself and then too hysterical in the aftermath to tell the truth. He may even be able to argue she should never have been allowed to take the stand in her then frame of mind. That if she had been able to afford legal guidance, she would have been told to plead temporary insanity.'

'Will it work?' Hope shone in Ada's words, and Louisa pushed down her bitterness. It would not do to be jealous of Mabel Spencer and all that she had been through.

'There are no guarantees, but he is hopeful.'

'Mabel could be free.' A wondrous whisper, like a prayer, and it rubbed against all of Louisa's self-restraint.

That is what I want, too. It is why I put these actions into motion. This is not about me or Ada, but about righting a wrong.

It was what she kept telling herself, but she knew the last for a lie every time she thought it. It was always a little about Ada. About the joy it would bring her, no matter how bitter it tasted now.

'But none of that explains any of...' Ada waved a hand in the bathroom's direction.

And telling her Mabel might be freed had been the easy bit. How to explain herself and all her traitorous doubts?

'Oh,' Ada muttered, and there was so much understanding in that small sound. Louisa did not have to explain. She had figured it out for herself and was not impressed by her deductions. 'You think what? If Mabel is free, I will go back to 'er, because she's not...like you.'

Louisa's words all caught in her mouth.

Her silence must have spoken for her because Ada shouted, 'Mabel being free won't change a bloody thing between us!'

And that was such an obvious lie it was intolerable. 'Of course it would. You could have a chance for a normal relationship. Or as close to normal as a woman like you can have.'

'And you think that's what I want?' There was a snap to Ada's voice. 'Mabel gets out of gaol, and we just disappear int' sunset together and leave you behind?'

'No, no, that's not what I think. I don't think that's what you want, not now, here, in this moment. But if we succeed, if she's free and in your life again... would it not make more sense?' It seemed every time Ada had called her clever was a lie. She wanted to scoop the traitorous words up the moment they left her mouth.

Ada scoffed. 'Since when did love 'ave to make sense?' She waved her arm toward Louisa's bookshelves, to where her many fiction books were shelved. 'Have you not read any of these books you hoard?'

'But this is not fiction, Ada.'

'No, this is our damned lives. Do you think I would be 'ere if I didn't want t' be?'

'You're right. I know you're right. I am not proud of myself for these thoughts. I told myself everything you are telling me now, but they did not go away. I do not wish to doubt you.'

'But you do.'

'I doubt myself.'

Ada's anger deflated a little. She frowned, head tilted to the side. 'Why? Do you think you are not enough? That what? The way you are lessens your value?'

And despite herself, despite hating herself for the truth laid bare in front of her, Louisa nodded.

Ada paused, and for one excruciating moment, Louisa thought she would agree. 'For such an intelligent woman, you can be rather silly sometimes.'

'Is that supposed to cheer me up?' But it had. She would have guessed Ada's nonchalance at her revealing such a shameful inner fear would infuriate her, but instead, it was reassuring. She really was just being silly and had nothing to worry about.

Ada reached across the desk and interlocked their hands. It was astounding how well they fit together. 'If you were a man, I'd marry you.'

Now there was an idea to take Louisa's breath away. 'Me too. I want to spend the rest of my life with you, Ada.'

'Then we're in agreement.' Ada leant across the desk, and Louisa stood to meet her. The kiss was short and chaste and sweet and meant a million times more than whatever Louisa had tried to do in the bathtub.

'Now come on.' Ada stepped backwards. 'You need to get out of that wet corset.' She held a finger up. 'And that was literal, not a flirtation.'

Louisa smiled but held back the tease that came to mind. This was not the right moment.

Ada's eyes narrowed. 'Oh God, what are you thinking? Come on, out with it. It can't possibly be worse than owt else that's been said this evening.'

Well, really, she had asked for it now. 'Just that I would never flirt with a married woman, Mrs Wilkinson.'

Ada stared at her, mouth agape. 'Did you just... did you just make that joke?'

'I guess I did. In my defence, you told me to say it.'

'Yes, I did. I should not have done that. I was wrong. That was worse.' She shook her head, mouth still open, but the corners now curled upwards as though she could not prevent her smile.

'Don't forget your cocoa.' Ada's drink sat forgotten on the tray, and Louisa had barely drunk any of hers, using it more like a hot water bottle. She took a big sip now and revelled in the warmth. Ada was right. She really did need to get changed.

In their bedroom, they left the drinks on the vanity table, and Louisa shrugged off her dressing gown.

'There is one more thing I need to tell you.' Ada tugged at Louisa's corset strings. 'I got distracted by...'

'Me making a complete fool of myself?'

'I would not word it quite that harshly, but yes. When I was at my parents', I promised my mum I wouldn't let Pete get arrested.' Ada's confession was a mere whisper.

Louisa spun around, corset strings be damned. 'Ada, what if...'

'He did it?' Ada shrugged, a gesture supposed to be casual, but it came across as anything but. 'I can't let Pete go to gaol or even a borstal. Whatever else he is, he's my little brother.' There was a lot more going unsaid, some emotion unknown to the sibling-less Louisa. 'I made my mum a promise, Louisa. I can't break it.'

I want to marry you. I want to spend my life with you.

This was why marriage vows contained for better or for worse.

Had Ada not just accepted her at her worst?

She cupped Ada's cheek in her hand, running a loving finger down her mark. 'Then we will make sure he does not.' Ada's hand reached up to cover her own, and her eyelids fluttered shut.

It was not a promise Louisa should have made—her father's voice rang loud in her head, cursing her for being a lawbreaking fool—nor one circumstances might allow her to keep, but she was going to try her hardest.

It would be a lot easier, though, if Peter Chapman turned out to be involved in a much smaller, pettier crime. They needed to get him off their list of suspects and quickly.

Artie. Miss Franklin. Peter. They had an increasing list of who they did not want it to be. But their possible suspect pool outside of those candidates was both too small and too wide. They needed to narrow it down to a likely person.

'If Mrs Green did send that note to Miss Franklin, then

we need to figure out who Adam Richardson was blackmailing.'

Ada's eyes blinked open. 'But how?'

And wasn't that the question. Louisa did not have an answer.

'Tomorrow,' Ada whispered, squeezing the hand under hers. 'We can figure it out tomorrow. It has been a long day.' She stepped out of their embrace and made a twirling gesture with her finger to tell Louisa to turn around again. When she complied, Ada tugged loose the last of her corset strings, and Louisa shrugged the wet garment off with relief.

'Better?' Ada let go, moving to the vanity table. 'I need to sort my hair out. I didn't get a chance to brush it earlier.'

'Let me.' Louisa swapped her still-damp chemise for a nightgown. 'You should drink your cocoa.' She passed Ada her drink and picked up the hairbrush. 'And you have still never let me see what your hair looks like when brushed dry.'

Ada's eyes narrowed in the mirror. 'And I never will. Even if we both live to a hundred.'

A hundred. Now there was a thought. Her and Ada growing old together. She had never allowed herself to consider that far ahead. Had she always been waiting for the other shoe to drop, for Ada to grow tired of her, and she never even realised?

I want to spend the rest of my life with you.

Louisa lifted a section of Ada's hair, brushing the ends first like Ada had taught her.

Tomorrow. And the day after. Until we are a hundred.

Chapter Seventeen

A Confession

The clock on the mantelpiece, just visible in the moonlight sliding in between the curtains, said quarter past three when Ada finally gave up on sleeping and crept downstairs. She flicked the light switch on and then, blinking and cursing her clever idea of convincing Louisa to install electricity, flicked it off again.

Other sleepless nights had been spent in her painting room, but as soon as she entered, she knew her mind was racing far too much for even her art to distract her. So, she grabbed the bottle of gin she kept in there and came downstairs, where at least there was less chance she would wake Louisa and Sophie.

Mabel could be free. Ada took a swig of the gin, neat out of the bottle, and winced. How many times had she dreamed of this when Mabel had first been arrested? When, despite all the evidence to the contrary, she had so desperately believed she was telling the truth. Even after she had accepted Mabel was lying, even after she stopped visiting, there had been some secret, foolish part of her that had hoped for a miracle.

And now Louisa may have done it.

She took another swig and grimaced. She should swallow her pride and ask Louisa to include a bottle in their groceries because she would never purchase anything this cheap and vile.

It's as bad as the stuff we used to steal from Mabel's mother.

And there was a part of her who wished she could go back there. Be that girl once more, with no idea of what was to come, even whilst an equal part of her wanted to cling to the life and the love she had built here.

She had not lied to Louisa. She could not imagine being with Mabel again – in or out of gaol. There was too much history between them. And it would mean hurting Louisa, and that was the last thing Ada ever wanted.

It did not stop her from doubting me. Or was she merely doubting herself? Or both?

Ada took another swig of the gin. The alcohol was having an effect now, her head swimming, her limbs heavy. She wanted a cigarette, but her bag was in the hallway, and getting there would be far too much effort.

I should go back upstairs.

But that was even further.

Will Louisa think I'm mad at her if she finds me asleep in the sitting room?

And she was not mad. It was just a lot to process. Mabel's possible release. Louisa's worries about her sexuality. And she understood them—she did. She had been taken back when Louisa first told her on that walk two years ago, the words tumbling from her lips like a sordid confession. It had taken some adjusting to, rearranging her expectations of what their relationship would be. And, of course, it would have been easier if Louisa desired her in the same way, but that was not the sort of thing a person could change. It would be like asking Ada to take a fancy to a man.

If you love someone, you have to love all that they are. It had been a line in a music hall show, of all things, snuck in amongst the coarse jokes and slapstick, but it had stuck with her, nonetheless. She had to love Louisa because of who she was, not despite it. And now, she could not imagine their relationship any other way but what it was. Not perfect – this evening proved that – but something wonderful.

But does Louisa think I have regrets?

Hopefully, she had made her opinion on that clear enough. It had not taken long, back at the start of their relationship, to come round to the idea because why shouldn't Louisa experience desire differently? People told her she shouldn't desire the way she did, but the world was much vaster and more complex and more wonderful than that. Louisa's sexology texts were proof, and Ada suspected they only showed a narrow selection of a broad array of people, hiding in the shadows, pretending at some idea of 'normal'.

Or being who they are the best they can.

It was all they could do. It was what she and Louisa did. What she and Mabel had done. What Sophie did. What the Richardsons and Mr Taylor had done.

She took another swig of gin and regretted it, lying down on the sofa, watching the ceiling spin to match her whirling thoughts.

If Mabel gets out, what will become of her? Where will she go? I can't invite her here – that's a step too far. But her mum is gone, and her siblings want little to do with her. Will they change their minds if she is pardoned? No, not pardoned, paroled. She'll still be a released convict. What happens to released convicts?

Nothing good.

But she'll be free...

———————

A loud squeal of delight jerked Ada awake, and she choked on a mouthful of fur. She sat up, spluttering, and a blanket slipped off her shoulders.

Blinking in the pale dawn light, the sight of the sitting room slowly filtered its way through a sore head into her consciousness. A disgruntled Gal glared at her from the floor and jumped onto the windowsill, curling into a tight ball. Ada must have fallen asleep on the sofa, and the cat had made herself comfy during the night.

Someone else was awake, though. Excited voices filled the room from nearby – a man and a woman, though Ada's foggy brain couldn't distinguish the words.

A man?

'The hell's going on?' Ada muttered.

There is definitely a man in the hallway in our fully female household. Ada cocked her head, listening. The voices were louder than before. *More like a boy. Wait, that sounds like Artie Dixon?*

She pulled her stiff limbs off the sofa and into the hallway, where two figures turned to face her.

'Oh, miss!' Sophie exclaimed with a grin. 'Look! They've let Artie go!'

And yes, the boy stood next to Sophie – an inch shorter than her, Ada's sleep-befuddled mind noted – was Artie Dixon.

'So, they have.' It came out more confused than celebratory, but surely that was reasonable in the circumstances.

'That is good news indeed.' All three of them turned to where Louisa made her way downstairs, taking in the scene in front of her, looking slightly more dishevelled than usual. Her hair was in a simple plait, crudely done, and her feet were stockingless. She was at least dressed, unlike Ada. 'I am glad to see you free, Mr Dixon, but I have to ask—'

'How int' world you've managed it,' Ada finished for her.

'Miss Franklin confessed.'

Whatever answer she might have expected, it was not that.

She stared, dumbfounded.

'I know,' he said. 'I was shocked, too.'

'Perhaps we should go into sitting room,' Ada said. 'I suspect you have a story to tell, Mr Dixon.'

'Shall I get a pot of tea, miss?' Sophie asked.

'Yes, that feels very necessary.' Ada rubbed at her forehead. 'And a cup for yourself, too. You should hear this.'

Sophie glanced in Louisa's direction.

'Yes, tea, for all four of us. If you would, Sophie, please.' The maid headed towards the kitchen with one last smile in Artie's direction. He watched her retreat before snapping his attention back to them.

Ada led him into the sitting room, where his eyes roved around its walls and furniture. She hurried to pick the blanket off the floor and folded it neatly. Either Louisa or Sophie had tidied the gin bottle up, presumably when they gave her the blanket. She wasn't sure which of those options was worse.

'It's nice in here, miss. Sophie says you did place out when you came to live here.'

'I did. Thank you.'

Louisa sat on the sofa and placed her hands primly in her lap, looking composed, messy hair and bare feet aside. All the impatient questions that must be bouncing around her mind were well-hidden.

'We met your sister,' Ada said, for want of anything else to say, and sat beside Louisa.

'She mentioned. She was one who told me I should come 'ere as soon as I could, not just to let Sophie know I was out, though I was going to do that, of course, but to let you know I was safe. And to, um, to tell you about Miss Franklin.' Artie remained standing. He shook his head when Ada gestured at the armchair. 'I'll leave it for Sophie.'

Louisa asked, 'And you are sure Miss Franklin did not fire that gun?'

He fiddled with his sleeve cuff. 'I was there, ma'am. Next t' her. The shot alone would have deafened me. I've thought that evening through so many times, and I can't see 'ow Miss Franklin could be one t' kill 'im.'

'Then why confess?' Ada asked.

'I don't know, miss. I only met 'er that night. And it turns out no one really knew 'er. Hettie said she was a spy. Working for 'er uncle, that detective who let you speak t' me. Which makes a lot of sense, now I think about it.'

Inspector Lambert will not be pleased about this. Ada wasn't sure how she felt about that. There was little love lost between them, but it was hard to revel in the man potentially losing a family member.

And his wife, too. What has she done to deserve this? Except for everything she could to keep her late sister's daughter safe, if you believe the rumours.

Sophie returned with the tea, and the conversation paused as she poured.

Artie smiled at her. 'I left the seat for you.' He moved towards her, arm outstretched, before snatching it back, like he was about to take her hand and thought better of it. He busied himself with fetching his tea instead.

Ada covered her mouth to hide her amusement and busied herself with adding sugar and milk to her cup. She added an extra sugar lump; she deserved it this morning.

'We were just discussing Miss Franklin,' Louisa told Sophie and lifted her own tea, black and unsweetened, to her lips.

'About her spying.' Artie moved to stand beside Sophie's chair rather than in the centre of the room. His spare hand rested on its arm, mere inches from hers.

'I can't understand her,' Ada continued to the group as large. 'She joins the suffragettes t' spy for her uncle. Becomes a true believer in the cause. Possibly steals suffragette money t' buy gunpowder. Gets arrested for a murder she didn't commit and then four days later confesses to it, as if her uncle hasn't swallowed all his morals and propriety t' try to prove 'er innocence.' The more she tried to understand Emma Franklin, the less she did.

Sophie's brow furrowed. 'Do you know who else it might have been? Have you found anything new in your investigation? I, um, didn't get the chance to ask yesterday.' *Dear Lord, how much did Sophie overhear of what happened last night?*

'There are no clear suspects,' Louisa said, her cheeks pink. No doubt she, too, had picked up on Sophie's words. 'Mrs Green, maybe. Or Mrs Jennings,' she turned to Artie, 'you said they argued, but that is a tenuous link.'

'Pete,' Ada said. 'Though he has no motive, thank God.'

'Kitty's sweetheart?' Artie asked. 'He'd do it if she asked him to. Do owt she asked. He gave her all that fake money months ago. She was showing it off t' me.' Artie kept talking, but Ada heard none of it.

Fake money. Ada closed her eyes and sighed, her cup frozen halfway to her mouth.

Artie was still babbling about Kitty and Pete, but Ada spoke over him. 'Louisa, tell me I cannot murder my brother.' She said the words calmly, with no real anger, though that was no doubt to come once her shock subsided.

'Your brother?' Artie exclaimed. 'Oh shit, yes, Chapman. I didn't realise, miss. And I'm sorry for swearing, ma'am. I...'

'It is fine. And you cannot murder your brother, Ada.' A touch of an order to her words. In any other circumstance,

Ada would have bristled at that. 'Maybe it is not what it sounds like.'

'It sounds like my brother's been using the WSPU to rinse forged money.'

'That Miss Franklin then herself stole,' Louisa added.

'And police now think it is being produced by the WSPU.'

'The police think WSPU are forging money?' Artie asked.

At the same time, Sophie asked, 'But what does any of that have to do with Mr Richardson?' which was a pertinent question, but Ada could not bring herself to care about Mr Richardson.

I cannot have my son in gaol.' She had made her mother a promise. And Artie was free. And Miss Franklin had confessed. Would it be better, now, to step away?

'I do not know.' Louisa's words came from a long way away. Ada should open her eyes. Re-join the conversation. 'Except Mr Richardson was paid with that forged money.'

Inspector Lambert still knows about the forged money. He will keep digging on Miss Franklin's behalf. If we can uncover the connection, so can he. Or he might just arrest the suffragettes and damn the consequences.

'We do not know what she knew,' Louisa said. Ada had lost the thread of what they were discussing. She should open her eyes and pay attention. See if something in all this could help her save her foolish, twice-damned little brother.

Oh Pete, why couldn't you stay small and cute and 'boisterous,' when the worst thing you did was put a dead mouse in my shoe?

She never thought she would be nostalgic for that dead mouse in her shoe.

Ada opened her eyes. 'It could still be irrelevant, couldn't it? The money. We have no reason to believe Mr Richardson knew owt about it. No reason anyone involved would want him dead.'

Louisa hesitated.

But Ada knew the answer. Her previous question had been more of desperate hope than an actual observation. 'Unless Mr Richardson did know about it. That could be what he was blackmailing someone about. Kitty Jennings, for example. Pete can't be running this scheme alone. And Mr Richardson was desperately trying to get as much money as possible, according to Mr Taylor, so a double pay-out. The money from Miss Franklin for the gunpowder and blackmail money from Miss Jennings.'

And then Pete shot him for blackmailing his sweetheart? Or for uncovering his forgeries. Or both.

'Blackmail?' Artie asked.

Louisa's hand moved to Ada's wrist, a gentle clasp, a soft reminder she had someone by her side. It remained there as Louisa briefly explained to Artie about Mr Richardson and his "big suffragette pay-out". Once she'd finished, she added, 'But why would Miss Franklin confess now? It's been four days since your arrest. She was maintaining her innocence until yesterday evening.'

'To save me from the noose?' Artie's voice was soft.

Sophie's hand moved the few inches to close the gap and sit on top of Artie's. He dared a glance towards her, a soft rose blush spreading across his cheeks. Something warm snuck its way around Ada's heart, even as she refrained from saying 'aww' out loud like she was at a pantomime.

'Maybe.' Louisa didn't sound convinced of Miss Franklin's intention, and Ada agreed. 'And we have still not confirmed who was threatening Miss Franklin, though we have our suspicions.'

'Someone was...' Artie muttered to himself. 'Bloody 'ell! There's been a lot happening.' He stopped and stared at Lousia. 'I mean, sorry, again, ma'am, for the language.'

'I have heard Ada say worse.'

'Hey!' A half-hearted protest.

And one Louisa rightly ignored.

'And you don't think it was Mr Richardson threatening Miss Franklin? Especially, if he's...blackmailing someone?' Artie asked slowly like he was trying to figure it out or treading carefully.

'The person threatening Miss Franklin is a woman.' Ada did not explain how they knew that. They still did not know how much Artie knew about the pair of them or Sophie's own past.

That may be another awkward conversation we have to have. Or perhaps not so awkward if our last conversation on the topic is owt to go by.

'Though we cannot rule out the possibility he was working with a woman – probably a member of the WSPU – to blackmail her,' Louisa added.

'Could that relate to her confession? Whether or not Mr Richardson was involved, and whether or not she played a part in his death, if someone else was involved and threatened her, someone still alive and potentially dangerous, maybe she is safer in gaol,' Artie said.

'You make a fair point,' Louisa agreed.

The boy smiled proudly.

'But isn't it most likely to do with her spying?' Sophie asked with some hesitance. 'You mentioned her being called a traitor. Could she not go t' Inspector, no matter how bad their relationship is, and tell him? That must be better than gaol?'

'That is...also a fair point.'

Sophie's smile was a lot subtler than Artie's.

'It is,' Artie said, looking straight down at Sophie.

She blushed.

The inner pantomime audience in Ada wanted to cheer.

'We are going around in circles,' Louisa said.

And does any of it matter now?

'And none of it changes the fact Miss Franklin confessed.' Ada's voice came out flat. She turned to stare into the empty fireplace, not lit on the warm summer's morning. 'We don't know what she said. Or how she claims to have done it. Maybe she is telling the truth. Maybe she thought Mr Richardson was the one who knew about her spying and killed him for it.'

Artie shook his head. 'She didn't fire that gun, miss. I'm sure.'

'Still, it no longer needs to be our concern.' She quickly glanced over at Artie and then to Louisa, hoping she would understand. Artie was free. Pete was still free. They had done what they needed to do for the people they loved. Digging deeper could only make it worse. She would not help lead Inspector Lambert to her brother.

Louisa's brow furrowed, and she bit her lip. If she had understood the message, she was no happier about it than Ada was. Ada couldn't watch her any longer – for once cursing at how good she had gotten at reading the multitudes of emotions beneath Louisa's serene mask – and turned to stare into the fireplace once more.

Can I allow a potentially innocent woman to go to gaol? Can I allow my brother to walk free if he murdered Mr Richardson, if he took a child's father from her, and in doing so, also took a man who was like a father to her in the aftermath?

But she had made her mother a promise.

For fuck's sake, Pete. You foolish, foolish boy.

She closed her eyes again but that did not make her decision go away.

'A-da! A-da! Look!' A toddler with his wooden blocks piled high, the paint chipped from years of rough play from the older siblings who'd gone before him. Just past his third birthday and still alive. Mum had finally stopped staring at him in disbelief, like he could drop dead at any moment. 'Look!' A chubby hand pushed the blocks over with a clatter, and Pete beamed with pride. Ada laughed and picked him up, swinging him into the air as his giggles filled the attic.

'This is the end of it, then.' Louisa's voice cut through the memory.

Ada opened her eyes into the silence that followed.

'I'm grateful for your help, Miss Knight, Miss Chapman.' Artie shuffled in his spot clearly unsure if he should go or not.

'Of course,' Louisa said. 'Please stay as long as you like. I would like to get to know you better.'

Kindly meant, but it only made Artie shuffle more, uncomfortable with the attention.

Ada searched for a new topic to help relax him. Sophie had mentioned him talking about his job with some passion. 'You're an apprentice gardener, Sophie said.'

But that only made him squirm more. 'Oh, um, I was, miss.'

'Ah,' Ada said. 'Yes, I can't imagine the three-day absence went down well.'

'No, miss. It didn't. Nor the reason for it. I'm hoping they will at least give me a reference.'

'Did you lose your job, Artie?' Louisa asked. Had she only just followed the thread of the conversation?

'Yes, ma'am.' Artie failed to meet Louisa's gaze, studying the carpet intently, red creeping across his face again, but his cheeks were stained by shame this time.

Did Sophie move a little closer? Hold his hand a little tighter? The movements were so minute Ada could not be sure of them, but she suspected she did.

'Because of your arrest?' Louisa continued.

A small reluctant nod. He still wasn't meeting her eyes. 'Even though it was a wrongful arrest, I still wasn't at work for three days. And I have a "criminal connection."'

'They are calling being falsely arrested *criminal*?'

'They meant my sister, ma'am. They know she's a suffragette now.'

'And that's reason enough to fire you?' Was that disbelief or anger in Louisa's voice? Or both.

He nodded. 'Yes, ma'am.'

'It's not unheard of, ma'am.'

'It's not that surprising, Louisa.'

Louisa took a moment to digest that information.

'We should go back to the WSPU.'

Which was not at all what Ada had expected her to say next. 'Why? If the case is closed?'

Did we not just decide to leave well enough alone?

'I have made my mind up. I want to join the suffragettes.'

Chapter Eighteen

An Inspector Calls

The determined glint in Sophie's eyes told Louisa she would not be swayed, and so she swallowed her concern for the girl. What choice did she have, sat here in the embarrassing realisation Artie Dixon's dismissal had surprised no one else in the room? And if he could be dismissed because his sister was a suffragette, then how many of the women sat in the WSPU'S headquarters had lost their jobs? How many nationwide? Was this why so many of the suffragettes were women like her—upper-middle-class and with no jobs to lose? How many women dared not speak up because it would cost them everything? Their jobs, their husbands, their children.

And how had it taken her so long to consider that? Shame crawled across her skin. She had been so caught up in her own morality, she never realised she had a chance to fight back where many did not.

She could hardly condemn such injustice than perpetuate it not ten minutes later.

'Of course you can come with us, Sophie.' Ada chimed in before Louisa could. A challenge. A dare to disagree. Did this mean Ada was on board with her plan?

Still, Sophie turned to her. As she always did. 'Of course,' Louisa said, and the maid relaxed.

'I want to come, too,' Artie said. 'I know I can't officially be a member, but I've nowt to lose now. And the argument is that if women get the vote, they'll have to give it t' all men, so...' He shrugged.

Louisa nodded. 'That's agreed then. Let us get ready and have breakfast, and then we shall head into town.' She stood.

'Oh!' Ada exclaimed as she also stood, looking down at herself. 'I've done this entire conversation in my nightgown, haven't I?' She turned to Artie with a smirk. 'You must think me awfully crude.'

'Oh, um, no, miss.' The boy was turning red again, though this was an entirely different type of embarrassment. 'I did wake you up. So, it's my fault, really. I just wanted t' tell Sophie as soon as I could, that is...'

Louisa flicked her partner's arm. 'Come, Ada. Stop teasing the poor boy.'

'I'm going to make a start on breakfast,' Sophie said. 'Why don't you come down t' kitchen, Artie?'

'Yes, great idea.' He turned to Sophie, his relief palpable. 'Have I told you I know how to cook? Not very well, surely not as good as you, but Hettie taught me a bit...' His voice trailed off as he followed Sophie out of the sitting room.

'I like him,' Ada grinned. 'Can we keep him?'

'He is not a pet, Ada.'

'I dunno. He's more likely to listen to us than Gal.'

The cat snoozed on the windowsill, oblivious to the revelations of the morning.

'Well, true as that might be, he is still a human with a human's free will. But...a human I am considering offering a job.'

Ada smiled. 'I like that idea. However, we do not need a gardener. It's only a small space, and between us and Sophie, we have it under control.'

'By which you mean I let the artist run riot in a plant nursery?'

'We have an excellent colour scheme.'

'Until the wildflowers grew.'

'They add to the ambience of the scene.'

Louisa raised her eyebrows at that. 'We shall have to get the apprentice gardener with a passion for flowers to give his opinion on that. As for a job for him, we can iron out the details later. And I will need to talk to Sophie first.'

'Yes, probably for the best to check with her.'

'Indeed. Now come. Let us get you out of that... No, I am not finishing that sentence.' She caught what she was about to say in time. She was getting better at that.

Ada's face scrunched up for a few seconds, and then she laughed. 'Later, perhaps?' And Louisa knew that was a genuine question that she could always answer in the negative, no hard feelings.

'Later, perhaps.'

Ada's thumb stroked across her knuckles.

They both jumped at the loud, impatient knocking on their front door. Galapagos meowed from the windowsill, disgruntled at being awoken.

'I guess I really should get dressed if we are to have more guests.' Ada glanced at the clock. 'And it's still not even past breakfast.' With one last squeeze, they parted, and she left the sitting room.

Louisa checked her reflection in the mirror hung in the hallway. She had dressed in a hurry earlier, but she was at least half-presentable, even if her hair was a little more array than she would have liked. Her bare feet needed to be covered, though, and she grabbed a pair of shoes off the rack and shoved them on, unbuckled. Their visitor knocked again, louder. She would have to do. Sophie was downstairs cooking, and what did people expect if they arrived on the doorstep at such an early hour?

She opened the door to find Inspector Lambert on the doorstep and found herself not at all surprised. He had the haunted look of a man who had not slept – dark circles under his eyes and an unshaven jaw.

'Ah, good morning, Inspector.' Surely, she should say something else, but what? Sorry about your niece confessing to murder?

'Miss Knight.' He nodded. 'I need to speak to you and Miss Chapman.'

He still believes her to be innocent. He was not giving up yet. Why else would he be here? He would not come to them to drown his sorrows.

'Come in, Inspector.' She stepped aside to let him pass and could not help but remember the last time he was here. 'Just so we are clear, you are not here to arrest us this time?'

He sighed. 'You and Miss Chapman certainly know how to hold a grudge.'

'Most people would hold a grudge if you falsely arrested them.'

'Can confirm.' Artie stood in the dining room doorway, eying the inspector warily. Then he turned to Louisa, 'Sophie sent me t' tell you breakfast should be ready in ten minutes, ma'am.'

'Ah, young Mr Dixon, I need to talk to you, too. You already being here simplifies matters.' The inspector removed his hat and jacket, both water speckled. It was drizzling outside; he had come here in the rain.

'There's nowt else for me to say...sir.' Artie made the honorific an insult.

'Shall we all head into the sitting room? Though, as Artie said, breakfast is ready soon. I am sure Sophie could make some more if you would like.'

'No, thank you.' Then he paused, thinking. 'Actually, yes, please, if it's not too much of an imposition. I haven't eaten since... well... in a while, shall we say.' He dragged a hand down an unshaven cheek.

'Artie, could you go tell Sophie that Inspector Lambert will be staying for breakfast, please?'

He paused for a second, glowering at the inspector and reminding Louisa that despite her plans, she did not employ him yet.

This is still my house. Or should I be treating him as a guest? How does one behave towards your maid's sweetheart? It was not information that was ever included in etiquette books unless "always maintain a strictly professional relationship with servants" counted, and that was already blown far out of the water.

But even as the question formed in her mind, he said, 'Yes, ma'am,' and hurried away.

The inspector watched him leave, frowning, before turning his attention back to her, his frown still in place.

'Shall we?' She gestured at the sitting room and led him through, nearly tripping in her unbuckled shoes. 'Please sit.' Neither of the officers had sat the last time they were here. Ada had deemed it as "looming over her" in her retelling of the event.

'I'd rather—'

'Sit.' The harsh order came out before she could stop herself.

A perplexed expression crossed his face. *Has he ever been ordered quite so directly by a woman before?* He glanced at the armchair, where Galapagos had taken up residence in the five minutes since Sophie vacated it, and took a seat on the sofa, straight-backed and tense like he might jump up at any moment.

Louisa—having started what she guessed was now a power play—remained standing.

'I assume this is about your niece.'

'Yes. Since Artie Dixon is here, you know she confessed.'

Louisa nodded.

'And that he still claims he never saw her with a gun.'

'Inspector, do you know exactly what it is she has confessed to?'

'What do you mean?'

'Has she confessed to being the one who fired off the shot?'

He nodded. 'She claims Artie was too distracted to notice, focusing on Mr Richardson's retreat. And then she dropped the gun down a drain when my officers were not paying enough attention. It's all ludicrous, of course. But it's a confession, nonetheless.'

'Do you think it is a forced confession?'

'No. The police do not do such things, Miss Knight.'

She did not dignify that with an answer, merely stared at him, disbelieving.

He relented. 'I cannot see them forcing Emma to confess. She was our spy.'

'It would not cast you or Leeds City Police in the best light, should the press get hold of it.'

The door opened, and Ada entered, wearing one of her plainer day dresses. 'Oh, it's you. I mean—'

'Good morning to you, too, Miss Chapman.'

Ada crossed the room to stand alongside Louisa, staring down at him, and Inspector Lambert shuffled in his seat, clearly itching to stand. An awkward silence fell. Galapagos took this as her opportunity to jump off the armchair and sniff at the inspector's trouser leg, who tried gently nudging the cat away to no prevail.

'Gal, come here.' Ada bent down and picked up the cat, who gave an obligatory protest wiggle before settling into her arms.

Since Ada seemed to have no interest in filling the silence beyond that, Louisa ploughed on. 'So, she's choosing to make a false confession then?'

Beside her, Ada tensed, fingers buried deep into Galapagos' fur.

'Yes.' He jumped to his feet. 'Have you found any proof otherwise?'

They had not. Louisa hesitated. If she admitted that, Inspector Lambert would not give up. And chances are, if he kept investigating, he would find out where the forged money came from eventually.

'I shall take that as no.'

'Does she mention her motive in this confession of hers?' Louisa asked.

'She said he found out about her spying. What?' He barked, turning to Ada. 'I know that look of yours, Miss Chapman. What did you find in relation to her being a spy?'

Ada only glared in response, its effect unhampered by the cat in her arms, so Louisa answered, forcing down her own irritation at the way he spoke to her partner. 'You already know someone threatened her. And we have discovered that Mr Richardson was blackmailing somebody in the WSPU.'

'It's an understandable motive for murder.' And was Louisa the only one who heard the desperation leaking into Ada's tone?

'No.' He shook his head. 'No.' If Ada's desperation was leaking, then his was pouring out.

A gentle knock on the door interrupted them, and Louisa called for the person to come inside.

Sophie entered. 'I'm about to serve breakfast, ma'am.'

'Thank you, Sophie.'

The inspector turned to the maid. 'Tell your sweetheart I need to speak with him whilst we eat.'

Another prickle of irritation. This definitely was still her house, and Sophie was her staff.

'Yes, sir.' Sophie blushed, most likely at the word sweetheart.

'We?' Ada said at the same time.

'Your mistress invited me to eat.' And did she imagine the sly way he said 'mistress'?

Ada turned to her, her expression saying *why the hell would you do that?* but the words that left her mouth were, 'Oh, well, alright then.' She placed Galapagos back on the armchair and received a protesting 'meow' in response. 'Sorry girl, no titbits today. We have company.'

'Shall we?' Louisa led their small group into the dining room, being careful to shut the door behind her, so Galapagos could not follow and beg for scraps.

Sophie had set the table for three. *When did we last have a guest?* Louisa had no family and only limited friends and acquaintances, whilst inviting any of Ada's friends or family would only make the companion lie shakier. *Have I isolated Ada out here?*

But no. No. She would not have any more doubts.

Silence fell again as they sat, and Louisa did not have the energy to fill it, focusing instead on her breakfast.

It lasted until Artie made his appearance. 'Sophie said you want to speak to me, sir.'

Inspector Lambert swallowed his mouthful of food. 'Is there any chance Emma could have held the gun without you seeing it?'

He shook his head. 'I mean, I wasn't looking directly at her, but it would have deafened me. I was standing right next to her. I'm certain the shot came from behind us.'

He waved the boy away, but Artie hesitated, hovering in the doorway.

'Yes?' Inspector Lambert barked.

'She's not a murderer, sir. I'm sure. Whatever else she was or wasn't, she didn't kill him. I thought you should know that.' He turned and fled the room, leaving the inspector staring at an empty doorway.

'To save me from the noose?' His earlier question repeated in Louisa's mind. Was this his way of returning the potential favour? Was Miss Franklin that self-sacrificing? It did not fit the picture of her character Louisa had built up in her mind. Perhaps she was wrong. She had spoken to the woman for fifteen minutes, after all. And all that brimming anger was at her uncle and men like him, not a boy like Artie Dixon, who had no power or real consequence in the world, not even a vote, same as them, just an apprentice wage and his love and loyalty to offer.

And he no longer has the wage anymore.

With a jerk of his head, Inspector Lambert turned back to Louisa and Ada. 'You see? There is no way this confession is true.'

'Then why make it?' Ada stabbed at her sausage.

Inspector Lambert opened his mouth, but no answer came. 'I do not know.'

'You want us to keep investigating, don't you?' Ada pointed her sausage-laden fork at him, egg dripping from where she must have dipped it.

'Why?' The same question she had asked with such anger three days ago, but more incredulous now. 'All this effort for a woman who wanted t' blow your police station up?'

'Family, Miss Chapman. I thought you might understand, your little brother being what he is. Do you want to see him arrested?'

Ada bristled. 'What do you know about Pete?'

'What do you?' It sounded so much like a threat.

'Peter Chapman is not our concern here,' Louisa interrupted. It would not do to let the inspector see how successful that threat could be. 'Have you considered, Inspector, that all this is Miss Franklin's choice, and we should not intervene? Family or not.'

'Sometimes, you have to let family make their own mistakes,' Ada added. 'Ask Walter. He'll tell you all about that.'

'I presume that must be your law-abiding brother since I don't recognise the name. And whatever *choice* you think my niece made, if she was not the murderer, then there is still one out there.'

'And you think we're better equipped to find them? That is, quite frankly, your job,' Ada snapped.

'You said he was blackmailing a suffragette; you still have a better chance of finding them than me.'

'And if it was your niece?' Ada demanded.

'Please,' was all he said in response. He paused, he and Ada staring each other out. 'Please...she's like a daughter to me.' Softly spoken and pain-laced. Not a confession one expected to hear over sausage and eggs, but no less true for it, Louisa was sure.

A daughter who had turned away from all he believed in. Louisa felt a sudden affinity with Miss Franklin and her anger at the discovery the world was not how she had been taught it was. That those she loved had lied to her, including a man who was like a father to her.

This is revenge. The insight hit lightning fast and rooted itself inside her mind, unshakeable.

What if she did this to hurt you? The question was on the tip of Louisa's tongue when Ada spoke first, her voice as soft as the inspector's had been.

'He had a daughter, too, Mr Richardson.' She thought of the girl screaming as she was removed from her home—an orphan taken from the care of a man who loved her. If Louisa should be feeling an affinity with anyone, it should be that girl. 'She deserves the truth if nowt else. Deserves more, certainly, than whatever game your niece—your *daughter*— has turned her father's murder into.'

He nodded stiffly. 'You are right, Miss Chapman. I will not defend Emma on that. But this means you will keep investigating?'

'For a price.' Ada put down her knife and fork and stopped eating, her gaze locked intently on Inspector Lambert.

This was clearly not the answer the inspector had expected. Louisa, too, felt a stab of trepidation.

'Name it. Within reason.'

'Whatever you think you know about my little brother – forget it. Stay away from 'im. He's of no interest to you or the law.'

Oh, of course. It was, in fact, quite a clever plan. Inspector Lambert had already played his hand in revealing he knew at least something of what Peter Chapman was involved in. If they kept investigating instead of the police, it might keep the inspector away from the knowledge of the forged money's origin, as well as get him to agree to stay away from Peter in general.

Unless he is our murderer.

Inspector Lambert stared Ada down with that watchful gaze of his. 'I said, within reason. If he kills someone with that gun of his – and yes, I know about that – I will not let him get away with murder. If your brother killed Mr Richardson and that is why you are asking, I will find out, and I will arrest him, whatever deal we make today.'

'My brother didn't kill Mr Richardson. At least, we 'ave found nothing that points t' him.' Which was not entirely the truth and yet not entirely a lie.

'Then we have an agreement, Miss Chapman.' He held his hand out over the breakfast plates, and she shook it.

Was it strange that Louisa was proud of Ada at that moment? As she made a backhanded deal with a police inspector to keep her troublesome—in fact, he had graduated up to law-breaking—little brother out of gaol.

But it was cleverly done. And done for the right reasons. For the sake of Mrs Chapman and the continued survival of the child she did not lose after so many hard years.

'Then there is something else,' Inspector Lambert said.

Louisa's heart sunk. *What now?*

He patted his waistcoat and stood, muttering something about his jacket pocket.

Ada used his absence to share a befuddled look with Louisa, but she had no reply except to return the sentiment.

He returned with an envelope in his hand. He turned it over in his hand, staring at it like he suspected it might contain some of the suffragettes' letter bombs. 'If there is anyone I can trust to keep this a secret, it is the two of you.'

Which only heightened Louisa's curiosity. Still, he hesitated to hand it over, and she had to bite down the impulse to grab it from his hand. She checked to make sure her partner wasn't about to do just that. Ada's eyes were on the envelope, her hands gripping her chair's arms.

Eventually, he shoved his hand towards them, holding it out. Louisa moved to take it, but Ada was quicker, opening it in such a hurry, it would surprise Louisa if there was any envelope left.

'Oh. *Oh*.'

That was it. Louisa could not wait any longer and shuffled her chair closer to Ada, leaning over her shoulder.

Dearest Camellia,

More flowers. The rest of the letter read much like the one they found in Miss Langwith's drawer. Full of desire and passion and all the words Louisa would never say to Ada.

'You wouldn't be you, and we wouldn't be us.'

Louisa held those words close to her and focused back on the letter. On the puzzle. 'Where did you get this?'

'I'm assuming you're not Camellia,' Ada smirked.

'No. It was...hidden...in...'

'Miss Franklin's room.' Both Louisa and Ada finished for him.

He grimaced but nodded.

Is it the same writer?

'May I?'

Ada passed her the note, and she peered at it. Maybe. They would have to compare the letters.

'You realise a woman wrote this?' Ada asked him.

He grimaced. 'Yes. Its contents make that...clear.'

'Is this not the part where you tell us such a thing is unthinkable?' Ada was enjoying this.

'Let us skip this song and dance, Miss Chapman. You look to your sins, and I shall look to mine.'

Your sins.

If there is anyone I can trust to keep this secret, it is the two of you.

Louisa had not imagined the inspector's insinuations. Strangely, she was less panicked by this confirmation than any of her previous suspicions. A calm overtook her. He knew, and the world had not fallen apart.

Or our world, at least.

'May we keep this?' Louisa lifted the letter in her hand. 'It may have a part to play in our investigation.'

He nodded. 'Whatever you find, where it relates to that letter, I do not wish to know the details. Just find whoever killed Mr Richardson and prove my niece's innocence.'

'We will try,' Louisa said.

'Thank you, I will leave you to finish your breakfast.' He placed his knife and fork on his half-finished plate and, with a short half-bow to them, left.

Ada took a large slurp of tea. 'This is already a long day, and it's not even nine o'clock yet.'

In the hallway, the front door slammed shut behind the inspector.

'It was well-played,' Louisa said. 'Making him agree to leave Peter alone.'

Ada smiled. 'Thanks. I didn't think you would approve.'

'More and more, I find you are becoming my moral compass.'

'Well, that's terrifying.'

'Indeed. But I shall worry about that at a later date.' She held out the letter Inspector Lambert had left. 'First, we need to compare this.'

Ada stood. 'If it matches, and I suspect it does, that means the same woman was having an affair with both Miss Langwith and Miss Franklin, and then threatened Miss Franklin.'

'It does indeed.'

'That is...complicated.'

Upstairs in Louisa's study, they confirmed their suspicions. Both love letters and the note were all written by the same woman.

'It appears we are still to the WSPU, if not for the reason we had planned.'

'You know they'll hate us, right?' Ada said it conversationally; how much effort had that taken her? 'If it turns out a suffragette did this, and we sell them out t' police. Our chance of helping the movement will be gone. All for the sake of my foolish little brother.'

But you promised your mother. And I promised you.

It was a bitter pill to swallow, nonetheless. She had dragged her feet for so long, and now she was un-blinkered, it only meant she was making this decision knowingly.

Selfish, again.

She said none of that out loud. 'The WSPU has managed fine without our help so far. I am not so conceited to think they cannot do it without us.'

A ghost of a smile graced Ada's face. 'True. You have to be the one to tell Sophie she's not coming with us now, though.'

Chapter Nineteen

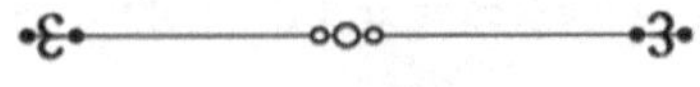

A Decision

Sophie came with them. As did Artie Dixon. Any illusion Louisa had control over her household had gone up in smoke, a fact Ada had been quick to point out.

At the front desk, Sophie blurted out, 'I want to join.'

Which was not what Louisa had been expecting.

The woman manning the front desk peered at her. 'How old are you?'

'Seventeen.'

'Same as Dora Thewlis,' Artie added from beside her. 'And she was a member of the WSPU.'

The woman pursed her lips. 'One baby suffragette was enough.'

'Is it?' Ada said. 'If Huddersfield can have one, why not Leeds?'

The woman must have sensed a losing battle because she stood with a sigh and told them to follow her.

At the doorway into the main assembly room, they nearly ran into one of the mill girls, who dodged around them. She broke into a smile. 'Artie! It's good to see you free. How are you? You going t' ask for one of our prison badges?'

Artie laughed. 'I am well, thank you, and proud as I would be to wear one, aren't those for hunger strikes? I didn't do owt nearly as brave as that.'

The girl chuckled and asked, 'Who are your friends?'

'Oh! You won't have met Miss Dawson before.' He took hold of Sophie's hand. 'She's here t' join you.'

'Miss Dawson? No, we haven't met.' She turned to Sophie and smiled. 'Though, I have heard all about you.'

'You have?' Sophie squeaked.

'Ahem,' the woman from the front desk interrupted. 'Do you wish to speak to Mrs Cohen or not?'

The mill girl waved them off. 'Please, don't let me stop you. Oh, and Artie, your sister is here – she's helping young Miss Jennings wit' one of her sewing projects.'

In the main assembly room, Mrs Cohen was called over. There were questions in her eyes as the situation was explained to her, including a querying glance in Louisa's direction, but she led Sophie to her office readily enough.

Only a few other women were at the headquarters, as expected, dotted around the room at various tasks. It was still early in the day, and for those who still had employment, this was a workday.

Kitty Jennings sat with Miss Dixon, a large cloth banner in the suffragettes' colours spread on the table in front of them. The word 'VOTE' was already sewn onto it in purple fabric. Louisa sincerely hoped she was not about to have to assist with sewing.

'Artie!' Kitty squealed. 'You're free.' She rushed over and enveloped him in a hug, which he tentatively returned. He sent a nervous glance towards where Sophie had gone as he let go, though she was no longer in sight. What was it he had said earlier? Something about Kitty trying to make him jealous by showing off the forged money Pete had given her? Louisa had been distracted by Ada's brother being the one responsible for the forgeries, and Ada even more so. Was that something 'normal' people did? Trying to make each other jealous?

Maybe they were not so normal after all – perhaps they were the ones who should be studied, for that seemed like much queerer behaviour.

'I see Artie has shared our good news,' Miss Dixon said with a smile. 'But what brings you here?'

'Sophie's gonna join the movement,' Artie told his sister, brimming with pride.

'Oh? We don't have many domestic servants on our lists. Most could never join us without risking their position.' She glanced at Louisa as she said it – an unasked question.

'It would be rather hypocritical of me to tell my maid she cannot support the same movement as I do.'

'I thought you were a *suffragist* but not a *suffragette*.'

'What Pete said,' Kitty added.

'Yes, well, shockingly enough, Peter Chapman does not have an insight into my beliefs and actions.'

'What about that one?' It was the same young woman who had taken such offense to Ada's presence during their first visit. She glared with the same resentment she had previously. 'He knows about '*er*.'

Ada scoffed. 'The list of things my little brother doesn't know about me is long and varied. I wouldn't believe a word he says, particularly if it relates to me being supposedly married. I can tell you for a certain that is a lie.'

She turned to Miss Jennings, who shrugged, unrepentant. 'What I was told.'

'"We're supposed to just believe you haven't actually been spreading your—'

'Sally!' Miss Dixon interrupted.

'Believe me or don't,' Ada said. 'I know the truth either way. And Kitty,' she turned, 'feel free to tell my brother he was wrong.'

'Huh, imagine that,' another young woman joined their group. It was the other mill girl they had spoken to, though Louisa could not remember her name.

Why are they here during the day? Have they, too, lost their jobs?

A wave of sympathy flooded her, even as Sally's glare at Ada did not lessen.

Did they have families? How were they getting money in? Or had the girls been kicked out – by fathers, brothers, maybe even husbands? Were they, too, sleeping at headquarters?

And what can I do about that?

She could not hire every person fired because of their political beliefs.

But I can help them fight.

The conviction seized her, its fingers clutching into the very core of her being, what she would call a soul if she believed in such things.

'Excuse me. I need to speak to Mrs Cohen.'

Ada frowned for a second, confused. *Sorry, Ada, my dear. It is my turn to be the impulsive one.*

She would explain later. Ada would understand. And she did not have to follow. If she wished to keep her promise to Mabel, Louisa would not say a word of censure.

When she knocked on the door of Mrs Cohen's office and was called inside, Sophie greeted her by scrambling to her feet. 'Can I help, ma'am?' She had forgotten the maid was still in here. No matter; this was as much her fight as Louisa's.

'I am sorry to interrupt.' She turned to address Mrs Cohen. 'I wish to join, too. To become a full member of the WSPU.' She tried to ignore how Sophie's eyes widened, and her face split into a grin. 'But first, there is more we need to tell you. About Miss Franklin and Mr Richardson.'

This was the decision she had made. She would join, but she would do it honestly. And that included sharing the fact they were still searching for a killer in their ranks.

'Well, this is an unexpected turn of events. Will Miss Chapman be joining us?'

Louisa paused. It would be better for Ada to be here to help her explain. Yet she was talking to Kitty – hopefully getting information about Peter and his forged money – and it would appear suspicious for them all to conspire in Mrs Cohen's office.

'Miss Chapman is currently otherwise occupied.'

'Then tell me what you need to tell me, Miss Knight, and I will give you the forms you need to fill out.'

The entire conversation with Mrs Cohen went easier than expected, and afterwards, Louisa sat in the treasurer's office. Officially a member of the WSPU. That fact had not quite sunk in yet. Nor the fact Ada still did not know – it was a conversation to be had privately. But when Mrs Cohen had suggested she could be of use speaking to Miss Langwith and investigating the figures, she had seized at it.

'So, let me check if I have understood this correctly.' The treasurer took her glasses off and pinched the bridge of her nose. 'You think Peter Chapman, assisted by Kitty Jennings, has been stealing our money and replacing it with forgeries? And Miss Franklin stole that money to pay Mr Richardson for explosive powder?'

Louisa had told her as much. She needed to know if she was going to be any help with the forged money. Whilst she was still potentially a suspect because of the love letters between her and Miss Franklin's potential blackmailer, she was low on the list, and there was no investigating the missing money without her. Perhaps the relative honesty would help gain her trust, especially since Louisa also needed to find a way to get her letter's author from her. They still needed confirmation it was Mrs Green, as they suspected. And if she was involved, this would warn her they were getting close, and people got sloppy once they thought they were close to being caught. Or at least they did in Louisa's detective novels.

'Yes.' It was a concise summary. 'Is there anything that would suggest that is not the case?'

Miss Langwith nodded and reached down into one of her desk drawers – one of the unlocked ones – and pulled out a leather-bound book. 'What about the small amounts? As I just mentioned the books had not been balancing for a while prior to the large-scale disappearance.' She flipped through till she found the page she wanted, laying it open on the table to reveal a set of neatly written accounts. 'So, either Miss Franklin's stealing dates further back than you realised, or Peter Chapman and Kitty Jennings were doing more than swapping out the notes.'

'That does not sound wise. It sounds like a good way to draw attention to your money laundering scheme if anything.'

'Neither strike me as the smartest of people. Greedy, perhaps. And young. Foolish.'

All excellent words to describe Peter Chapman.

'I struggle to believe this of Kitty Jennings, though. She is no criminal mastermind. I will not pretend to have any real fondness for the girl, but she does not strike one as the sort to steal and cheat. Unless the boy is... Excuse me, I know he is your friend's brother, but he could be a...'

'Bad influence?' Louisa finished.

Miss Langwith nodded, looking relieved Louisa had said the words for her.

'Please do not hesitate to insult Peter Chapman around me – I will not be defending him.'

'And his sister?'

'Is still his sister.' *And is risking a lot to try to save his sorry hide.*

She gave a slight smile. 'I used to wish for siblings as a child, but it is times like this I am glad that wish was never granted.'

'I have had similar thoughts.' Usually in relation to Ada's troublesome little brother. It was strange to have her own sentiments echoed back at her.

Miss Langwith smiled, but her face turned contemplative. 'You and Miss Chapman. You come across as very different people.'

'I suppose we are. Yet I find it a beneficial aspect for a *companion.*' She emphasised the word for once. 'She's pretty, spirited, *lively.*' Louisa fought not to cringe at her own words. For all her accidentally saucy turns of phrase, when she tried to make double entendres, the words sounded ridiculous on her tongue.

Miss Langwith frowned. Was she panicking on the inside? Did she, too, share Louisa's constant fear of people finding out the truth of who she was? 'I am sure Miss Chapman makes for enjoyable company.' Was that sincerity, or was she, too, terrible at using double meanings?

'She certainly keeps my life interesting.' That one was not even a double entendre; it was just a fact.

As if to emphasise that point, the door flung open to reveal Ada, dressed in a paint-splattered apron with her hat askew. As soon as the door closed behind her, she turned to Miss Langwith and announced. 'You were having an affair with Mrs Green, as was Miss Franklin. Tell me, did you find out about it and decide to have her framed for murder?'

Chapter Twenty

Sapphic Affairs

Miss Langwith stared, mouth agape, like the Edvard Munch painting Ada had seen a print of once.

Louisa looked no less stunned, though her mouth wasn't open quite as wide.

'That is quite the accusation, Miss Chapman.' Miss Langwith had finally closed her mouth and forced out a convincing-sounding denial. She could do the same haughty dismissal as Louisa with her accent.

'It is certainly a bold statement, Ada.' Which translated to 'how have you confirmed that?'

She answered the unsaid question. 'I just had a very illuminating conversation with Kitty. She was quite apologetic about spreading rumours, and so, of course, I forgave her. After that, she was eager t' tell me about all the things she hopes to do for the WSPU one day. How the women here have taught her so much, including Mrs Green, who taught her a thing or two about bomb-making and the science behind it. And isn't that funny? Because the other thing Mrs Green taught her – some poetic whim or other, a moment of boredom – was the language of flowers. It seems she learnt it during her brief time at finishing school.' Miss Dixon had shared that bit of information. Prior to Artie's release, she and Miss Jain had kept digging for any more information the suffragettes had on Mrs

Green. Her rich father had paid, but when he died unexpectedly, his widow felt no need to keep paying a bastard's school fees.

'How does any of that relate to your accusation? Not all of us share your...unusual persuasion.'

The insult did not sting as much as usual, but it would still grow tiring quickly, so best to bring all this denial to an end. Ada reached into her bag and withdrew the letters to Miss Langwith and Miss Franklin, tossing them onto the desk in front of the treasurer. 'I imagine finishing school is also where she picked up such fancy handwriting.'

Miss Langwith picked them up tentatively.

'One, you should recognise. T'other one was found in Miss Franklin's room.'

'How did you get these?'

'Broke into your desk drawer last time we were here.' *Hopefully, that should distract her from the fact we got the other one from a police inspector.*

It did. 'You...*broke* into my...*desk*?' she sputtered.

'Ada's very handy with a hairpin,' Louisa joined in. Perhaps she had realised Ada's misdirection. 'Like I said, she keeps life interesting.'

It was absurd, but pride blossomed in her chest, nonetheless.

Wait, why were they discussing me?

'You condone this criminal behaviour?' Miss Langwith demanded of Louisa.

'Says the suffragette,' Ada interjected.

'You never answered Ada's question,' Louisa added.

'And what question was that?'

'Did you set Miss Franklin up for a murder she did not commit?'

Miss Langwith launched to her feet. 'I am not answering these questions. Excuse me.' She bustled out of the office, the door slamming in her wake.

Louisa turned to Ada, her tone droll. 'I think I may be about to be ejected from the WSPU only half an hour after joining their movement.'

'You joined the suffragettes?' Ada's voice came out louder and shriller than intended.

'Ah, that was not quite how I planned to inform you.'

And all Ada's fears were still bubbling away under the surface, but rising above them was a great tidal wave of amused hysteria. 'I cannot believe I spent two years listening to you explain why a peaceful suffrage movement was the best option, only for you to join the WSPU before me. I am going to join. Right now.'

Even as the words left her mouth, she remembered her promise to Mabel. But *Louisa* had joined. And when else would she get this chance? To fight. To make a difference. To do some good in the world.

And Mabel could be free soon. The small matter of her joining the suffragettes would pale in the wake of that.

'If you don't get removed for saying their treasurer was involved in a conspiracy to murder.' But behind her continued drollness, Louisa had not quite hidden her pleased expression when Ada said she, too, would join. 'You realise Mrs Green's knowledge of flower language alone is flimsy proof?'

'And there's my sensible Louisa.' But Ada said it with a smile.

'Sensible, meanwhile, has never been your forte, has it, Miss Chapman?' She spun round at Mrs Cohen's voice.

'Says the suffragette,' Ada muttered again. But really, was she seriously being lectured on being sensible by someone who famously snuck into one of the most secure locations in the country with a crowbar?

Mrs Cohen smiled at that, though her next words were serious. 'Miss Langwith is quite cross with you. Something about a murder accusation?'

'Technically, I accused her of setting someone else up for murder.'

'Miss Chapman.' Ada would never tell Mrs Cohen how much her exasperated tone of voice reminded her of Inspector Lambert.

'So, I guess now isn't a good time to say I would also like to join?'

'I was rather expecting that. Or at least I hoped. It would be a strange turnaround for the books if Miss Knight joined, but you didn't. But please leave your murder accusations until you have proof.'

'Until we have proof?' So, not stop altogether.

'Mr Richardson – whatever else he was – was a friend and a father. If someone killed him, they cannot be allowed to walk free. Even if it is one of our sisters.'

Ada nodded. 'So, where do I sign?'

Once she'd signed all the necessary papers and paid the membership fee, Ada returned to the main room. There was no sign of Louisa – she must still be hidden away in the treasurer's office, trying to make sense of the figures and smooth over Ada's deliberate faux pas. She might even learn more about Mrs Green from her former lover in the process.

Ada headed back towards the banner she had been working on earlier, but all thought of art fled her mind when she spotted Pete sat amongst the suffragettes, bold as brass at Kitty's side.

She marched over.

He glanced up, bored, at her arrival. 'So, I hear you're finally a suffragette? And Miss Knight and her mousy little maid.'

Kitty giggled. 'Don't be mean, Pete. Artie Dixon seems quite taken with her,' she added sniffly.

'There's no accounting for taste.'

'We need t' talk.'

'So, talk.' He waved at a chair beside him. 'If you're here to scold me over the marriage rumours – it was just a joke, Ada.'

'Hilarious,' she said drily. 'But it's not that. I need to speak with you privately.' She turned to Kitty. 'Family matters. I'm sure you understand.'

Kitty smiled, flashing the gap in her teeth. 'Of course. Talk t' your sister, Pete.'

'Outside.' Ada grabbed his arm and marched him out of the assembly room. When they made it to the corridor, Pete shook his arm free, leaned against a wall, and lit a cigarette.

Ada mirrored him. She would need it for this conversation.

'Is it true you've lost your job?' he asked.

Thrown by the question, all she answered was 'what?'

'Your police sketch work – it's gone?' He took a drag of his cigarette and coughed. Once. Twice. Three times.

Not so used to smoking then, little brother.

Ada nodded in answer to his question, even as she tried to hide her smile. The one sketch she did for the police recently didn't count. When this was all over, Inspector Lambert would want to wash his hands of her even more.

He frowned. 'Do you need money?'

Ada tilted her head, confused. She put the cigarette back to her lips to delay answering, trying to work out her brother's reasoning for his questions. 'I still have a roof over my head and a bit saved up.' Not much, but all that meant was having to be a little frugal in her luxuries, so she could not complain.

'You're more reliant on Miss Knight's charity than ever before,' he said with genuine concern. It was disconcerting.

'It's not charity, Pete.'

'Prostitution then, if you'd prefer.'

Why am I trying to save his sorry hide again?

'You couldn't be any further from truth if you tried, Pete, so can I recommend you stop speaking on matters you do not understand.'

'Sorry, did I strike a nerve?' He smirked. 'I am trying t' offer you help here.' He flicked his cigarette stub away – he had not smoked anymore of it since his coughing fit, letting it burn down.

'In the most obnoxious manner possible?' With nothing suitable to use as an ashtray, she stubbed her own cigarette out on the wall, sending a silent apology to whoever owned the building.

He shrugged. 'Just let me know. If you do find yourself in need of cash.'

'I don't need your bloody forgeries, Pete!'

His face fell, all his swagger draining out of him. 'You know about that? Did Rosie tell you?'

'Rosie? Pete, for the love of God, please tell me you did not drag our nine-year-old sister in t' this mess of yours?'

But Pete ignored her, fear pitching his voice high and frantic. 'Do police know?' And at that moment, he looked so very, very young. An adolescent boy in over his head.

Ada took pity on him. 'Inspector Lambert found your forgeries in his niece's bedroom. I don't know if he's made the connection. He does know about that gun of yours, though, and no, I didn't tell 'im.'

Pete let loose a string of creative curse words.

'He's not gonna come after you for it,' Ada said. 'Not if I can help free his niece.'

'What?' Pete's face twisted into a mask of confusion.

'I made a deal.'

'For me?'

'For Mum. Who you need t' go and see, by the way. Where have you even been living?'

'Friends.'

'Go home, Pete. Or at least let Mum know you're alive.'

He scuffed his shoes against the carpet. 'Fine.'

'And tell me how Rosie fits into this.'

'She found my stash. We made a deal.'

Ada stared at him, waiting.

'I paid her to keep quiet.'

'You bribed our baby sister?' Ada gasped as realisation hit. 'The necklace. I should've known Mum and Dad would never have bought her that.'

'I should think not. It cost me a pretty penny, too.'

Was it real silver, after all?

'Great,' Ada deadpanned. 'My brother is a forger and my sister a blackmailer.'

Maybe she wrote the note to Miss Franklin. Ada let out a snort of hysterical laughter at the ludicrous thought.

Pete eyed her warily. 'Are we done here?'

'One more thing, since I'm helping you, you need t' help me.'

'I offered you money.'

'Not that, Pete. Mr Richardson's murder. I can't protect you if you were the one who shot 'im. Do you understand that?'

'You think I...' Ada spotted a genuine glint of hurt in his eyes, before he smothered it with outrage. 'Why would I do that, hmm, Ada?' I don't know this Mr Richardson. Why would I want 'im dead.'

'So, he wasn't blackmailing you and Kitty then?'

'What? No!' His shock appeared sincere, and relief flooded Ada. 'Honestly, Ada, I know nowt about any blackmail. If someone was blackmailing us, they'd know about it.'

'That does not make you sound innocent, Pete! And I'm guessing by "us", you don't mean you and Kitty.'

He crossed his arms and said nothing.

Ada sighed. 'Just tell me you have an alibi, please.'

'When was it?'

Ada told him the date, and he thought for a moment. 'We went t' that picture house in Headingley.' He reached into his jacket pocket and pulled out an assortment of rubbish – coins, receipts, a button, several sweets, and a handkerchief. Their mother's tidiness had not been passed down to him, either. He poked through it until he muttered a quiet, 'Aha, here' and held out a ticket stub.

Ada took it, scanning it quickly, and a fresh wave of relief washed over her. He had been at a picture showing on the evening of Mr Richardson's murder. It was not feasible for him to have got from Headingley to town in time to have killed Mr Richardson.

'*A Militant Suffragette*?' Ada said the film's title questioningly. She had dragged Louisa to see it two months ago, intrigued by the title. However, its portrayal of the suffragettes had left her unimpressed, as had its heroine choosing her anti-suffrage aristocratic lover over the women's cause. Though, she should not have been that surprised – there were few films that showed the suffragettes in a positive light.

'Kitty's choice.'

'Did she hate it as much as I did?'

'She found it funny.'

'Well, I guess I can see how it could be considered amusing.'

'Speaking of Kitty, I should head back in.' He hesitated. 'But I meant it, Ada. If you need money…'

'I do not need your help, Pete, or your fake money.'

He rolled his eyes and walked away.

'And *I* meant it,' she shouted at his retreating back. 'Go see Mum!'

He gave a wave of his hand above his head she presumed was an agreement – or at least acknowledgement – and disappeared through the doorway.

Ada placed her head against the wall and sighed.

So not Pete. And not Kitty. Mrs Jennings is still a possibility. But Pete's surprise at the idea of Kitty getting blackmailed had appeared genuine, though there was always the possibility she didn't tell him. Or Mrs Jennings had been the one blackmailed about her daughter's actions and never told her. They did not seem like a mother and daughter who confided in one another.

There's also Mrs Green. Had she been aiming for Miss Franklin, the spy who became her lover, and missed terribly? *Which does not bode well for her future as a bomb-maker.*

Or it could be a different suffragette entirely Mr Richardson was blackmailing. *How many traitors do they have? What sort of union have I just joined?* Because she was one of them now. She gave a shaky laugh, alone in the corridor. She was a suffragette. So was Louisa. And Sophie. This was not how she had expected the day to go when she woke up with a sore head and a mouthful of cat fur.

She should go back inside. She had a murder to solve, an ungrateful – or maybe not entirely ungrateful? Why had he offered her money? – little brother to save, and then they could look to the future

---

Ada and Louisa left the WSPU headquarters several hours later. They'd convinced Mrs Cohen to give them Mrs Green's address, though she had warned them that all they would find there were 'two of the most miserable men in existence,' and left Sophie and Artie with Miss Dixon. Sophie had, in her half a day as a member of the WSPU, already taken charge of their kitchen, which was quite an achievement for a seventeen-year-old girl in a room full of matriarchs.

Kitty Jennings kept sending her curious glances but said nothing more than a throwaway comment to Artie that Sophie was 'quite the gal'. Pete had disappeared not long after their conversation. Hopefully, to visit their mother.

As they turned the corner where New Briggate reached Lowerhead Row, a large group of both men and women were gathered on the pavement. They kept stopping every passerby and attempting to hand them a piece of card. Some shook them off; others took the offering politely. One passing woman shouted at them before being pulled away by her male companion.

'Who are they?' Louisa asked. Her face scrunched up in the same manner as when she was struggling to understand a particularly taxing book.

'Nowt good,' Ada replied.

As soon as they approached the group, a woman shoved her arm in front of them, waving a colourful postcard in their faces.

Ada had seen enough anti-suffrage propaganda to assume

that was what it was, especially so close to the WSPU's headquarters.

'We need to stop this scourge,' the woman declared. Even amid her mania, her eyes did the brief flicker to and away from Ada's marred cheek.

But Ada was much more interested in the card she was offering them, plucking it from her hand. 'Oh, I entirely agree,' she said in her plummiest voice. 'All these miscreants blocking up the pavement, disturbing good citizens trying to go about their day, it's a disgrace.'

'I, well, I never,' the woman blustered.

Ada grabbed Louisa's arm and hurried away before the woman could form a coherent retort, weaving their way around their fellow pedestrians. 'Now, let's see what we have here.' Ada waved the card in her hand. 'I'm going for a man being forced to do some cleaning. Do you want to take a guess?'

'I will say... a woman wearing trousers?' Amusement glinted in Louisa's hazel eyes.

'Oh, the horrors,' mocked Ada, who regularly wore an old pair of men's trousers when painting.

She glanced at the card to see which stereotype they had chosen, and a peal of laughter burst from her. Several passersby sent her curious glances. She tried to stifle her amusement, but each time she nearly had it under control, a new set of giggles overtook her until she had to pause and lean against an unlit gas lamp.

'What could possibly be so funny?' Louisa held her hand out for the card, but Ada was laughing too much to hand it over. 'I highly doubt the anti-suffrage movement has suddenly gained a sense of humour. Though, I suppose some of their attempts have been unintentionally amusing.'

'Oh, we're definitely in unintentionally amusing territory here.' Her giggles finally subsided, and Ada passed Louisa the card.

Louisa's laughter was a lot more restrained than Ada's had been. She raised a hand to cover her mouth and unconvincingly turned it into a cough. Leaning over to Ada, ever so slightly closer than she usually got in public, she whispered, 'Entirely wrong audience, really.'

The postcard depicted two women kissing, with a tagline underneath declaring that 'Women will be doing all the men's jobs soon.'

Neither of them appears particularly sad about it. Someone should tell the anti-suffragists their propaganda probably shouldn't be implying that women would be perfectly happy without men.

Ada released another burst of laughter, but when she turned to share this insight with Louisa, her partner's face was sombre.

In a much more urgent whisper, Louisa asked, 'Do you think they knew?'

Ada's amusement dampened, 'I'd guess not – the intention is to scare men and scandalise upstanding women. As you said, we're very much not the intended audience.' Her nonchalant words didn't stop the uneasy feeling in her stomach. Already twice today, the true nature of their relationship had been laid out in front of them. They were skating on thin ice and could fall into the freezing waters of social ostracisation below at any time, but she would not acknowledge that fear. Louisa worried enough. Trying to lighten the mood, she joked, 'Maybe we should have it framed. Hang it on the wall.'

'I am not convinced it would be the wisest thing to display in the sitting room.'

'We could put it in your study. It'd be out of the way of prying eyes up there.' Ada let the 'and imagine how your father would have felt about that' go unsaid.

'Perhaps your painting room would be a better option.'

'No, your study is definitely the right place for it.'

'In the fireplace, perhaps.'

Ada smiled and held her hand out. Once Louisa passed the card back, she tucked it away in her bag. She could create a return cartoon to mock it – one of her new contributions to the suffragette cause.

That thought lessened her fear a bit. Finally – *finally* – they were fighting back.

For all her questioning and worrying, now she had decided – and *Louisa* had decided – it felt freeing. They could face whatever there was to come.

'Do you think they do actually know, though?' Louisa whispered, though their tram stop was empty. 'Not about us, specifically, but about people like us, like Miss Langwith, Miss Franklin, Mrs Green. They are not wrong to say people of a...sapphic persuasion...are part of the suffragette cause, not that I am fool enough to believe the vote could change our standing in society.'

'Who can say. They certainly do not approve of the idea of us.' Ada patted her bag where the postcard was. 'We go against *the natural order of society.*'

'The vote will not change that.'

'No. But it is a step in the right direction. We are still women, and we will always have to live as women who do not fit the right mould. Men like us – they have to hide and lie, and they are in much graver danger if caught – but at least if they keep it secret, if they can give the appearance of what people think a man should be, then they are still given respect due to men. Positions due to men. Pay due to men. But we will always be treated as women and inferior women at that. Surely, improving the rights of all women can only help us in the end?'

Louisa smiled. 'You are right. Rather insightful, if anything.'

'No need to sound so shocked.' But her tease had no bite. 'Ah, the tram is here. I shall have to continue being insightful later. We have to make the acquaintance of two terrible men.'

Mrs Cohen's description of Mrs Green's husband and stepson had not been exaggerated. Mr Green resented his wife, the suffragettes, and by all accounts, the whole world and everyone in it. He was perhaps the most miserable man in existence, except for his adult son, who hated his stepmother even more than his father, which was quite the achievement.

'I mean, I understand why she wanted to be as far away from them as possible,' Louisa said to Ada as they walked away from the house.

'I understand why she started bedding women.'

'That's not—'

Ada grinned at Louisa to stop the forthcoming sexology lecture before it even began.

Louisa shook her head, smiling affectionately.

'Shall we take a hansom home? I believe there is a rank nearby.'

Ada agreed readily. Her feet ached, and she was ready to get home, collapse onto the sofa and not move. They found the rank with no issue. Both of them sat quietly in the cab, watching the world go past, but Ada's mind was full of circling thoughts, and she imagined Louisa's was, too.

Pete and Kitty have an alibi, but we do not have one for Mrs Green. Is the forged money going to be irrelevant, after all, or is that wishful thinking on my part? Or is it the sapphic affairs that are not relevant? Or are both relevant, like both Mrs Pearce and Mrs Parks were? Though, there were not two bullet holes in his body.

Ada sighed with frustration, and beside her, Louisa gave a small chuckle. She moved to close the gap between their hands. There was a time – not so long ago – when she would not have dared to be that bold in public, even in the relevant privacy of the back of a hansom cab. Ada gave her hand a slight squeeze in response.

It was still light by the time they stepped out of the cab, though Ada's stomach told her it must be nearing teatime, if not past. *Will Sophie be home yet?*

She got her answer immediately upon them entering the house.

'She's dead.' Sophie's face was grave.

'Excuse me?' Louisa said.

Miss Franklin?

'Mrs Cohen got a call from London office. Miss Davison, the woman from that derby, who was so brave and ran in front of King's horse, and papers were so cross about it. She died earlier today. Mrs Jennings said she's a martyr. Kitty said that's a load of... rubbish.'

I suspect she didn't say rubbish.

It was not surprising news. Everything they had heard or read had implied Miss Davison was too injured to survive. Still, it was like a rug being swept from under her feet. Miss Davison had believed. She had wanted to fight and taken risks for her cause. And she had died for her cause. The cause they had just joined.

'Is she a martyr?' Sophie looked back and forth between the two of them.

'She was a brave woman who died fighting for something she believed in.'

'God rest her soul,' Ada muttered. All those years of Sunday school had left their mark.

'Amen,' Sophie added.

'I hope she is at peace now.' A tactical response from the atheist Louisa, but Ada doubted it was any less sincere for it.

'What does it mean?' Sophie asked. 'For the WSPU? For... us.'

Ada, at least, had an answer for that. 'It means we make sure she didn't die in vain.'

Chapter Twenty-One

The Sacrifices Made

Armley Gaol loomed over them. Beside Louisa, Ada stiffened. Was she, too, thinking how someday soon they might be imprisoned here? Was she thinking of Mabel and the promise she had broken?

By the visitor's entrance, Inspector Lambert waited with a younger woman beside him, who must be his wife. At an estimate, she was a few years older than Louisa, which still made her roughly twenty years her husband's junior. She was dressed like she was attending church, not visiting a prison – a pink silk dress and her blonde hair swept up beneath a large picture hat adorned with matching flowers. Inspector Lambert, meanwhile, wore his usual bowler hat and black suit beside her.

They had received the phone call from the inspector earlier in the morning. Three days had passed since Ada struck a deal with him, and they were no closer to finding Mr Richardson's killer. He had secured a visit with Miss Franklin for him and his wife, and he wanted them to come, too. With no better leads to follow, it made sense to agree. Besides, the question of why Miss Franklin confessed continued to irritate Louisa.

'Good morning,' he greeted them, and they echoed the sentiment. Mrs Lambert only gave them a forced smile. She appeared even more tightly wound than Ada.

After a few quiet words from the inspector, they followed a warden through the gloomy corridors of the prison. It was cold inside, despite being a bright sunny day outside, and Louisa suppressed a shiver.

This is where they will lock us up if we continue down the path we have started. The thought came back to her unbidden. Mrs Cohen and others had served sentences inside this very building, starving themselves as a continuation of their protest. Of course, she had known, when joining the suffragettes, what their fight entailed and how it could end. It was a different matter entirely to walk through the gloom of the prison behind a surly-faced warden and be unable to ignore her gratefulness that she was only a visitor.

What was it Mabel said to Ada? This place breaks everyone eventually. Even the suffragettes, no matter how they wear their imprisonment pins with pride once they are on the outside.

The warden showed them into a small room with a metal table and a scattering of chairs. A small, barred window allowed in thin streaks of light that barely illuminated the room. There were no gas lamps.

The warden announced he would return shortly with the prisoner and Mrs Lambert flinched at the last word. Her husband placed a soothing hand on her arm, guiding her to a chair.

Louisa, too, moved to sit for want of a better option. Ada did not follow, pacing the tiny constraints of the room. She would not fare well in an actual gaol cell.

Her decision. Her decision. Louisa would not feel guilty for this road they had started down together. Still, she watched her partner's frantic movements, wishing she could reach out and comfort her, mutter soothing words, but she could not with Inspector Lambert and his wife so close. He may know, but it still did no good to flaunt what they were so openly.

Ada finally came to a stop as the door re-opened, and the warden returned with Miss Franklin. Prison had muted her. She was dressed in grey cotton, her hair in a simple plait, and her expression dull. Handcuffs secured her wrists.

Mrs Lambert made a distressed noise.

'The cuffs are unnecessary,' Inspector Lambert said, with every inch of authority he could muster in his voice.

The warden opened his mouth as if to argue, but then he shrugged and reached for a ring of keys. With a gentle click, he unlocked the handcuffs. Miss Franklin winced as he removed them.

The warden did not appear to notice, and with a tight nod at Inspector Lambert, he turned his heel and locked the door behind him.

Ada moved to stand behind Louisa, her hands gripping the back of the chair.

'Well, this is quite the welcome committee,' Miss Franklin said into the silence, rubbing at the red marks on her wrists.

'Emma!' Inspector Lambert scolded, as his wife said tearfully, 'That's not funny, Emma.'

'How are you?' Mrs Lambert continued.

Miss Franklin stared at her, disbelieving. 'Why are you here?'

'To see you.'

She turned to face Louisa and Ada. 'And why are you here? Your investigation is over.'

'I am not so sure it is,' Louisa said.

Miss Franklin scoffed. 'If you wish to waste your time, be my guest.'

Inspector Lambert spoke before Louisa could reply. 'You did not fire that gun, Emma. So, tell me why you are lying.'

She stared her uncle down. 'I am not lying.'

Mrs Lambert sobbed. 'Why are you doing this?'

'Telling the truth? Is that not how you raised me, Aunt Ethel?'

'I did my best for you.' It was barely a whisper, but there was a lot of meaning in those words. If Miss Franklin had been in her care since she was a child, Mrs Lambert must have only been young herself when she received custody. How much had she sacrificed to help care for her late sister's child?

Exactly how long have the Lamberts been married?

'*We* did our best for you,' Inspector Lambert added.

'Do you want my snivelling gratitude? Oh, you wedded and bedded an eighteen-year-old. So gracious of you.'

'Emma!' It was both her relatives who shouted her name this time—Inspector Lambert on the verge of bellowing at her, Mrs Lambert on the verge of tears again.

And none of this helps us.

She was trying to formulate a question when Ada spoke from behind her. 'We get it. You hate your uncle. He's not one of my favourite people, either. It's still not a good enough reason t' confess t' a murder you didn't commit. And please spare us your insistence of guilt. No one believes you. Maybe you think you're making some great, grand gesture, a dazzling act of defiance, but I have a friend trapped in this gaol, as I think you know, and she told me this place breaks everyone, eventually. Even you, Miss Franklin. Are you really willing to break yourself just to devastate your aunt and uncle in the process?'

'I...'

Ada had knocked the winds from Miss Franklin's sails. It had been an excellent speech, but Ada often had a way with words and people that Louisa both admired and envied.

'That is not what this is.' Miss Franklin dropped her gaze to her wrist, her fingertips tracing those red lines again.

'Then what is it?' Mrs Lambert asked softly.

'It...' She shook her head. 'You would not understand.' She looked back up, directly at her aunt this time. Tears pooled in her eyes. 'You did what was best for me – or what you thought was best for me – and I am aware of that. I am grateful for that. I have had a lot of time to think these past few days. You sacrificed your life for me – or at least your choices in life – and I am sorry if you think I have repaid that sacrifice poorly, but...' she sighed. 'I...' Her fingers twitched, but no more words came.

Louisa dared not speak into the silence that followed.

Behind her, Ada gave a soft, surprised 'oh', and Miss Franklin's head jerked round to her. 'This is a sacrifice.'

Miss Franklin stared – wide eyed and open mouthed – before quickly trying to smother the expression. It was too late. Those few seconds of honest reaction were all the answers anyone needed.

'A sacrifice for who?' Mrs Lambert jumped to her feet. 'For who, Emma?'

But Miss Franklin shook her head wildly, strands of hair falling loose from its plait. She jerked her arms across her chest, trying for defiance but only hugging herself close.

'The woman who sent you that letter?' Inspector Lambert asked.

Again, her reaction betrayed her. For a few crucial moments, her surprise and horror were writ large across her face for all to see.

'What letter?' Mrs Lambert asked. 'What woman?'

Mrs Green. They had not shared that information with Inspector Lambert, not yet. *The woman who wanted to escalate the violence, who encouraged Miss Franklin to blow up her uncle's police station.*

It should be a simple choice. Say her name and damn her. Yet indecision held Louisa in its grip.

Mrs Green spoke so passionately about the rights of working women. Whatever her methods, her belief is genuine. Her desire to improve the lot of women like her, dealt a poor hand in life.

She would not be able to continue any of that from gaol. Nor was she the only suffragette whose actions had led to deaths. *But this was a cold-blooded murder. And Miss Franklin, its potential intended target. She is sacrificing herself for a woman who might have tried to murder her. If this is her choice, let her make it fully informed.*

'Mrs Green.'

All eyes turned to Louisa, but she focused on Miss Franklin. 'She wrote the note, too, the one threatening you. She tried to murder you, and yet you sacrificed yourself to save her.'

Miss Franklin's face crumpled. She shook her head frantically. 'No. No. No. You are lying.'

'Can a confession be rescinded?' This was Mrs Lambert to her husband.

'It is difficult.'

'NO!' Miss Franklin screamed at them both. 'NO! GET OUT OF HERE! LEAVE ME ALONE!' Her tears streamed, her words punctuated with heaving sobs. 'I DID THIS! I KILLED HIM! YOU ARE ALL WRONG!'

Sometimes, Louisa wished she understood other people better. That she could peel back their skin, crack open their skulls, and peer into their minds. Compile notes and analyse them until she could rationalise why people's actions were often so alien to her. What she would not have given to read Miss Franklin's mind at that point, to understand what exactly compelled her to act that way.

But she could not. She could do nothing but sit there, dazed, as Miss Franklin's shouts mingled with her uncle's bellows and her aunt's sobbing. The noise pressed in on Louisa, battering her from all sides. She wanted away from this tiny room and these people and their racket and their incomprehensible choices.

Why was Miss Franklin not begging them to rescind her confession now she knew Mrs Green had been the one to threaten her? How had Mrs Lambert been willing to sacrifice herself and her body into marriage when Louisa could not even give herself over to a woman who she loved? And why had Inspector Lambert agreed to any of this? Why had he chosen his own niece as his spy? This girl who he said was like a daughter, who screamed at him with such fury.

The door crashing against the wall broke through their noise, and they all jumped. 'What the bloody 'ell is going on 'ere?' The warden from earlier stood in the doorway, his face like thunder.

'We were just leaving.' Inspector Lambert stood with an attempt at dignity.

'Good. Go,' Miss Franklin spat at him. Louisa had thought she understood her anger, but now she was not so sure. It was a savage thing, and Louisa had never been so wildly infuriated in her life. Even yesterday, joining the suffragettes, it had been a cold anger that led to a calculated decision.

No one spoke as the warden led them back down the miserable corridors. Once outside, Inspector Lambert turned to them both and said, 'This Mrs Green... Where is she?'

'Down south somewhere, and that is all we know,' Ada said.

'Then find her, prove her guilt, and I will make Emma see sense.' He spoke with the same iron authority he had used on the warden earlier.

'She's beyond sense, Oliver,' Mrs Lambert muttered. 'I don't...' she shook her head, dazed. 'Why is she... Why would she...' She wiped at the tears pooling in her eyes.

'We should be going.' Inspector Lambert took his wife's arm and led her away, still crying. Her tears, Louisa understood, at least. She had done her best by her late sister's child, and it was not enough.

'What in God's name was that?' Ada asked the second they were out of earshot. Or Louisa hoped they were. They had not walked far, and Ada had not spoken quietly.

'My thoughts exactly.' It reassured her she was not the only one befuddled by what had occurred.

'They make my family look functional.'

'They make me quite happy I only have distant cousins I never speak with. And certainly, happy I never married one of them. Did I tell you about that? I had never even met the man. Father threw the letter in the fireplace and said nothing of the sort would be happening.' He had been her ally in that, having no issue with a spinster daughter, despite his many speeches on how the structures of society must be upheld.

Or he was a hypocrite who did not want to be left alone.

The thought was a knife to her chest. It seemed no matter how many times she uncovered her father's flaws, it hurt no less.

'Fair play to your father,' Ada said. 'I'm rather glad you're not married.'

'You and me both.' And she wished desperately to lighten the mood, hoping laughter would ease the pain in her heart, so she added, 'I wish I could say the same about you, Mrs Wilkinson.'

Ada's eyes narrowed. 'I can't believe you made that joke again.'

Louisa grinned. 'It is the joke that keeps on giving.'

'If I was married to Davey, I wouldn't have to put up with this nonsense.'

'Having met Constable Wilkinson, I highly doubt that. The man's taste in humour is...acquired.'

'That is a fair point.'

Louisa laughed. And if it did not ease all her pain, it at least helped.

'If you are quite done,' Ada said in a faux-prissy accent, 'we still have the problem of Mrs Green to solve. I have an idea, but, well, I hate it.'

'Is it terrible?'

'Distasteful.' At Louisa's querying expression, she continued, 'There's going to be a funeral procession for Miss Davison in London. The WSPU is asking its members from across the country to honour her... well...'

'Sacrifice?' Louisa said.

'It felt like an ironic choice of word.'

'But no less true for it.'

Ada nodded. 'Wherever Mrs Green is now, I imagine she will be there, and... I dislike the idea of using a funeral procession in such a way, but I was hoping we would go anyway. I want to...'

'Walk with the suffragettes? Show our respect for Miss Davison?' Louisa nodded. 'Me too. We will have to speak with Mrs Cohen about the arrangements being made for the

Leeds Branch.' She paused, then added, 'And what if we find her, and we get her to talk, and Mrs Green is responsible?'

'I will tell Inspector Lambert,' Ada said. 'I'll take no joy in it – but we made a deal. It will be up to him to see if he can free Miss Franklin. I cannot imagine her testifying. She must really love Mrs Green, despite everything.'

And there it was. What Louisa had been missing earlier. Miss Franklin loved Mrs Green. Furthermore, Mrs Lambert loved Miss Franklin. And Inspector Lambert loved her too, his daughter-in-all-but-name. Did he love his wife? Or had he loved her dead sister, like the rumours Bertie Smith spread? Either way, he appeared to care for her. Perhaps loved her even if he was not in love with her.

Love can be the most amazing thing and the worst, but it drives so many of our actions. Was that not the moral of so many of the novels Louisa had secretly and then not-so-secretly devoured in her lifetime?

Such as not wanting to let your only daughter out into a world that could hurt her.

Or the tug to still respect a dead man's wishes, even though she disagreed with so many of them now.

Or like Ada protecting her little brother, who had done little to deserve it. And Miss Dixon, trying to save her little brother because they were all each other had left in the world.

She glanced up at the prison walls. *Or visiting an old lover because they deserve better than what life has given them.*

Or doing what you could to save a sweetheart in trouble, even when you were a young woman at the very bottom of the power structure of society like Sophie.

If it had been Ada's life on the line, Louisa would make whatever sacrifices had to be made.

Maybe she understood other people better than she thought. Sometimes. Or maybe Ada helped her with that.

'Louisa? You look like you are having an epiphany. It's kind of concerning.'

'I love you.'

Ada frowned even as she said, 'I love you, too. Though if that's your epiphany, I'm slightly disappointed. That is not a new revelation. Or so I should hope.'

Louisa laughed ever so slightly. 'No. But it needed to be said.'

'Alright,' she said uncertainly, still watching with a puzzled expression. 'Are you going to explain beyond that?'

'Ada, my darling, I do not think I could if I tried.'

'That's not at all worrying,' Ada replied drily. 'Also, your darling, am I?'

'Yes,' Louisa grinned at her. How she wished to kiss her here on the street. But they could not, of course, and there would be a grim irony in doing so in the shadow of a prison.

Ada smiled. 'I like it. And I hate to ruin the mood, but...'

'We need to head to the WSPU again.'

Is it love that fuels at least some of the WSPU, too? Love for their daughters, the hope of a better world for them someday.

Emily Davison had no children – or at least not according to any of the papers, including *The Suffragette*. But could her actions be interpreted as love for herself and her fellow women? A demand that they deserved better.

She did not jump for the sake of her lover or her family, but was this a sacrifice of love as much as Miss Franklin's or Mrs Lambert's?

Perhaps love was too big a thing to understand and certainly not something she could compress into her notebook, not something she could ever define in words.

But she linked her arm through Ada's and was glad of it, nonetheless.

But is Miss Franklin? Alone, imprisoned, betrayed by the woman she sacrificed herself for and yet still lying to protect her.

That, Louisa could not understand.

Chapter Twenty-Two

The Martyr's Funeral

City of Westminster, London
June 1913

The sprawling capital of the British Empire – bigger, louder and busier than Leeds could ever hope to be – made Ada feel like a country bumpkin, a girl from the prairies, even though she'd lived her entire life in the centre of Yorkshire's industrial bustle.

How she dreamed of exploration as a girl, of sights unseen and places not yet travelled. She would have jumped at the chance to leave her damp and smoky little northern city behind – to see London, Europe, the world.

This was not how she pictured those travels. Attending the funeral procession for a woman she had never met, yet mourned, to investigate the murder of a man she found she could not mourn. Any sadness she had for Adam Richardson was for his daughter and his 'roommate'. Not for the man himself, who had slung insults at Miss Dixon and was blackmailing a woman from a cause he once believed in.

The WSPU were out in full force for their martyr. That was what *The Suffragette* called her in their headline on her death, though other papers had been less generous. Only a few women had made the journey from the Leeds branch – Mrs Cohen, Mrs Jennings, Miss Langwith, Miss Jain and

Miss Dixon – the rest constrained by jobs or money or family. Louisa had asked Sophie if she wished to join them, and she jumped at the chance. She stared around with wide eyes that suggested she felt even more out of place than Ada did.

Artie Dixon was here somewhere towards the back, where he and Mr Cohen had been told the male supporters would follow the women. He had thrown a worried glance at first his sister, then Sophie before leaving, but both had insisted they would be fine. For though Miss Dixon leaned heavier on her cane as the march progressed, she was as determined as any of them to be there.

They were one tiny part of a long line that progressed through the streets. Some wore mourning black, others white summer dresses with green and purple sashes, including the women from the Leeds branch. The sweet scent of lilies hung in the air, itching Ada's nose, as many of the women carried a bouquet in their hands. They had not thought to buy some in Leeds, and all the florists near the progress' starting point in Victoria had been sold out. Some women also wore their hunger strike badges like military medals, giving the proceedings the air of a state funeral, except the banner Mrs Cohen and Mrs Jennings held aloft proclaimed GIVE ME LIBERTY OR GIVE ME DEATH. Ada was quite pleased with how her artwork had turned out on the banner. Not only did the figure actually resemble a woman, but Ada had captured her face perfectly. That expression which spoke of defiance and determination mirrored on the faces of the surrounding women.

The Death March – played on the drums – kept disappearing in and out of earshot, travelling on the wind. They must have been playing it further up the progression, nearer to Miss Davison's coffin.

Crowds gathered to watch them pass, some with curious faces, some with heads bowed in respect, others not even bothering to hide their sneers.

Had Miss Davison intended to become a martyr? What had she thought as she ran across that racetrack? Or had she not thought at all, an impulsive decision?

'You ran in front of a horse.'

She had told Louisa she would not do that. Yet now, as she imagined herself in Miss Davison's shoes – stood at the racecourse, watching the king's horse approach, the idea implanted in her brain – the conviction struck Ada. She would have run if it had been her. The wild rush of a decision made, an idea seized. Not with any intention of dying, but with all the intention of living, of doing everything she could. If she had been at that derby, it could easily have been her coffin these women now followed. That Louisa now followed.

Louisa would have stopped me.

But would she? It was Louisa who had set them on this path they now tread. If it had been Louisa – this newly emboldened Louisa – who had stood by the racetrack, would she have run out in front of the King's horse? Would they follow Louisa's coffin through the streets of London one day?

Ada tried to blink the image away. It was not her or Louisa but Miss Davison who had run onto the racetrack. Miss Davison's body that made the procession through the streets of London and would journey up to Newcastle, not Leeds, where she and Louisa would return very much alive.

Ada's mother had always said her impulsivity would be the death of her one day. She didn't want it to be true. She wanted to fight, but she didn't want martyrdom. At the end of it all, she wanted to return to her home and Louisa's arms.

Does that make me less brave than Miss Davison?

The conversation with Louisa last week came back to her full force. Maybe she had been a coward in the past. But now, without Louisa's former hesitancy to hide before, she had to face the reality of the choices she was making. Prison. Social exile. The breaking of Mabel's promise.

Could she die?

She saw again Miss Davison, a figure racing onto a racecourse. She had lingered afterwards, critically injured but alive. Had she been conscious enough to think? Had it been worth it?

Would this be the turning point that gained women the vote?

If that was the case, if Miss Davison was looking down from Heaven – if Heaven existed despite what Louisa believed – she must be proud of her actions.

And if it didn't make a difference? If the men of Parliament shrugged their shoulders at her sacrifice, held her up as an example of the instability of women, what would the heavenly Miss Davison think then?

In her place, Ada would rage. She would want to come down from on high and give each of the so-called Right Honourable Gentlemen a good smack round the back of the head.

Actually, it'd be quite nice to do that in real life. She laughed to herself, gaining a questioning look from Louisa. Ada shook her head, knowing full well her train of thought was too convoluted to explain. And not at all suitable for the sombre setting.

Their movement was slow with such a large group of people hemmed in on both sides by constables in their blue uniforms. The Metropolitan Police were the big guns of the policing world, and they had shown up in force to make sure the whole procession went smoothly. Or that they arrested every suffragette at the first sign of violence.

The police had already made their first move this morning, arresting Mrs Emmeline Pankhurst. Supposedly, she was due to return to prison under the Cat and Mouse Act, but even the most strident of anti-suffragists would have to agree the timing was suspicious.

'That's the church,' Mrs Cohen said as they approached a white stone structure with classical columns. A strange church, in Ada's opinion, but then again, people did always say London was a strange sort of place. So far, that was holding up to be true.

Ada's understanding of the procession was that there was to be a service, and afterwards, the coffin would progress down to King's Cross. From there, a train would take Miss Davison's body up north to her final resting place – a place called Morpeth in Northumberland, where both her parents had hailed from.

The progression came to a halt, and many of the people near the front headed towards the church, whilst those closer to the back paused outside on the road. A hush fell, and Ada got her first glimpse of the coffin as they carried it into the church. It was draped in a purple banner and topped with a large display of lilies, a WSPU guard of honour on either side. Some of the men watching removed their hats as it went past.

Ada bowed her head and prayed Miss Davison hadn't died in vain.

We will make sure of it.

It was a promise to a dead woman she had never met, yet already it felt easier to keep than the promise she had made to her mother or Mabel.

Who will visit Mabel in prison if I am dead or imprisoned beside her?

'We should find a place to wait,' Mrs Jennings said once the coffin was out of view. The church was not large enough for the entire progression, so it was only friends and family allowed inside.

As she spoke, a commotion happened further down the road. Ada stared, trying to comprehend what was happening. A group of men lined the pavement, leering towards the nearby suffragettes, who appeared to be sneezing.

The police rushed forward towards them.

'Come on,' Mrs Cohen said. 'Let us be scarce. I do not want t' clash wit' police today.'

Their group turned away, fighting through the crowd.

'Three cheers for the King's jockey!' a man's voice shouted.

Ada's head whipped round. She could not tell where it had come from – that entire section of road was already a chaotic mess of people. The police constables had formed a line, but the suffragettes were pushing back. Why? Were the police protecting the shouter?

Louisa tugged at her arm, and Ada turned. She took Louisa's hand – Sophie had the other – and joined where the rest of the Leeds branch waited further up the street, away from the chaos. Groups of both observers and suffragettes were standing around, more intermingled than before. There were a group of women in silk kimonos who were being given a wide berth by both groups.

'Ladies of the night,' Miss Jain said in a faux-scandalised voice, following Ada's gaze.

'But it's day?' Sophie also stared in their direction.

Miss Jain giggled. 'You're right. It is. My mistake.'

Sophie's face crinkled in further confusion.

Louisa sent a glare at Miss Jain that told her to drop the subject.

One woman must have noticed Sophie's stare because she turned and winked at her, flashing a saucy grin.

Sophie, predictably, went bright red.

The woman was admittedly rather attractive. Well-suited for her job and no doubt wasted on men.

And these are not the right thoughts for a funeral.

Miss Dixon swatted her friend's arm and explained to Sophie in a quiet voice. 'What Aisha means is that they are prostitutes.' She frowned. 'You do know, what a—'

'Yes.' Sophie, somehow, only turned redder. 'That is, I've 'eard about them. There was a girl, from my school, she had a baby, when she was still young and unmarried, and then, well...'

'Can you blame the girl for her confusion?' Mrs Jenning asked. 'Why are they here?' Her voice oozed with disdain.

'They are women, are they not?' Miss Jain said. 'Why would they not come to pay their respects?'

'Hmph,' was all Mrs Jennings said in reply and turned to strike up a conversation with Miss Langwith.

Miss Jain looked ready to force the issue, but Miss Dixon squeezed her arm. 'Aisha, don't make a fuss. Please. Not today. I would like us both to make it back to Leeds safe.'

She deflated. 'Can I at least make a fuss once we're back in Leeds then?'

'As much as you want,' Miss Dixon said with a smile. 'Now, come, help me find a bench.'

The two walked away, Miss Dixon's limp more prominent than usual. With the other pair gone and Mrs Jennings studiously ignoring them, Ada and Louisa talked idly to fill the time until they were to continue onwards. Sophie remained quiet beside them.

It was as the progression reformed that their major problem for the day solved itself; Mrs Green came over and joined their group. She walked up to Miss Langwith and took her arm, bold as brass. Miss Langwith stiffened but didn't shrug it off. Keeping an eye on them as the march restarted, Ada observed how Miss Langwith's resistance melted, her stance slowly relaxing until she was leaning into the other woman.

They made uneven progress. Sometimes grinding to a halt, sometimes having to move so fast Mrs Cohen and Mrs Jennings struggled to keep the banner upright. It gradually became less of a procession and more of a mass of people.

'I think we are near King's Cross,' Mrs Green said.

A nearby woman fell into Ada, apologising profusely as she righted herself. What had once been a well spread-out line was now clustering together, jostling for position, the heat and sweat of thousands of bodies pushing close.

They had only moved a few more inches forward when a line of women forced their way past Ada, pushing her away from the rest of the group. She grabbed hold of Louisa's arm so they remained together. Sophie, thankfully, still had the other hand.

'We should get out of here before the progression becomes a crush,' Louisa said as the crowd pushed them further away from their group. Her grip tightened on Ada's hand, nails digging into her skin. She was not one for crowded spaces. 'We are near the end if that is King's Cross.'

'Where are the others?' Ada craned her head to find the banner, but she could barely see over the crowd.

'I cannot see them.' The taller Louisa stood on her tiptoes to give herself a further advantage, even as people continued to jostle around them. Ada's heart sped up. They were alone in this alien city.

'The banner?' Even as Ada asked, she stumbled backwards and squashed something underfoot. It was a different banner from the one she had helped paint, but it didn't bode well for her art's chances of surviving the afternoon.

'Miss Langwith,' Louisa shouted, waving. Ada joined her on her tiptoes, but saw nothing until a minute later when the woman in question and Mrs Green pushed their way through the crowd.

'Have you seen the others?' Miss Langwith asked.

They all shook their heads.

'We should get out of here,' Louisa repeated. She checked her watch without letting go of Ada's hand. 'We agreed to catch the four o'clock train home. We can regroup at the station later.'

'That sounds like a good plan,' Miss Langwith agreed.

Someone's elbows made close contact with Ada's stomach, and she let out a high squeal of surprise. 'Yes, let's get out of here, please.'

An agreeing squeak came from Sophie, clinging onto Louisa's other hand for dear life.

They turned away from the station and the front of the procession, forcing their way through the crowds till they thinned. They made their way onto the pavements, where spectators were also beginning to leave. When they reached the gates of a park, Ada suggested there might be a bench inside where they could sit and catch their breath.

And talk to Mrs Green.

The funeral over, they needed to focus on that one task before they could truly dedicate themselves to the suffragette cause.

Everyone in the group agreed readily except Sophie. Her head twisted around, searching the crowds for something.

Or someone.

Miss Langwith and Mrs Green had already turned into the gates and were walking away, but still, Sophie hesitated.

'I don't know where Artie is. Or his sister. What if Miss Dixon is hurt? Are they not less likely t' find us int' park?'

Ada searched the crowds, too, as if they might appear out of nowhere.

They did not.

'Artie was with Mr Cohen and the other men. They were near the back.' Louisa glanced around. 'They may have not even made it to the station yet.'

'And Miss Jain will not have let Miss Dixon out of her sight,' Ada added. 'She will take good care of her.'

'We will meet them at the train station later. The chances of finding them in these crowds are slim. I would not worry, Sophie. I am sure they are both fine. And,' Louisa glanced down the path at their companions' retreating backs. 'We need to speak to Mrs Green.'

Something unreadable flashed across Sophie's face, but she nodded, and that decision made, they turned into the park gate. A sign declared it to be The Regent's Park. Ada remembered enough history to know the Prince Regent had died roughly a hundred years ago. He had been obsessed with building all manner of fancy architecture, so it made sense he had built a park as well. What was more surprising was that they were allowed into a royal park, but it was open to the public. On any other day, their suffragette sashes would have looked misplaced, but there were a few other women dotted around wearing them, having had the same idea. If a few men glared in their direction, it was easy to shrug them off, surrounded by so many fellows.

'I'm tired,' Mrs Green declared. 'Let's sit.'

'Where?' Miss Langwith asked, scanning the nearby area. All the benches were already taken.

'Here!' Mrs Green knelt to sit on the floor, legs stretched before her, her skirts raised ever so slightly to show a flash of white stockings.

'Lydia!' Miss Langwith knelt next to her and pulled her skirts down.

Ada's legs ached, and she was more than willing to copy Mrs Green, flopping down onto the floor. Louisa eyed the grass with distaste but sat – with a lot more grace than Ada had managed. Sophie copied her.

Miss Langwith, meanwhile, was standing again, scowling down at Mrs Green.

'Oh, do sit, Georgie.'

Georgie? Miss Langwith didn't look like a Georgie.

'Georgiana,' she said primly. She took a step back. Whatever ease she'd had around Mrs Green earlier, it was gone now.

'Speaking of names...' Mrs Green turned to the three of them. 'I do not believe we've met.' Her gaze lingered on Ada's cheek. 'Though, actually, I think I do know who you are. You're Miss Chapman, aren't you?'

'Yes. How—'

Mrs Green smirked again. 'I hear you don't prefer Mrs Wilkinson.'

I do not want to kill my brother; I am trying to save his ungrateful hide. The thoughts did nothing to stop her flare of frustration.

'You heard right, considering it's not a name I have any right to, nor have I ever wanted it. I wouldn't believe a word that comes from the mouth of my no-good little brother.'

'I told you that rumour wasn't true,' Miss Langwith muttered. 'Just Kitty Jennings causing trouble as usual.'

But Mrs Green ignored her, still focused on Ada. 'It would make quite the scandal, really. The policeman's secret wife, now a suffragette. Don't you think, *Georgie*?'

Miss Langwith bristled, and Mrs Green smirked.

'Oh, do shut up!' The words came from Sophie, of all people.

'Sophie!' Was Louisa's exclamation a scold or mere surprise?

'Excuse me?' Mrs Green said.

'Someone who loves you is in prison because of you. Someone I loved nearly went to prison because of you. You killed a man, and now you sit here int' middle of a park like it never 'appened. What is wrong with you?' She screwed her hands up into balled fists. Hard to imagine quiet, sweet Sophie ever punching someone. But not impossible, from the raw disgust on her face.

Mrs Green stared incomprehensibly.

Ada dared a glance at Louisa, who gave the minutest of shrugs as if to say 'let us see how this plays out.'

It was Miss Langwith who recovered first. 'More murder accusations? Truly? Do you plan to point the finger at us all by the time this so-called investigation of yours is done?'

'She saw you,' Ada said to Mrs Green. 'Miss Franklin, that is. She's protecting you. She might hang for you. She confessed, you know.'

'What?' Mrs Green shook her head. 'No. I don't understand.' She sat up, pulling her limbs into herself, making herself small. Hard to imagine this woman was the same one who had spoken with such fire on the day they first saw her.

'Mr Richardson's murder,' Miss Langwith added. 'Your precious Emma confessed to it.' There was a sneer there, a hatred. *She had her suspicions about what was happening between the pair of them long before I shoved those letters under her nose.* 'And her a police spy, too.'

'How's that for a scandal?' Ada added, with perhaps a little more merriment than necessary. 'The suffragette and the police spy. Perhaps that is why you threatened her.'

On cue, Louisa reached into her bag – they had mutually decided she was less likely to lose these tiny scraps of evidence whilst journeying down to London – and pulled out the crumpled note.

Mrs Green leant over and snatched it from her.

'That's your handwriting.' Miss Langwith peered over her shoulder. 'I would know it anywhere.' The last muttered so quietly, she might not have realised she'd said it out loud.

Mrs Green jumped to her feet, the note clutched in a tight fist. 'What is this? Some kind of ambush?'

'Were you and Mr Richardson working together to blackmail her?' Louisa asked. 'Perhaps he got greedy. Perhaps *you* got greedy. Either way, you decided to solve the problem permanently.'

'No.' Mrs Green shook her head. 'I wrote this. I'll confess it. I was so mad at Emma. I'd thought we were alike, kindred spirits. That she understood. We wanted to change the world. Then Kitty came up to me one day, all full of herself like she gets when she has gossip to share, and says she saw our Miss Franklin at Millgarth Station with some police inspector and his wife. So, I did some spying of my own. And I left her that note at her uncle's house, so she would know I knew. And I didn't show up to our planned meeting with Mr Richardson. I'd presumed that was a police set-up.'

'Where were you?' Ada asked. 'The night Mr Richardson died?'

Mrs Green glanced at Miss Langwith, who stared at her with dawning horror in her eyes. 'That's why you came to me. Why you... you...' she stuttered over her words.

'Georgie, Georgiana, it isn't what you think.'

'She was your...'

'Lover,' Ada finished for her.

'No!' Mrs Green insisted.

Ada turned to Louisa, but it was unnecessary. She had already reached into her bag again and removed the letter Inspector Lambert had given them, holding it out to Mrs Green. 'Same handwriting.'

Mrs Green didn't take it. 'Who exactly are you, and what else do you have in that bag of yours?'

'Miss Louisa Knight, and my purse, my keys, my notebook, a pen, and a copy of the train timetable back to Leeds.'

Ada let loose a quick burst of laughter.

Mrs Green glared at them and stormed off. A pair of labourers – working on one of the park's fences – gave a high whistle as she passed them.

'Should one of us go after her?' Sophie asked. She eyed the men with distaste.

'Lydia is more than capable of looking after herself,' Miss Langwith muttered. She stared at Mrs Green's retreating figure.

'Is it true?' Ada asked. 'She was with you the night Mr Richardson died?'

Miss Langwith stiffened. 'Yes.' Her answer was curt, clipped. She did not want to have this conversation—that much was clear.

Unfortunately, we must have this conversation.

'And you're not saying that to protect her? She's not worth protecting. She was with Miss Franklin behind your back.'

'Yes, Miss Chapman.' Miss Langwith spoke through gritted teeth. She still had not turned to look at them, her posture frozen, her gaze locked on where Mrs Green had walked away. 'You have made that abundantly clear. If I thought Mrs Green was your murderer, I would not cover for her, but I am ashamed to admit she was with me that night.'

Going to the lover she betrayed to recover from the betrayal of another.

'Now, if you will excuse me, I have nothing more to say.' She walked away in the opposite direction from Mrs Green.

'Do we believe her?' Ada asked Louisa.

'I think so.' Louisa watched Miss Langwith stride away from them.

'But then who's left, ma'am? If it's not Mrs Green, and it's not Kitty Jennings, and it's not Peter Chapman...'

'Mrs Jennings?' Louisa suggested. 'Though we have little evidence for that. And the only possible motive is the potential blackmail of Kitty. Alternatively, maybe we are entirely wrong?'

'How did you know, anyway, Sophie, about Mrs Green?' Ada asked.

The maid blushed. 'You, um, you don't talk quietly, miss. And it's not that large an 'ouse.'

Ada laughed. 'I guess I don't.' Everyone knew domestic servants listened to their employers. Even if in the natural order of society, Ada was the one listening in, not the other way round.

And I would listen in at every keyhole I could.

Had Sophie been listening in at keyholes? And could Ada blame her if she had been? She and Artie were tangled up in this, too, no matter how much they didn't want to be.

'What I don't understand, ma'am, is why Miss Franklin would think it was Mrs Green?'

'Maybe she made a mistake. She could only have had the briefest glimpse of the gunwoman.'

'Or she tricked us,' Ada added. 'Is it possible she tricked us and led us on a merry goose chase?' *Though it was an amazing performance, if that is the case.*

'That is...possible, I suppose.' But Louisa didn't sound convinced.

'I don't like her very much.' Coming from Sophie, that was the cruellest of cuts. 'Based on everything you and Artie have told me.'

'Me neither,' Louisa agreed. 'But that is not a good enough reason to leave someone to the hangman.'

'I mean, technically, she has left herself for the hangman.' Ada sighed. 'We should at least try to get a message to her that Mrs Green is not guilty. Maybe we should tell the inspector. If we can't give him his killer, at least we can give him information that might convince her to drop her false confession. Will that be enough, do you think, to get him to keep his end of our bargain?'

'Even if he does not, you have done more than enough for your brother, Ada. You promised your mum you would do what you could to protect him, and you have.'

'It's true, miss,' Sophie chimed in. 'He's lucky to have a sister like you. Not that he appears to appreciate it.' She said the last with some feeling. Sophie had two elder sisters, and as far as Ada knew, neither spoke to her anymore.

'Here, here,' Louisa called.

'I mean, do you really need to keep investigating, ma'am? Artie's free. If Miss Franklin tells truth, then police will have to re-open their case. Inspector Lambert will make sure of that. Do we need to be involved anymore?'

'Perhaps not,' Louisa said.

'I mean, you meant it, didn't you, ma'am? When you joined the suffragettes? It wasn't just about this case?'

'No. No, it was not,' Louisa said with conviction.

'Then should we not focus on that? I'm grateful, truly, for you being willing to help free Artie, but...'

'But we have done enough,' Louisa finished for her.

'I don't know,' Ada said. 'Like Sophie says, we're suffragettes now. I would say we haven't done enough yet. We're only just getting started.'

***

The train chugged its way through the green fields and grey cities of England. Theirs was a subdued group. As Louisa predicted, they had been able to regroup at King's Cross Station prior to their train leaving. Sophie had been greatly relieved to see Artie waiting with his sister. The boy had shyly produced a small pink flower from behind his back, which she had taken with a coy smile. He proceeded to tell them all some complicated Latin name that Ada had already forgotten.

Mrs Green, however, had not re-joined them. A less than subtle question put to Mrs Cohen informed Ada she was to remain down south, where she could make the contributions she wanted to the cause.

They had removed their sashes and stashed them in a canvas bag. It was the same one Mrs Jennings had brought the banner in since it had not survived the crush near the end of the progression. There was no need to draw undue attention, particularly as they wished to be allowed to board the train home without being arrested on suspicions of planting a bomb.

All of them were seated in the third-class carriages. Louisa could have paid for first-class but had decided it would come across as snobby and distanced them from the many working women of the Leeds branch not long after joining. Miss Langwith possibly could have, too, though Ada did not know the reality of her financial situation behind her posh accent. Thankfully, whilst the train was busy, it was far from the worst she had been on – they had all got seats, at least. They were hard, wooden seats that quickly numbed the buttocks, but they were seats. If it was not the luxury of first-class, at least it did not come with the guilt of living on Louisa's money.

Ada flicked through her sketches. She'd drawn them whilst they sat in the park, waiting out the time till they needed to be at King's Cross by attempting to capture the day on paper. They were all missing something – too static, lacking in emotion, a bland recollection of a day of collective mourning. She slammed the book shut in frustration. They would neither help her honour Miss Davison nor impress Frank Rutter.

She would need something more if she wanted her work on the walls of the art gallery. And she wanted that more than ever – seized by the idea that she could capture the spirit and courage of the suffragettes and hang it on the walls for all to see. She suspected Mr Rutter would approve of that plan if only she could come up with a worthy painting. Her lack of formal art education had never felt so stark.

'You can work on it some more once we are home,' Louisa whispered, her fingers a soft touch on the top of her hand, hidden by their skirts. Some of Ada's doubt crept away.

By the time they stopped at Peterborough, any conversation between their group had lapsed entirely. The long day crept over them all, making them weary, and Ada yawned.

Opposite her, Sophie sat next to Artie, the flower tucked behind her ear. The pair of them watched the world go by out the window, pointing out the occasional building or animal to each other with an excited awe. They had done the exact same on the way down and yet did not appear any less excited by it. Had either of them ever left Leeds prior to today? Ada doubted it, and their joy was a simple pleasure to behold.

On the other side of the aisle, Miss Dixon slept on Miss Jain's shoulder, who caught Ada's eye as she turned to them.

'She must be very tired,' Ada said.

'It's been a long day.' Miss Jain brushed a strand of hair away from her friend's face. It was an oddly tender gesture, one familiar to Ada.

Could Miss Jain and Miss Dixon...

Ada turned away and copied the action, resting against Louisa's shoulder. Maybe she was reading too much into the gesture. Seeing Sapphics wherever she went. Though they had been right about Mrs Green, Miss Langwith and Miss Franklin.

She yawned again and closed her eyes. When it came down to it, it was none of her business. Good for them, if they were, and she wished them the best. A happier ending than the other three suffragettes, certainly. Happier than Sophie and her fellow maid. And definitely happier than her and Mabel. But it didn't have to end in tragedy or heartbreak – she and Louisa were proof of that.

Even if we spend a bizarre amount of our time chasing mysteries.

Louisa's voice, soft in her ear, cut into Ada's conscience. A hand lay on her shoulder, gently shaking her awake. She blinked her eyes open to be greeted with the familiar tracks leading into Leeds' central train station, backlit by a soft pink sunset.

'Are we home?' She sat up and stretched, her neck protesting her awkward sleeping position. 'Did I sleep through the entirety of the Midlands?'

'Best thing for it, I think. Though you missed an interesting conversation.'

'I did?' They had not seemed like a group about to have an interesting conversation when she fell asleep.

'You did.' Louisa stood. 'Let us get off this train, and I will tell you all about it.'

Ada also stood, joining the queue of people waiting to exit the train.

Once they had made it out of the crowd and said their goodbyes – a blushing Artie kissing Sophie's cheek – Louisa led the three of them to the hansom stand. Once inside, she explained in a quiet voice, 'Mrs Cohen came to sit next to me. She asked what we had discovered so far, and I told her all. But she also said that, while she wants answers as much as us, they are other matters to consider, now we are members of the cause.'

'Such as?'

'She met with several Northern suffragette leaders after the procession. They are all agreed in wanting to up the ante now, following Miss Davison's lead. They are planning a big co-ordinated attack across cities – window smashing, fires, bombs. No deaths—Mrs Cohen was strident about that. The bombs and arson will target empty buildings, and checks will be made to ensure the buildings are, indeed, empty.'

'No repeat of the Bradford fire,' Ada said. *But there is no guaranteeing that.* Mrs Cohen may have wanted to target property, not people, but some of the previous bombing targets made it clear not all within the WSPU agreed with her.

'Exactly. But still, something large enough that even Westminster has no choice but to pay attention to the women of the North.'

'To the working women of the North,' Sophie added. 'That's what she said. Ma'am.' She looked down, fiddling with a loose string on her dress. Was it correcting Louisa that had brought on the reaction? Or was she worried about the suffragettes' plans and her potential part in them?

For all she had been full of surprises in the last few days, it was still not possible to imagine her planting a bomb or committing arson.

'And us here in Leeds? Did she say what we will do?'

'Mrs Cohen said she will tell people they can do whatever action they choose – within reason.'

'So not blowing up Millgarth, essentially?'

'Essentially, yes. She suggested we could help with targeting the Town Hall – a window-smashing campaign, as there is no way to guarantee an empty building. Our city council may not have the power to grant us the vote, but it is still the clearest symbol of authority in the city. I agreed. I assumed you would not take issue.'

'You, Louisa Knight, want to smash up Leeds Town Hall?' Ada had to say it out loud to make sure it was true.

This was really happening. They were going to take a stand.

And be arrested. And be imprisoned. And go on a hunger strike.

But this was no time for cowardice. This was bigger than her. She could face those fears – thousands of women around the country already had.

'I do,' Louisa said with a grim smile. 'I am tired of doing nothing. We need to make sure Miss Davison's death matters. That the actions of women across the country – who have protested and starved and been tortured – matter.'

Ada's matching smile was surely just as grim. 'Then we will.'

Chapter Twenty-Three

Cracked Glass

Louisa took the envelope from her desk drawer and turned it over in her hands. Once this last action was done, everything was set in motion. She was admitting she may not come home tonight. With a deep breath, she stilled her hands, steeled her nerves, and went downstairs.

The sitting room windows were wide open, and the net curtains billowed in a gentle summer breeze. Galapagos sat nearby, hissing every time they blew near her and swiping ineffectively with her paw. Louisa chuckled at her antics.

'I tried to get her to move, but she was having none of it.' Sophie stood by the mantelpiece, polishing the clock. 'It's a nice day, ma'am. A good day to air the rooms, especially with yourself and Miss Chapman heading out. I'm sorry. That I won't be joining, I just...' She tugged at her apron.

'We all have our own skills, Sophie, and our limits. In relation to that, Miss Chapman and I have been talking.' She passed the envelope to Sophie, who took it with a   puzzled frown. 'In the event we do not return tonight, and the house is to be empty for a bit, I want you to offer it up to the WSPU as a safe house. There should be enough money in that envelope to cover the cost, including your wages.' Louisa paused, pushing down the nausea clawing at her throat. 'There is a reference in there, too, should you need it.'

Sophie's frown deepened. 'Why would I need a reference? I don't intend to leave, ma'am.'

'Just in case.'

Just in case I die. It was an off chance. A tiny possibility. Emmeline Pankhurst's sister, Mary Clarke, had died not long after being released from prison in 1910. Her hunger strike and the subsequent force-feeding were never proven to be the cause of her death, but anyone with even a rudimentary understanding of biology would know it had contributed. Even with the Cat and Mouse Act in place and force-feeding banned, it did not hurt to take precautions. She had checked her will was up to date, guaranteeing Ada the house and its goods and most of her money, less that which she had earmarked for Sophie.

'You do intend to come back, ma'am? This isn't... you're not... that is... I know you admire Miss Davison's bravery.'

'I do. But I have no intention of following in her footsteps.'

Sophie sagged with relief. 'Good luck then.' She said it with a slight smile.

Louisa had the strangest compulsion to hug the girl, but that would have been a step too far even for their unusual maid-mistress relationship, so she nodded in acknowledgement and walked away. Sophie still held the envelope of money limply in her hand.

It was the last end she had to tie up. She was ready for whatever the day – and the coming weeks – brought.

If someone had told me a year ago that I would be determined to throw stones at a council building, I would have greeted them with derision.

At least it was only throwing stones – for the time being. They had attended a WSPU meeting last week, a few days after the funeral, and even with Mrs Green absent, there had been members advocating that they needed to escalate their actions. There had been several bombings across the country following Miss Davison's funeral – in London, Kent and Birmingham. All of them had avoided the worst possible damage, but from what the newspapers reported, that appeared to be bad luck on the suffragettes' part rather than intention.

Not that the newspapers are a reliable source of information. Another institute she had to teach herself not to trust.

Ada joined her in the hallway, her mouth set in a tight line. When their gazes locked, she gave Louisa a smile that was more of a grimace. 'Your last chance to stay home.'

'Do you want to stay home?'

'No.' She reached for her shoes, and Louisa copied her.

As they stepped outside, Louisa took her hand, not caring if anyone saw. It felt like such a trivial thing now.

Ada turned at the gesture, head tilted, questions written all over her face.

'Time to face the day,' Louisa said.

'Time to fight back.' Ada's voice was full of quiet conviction.

Fear, sudden and overpowering, choked any more words from her throat, but Louisa squeezed her hand in response.

She could not let nerves stop her now. It was far past the time for doubts.

She took a deep breath. *Time to fight for those who cannot.*

———

Mrs Cohen led them to the heart of the city centre, past the Victorian municipal buildings, towards the Town Hall that dominated the skyline with its clock tower.

They were a group of six – the two of them, Mrs Cohen, Miss Dixon, Miss Jain, and one of the former mill girls, a Miss Lewis. Both Miss Jain and Miss Dixon had been insistent – Ada had briefly tried to dissuade them and been put in her place. It seemed they, too, were inspired by Emily Davison to do more. Or had they just grown so tired of the status quo that they saw no other choice?

The other members of the WSPU would cause their own chaos elsewhere whilst the police came running to this very public demonstration.

'You ready for this, Miss Knight?' Miss Jain asked with a grin.

'Not particularly,' Louisa answered. 'But I doubt I ever will be. No time like the present, as the saying goes.'

'And you, Miss Chapman,' Miss Dixon added. 'Not gonna go running off t' your sweetheart int' police?' Her grin was even wider.

Ada rolled her eyes, and Miss Jain playfully tapped her friend on the arm. 'That is the kind of joke you would scold me for saying.'

Outside the Town Hall, Queen Victoria still sat atop her stone throne, sans suffragette flag this time, looking down on them with disapproval. When the women spread out, Louisa stayed close to Ada, choosing a spot on the eastern side of the building. The street was quiet except for them, the people of the city at work, with only the occasional cart or car passing by. Louisa reached into her pocket and clutched the stones there but it did not stop her hand from shaking. Despite all her best intentions, nerves still etched their way across her body, into her heart, her stomach, and her fingers.

'When the clock chimes ten,' Ada muttered.

Louisa had to crane her head back to read the clock face; its minute hand sat between eleven and twelve. The Town Hall had never been so imposing before. Were the windows always so high? From its stone plinth, a lion statue judged her. What was the ridiculous story Ada told her once? That, at night, the lions left their position guarding the Town Hall's wide, columned entrance and prowled the city. Would they come alive now to protect their building from this act of vandalism?

Political protest, Louisa reminded herself.

She squeezed the stones in her pocket again, rough against her hand, until it hurt.

A gentleman passing by gave them a curious look. 'I say, are you ladies alright?'

The clock chimed. The first smash came a few seconds later, and he jumped.

'Quite alright.' Ada threw a stone, and it hit a window with a crack.

The man ran.

'I doubt we will have to wait long for the police.' Louisa squeezed the stones once more and pulled one from her pocket.

This is it.

The stone travelled in slow motion, a graceful arc, and clattered against the wall. She threw several more in quick succession, growing increasingly frustrated with her poor aim, till she was rewarded with the shatter of broken glass.

'Bravo!' Ada called. 'Votes from women!'

'Votes for women!' Louisa echoed.

There were several more scandalised shouts from around them and a lot of muttering. They were gathering a crowd, an assortment of middle-class women pulled from their shopping by the ruckus and clerks pulled from the building they assaulted and those surrounding it.

Then let them watch. That was the point. A message so loud even Westminster must take notice of the North.

She threw another stone at the same time as Ada, and they both clattered into the same window with another satisfying smash.

Ada cheered and repeated the slogan, shouting at the top of her lungs.

A whistle blew.

'Run!' The high-pitched shout came from the crowd, which made no sense, but Louisa was still not going to argue. She seized Ada's hand and turned southwards, away from the whistle.

'No!' The scream came from the right, in front of the Town Hall, near to the statue of Queen Victoria. Louisa's head jerked round. Miss Jain was sprawled on the floor, a police officer standing over her, truncheon raised. Beside this tableau, another officer already had hold of Miss Dixon's arms, who struggled against his grip, wincing, her cane nowhere to be seen.

We must help them. We cannot help. We need to run.

'No!' Ada darted right, rushing towards the officer, as the truncheon came down on Miss Jain's arm with a nauseating crunch.

Louisa followed. What choice did she have? Together. They were in this together.

Ada grabbed the officer's arm as it was mid-swing for another hit, and he turned to her with furious eyes that melted into confusion. He had a baby face at odds with his actions.

'Miss Chapman?' The truncheon lowered a little.

Miss Jain took this opportunity to push herself further away, hissing with pain as she did so.

Louisa bent and offered her hand.

Behind her, Ada said, 'Bertie, you have to stop!'

Bertie. Bertie. Which one is Bertie?

Miss Jain struggled to her feet with Louisa's help, clutching her arm and cursing.

The officer's next words were angered. 'Because you said so? Why are you here?'

Ada gasped, and Louisa turned round to find her struggling in the constable's grasp.

'Let her go!' Louisa grabbed his hand, scrabbling to pull it loose, but he shook her off.

'Bertie! Ow!' Ada winced in pain as his grip tightened on her wrists. 'You're hurting me!'

Bertie. Constable Smith. The young lad who liked to gossip and had such an obvious fancy for Ada, even I noticed it.

Clearly, that was gone now.

Fighting him off would not work. She tried to reach for calm. 'There is no need for violence, Constable Smith. No one is resisting arrest.'

'Is that so?' He sneered at her. His grip on Ada's wrists did not lessen, and the way she struggled to be free almost certainly did count as resisting arrest.

Miss Jain groaned as she limped a few steps. Could she run whilst Constable Smith was distracted by Ada?

'Where's Hettie?'

She will not leave Miss Dixon any more than I will leave Ada. And they had already seized Miss Dixon.

Another officer approached.

'You're under arrest.' Constable Smith probably intended his voice to have authority, but it was too high and shaky for that. He twisted one of Ada's hands behind her back, causing her to yelp in pain, and reached for the handcuffs. Anger boiled through Louisa's blood. She wanted to get his hands off Ada and damn the consequences.

Calm. Calm. I need to remain calm. Violence will not help, nor will losing my temper.

It took every inch of self-control she possessed to keep her tone even. 'I said she is not resisting arrest.' Louisa pitched her voice loud. Behind the constable, a small crowd was still gathered, and she wanted them to hear. 'There is no need for force.'

'Wilkinson.' Constable Smith turned to the approaching officer, and Louisa's stomach dropped at the name. There, indeed, stood David Wilkinson, an unreadable expression on his face. 'Come get these other two.' Constable Smith pointed at her and Miss Jain, who was still there, shocked and scanning the crowd.

She needs to run if she can.

'They've already taken her,' Louisa muttered to Miss Jain, her gaze not breaking away from where Constable Wilkinson ignored his colleague's order to arrest them. 'Run. Now. Whilst they are focused on Ada.'

Miss Jain did not move.

'Ada?' Constable Wilkinson stared at her like he had never seen her before. 'Ada, you goddamn fool!' He turned to his fellow officer and added in a harsh whisper, 'Smith, loosen your grip, you idiot. There's a crowd watching.'

'Or is it just because it's your little sweetheart?'

'Wife,' Miss Jain called.

'Huh?' Both police officers turned to her, bemused.

Ada broke free of Constable Smith's loosened grip, stumbling backwards. He jolted back round, but she stared across at Louisa, pinning her with a beseeching gaze. 'If you ever loved me, run.'

'What?' Louisa stepped towards her, but Constable Wilkinson grabbed her arm, forcing her to a halt. Her skin crawled, all her hatred for being touched rushing over her in that moment.

It will be worse in prison.

She tried to reach for calm once more. She would hold her head high and keep her wits about her, like she had last year, and not give David Wilkinson the pleasure of seeing her scared.

Constable Smith had nearly caught up to Ada, who locked eyes with Louisa, her face wild. Her next words were both an order and a plea. 'Please don't panic and run!' She dropped to the ground like a marionette doll cut from its strings, landing with a sickening thud.

Louisa screamed. She started to run forward, but a hand caught her arm and pulled her away. Away from Ada, still on the floor, the two police officers surrounding her. Constable Wilkinson must have let Louisa go at some point.

Probably when Ada hit the floor like a sack of potatoes.

'She said run!' It was Miss Jain who had her arm now. And she was right. Ada had said to run, so Louisa fought every instinct screaming at her and ran.

There was no plan, no thought to her action. She allowed Miss Jain to pull her away from the Town Hall, down an alleyway and through a public house where their arrival was greeted by at least one whistle.

This was wrong. This was all wrong. She had to go back. She tugged at Miss Jain's hand, and the other woman let go.

'If you want to be another martyr, I won't stop you, but I'm not going with you. It's too late. They have your friend as they have mine. You're clever, right? You know the law? You're much more use t' her on outside. And Hettie, too, come to think of it.' Miss Jain seized her wrist again. 'So change of plans—I'm not letting you go.' She ran again and pulled Louisa along in a haze, still not comprehending what had happened.

Ada. I left Ada. To be arrested and thrown alone into gaol.

———

Louisa spent the rest of the day at the WSPU headquarters waiting for information, though it was an obvious place to be should the police come looking for her. News had trickled in as the hours passed. Ada and Miss Dixon were not the only women under arrest after the day's events. Miss Lewis had also been arrested at the Town Hall, and several women were caught fleeing from an arson attack on an empty warehouse by the river. Mrs Cohen had avoided arrest this time, and Louisa joined her and her husband in trying to find a legal loophole similar to the one they had used to free her several months previously, but to no avail. Prison sentences would be inevitable.

By the time she got home, it was late. Sophie rushed into the hallway but stopped as soon as she looked at Louisa's face.

'Where's Miss Chapman?'

'Armley Gaol by now, I imagine.'

Or so I hope. Her mind kept replaying those last moments, Ada collapsed on the ground. But she was play-acting, distracting them. She was not actually hurt.

She was so still. And she landed with such force. She must have injured herself.

'Oh,' Sophie muttered.

Oh, indeed.

Louisa reached down to unbuckle her shoe, and the strap caught, refusing to move no matter how much she pulled and turned it.

'Fuck!' The word slipped from her unbidden. The first time she had ever said it out loud.

'Ma'am? Do you need some help?'

'I am fine, Sophie. I am fine. Can you go fetch some supper, please?'

The maid hesitated a moment before heading towards the kitchen.

Her stubborn shoe finally came off, and she flung it on the rack haphazardly. Once she made it into the sitting room, she could finally collapse upon the sofa, but that left her with nothing to do but drown in memories of what she had done.

Ada was in gaol.

She knew. We both knew the risks we were taking.

But I am not imprisoned, am I?

It should be the other way round. Ada was the one who dealt badly with captivity. Ada was the one who had already lost a loved one to the prison's high walls. Louisa should be in gaol, and Ada sat here.

Worrying about me.

Then we both should be in gaol. Together.

'If you ever loved me, run!'

What had been going through Ada's mind? As a man she had gossiped with, flirted with, held her arms in such a tight grip, and her oldest friend had been about to arrest her lover?

I should have done more. I should have got us both out.

Sophie returned with a tray carrying plates of bread and cold cuts of meat and cheese. 'Is there anything we can do, ma'am?' she asked as she placed it on the coffee table. 'For Miss Chapman, I mean.'

Louisa shook her head. 'Not until she is released. We will need to be there for her then. And other women, too, potentially. I still want to go ahead with making this a safe house.'

But if they release Ada on Cat and Mouse, she cannot hide here. It is the first place they will look for her.

'It's a good idea, ma'am. And I want to help. Do you want your envelope back?'

'Excuse me?' It took Louisa a few moments to register what she meant. 'Oh, yes. Leave it on my desk, please. And take the reference and this quarter's wages for yourself.'

'But I don't need them, ma'am.' She spoke with such forcefulness it sounded more like an order.

'Take them, Sophie. I have no plans to martyr myself. Martyrs do not run away.'

'That's why martyrs die, ma'am. I don't mean any disrespect to Miss Davison, but, well,' Sophie swallowed uncomfortably. 'You ran away?' There was no judgement in her tone, but it still irked Louisa.

She waved the maid away. 'That is all, Sophie.'

The girl paused for a second, questions still written across her face, but she curtseyed and muttered a quiet 'yes, ma'am.'

Louisa instantly regretted it. The quiet of the house pressed upon her. There was no Ada on the floor, surrounded by her drawings. Or sat next to her, pressed close, a teasing grin on her lips. Or at the gramophone, flicking through the records, determined to find the worst possible song to attempt a dance. She had a knack for finding the most terrible records in the store. Of course, she had to purchase them to torture Louisa with, declaring, 'We can waltz to this!' as the rudest Vaudeville song America offered played in the background.

The familiar ache of loneliness crept over Louisa.

The creaking open of the door announced Galapagos' arrival. She padded into the room and up into Louisa's lap, pushing her head against Louisa's cheek with a meow.

Louisa hugged her close. 'Oh, Gal.' Ada's nickname for the cat, the one she stubbornly never used. 'What am I going to do?' And she sobbed into the cat's fur.

Chapter Twenty-Four

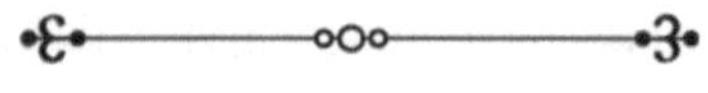

Regrets

It was quiet in the headquarters when Louisa entered, the main assembly room empty, giving it a haunted, abandoned feel. Many of their members were currently in prison, and Louisa assumed the rest were at home with their families. Even those without homes – like Mrs Jennings and her daughter – were absent. There was no meeting tonight, but the house was too quiet, and she could not remain there.

Miss Jain and Artie had been staying with Louisa – their landlady had learnt of Miss Dixon's arrest and thrown them out – but they were both out for the evening. Miss Jain had declared she had 'plans' with a wink. Louisa had given Sophie the evening off, so she and Artie planned to go to a picture house. They left the house in high spirits, and it was enough that Louisa could not regret her decision, even as the emptiness of the house taunted her. She had spent fifteen minutes searching for Galapagos, but the cat was nowhere to be found. Outside hunting, or whatever it was she did when she was not ruling over her newfound dominion.

In the three days that had passed since the attack on the Town Hall, there had been no news from inside Armley Gaol. The usual four-week rule against visitors remained in place. However, the plan had been for anyone who was arrested to go on a hunger strike, and there was no reason for that to have changed.

At least The Cat and Mouse Act is in place now. For all the suffragettes resented the act and its attempts to undermine their strikes, it did not stop their relief that force-feeding no longer occurred, hollow though it was.

'Hello?' Louisa called into the quiet. She had hoped for a distraction, at least. Something to concentrate on, something she could do.

The door to the treasurer's office opened, revealing Miss Langwith. 'Miss Knight, can we help you with anything?'

'I actually came to ask if I could be of help.'

'Invite her in. We need all the help we can get,' someone called from further inside the office.

'You like mysteries, do you not, Miss Knight? The plot has thickened on ours.'

Ours? Oh, the missing money. It felt like a long time ago. She had not given it, nor Miss Franklin, a stray thought since Ada's arrest. They had told Inspector Lambert that Mrs Green was not the murderer after returning from London, and he told them – no, ordered them – to keep searching. He had not been confident he could convince his niece to speak with him again. Whether he had succeeded or persuaded her to rescind her confession, they did not know, nor would he be contacting them again. Not after they had so publicly declared their new allegiance.

She was still vaguely curious, though, and it was exactly the distraction she came in search of, so Louisa moved over to the office, peering inside. Someone had trashed the room, drawers open, papers tossed, pens and stationery all over the floor, where Mrs Jennings was crouched, attempting to tidy it up. A pile of banknotes sat haphazardly stacked on one corner of the desk.

'Has someone broken in here? Looking for money?'

'No. The very opposite – they left us money.' Miss Langwith pointed at the stack of notes.

'That seems counterproductive. Who breaks in to leave money?'

'The tooth fairy?' Mrs Jennings commented.

Louisa had some vague knowledge of the tooth fairy, fuzzy memories of children bragging about their pennies on the playground. Enough to know it was the sort of fantastical nonsense her father could not stand.

'Is there anything missing?'

'Not as far as I can tell.' Miss Langwith crouched down to help gather the papers. 'It is like they made a mess to hide the fact they left the money, but I do not keep any cash here anymore, not since Miss Frank... not since the money went missing.'

'Perhaps whoever did this was unaware of that.'

'Very few people know. Only Leonora and Lydia, and probably Mr Cohen. And now the two of you.'

Louisa examined the door where she stood, searching for signs of forced entry. There were no scratch marks on the lock, no sign of tampering.

'Do you lock this door when you are not here?'

'Of course.' Miss Langwith sounded ever so slightly affronted.

'Someone had a key then.'

'Or picked the lock,' Mrs Jenning said. 'Shouldn't be hard with a couple of hairpins.'

Miss Langwith shot a pointed look at Louisa.

'That is Ada's forte, but even she is not talented enough with a hairpin to break out of Armley Gaol.'

'They confiscate hairpins,' Mrs Jennings said. 'You would know that if you had ever been imprisoned.' Her gaze swept over both Louisa and Miss Langwith.

That made sense, but Louisa had never considered it. For all that her thoughts lingered on where Ada currently was, she did not know the reality of it, as Mrs Jennings had less than subtly pointed out.

Is this what it has been like for Ada all these years? Whenever she thinks about Mabel. The difference being that Ada would be free within a few weeks at most, within the next few days if she was on a hunger strike, whilst, until recently, Mabel's freedom had appeared impossible.

Mabel will expect Ada to visit her this weekend. She needs to know why she cannot, even if she will not be pleased. But how do I even word that? Will she even want me to visit her? Perhaps it would be better to leave her be.

But that was a coward's thought. She just did not want to have an awkward conversation with her partner's former lover.

'I shall leave this mess to the two of you. I have *letters* to write.' Mrs Jennings stalked out of the room, shoulder barging against Louisa's as she passed to get to the door.

Louisa turned to share *a look* with Ada and was once more slammed with the reminder she was not there.

Miss Langwith's voice dragged her back into the current situation. 'Just ignore her.'

'What is the matter with her?'

Miss Langwith thought for a second. 'She is prickly and resents those she thinks have not suffered the same losses as if she is the only one taking risks. Lydia used to call her, and I emphasise these are her choice of words and not mine, "all gob and no action."' She gave a brief smile that faded as quick as a photographer's flash. It must pain her to speak of Mrs Green now.

'By letters, she meant letter bombs, right?'

'You are a quick study, Miss Knight. So, tell me, what do you make of this? Did our forger have a sudden fit of conscience?'

'That does not appear to be all the money that was exchanged.'

'Far from it. I did as you suggested and examined our money. They are more amongst the remaining notes that I suspect are forgeries.'

'And this?' Louisa pointed to the small stack of banknotes. 'Does it match the small amounts? The ones that went missing prior to Miss Franklin's theft?'

'A quick study, indeed!' Miss Langwith smiled, approving, and though her approval should mean nothing to Louisa, she drank it in any way. The only people who had ever approved of her showcasing her intelligence were her father and Ada.

'Kitty Jennings then?' Louisa suggested.

'But why go to all that effort to steal it, then bring it back?'

Louisa's eyes strayed to the closed door.

'Unless Mrs Jennings found out what her daughter had done.' Miss Langwith had followed her gaze. 'Stolen from a cause she has lost everything for.'

'We cannot prove that, though.' Unless there was a tangible link – something that proved Mrs Jennings had been here. Except she lived here, so of course she would be.

Louisa sighed, and Miss Langwith chuckled.

'Do you drink, Miss Knight?' Which was not a question Louisa expected, and it took her a few seconds to comprehend it and supply an answer.

'The odd glass now and then.' Usually at Ada's suggestion.

'I am the same, but more and more, I think it is a good time to start.' She opened a drawer in her desk and pulled out a bottle of clear liquid.

Louisa studied the label – gin – and tried to keep her expression neutral.

'I know. I say I rarely drink, and then I pull a bottle from my desk. It was a gift from Lydia. I have not opened it yet. No time like the present, though? We will need glasses. Excuse me a moment.' She stood and paused in the doorway. 'Are you likely to snoop without your friend here to encourage you?'

Louisa gestured to the messy piles of papers on the desk. 'I would not have the time to even make a start.'

'Fair point.' And she left.

Louisa could have tried to search through the mess, but what was the point? She as good as knew the answer. Kitty Jennings had stolen the money, and Mrs Jennings had found out and tried to put it back. But Louisa could not prove it, and that rankled.

But what does it matter? I can hardly report Peter Chapman's forgery to the police. The suffragettes are not getting that money back.

Miss Langwith returned, brandishing two glasses, and poured a measure of gin into each.

She passed one to Louisa, who took a sip and pulled a face at the bitter taste.

Miss Langwith did the same. 'How do people drink this?'

'Beyond me.' Yet she took another sip.

'Have you heard our latest tale? About Miss Lenton? I do not believe you will have met her?'

'I have heard about her. They released her from Armley Gaol a fortnight ago after a hunger strike?'

Only a few days. She was only in there a few days – it will be the same for Ada.

'She's been staying at Mr Rutter's house – the gallery director – since her release, and yesterday, the police came to find their mouse.'

'She has been re-arrested?'

Miss Langwith smiled. 'Oh, no. They snuck her out of the house in a delivery van. Leonora drove it, dressed as a baker's man, and Miss Duval was dressed as an errand boy. She and Miss Lenton swapped places. She should be on her way to Scarborough now and France from there. A little beyond the reaches of the Leeds constabulary, would you not say?' Her smile became a smirk.

Louisa matched it and held up her drink. 'Well, cheers to that.' Their glasses clinked.

Ada will laugh herself silly at that story when I tell her. A fresh tide of worry washed away her brief amusement. *Just a few days. Just a few days.*

'Are you worried?'

'Excuse me?' The words came out tarter than intended.

'About your friend.'

'Of course.'

'But you ran?'

It still needled. Yet it was the truth. 'Yes.'

'Miss Jain said that was Miss Chapman's doing.'

'She told me to run.' The truth fell from her lips. This was why she did not drink. She had been sipping all the time Miss Langwith talked, her glass nearly empty. 'If you ever loved me, run.' It did not hurt as much to tell Miss Langwith, harbouring her own secret heartbreak.

'Yet she must have known how it would end when the two of you set off that day.'

'Yes. Yes, she did.'

We were supposed to be together, Ada. Yet how could she possibly be mad that she was not currently imprisoned?

'Then why tell you to run?' Miss Langwith drained the last of her glass and reached for the gin.

'I wish I knew.' Louisa nodded when Miss Langwith moved the bottle towards her glass. One more should not leave her too drunk. She still needed to get home, and alone at that.

To my empty house.

No, not empty, not forever. There was Sophie. And Miss Jain and Mr Dixon. She had friends for the first time in her life.

'Mrs Cohen said Miss Chapman always called you a suffrag*ist*.' She slurred the last syllable. 'Peaceful. A law-keeping type.'

'And I was. Were most of us not to begin with? What about you? You come across as quite...conservative.'

Miss Langwith laughed. 'And so I am. Or was. My mother—now *she* was conservative. She had a lot of opinions on what I should or should not do. Which was odd for a woman who always told me never to have opinions.'

'I never knew my mother.' When was the last time she spoke about her mother? Ada had asked about her, but what was there to say about a woman she had never met and her father barely ever discussed. 'I killed her.'

Miss Langwith's glass hit the table with a clunk. She stared at Louisa, eyes wide.

'I mean...childbirth. I did not...'

'Right.' An awkward chuckle. 'That makes a lot more sense than you committing matricide. But dear lord, Miss Knight, you should be careful saying things like that.'

'Sorry.'

Miss Langwith shook her head. 'You are a mystery, are you not?'

Louisa's heart seized.

'You were a mystery.' Ada had said that once, flashing her most roguish smile.

'A mystery?' Louisa repeated, blindsided by the memory. She took another large gulp of her gin, wallowing in the burn at the back of her throat and the acid taste in her mouth until she coughed. Honestly, how did anyone like this stuff?

Miss Langwith filled their glasses again. 'Ironic, is it not? For a woman who claims to solve mysteries. But you are stoic... and fairly conservative yourself. For all she is known to have worked for the police, it is obvious Miss Chapman is the passionate one. Fire in her belly as bright as her hair.' An accurate description, but who was Miss Langwith to say so? Especially in such an awed voice. 'Lydia is like that, too. A brighter spark than...' She clicked her tongue and took another sip. 'A bright spark. We used to argue about that. She told me I need to commit more. That I could not remain scared and hiding in my office. But I cannot. I want to protest. To throw stones and bomb an MP's house... Oh, darn, forget I said that!' Her glasses were slipping down her nose, but she did not appear to notice. She stared at Louisa, worry flicking in her eyes.

'They are going to bomb an MP's house?' It was certainly an escalation. But whether it would help or hinder, only time would tell.

The time for polite words has passed.

'Some MP down south, yes. An escalation, is it not? But this is my point. We are not extremists, you and I. Why am I here?' She gestured at Louisa with the hand holding the gin, and some liquid slopped over the side onto the desk. 'Why are you here?'

'Because it has become blatantly obvious nothing else is going to work. And I can fight where others cannot.'

'If you had the tools, could you do it? The bombs? The fires?'

Louisa hesitated. She knew the answer she wanted to give.

'Or maybe I am just a coward.'

Images flickered through her mind: a building exploding; rubble and dust in the air, coating her lungs, making her cough; the panicked wailing of people in excruciating pain; and Louisa stood, unflinching, knowing she had brought forth this chaos.

Ada nearly lost her arm to a mill loom. Sophie was fired because she kissed another girl. Mabel rots in prison because her foreman thought he had a right to her body. And if my father had not been selfish enough to want to keep me at home, what would my life have been? Marriage and babies and a lifetime of my skin crawling when my husband touched me and never, ever knowing why. They lock women like me away in asylums and call it hysteria.

The vote would change nothing. Not immediately. But it would be a start. It had to be a start.

What price was she willing to pay for that start?

'I do not know.' A confession.

But Miss Langwith did not judge. She was watching Louisa intently. Her glasses kept slipping down her nose, resting near the tip like they could fall at any moment.

'Careful.' Louisa leant over and pushed her glasses back up. Halfway through the motion, the strange intimacy of it hit her. She rarely got this close to anyone but Ada. She straightened up, leaning away.

'Thank you,' Miss Langwith muttered. 'We are the same in that, you know?'

'Glasses?' Louisa's vision was not perfect, but she did not need corrective lenses.

An explosion of voices from next door interrupted whatever Miss Langwith was going to say next. Louisa tried to place them.

Miss Langwith got there first. 'Miss Jennings must be home. She and her mother are arguing. Again.'

'I told you! I told you that boy was trouble!'

That boy. Peter. Louisa jumped from her seat and had to reach out for the desk to steady herself. She had drunk far too much, far too fast.

'Whatever has happened to your friend's brother, there is little you can do about it now at,' Miss Langwith checked a wristwatch, 'half ten at night. Besides, it may be old news.' She gestured at the stack of money. Was Mrs Jennings confronting her daughter about her theft?

Louisa took a couple of wobbly steps towards the door. The voices had dropped out of hearing.

'And I cannot imagine young Mr Chapman would appreciate your help should you try. Nor would Mrs Jennings or her daughter appreciate you interfering in their affairs.'

All of which was true enough. Ada had done what she could to help her ungrateful sod of a brother. Whatever had happened was his problem alone.

A smash rang out from beyond the door, followed by a screech.

'Maybe I should...' She glanced towards the door again.

Miss Langwith waved her concern away. 'They will wear themselves out eventually. They always do.'

A door slamming shut and the quick fading thuds of someone running downstairs announced she was correct.

Louisa sat back down with a heavy flump, grateful for the solid chair beneath her unsteady legs.

No more alcohol.

'What were we saying?' Louisa asked. Somewhere in the distance, so faint she might have been imagining it, came the soft despairing sound of a person crying.

She tried to stand again, and Miss Langwith reached out an arm to stop her. 'She will not appreciate your pity either.'

She stopped trying to stand. 'No, I cannot imagine she will. Shall we return to our conversation...' she screwed up her nose, trying to think through the fog of alcohol. 'About glasses?' That did not sound right.

Miss Langwith chuckled. 'Not quite. I was merely commenting on our similarities.'

'Similarities?'

'Or perhaps not quite so similar. You, at least, had the nerve to go to the Town Hall.' She gave a short, self-deprecating huff of laughter. 'Would you believe me if I told you I joined with every intention of protesting, of fighting, of martyring myself? But then I ran scared. It turns out all I am good for is figures and numbers, hiding out in my office, except I am not even any good at that. I lost the money, then I got ransacked and had someone put money back, and whoever heard of such a thing, yet I am no closer to finding the identity of our thief. I have got nothing but a bloody button.'

'A button?' Louisa jerked upright. Had she mentioned a button earlier?

Miss Langwith laughed. 'Even drunk, you are still sharp, Miss Knight. I had decided not to tell you.'

'Am I untrustworthy?'

'No, no, I mean, a little yes. I do not know you. You came and prodded and poked at everything and upheaved my life. You helped ruin my relationship with Lydia.'

'Mrs Green ruined that all by herself.'

'You dislike her. I thought you, of all people, would understand what with Miss Chapman and her hairpins and her criminal brother.' She reached for the bottle of gin and poured more out, but Louisa shook her head.

'You sure? A little more will not hurt.'

She poured a generous serving into Louisa's glass.

'Miss Chapman is more than knowing how to pick a lock. She is...'

The best thing to happen to me.

And I left her face down on the pavement.

Louisa downed her drink.

Ada would be proud.

She laughed at the irony, a little too loud and bitter.

'Is that what Miss Chapman is?' Miss Langwith gestured at her empty glass, understanding writ large across her face, but she understood nothing.

'No. I do not want to talk about Miss Chapman.' She searched for a different topic. What had they been discussing earlier? *This is why I hate being drunk.* 'Aha! The button! Show me it, then. I have not forgotten.' She pointed a wobbly finger at Miss Langwith.

I wish Ada was here. She would find this hilarious.

But Ada was not here. Tears burnt the back of her eyes, but she would not cry. Not here in Miss Langwith's office, with far too much gin inside her.

Later. When she arrived home to the empty bed in Ada's studio – having offered the master bedroom to Miss Jain – she would let out her tears. Again.

But for now, she needed to concentrate. Ada would never let her forget if she found out Louisa had a chance to learn more in front of her, and instead, she went home and cried.

Concentrate, Louisa.

Miss Langwith was struggling to open the locked desk drawer – her fingers were clearly as nimble as Louisa's currently were – and muttered something that sounded suspiciously like 'hairpins'. Finally, the lock clicked open, and she slid the drawer forward, spending a few more minutes searching for what she wanted.

Finally, with a muttered 'there it is,' she withdrew her hand – a dark green button sat there.

Louisa picked it up, examining it. She had seen it before. Somewhere. She needed to think and cursed the alcohol clouding her brain. If she was sober, she would know where this was from. She would remember it.

But nothing would come.

'May I keep this?'

'If you wish. It is a needle in a haystack, though. Or a button in a haystack.' Miss Langwith chuckled at her own joke. Ada did that. Often at jokes whose only hilarity came from how comically bad they were.

The hole inside her ached a little more, tears burning her eyes once again. Perhaps it was time to go home and cry.

Rather rude, though. To take the button and leave.

'You are thinking of Miss Chapman.' It was not a question.

'Yes. Do you not think of Mrs Green?'

'I do, yes. Every day. I doubt she thinks of me, though. She is *busy* now.'

'And if she dies?' The question was out of her mouth before Louisa could stop it.

'Then she dies a martyr, like Miss Davison, and she will be happy with the outcome. I wonder if Miss Davison had a family, though. A lover who will mourn her.' Miss Langwith's eyes dropped to the desk, and she fiddled with the empty glass. 'What would you do? If it was Miss Chapman?'

'Hmm?'

'If it was Miss Chapman... playing with explosives?'

This time it was Ada in the rubble amongst all that noise and ash and anguish. 'No.'

Miss Langwith raised an eyebrow.

'I mean... that is...'

What if Ada came out of prison fired up with fresh determination and angrier than ever? It was not outside the realm of possibility. If anything, it was very plausible.

Will we stand in the ash and rubble together?

Though if they were setting bombs, they would not be there when they exploded. Not if they did a good job. Her drunken imagination was getting the better of her. She leant back against the chair, head tilted upwards, and closed her eyes. She opened them when the spinning of the world around her made her nauseous.

'It hurts you to think of it...' Miss Langwith's voice came from a great distance.

What was she talking about?

Ada. Explosives. After prison.

Louisa had told Sophie she was no martyr, and it was true. But Ada?

What would Ada want, fresh out of gaol?

'I do not know,' Louisa said. 'Sometimes Ada...scares me. She is too...free. She never stops to bloody think.' The words tumbled out. True, but never before voiced aloud.

And I stop to think too often and too much.

'It is hard, is it not?' Miss Langwith leant forward like she was going to whisper words for Louisa's ears only. 'I was scared all the time with Lydia. Scared of her getting hurt. Scared of her leaving for someone who could match her fire. And I was right to be. Do you ever think you could...' She moved closer. Too close.

Louisa tried to move backwards, but she was met with the solid resistance of the chair. 'Could what?'

'That it would be better...' Miss Langwith shook her head and moved away, and Louisa dared to breathe again. 'Never mind. I am talking nonsense. The alcohol, no doubt. We should head home.'

Louisa nodded. She stood and instantly regretted it as the floor rocked underneath her. She placed a hand on the desk to steady herself and waited for it to right.

It did not. Just kept spinning. Round and round and round.

'Miss Knight, are you quite alright?'

'I will be fine in a minute.' She collapsed back into the chair.

Miss Langwith moved and knelt next to her. A warm hand slipped into hers.

No. That is not right. That should be Ada's.

Louisa tried to wriggle her hand free, the contact burning her, and whilst Miss Langwith let it go, she did not move. She was far too close again.

'Do you ever think you would be better off with someone more like you?'

Sometimes, yes. The thought came unbidden and treacherous, and when Miss Langwith smiled, she realised she had said it out loud.

Chapter Twenty-Five

Hunger

Hunger clawed at Ada's stomach, demanding her full attention. She tried to distract herself with happy memories, but everything came back to food, eventually. Trying to focus on her favourite memories of Louisa, she inevitably arrived at the two of them at the dining table on Christmas Eve, a large spread of food before them. Beef, roast potatoes, Yorkshire puddings, carrots, peas, parsnips, and Brussels sprouts, all topped by thick meaty gravy. And a flaming Christmas pudding afterwards, so sticky it clung to her teeth. Last year, Louisa nearly swallowed the shilling hidden within, and Sophie had been so apologetic, as if the girl could have predicted that happening. In the end, Ada had poured her some port and told her to sit and drink with them. They had mince pies for supper, all any of them had room for, paired with more port. She'd been a little tipsy by the end of the night, and Louisa even more so. Ada's tolerance for alcohol was not the best, but it was by far the best in their household. She ended the day joyful and stuffed, which was the best way to spend Christmas Eve.

And there was goose and even more pudding at her parents' for Christmas the next day. Rosie found the shilling that day and squealed with delight. At least some of her enjoyment was because it clearly irritated Pete he hadn't, even though he tried to hide it. And John and Abigail brought chocolate bars for everyone – they must have saved up to buy so many all at once. Even Walter smiled at that, if only because his kids were so excited.

They even brought one for me to take home for Louisa. A kind gesture – but John has always been the kindest of my brothers.

What she wouldn't give for roast dinner and pudding and chocolate right now. She had thought she knew what hunger was from those nights as a child when Dad was out of work and there were six mouths to feed. Or had it been five? Or seven? How many siblings did she have that winter when her father was laid off? Was George still alive? Had her mother been pregnant? No, there was a baby, she was sure. Just the one. Had it been George? How bad was it that she could not even tell her dead siblings apart? But they were babies, just babies, and everyone knew babies died, especially in a cold, hungry winter.

But summer came, like summer always comes. And Dad found more work, and there was food again, and children alive to eat it. Her mother made a cake, a Victoria Sponge, to celebrate that first pay packet, and Ada had never tasted anything so delicious.

God, she wanted a slice of cake with a nice sugary cup of tea to wash it down.

Hunger twisted in her belly. If she shouted for food, they'd bring it. It would be gruel or something equally unappetising, but it would be food, and it would end the ache in her stomach, the shake in her limbs, the pain in her head.

The guards would crow over it, though. Earlier, a suffragette in a nearby cell had given up and asked for food. The guards had lorded her weak will over her, shouting for the other women to give up their silly protest. Ada had tried to place the woman's voice, but it had been too quiet, the guards too loud, and her head too fuzzy.

And eating would mean not being able to leave anytime soon. If she could hold out that little longer, they might send her home, back to Louisa. The suffragettes had hidden people before, preventing the police from returning them to gaol. She needed to last only a little longer. Once Ada was out, she and Louisa could make a plan. Louisa would solve it. She always knew what to do.

And Sophie would cook. The maid made the best chocolate pudding Ada had ever tasted – though she would never confess that to her mother. She'd ask Sophie to make a whole batch of them, and Louisa would tease her as she ate them all and jokingly refused to share.

Soon. Soon. Soon. Just a little longer.

The heavy clink of footsteps echoed down the corridor. She lifted her head and forced herself to sit up straight. They wouldn't find her sprawled on the floor.

Soon I will be home. Soon this will be over. Soon I'll be back in Louisa's arms, where I belong.

This place would not break her. She would prove Mabel wrong. God, Mabel, who was in here somewhere, who would believe Ada had given up on her again when she did not show up at visiting hours. She promised to make it every fortnight.

I promised not to join the suffragettes. I promised her years ago that nothing would ever separate us.

Was she destined to always break her promises?

Was Mabel nearby? If Ada shouted, would she hear it?

All that came from her throat was a croak.

At least I kept Louisa out of here. Though her little stunt had gained her Constable Smith's ire and an impressive collection of bruises. Davey had left without a word once she was off the floor.

The footsteps were nearly at her cell. Were they coming for her? Was this it? Was she ill enough to leave?

Or are they here to hold me down, ram a tube down my throat and force me to stay?

Fear raked across her heart and up her throat, choking the air out of her lungs. *No. They don't do that anymore.* There had been too much anger. People might not want women to vote, but they did not want the poor, confused dears tortured either.

It did little to ease terror's grip on her chest.

The footsteps came to a stop, and a man stood by the bars of her cell.

She would not show him her fear.

Soon, Louisa. I promise.

This promise she would keep.

Chapter Twenty-Six

Consequences

I t took four cups of tea for Louisa to feel even remotely human. Sophie kept a steady stream of them coming up to where she hid in her study as if by cosseting herself away from the world, she could stop it from existing.

Despite her best efforts, her memories of the previous night were blurry at best. Miss Langwith. Gin. The room spinning and a woman who was not Ada far too close. A hurried slur of words that she had to go, she had to leave, and then, nothing. She did not even remember how she had gotten home. A hansom cab, presumably, an unsafe choice for a woman alone and inebriated.

Are there any safe choices for a woman alone and inebriated? I got lucky. I made it home. She should have known better than to drink that much. She knew how much she hated it. And there had been no Ada to look after her this time.

Sometimes, yes. Treacherous, treacherous words.

'But you would not be you, and we would not be us.' Was that not true of Ada, too?

Would Louisa's life be easier if Ada was a little less impulsive, a little more like her? Yes.

Would her life be better? No.

Perhaps that was why she ran from Miss Langwith. Her mind had not been coherent, but she still knew it was wrong.

That it was not what she wanted.

Why would Miss Langwith – a woman recently scorned – want me to cheat on my own lover?

She had no answer there.

She took another sip of tea, wishing Ada was there to ask, even though that was not a question she could ever ask her partner.

I will never understand people. Her head throbbed. *Or the appeal of alcohol.*

Her fingers drummed against the book beside her – *Pride and Prejudice* by Jane Austen. An old favourite, she used to keep this tattered copy hidden behind her bookshelf, out of her father's view. In fiction, people's true motives were always revealed, even if the characters themselves were more complicated. Mr Darcy was a good man who made a bad first impression, flawed but willing to improve upon his shortcomings. Mr Wickham was the villain with an ability to charm, and Elizabeth Bennet was the heroine who learnt from her mistakes. Real people were harder to understand, and, unlike Mr Wickham, sometimes their motives were never revealed.

Louisa sighed as someone knocked on the door. The tempting smell wafting in told her the person had brought a fried breakfast, and her stomach rumbled, her earlier nausea replaced with hunger.

'Come in, Sophie.'

'It's Artie, ma'am.'

'Oh, well, come in, nonetheless.'

The boy entered, carrying a tray with yet another cup of tea and a plate containing a Full English breakfast.

'I thought you might appreciate some food.' Presumptuous but well-intended.

'A little late for breakfast, is it not?' But Louisa took the tray.

'It's what my dad always wanted. He used to...drink...sometimes.' There was a lot left unsaid in his pauses, but Louisa did not push him on them. That much, at least, even she understood. His father had been an alcoholic.

Was he drunk the night of the fire? Did he burn their house down, either by accident or drunken negligence, killing him and scarring his daughter for life. It was an unfortunately common occurrence, requiring only a lit candle and a moment of clumsiness.

'Thank you. Was the tea your idea, too?'

'No, that was Sophie. She claims it makes everything better, or at least that's what her mother used t' say.'

Louisa laughed. 'Ada works on much the same principle. She got it from her mother, too.' She took a sip of the fresh tea. 'I find I cannot fault it.'

'Indeed, ma'am.' He inclined his head and turned around.

Louisa removed the plate from the tray and picked up the knife and fork but paused. Artie still hovered in the doorway. 'Was there something else, Artie?'

'The button, ma'am? Have you remembered who it belongs to?'

Button? It took a few moments for the hazy memories to surface. The button Miss Langwith found in her ransacked office.

When did I mention that to Artie? Had it been here when she got home? Did Artie Dixon witness her inebriation? Shame rushed through her.

'No,' she said curtly. Then softer, 'Thank you for the breakfast... lunch... breakfast?'

'Dinner, ma'am.' It took her a few seconds to realise that, like Ada, he was using dinner to mean the middle meal, not the evening one. Before she could reply, he had closed the door behind him.

As she ate, Louisa obsessed over what she might or might not have said but came up with no answers. Her memory remained stubbornly uncooperative. Afterwards, she went in search of her bag, curiosity alighted by Artie's mention of the button.

Thankfully, it was hung in its correct spot – the hook beside her coat in the hallway. She grabbed it and retreated to her study unnoticed.

The button was as she remembered – green and shiny – and her certainty remained that she had seen it before, but where eluded her as much as the end of the previous night did. On Miss Jennings, perhaps? Or her mother?

She turned it in her hands, studying it from every angle as if it held some hidden secret in its metal. Her fingers stilled when the memory hit, confusion following in its wake.

The button was Ada's. They had purchased the dress from the modiste on the High Street – a birthday present for Ada. Though she was comfy in a paint-splattered man's shirt and trousers, she had a weakness for pretty dresses.

Then another memory hit, cutting through her sluggish thoughts with perfect clarity, and everything fell into place.

I know what happened. I know who our murderer is.

But what to do with that information? Should she call Inspector Lambert and tell him? Or say nothing and leave Miss Franklin to her chosen fate?

There was no Ada to ask. And no Father. Without them both, where was her moral compass?

This is ridiculous. I am capable of making a decision. I hired Sophie, did I not? There was no Father or Ada to guide me then.

But that was it, wasn't it? The one act she did because she alone thought it was right.

I chose Ada. I could have run away. I did not.

She turned the button in her fingers. She had to decide.

———

She had still not decided when there was another knock on her study door, and Miss Jain called her name.

'Sophie said this is where you were hiding,' she announced as she came in.

'I am not hiding, I—'

Miss Jain's derisive snort cut her off. 'Good night?' she asked with a smirk.

Did she witness my drunken behaviour, too?

She did not want to talk about last night anymore. 'I could ask you the same.'

'Oh, excellent!' Miss Jain's words were leaden with double meaning. She had been dressed to impress when she left last night, in clothes far beyond the price range for an out-of-work actress.

'Does it not bother you? Carrying on like that, with Miss Dixon imprisoned?'

In her mind, Miss Langwith leaned close again, too close, and Louisa uttered treasonous words.

Miss Jain frowned. 'Hettie would hardly expect me to starve just because she is.'

Louisa could not make heads or tails of that statement. 'Starve? No one is starving in my home, Miss Jain.'

'True enough. That does not mean I am going to let my only source of income dry up. Not when he is so...enjoyable as well, and that is a rarity, Miss Knight, though I suppose not one you would understand.'

'Please speak plainly, Miss Jain. I am too tired—'

'Too hungover.'

'Yes,' Louisa conceded. 'That, too.'

'I have a gentleman friend. He pays me well for my company, at dinner parties and theatres, and in his bedroom. Much better than I could ever hope to get on the stage or in a mill or with a needle. Is that plain enough, or do you need me to go into more details, an experience I cannot imagine either of us will enjoy?'

'No, that is clear enough. I had not realised... That is, Ada thought... Well, none of that matters. It is not my business.'

Miss Jain laughed, amused by her flustering. 'Tell me, what did Miss Chapman think?'

Louisa shook her head. 'It is of no concern.'

But after a few moments, Miss Jain clicked her fingers. 'Hettie! You mentioned Hettie earlier—that is what Miss Chapman thought, is it not? That our friendship was more akin to what the two of you share.'

Seeing no point in lying, Louisa nodded.

Miss Jain smiled. 'Now, I am going to say something that will truly shock you. I love Hettie, I will stand by her side, and I want her in my life, *as long as we both shall live,*' her smile twisted as she mimicked the wedding vows, 'but as a friend. I have no desire to woo her, to court her, or to live as woman and wife as you and Miss Chapman do, no matter what words you use for the outside world. It holds no interest for me. Not with Hettie, not with Mr Robbins – though I'll happily share his bed – nor anyone. I may marry someday if needs must, but it will be a practical marriage.'

Louisa stared at her, taking the words in. It was not like her, not exactly, in many ways the exact opposite, but it was still stepping outside of society's norms, a rejection of what was supposed to be desirable to all.

I do not want sex. And she does not want romance.

'I see I have shocked you, indeed. Shall you try to convert me? Tell me everyone must fall in love – it is part of what makes us human.'

'Not shocked, just surprised. I... that is, Ada and I... We do not have a standard relationship.'

Miss Jain raised an eyebrow. 'Well, yes, obviously.'

Louisa blushed. 'I meant besides the obvious.' But then, she could not continue. She had only ever told Ada. Would Miss Jain understand? Would she recognise the similarities?

This could help me in solving the question of why. Why am I like this? Why is Miss Jain how she is?

She just had to say the words.

Another knock, this time loud and from downstairs, interrupted her spiralling thoughts.

Who could be visiting us?

Grateful for the interruption, she listened as the front door opened, followed by Artie's voice, pitched loud, 'Miss Knight is not here, Constable.'

So, Leeds Constabulary has come for me, after all.

It was not surprising. Both Constables Smith and Wilkinson had seen her. If anything, she would have guessed they would visit sooner. She strained to listen, but the constable's voice was quiet. Should she hide? Where? Or would it be better to do her time and take a stand?

Miss Jain stared through the wall in the direction of the voices. She turned towards Louisa and asked sardonically, 'Shall I fetch the delivery van?'

Louisa could not muster up a laugh.

Another knock, quieter, on the study door and Sophie's whisper. 'Ma'am?'

Compelled by the maid's caution, she tiptoed to the door and opened it carefully. The hinges, of course, chose that moment to creak like they had never once known oil.

'Constable Wilkinson is downstairs. He insists he is not here t' arrest you. Artie didn't want to let 'im in.' Her tone in the last sentence implied Artie was not the only one.

'I will speak with him.'

Sophie frowned and opened her mouth to argue.

'I will not have the pair of you arrested for harbouring a fugitive.'

'Are you a fugitive, ma'am?'

'That might be overstating the matter, but the point still stands.'

'Well,' Miss Jain said from behind her. 'Let us go talk to your friend's peeler husband.'

'There is no need for him to know you are here, too.'

Miss Jain gave a mischievous grin. 'Oh, he almost certainly already knows. If I am to be arrested, at least let me have some fun first.' She pushed past Louisa and hurried down the hallway.

'Um... should we stop her?' Sophie asked.

'It is a little late for that.' Louisa set off towards the stairs.

Sophie followed. 'I can fetch more tea? Or something stronger? I feel you might need something stronger.'

Louisa's stomach flipped at the mere thought. 'Tea is fine, Sophie, thank you.'

The pair made their way downstairs, separating in the hallway.

The tableau Louisa walked into was plucked straight from the music halls where Miss Jain had once performed. Constable Wilkinson sat on their sofa in his civilian clothes, ramrod straight. He was pinned in by Miss Jain on one side, talking to him in the low sultry voice Louisa imagined she had used in her performances. On the other side, Galapagos stretched to her full length against his thigh, one paw claiming him as hers. Her head butted against his leg, and she purred at full volume.

'Sorry, am I interrupting?' Louisa said to announce her presence.

In the two years she had known him, Constable Wilkinson had never looked quite so happy to see her. He jumped from his seat, earning a betrayed meow from Galapagos and an amused smirk from Miss Jain. 'Miss Knight, thank heavens. Odd kind of 'ousehold you're running nowadays. You appear t' be taking in all sorts of strays.'

'I hope you're talking about the cat, Constable.' Miss Jain's voice took on a dangerous tone, and the way she threw his title at him made it clear she intended it as an insult.

'Cats, suffragettes, apprentices—it's all change round 'ere.' He turned to stare directly at Louisa. 'Including the fact that Ada is missing from this scene.'

'We both know where Ada is, Constable.' Louisa tried to mimic Miss Jain's tone but did not quite succeed.

'Though your concern for your wife is touching.'

He sighed. 'Is anyone going to explain that? Ada didn't make a whole lot of sense when I asked her. Just kept saying, "people really will think we're married now."'

The words were a jolt to Louisa's heart. 'You've seen Ada? How is she?' The words came out too quickly. A demand rather than a question.

'I visited her, yes. She's...not well. I tried to make her see sense but...' He sighed and scrubbed a hand through his sandy hair.

'Not well?' *The hunger strike.* No amount of logic could make the idea of Ada starving herself feel acceptable, no matter how much Louisa understood her reasoning.

'What do you mean "see sense?"' Miss Jain's question was steel sharp.

'I mean stop starving herself!' Constable Wilkinson's voice was equally dangerous.

'That's Ada's choice,' Louisa said. 'Is that all you came here to tell me, Constable?'

'Is that all you have to say? Do you have any idea how worried Mrs Chapman is? She begged my mum to convince me to visit Ada, which was no easy feat with the ban on visiting suffragettes. Did you know that?'

Louisa did not know that. She had not thought to visit the Chapmans since Ada's imprisonment. Should she have? Would they even have welcomed her?

He scoffed. 'No, you didn't, did you? This was a wasted journey.' He stormed out of the room in a rush, colliding with Sophie and her ladened tea tray with a crash, a scream, and a loud curse.

Louisa hurried forward. 'Sophie, are you alright?' The maid was wiping wet hands against her white apron, which had a large brown stain spread across it. The tray and its components had dropped to the floor, and at least one cup had smashed. One of the newer sets Ada had purchased, thankfully, nothing that had belonged to Louisa's mother.

'What the 'ell did you do?' The shout came from Artie Dixon, and he aimed it squarely at Constable Wilkinson.

'Artie!' Louisa said his name sharply. 'Can you tidy this up please whilst Sophie goes and cleans herself up? Sophie, you will need to apply cold water anywhere the water burned you. Go use the bathroom.' After only a second's pause, they both moved to do as she said, Artie bending down to the floor and picking up any stray shards of crockery and Sophie scurrying upstairs. Louisa turned to their guest. 'Constable,' she scanned his clothes, 'you appear to have survived the encounter unscratched, though you may want to look where you are going more closely in the future.' She gestured at the door. 'I believe you were leaving.'

Behind her, Miss Jain let out a low, quiet whistle of approval.

'And that's it, is it? You will leave Ada starving in prison and Mrs Chapman to her grief?'

'There is no need to hyperbolise, Constable. Did you really think I would help you with this?'

'I thought you were the sensible one, Miss Knight.'

'I like to think I am.'

She almost got a smile for that, but then his face turned serious again. 'But you won't help me convince Ada to eat? If you agree, I can help you visit her.'

Louisa shook her head before her emotions could betray her, and a silence hung between them, heavy and unyielding. Even Artie, still crouched on the floor, froze.

It was Miss Jain who broke it. 'Did you see a Miss Dixon whilst you were there?'

'Who?'

She laughed bitterly. 'Never mind.'

Constable Wilkinson frowned at her for a second and then turned back to Louisa. 'Pete was arrested last night.'

'Kitty's sweetheart?' Miss Jain said.

Is that why she and her mother were arguing?

Louisa should have had a stronger reaction to the news, but it was no shock. Peter Chapman had been heading towards trouble over the course of the last year, and it had finally caught up with him.

Despite Ada's best efforts.

'Your governor's words are not worth much, then.' *But then Ada broke their deal. She cannot save Miss Franklin from prison while inside it herself.*

He frowned at that. 'I don't know what that means. I suspect I don't want to. All I know is Pete's in our holding cells. That's why Mrs Chapman is so desperate. Two of her children arrested, including one imprisoned and starving herself. It's poor repayment for all she's been through.' He scoffed again. 'Do you even know about that?'

'I know enough.'

He stared at her a few seconds, shook his head, and said, 'So be it then, Miss Knight.' The front door rattled in its frame as he slammed it shut.

'So, what happened to Mrs Chapman?' Miss Jain said after he left.

'It is not my place to say.' Her reply to the constable had been true – Ada had told her some of her mother's struggles, but it was not something she spoke of often, and Louisa was shamefully glad of that. She had not known how to respond and had struggled to understand why Mrs Chapman had not taken the simple solution and stopped getting pregnant. Ada spoke of her father as a good man. Surely, he would have understood the need for that? She had enough sense to not say that out loud to Ada, suspecting there was some nuance she was missing.

It was the reason Ada gave for the promise she had made to her mother. A promise that was now in tatters.

A promise Ada would have tried to fix.

At least Louisa now knew what Ada would do if she was here. But she was not, so it would be up to Louisa.

She reached into her skirt pocket for the button still stashed there. Ada's button, from the dress she'd ruined with paint. The *forest green* button.

She turned to Miss Jain and Artie. 'I need to speak with you both about Kitty Jennings.'

Chapter Twenty-Seven

Two Prisoners

Surrounded by the dull bricks and familial misery of visiting time at Armley Gaol, Mabel Spencer bore little resemblance to the smiling girl in Ada's old portrait. The girl Ada once drew in the flush of life was a woman old before her time, dressed in the faded grey dress of a prisoner. She sat opposite Louisa and studied her, eyes roving from her head to her toes. It was not quite the same as how men did it sometimes, typically ending with a dismissive sneer. With Mabel, it was more of an inspection than a leer, but it still made Louisa want to fidget under her gaze. Instead, she clasped her hands in her lap and sat up straighter.

'Well, I must say, this is a surprise.' Mabel's tone was amused, her smile wry, a flash of that girl Louisa would never meet.

'You know who I am then?' She had to raise her voice as a baby a few chairs away chose that moment to cry.

Mabel nodded. 'Ada has mentioned you a lot. And speaking of Ada... I'm guessing you are 'ere because she didn't listen t' me?' She spoke with tired resignation, her voice barely audible over the screaming baby and the other background chatter. 'Is she...here? At Armley? Did she ask you to visit me as well?'

'She is here, but I have not seen her.'

'What did you say?' Mabel shouted over the baby.

'I have not seen her!' Louisa shouted back.

'You have not been to visit her?' There was a bite to Mabel's question, and Louisa hurried to explain.

'They do not allow suffragettes to have visitors for the first four weeks.' She had glanced around the room when she first entered, but as expected, there was no one she recognised. No sign of Ada, though she was in this gaol, somewhere beyond these walls, starving herself. Louisa was so close and yet so far away.

'You're even posher than I imagined.' Mabel's voice was lighter. It seemed Louisa's explanation had done its job. 'Ada really has done well for herself.'

'I would argue it is the other way around.'

'Good with words, too. Ada always liked pretty words. Pretty paintings. Pretty dresses she couldn't afford, though that seems to be less of an issue for her nowadays.'

Louisa did not know how to respond to that, and the noise of the room pressed into the quiet between them. The baby had been silenced, but a man behind Louisa berated his wife – a guard called from him to calm down or be removed.

How does Ada come here every fortnight?

Louisa tapped her fingers against her leg, unable to think of an appropriate response to Mabel's earlier comment. Her mind turned instead to how best to broach the other information she came here to share.

Mabel leaned forward. 'So, how can I help you, Miss Knight?'

'I thought you should know. Why Ada is not here to visit you, I mean.'

'That is kind of you.' There was no mockery in the statement, only sincerity.

Perhaps it would be best to say it plainly. 'And there is something else I need to talk to you about.'

Mabel raised her eyebrows and regarded her coolly. 'What more could you have to tell me, Miss Knight?'

'I have been speaking with my solicitor—'

'You have a solicitor?' Quiet amusement leaked into her voice. Ada had once responded similarly. Having a family solicitor was not, Louisa had learnt, a common practise amongst the working classes. Which made sense when she considered it. She had just never considered it before then.

'A family friend who is a solicitor. The point, Miss Spencer, is that he thinks you might have a chance of being released.'

At that, she went rigid and stared at Louisa. 'Is this a joke, miss?'

'No. Not a joke. It would not be a very funny sort of joke.'

'No, no, indeed it would not,' Mabel muttered, looking down at her hands. She glanced back to Louisa, 'Truly?' There was raw hope there, to the point where it made Louisa uncomfortable.

'Yes, truly, but it will require some...difficulty.'

'Difficulty?' Mabel peered at her. 'Miss Knight, whatever it is, please just say it.'

'You would have to tell the truth of what happened that afternoon to a panel of magistrates.'

'Men,' Mabel spat. 'I would have t' sit before a panel of men and be judged again. I have already done that once, Miss Knight. I 'ave no desire t' repeat experience.'

'Even for your freedom?'

Mabel opened her mouth, but no answer came.

'You do not have to decide now, but I wanted you to be aware it is a possibility. That you have this option.'

Mabel squinted at her. 'Why have you done this?'

'Excuse me?'

'This.' She gestured at Louisa. 'Speaking to your solicitor. Why would you try to get your—' Mabel glanced around the room, eyes skirting the other prisoners and their visitors and the guards. 'Well, we both know what we are and what was once mine. Why would you help me get free?'

Louisa considered her answer for a moment and decided on honesty. 'I would be lying if I said I have not had the exact same thought. But all other...*matters*...aside, you do not deserve to spend the rest of your life in this place. No woman does, not for defending herself.'

Mabel stared at her a little longer, taking the words in, and then nodded, like she accepted it for the plain truth it was. 'I will think about it, Miss Knight. You may think I'm a fool who should jump at the opportunity given me, but—'

'No.' Louisa shook her head. 'I do not think you are a fool. It is a hard request they would make of you, and I would be remiss not to tell you that there is no guarantee of success, even if you force yourself to go through with it.'

Mabel smiled tightly. 'Thank you. For putting this in motion and for the honesty.'

'You are welcome, Miss Spencer.' That could have been the end of the conversation – the visit – but Louisa hesitated.

Here is perhaps the only person to know Ada the same way I do. Who may know more about certain aspects of her life, the parts I struggle to understand.

'May I ask you something else?'

Mabel tilted her head, a curious gleam in her eyes that gave her a vitality that many of her fellow prisoners lacked. Regardless of what she had told Ada, Louisa doubted gaol had entirely broken Mabel's spirit. Which boded well for her ability to do and say what was necessary to secure her release.

'Of course,' she replied. She gestured at the surrounding room. 'I have nowhere else to be.'

Louisa smiled at that. And then she told her all she had figured out in the last few days and asked her the question that had been eating away at her. What was her best option? What would Ada do?

Together, they made a decision.

———————————

Her request to speak to a second prisoner did not impress the guard, judging by his frown, but a smile and the press of four half-crowns into his palm resolved the issue. Louisa was sure she had done the interaction clumsily. She wished – for the thousandth time – Ada was here beside her, not least because she would have dealt with the situation with the guard better. Hopefully, by the time he came back, her heart rate may have returned to its normal speed.

It was nearly there when Miss Franklin entered the visiting room, but it climbed again at the sight of her. Louisa may have decided, had even gotten Mabel's approval as a proxy for Ada, but it did not stop doubt from rearing its head once more.

The dark circles under Miss Franklin's eyes told their own story. Had doubts of her own plagued her since the visit with her aunt and uncle?

She sat in the same seat where Mabel had been and gave a quick, forced smile. 'Miss Knight, is it not? I cannot imagine what you have to say to me.'

'Have you spoken to your uncle since I was last here?'

'I have nothing more to say to him.'

'Then you will not have learnt that Lydia Green did not shoot Adam Richardson.'

Miss Franklin stared at her. She was so startled, she even

forgot to mention she already knew that because she – at least according to her confession – had been the one to do so.

Louisa ploughed onwards before she could recover. 'And neither did you. Please'—she held up her hand to stall the belated insistence of guilt—'do not waste both our time insisting you did. You have sacrificed yourself for nothing. Do you know where Mrs Green was at the time Mr Richardson was shot?'

Miss Franklin shook her head.

'She was with Miss Langwith. It seemed with your betrayal, she returned to her former *friend*.'

'That sour old cow?' Miss Franklin scoffed.

'She was at least not a spy. Mrs Green was under the impression that your'—she glanced at the watching guard and the few remaining prisoners and visitors—'*intentions* for your uncle were, in fact, a trap to ensnare her.'

'There was no trap!' She appeared genuinely insulted by the insinuation, and Louisa's dislike of her grew. The WSPU's bombing campaign was one matter. Trying to murder your own family was another.

But I am not here to argue the morality of her choices.

'Well, that is between you, your uncle, and your conscience.'

Miss Franklin opened her mouth to protest, and Louisa held up her hand again. 'But you did not kill Mr Richardson, so you do not belong in here.' That, at least, was still black and white when so much was grey nowadays. Even Ada and Father would agree with each other. 'But I need to know why you thought Mrs Green was our murderer.'

Miss Franklin hesitated for a second. 'Her dress.'

Louisa's heart jumped, and she fought to keep her face neutral. It was as she suspected.

'I only saw her – or whoever it was – for a moment. The briefest of flashes, but I know that dress, the pattern is quite distinctive.' She dropped her voice to a whisper. 'I've removed it from her many times.'

'That does not mean it was Mrs Green who was wearing it.'

'Why would she give someone her favourite dress?'

'Maybe she spilt paint down it.'

'Who would want a paint-stained... oh! Oh!' Miss Franklin's eyes widened, dawning comprehension spreading across her face.

'I think we may have reached the same conclusion.'

Miss Franklin uttered a string of curse words.

'Watch your tongue,' the guard called.

She glared at him with so much venom Louisa worried she was about to replace one murder she did not commit with another she did.

'Miss Franklin.'

Her head jerked back round to Louisa. Her voice was only just above a whisper when she asked, 'Can you get me out of here, Miss Knight?'

'I can, if you can be civil to your uncle.'

Miss Franklin's lip curled.

'Just until you are out. Then you are no longer my concern and can say whatever you want to him. If anything, I highly encourage you to do so.'

She smiled at that. 'Then do what you must, Miss Knight. And I will be the,' she put on a fake high-pitched desolate voice, 'devastated, misguided niece who took a wrong path and just wants to return to the family fold.'

It was nearly enough to make Louisa feel sorry for Inspector Lambert. Nearly.

But she had a plan to enact.

Chapter Twenty-Eight

Freedom

It was over. It was finally over. Ada tilted her head towards the sky, enjoying the warm sunshine on her face. The small group of suffragettes waited behind the gates of Armley Gaol in silent anticipation. Ada certainly had no energy for idle chit-chat. She barely felt like she had the energy to remain upright; every step was a shaky effort, and her stomach begged to be fed. Still, she had offered an arm to Miss Dixon, as had Miss Lewis, the former mill girl who had been with them at the Town Hall, for Miss Dixon appeared even closer to collapse than Ada. No one had returned her cane or supplied her with anything else to aid her.

'I just have to make it past those walls,' she had muttered earlier with steely determination. It was all any of them had said. Still, even in their silence, there was no denying the undercurrent of victory that flowed between them all. They had held out. They had won.

Once the gates opened, it'd be over.

For now.

The licence folded in her hand listed her date of return in a week and her home address. Even if she hid elsewhere, they would re-arrest her as soon as they caught her at another protest.

Would she be involved in another protest?

I broke so easily this time.

The idea of going through it again – of coming back to Armley Gaol and suffering through another hunger strike – chilled her to the bone. But what was the alternative? To accept the way of the world and their place in it? To be nothing more than second-class citizens? For their lives to always matter less and for them to not even try to fight back against it?

No. She couldn't face that either.

A sneering prison warden slid the gate open, and Ada bit down the impulse to stick her tongue out at him. Not now. Not when freedom was so close.

Not when Louisa is so close.

They hurried through as quickly as they could manage, and the gate banged close behind them with such a clang Ada winced, and Miss Dixon jumped, then stumbled.

She tightened her grip on Ada's arm and muttered, 'That was unnecessary.'

A group of women wearing suffragette sashes waited on the other side. Ada scanned their faces quickly till she found the one she needed to see. When Louisa's gaze met Ada's, she gave her a slight, almost shy, smile. Ada returned it with a grin as relief flooded her veins.

It's over. I'm going home.

'Well, thank God, that's over!' one of her fellow prisoners shouted – another one of the mill girls, Miss Lovell. She turned and made a rude hand gesture at the prison walls, eliciting laughter from those watching. Even Louisa smiled – a quick, fleeting thing, like she did not want to be caught laughing at a rude joke.

The waiting women surged forward, enveloping friends in greetings and hugs. Ada had only managed a couple of steps when Louisa made it to her side. She pulled her into a hug, made awkward by her still being linked to Miss Dixon and the other girl, though they only laughed. Ada did not care. This was what she had held out for.

Miss Jain was not far behind, pushing a wheelchair. Miss Dixon released their arms and fell into it with a wince and a sigh. 'You're a good 'un, Aisha.'

'I try.'

Ada turned away to give them some privacy and wished for more of her own.

'How are you?' Louisa took her hand, and Ada seized it, revelling in its soft warmth, grateful this small gesture could go overlooked.

'Ada?' Louisa awaited an answer – an overwhelming concern laced in the two short syllables of her name.

'I...have been better.'

'Of course. Oh,' Louisa reached into her skirt pocket with her spare hand. 'Here, this is for you.' She held out a small, rectangular box. It looked like a jewellery box, but why would Louisa be giving her a necklace?

With shaky hands, Ada opened it to reveal a medal with a white, green and purple ribbon. FOR VALOUR was inscribed on the clasp, and HUNGER STRIKE on the medallion.

'We can add your name and the dates to it.'

Ada clutched the box tight in her palm. She had earnt this.

'Here, I brought this, too.' Louisa tugged her hand free and reached into her bag, pulling out a brown paper package that looked remarkably like a wrapped sandwich.

Ada snatched it from her – the medal box tumbling forgotten to the ground – as her stomach growled, demanding the food she had denied it for days. She tore through the paper, ripping it to shreds, and took a huge bite out of the sandwich underneath. It was glorious – ham and cheese and bread spread with a thick inch of butter, just like she preferred.

It was gone far too soon.

'Have I told you recently I love you?' And before Louisa even had a chance to respond, she added, 'Any chance you thought to bring another?'

'No. You will make yourself—' Louisa stopped and continued in a softer tone of voice. 'It is not good for you to eat too fast and too much when you have not eaten for a while.'

'Are you sure?' Ada's stomach certainly considered it a good idea.

'I am sure.' Louisa held out the medal box again – she must have picked it up whilst Ada was distracted devouring the sandwich – and Ada took it back. 'However, I am not at all sure Sophie will listen to my advice. Chances are we are going to have a feast fit for King George himself waiting for us when we get home.'

'Oh, we will,' Miss Jain said from beside them. 'I told Artie to make sure of it.'

'Have you been ordering my brother around again, Aisha?' Miss Dixon still looked likely to fall asleep at any moment, but her voice was lively and teasing. She had a pile of similar brown paper in her lap and a matching medal pinned to her dress.

Ada tried to copy her and pin the medal to her dress – her own dress, not the awful sack they had made them wear, despite their protests of being political prisoners – but her hands refused to cooperate.

'Here,' Louisa took it and, with careful consideration, pinned it to her chest, fingers brushing against hers.

Ada preened. 'How do I look?'

'Like one of the bravest people I know.' The words were so sincere they stole any clever response Ada might make.

Miss Jain coughed, ruining the moment. 'I preferred it when you two were at least trying to be secretive around us.'

'"Trying" being the operative word,' Miss Dixon added with a grin.

Louisa blushed and stepped away, then cleared her throat. 'Shall we head home?' and then turned to Ada. 'Miss Jain and the Dixons are staying with us like we discussed.'

That took Ada by surprise. She had almost forgotten that discussion. It would not be quite the homecoming she had expected.

But it is good that we can offer them a home. We will find a way to make it work.

'Oh no,' Miss Dixon said, deadpan. 'I put the wrong address on my licence. How ever will the police find me if I don't return to prison?'

'Such a shame,' Louisa agreed, equally deadpan.

'Terrible, really,' Miss Jain added. 'Though that one's husband might grass you up.'

Ada forced a sigh – too tired to muster up any real frustration – even as the other three women laughed.

'Traitor,' she muttered to Louisa, which only made her partner laugh harder.

A fellow suffragette's husband offered them a lift in his cart, which made things easier for Miss Dixon as it had a ramp. Miss Jain kept up a gentle chatter with Louisa all the way home, allowing Ada and Miss Dixon a chance to rest.

Ada's heart soared when the cart stopped, and she stepped out onto the pavement, back at the house in Roundhay that had become her home.

Louisa squeezed her hand like she could read her mind.

The tantalising scent of baking hit them as soon as they opened the door and made Ada's hungry stomach seize.

'It would appear your servant listened to me and not you,' Miss Jain remarked with a grin.

Ada turned a laugh into a cough, and Miss Dixon didn't even bother to disguise her amusement, but Louisa just rolled her eyes. 'It would appear so.'

'Shall we head straight to the dining room?' Miss Jain asked her friend, and at Miss Dixon's nod, she pushed her in that direction.

Gal chose that moment to appear, rushing out of the sitting room with a series of elated meows and winding her way round Ada's legs with a loud purr.

Ada leant down to stroke her. 'I've missed you, too.'

Gal butted her head against her hand, demanding more strokes, and Ada complied.

Beside her, Louisa gave a low laugh. 'Should I be jealous?'

'Of me or Gal? Because you know she's my favourite.'

Louisa knelt and also stroked the cat, who purred even louder at all the attention. 'That is fine. She is my favourite, too.'

'How terribly rude.' Ada put on a fake wounded voice. 'I go to gaol, and I come home to find you have already replaced me.'

'Are you two coming in here or not?' Miss Jain called from the doorway. 'I will go raid your kitchen on Hettie's behalf if you don't hurry.'

Ada straightened as her stomach rumbled at the mention of more food. A dizzy spell overtook her, and she used the wall to steady herself as her head swam.

'Ada!' Louisa grabbed her arm.

'I'm fine. I just need to eat.'

'Of course. I will let Sophie and Artie know we are home.'

In the dining room, Ada collapsed gratefully onto a chair, breathing in the rich aroma of baking and salivating at the promise of what was to come. Gal followed, still meowing and brushing against her legs.

From downstairs, there came a surprised exclamation.

'So, shall we guess exactly how many cakes the two of them have baked?' Miss Jain asked.

'Ten, I hope,' Miss Dixon said.

'Twelve,' Ada said. 'Six each.'

'You mean two each,' Miss Jain corrected her and then laughed when both Ada and Miss Dixon glared in her direction.

Gal jumped onto her lap, something she was definitely not allowed to do at the dining table, but an exception could be made in the circumstances, and Ada scratched behind her ears.

'Oh, what a cute cat!' Miss Dixon exclaimed from opposite her.

'Cute pain in the backside,' Miss Jain muttered. 'Is Miss Knight mistress here, or is it Galapagos?'

'Galapagos?' Miss Dixon echoed, amused.

'I am never letting Louisa name a pet again,' Ada muttered. 'Don't you agree, Gal?' She scratched under her chin, and the cat purred louder. 'I think that's a yes.'

Miss Dixon laughed and leaned forward, arm outstretched to stroke Gal, but then she gave a yelp of pain and fell back into her seat.

Miss Jain rushed to her feet, but Miss Dixon waved her back down. 'After all these years, you would think I'd have learnt.'

'Are you in need of anything?' Ada asked. 'We have a medicine cabinet downstairs; I can go have a look, see if we have anything that would help?'

Miss Dixon shook her head. 'No, thank you. Food is what I need more than owt else. And we wouldn't want to disturb *Galapagos*.' She smiled at the cat.

The door swung open to reveal Sophie holding a cake platter containing the largest, most delicious-looking chocolate cake Ada had ever seen, its edge overhanging the base of the glass stand. 'Miss Chapman!' Sophie beamed at her. 'I made your favourite chocolate cake.'

'Yes, I can see that, Sophie!' The icing was a dark shiny brown that promised to be rich, and Ada could already taste it on her tongue.

Sophie placed it in the middle of the table, and Artie came in after her with plates and forks and a serving knife. It took every inch of self-control Ada possessed not to reach over and shovel the cake into her mouth with her hands.

Once Sophie had cut them both a massive doorstop of a slice, Ada tucked into it immediately. She was about two-thirds of the way through when the nausea hit, and she ran out of the room, knocking a screeching Gal off her lap, hand clasped to her mouth. Panicking, she ran to the first place that came to mind, the front garden, and she just made it before the cake came back up. Stomach acid burned the back of her throat as vomit coated their lawn and her skirts. When it appeared no more was coming, she wiped her mouth with her sleeve – which probably wasn't the cleanliest of choices, but the dress already needed a wash – and straightened up, muttering 'Shut it,' to Louisa, who hovered in the doorway.

'I did not say a word, dear.' Louisa held out a glass of water, and Ada took it with a small thankful smile. 'But you probably should stick to more plain food until your stomach is used to eating again.'

'You couldn't have said that five minutes ago?'

'Would you have listened?'

Which was a valid point.

'Oh, I didn't think of that,' Sophie's voice came from behind Louisa. 'I'm sorry, miss. I'll clean that up, and I'll make something plain.' She thought for a second. 'Toast, maybe? Toast should be alright, shouldn't it, ma'am?'

'Toast should be fine. Thank you, Sophie. Could you bring it upstairs?' She turned to Ada. 'Some privacy may serve us all well, and,' she glanced down at her stained skirts, 'you should probably change.'

Ada followed her gaze down to her dress, which had already been wrinkled and musty from its stay in the prison's storage room. She plucked at the fabric covering her chest. 'The smell of vomit and gaol, what an excellent combination.'

Louisa crinkled her nose but still held out her hand and led Ada back into the house. Gal followed with a meow and sat at the top of the stairs, watching as they climbed at a pace much slower than usual, Ada's limbs refusing to cooperate. Eventually, they made it to their bedroom.

Except it was not their bedroom. It may have still been the same room, but it did not look the same as it had when Ada last stepped inside. It was a mess, scattered with clothing and hats and shoes and cosmetics and perfume, none of which belonged to either of them.

'So, I was only joking about you replacing me...'

'Excuse me?' Louisa stared at her incomprehensively for a moment. It was clear when she understood, eyes narrowing in Ada's direction. '*No.* I've been sleeping in your studio. Miss

Jain has been staying in here, but your clothes are still in the wardrobe.'

'Ahh, hence the explosion at the textile factory.'

Louisa snorted and covered her mouth.

Gal settled herself down on a discarded coat on the bed, watching Ada with caution. Her tail flickered.

'Do you think she will forgive me for her sudden trip to the floor?' Ada asked lightly but turned to the wardrobe, searching through her dresses for her oldest and most comfortable.

'Oh, absolutely not.' Louisa lifted Gal from the coat, who gave an obligatory meow of protest, but then happily settled into her lap as she sat on the edge of the bed.

Ada busied herself with getting changed, forcing her protesting limbs to work, and shaking off Louisa's offer of help.

Louisa gasped softly when she removed her dress. 'Is that from when you fell?' She pointed at the bruises on her arms and legs. Some were still a spectacular dark purple, others turning a sickly yellow and green. 'You scared me, you know.'

'I thought I might have. I'm sorry, I just... I wanted to give you a chance to escape. I couldn't face the idea of someone else I love behind bars.'

Louisa's face twitched but smoothed over. 'I understand. Please never do that again, though.'

'I'm afraid I can make no promises.' But Ada did not want to think about her potential future of being in and out of prison. She would face it once she had clean clothes and some food in her stomach.

When she finished dressing, she turned back around to find Louisa still watching her intently. There were many saucy comments she could have made, but she hadn't the energy, not even to make Louisa blush. Instead, she came and sat next to her, leaning her head against her shoulder, savouring her warmth and breathing in the familiar, comforting scent of her favourite orange blossom perfume. 'I missed you.'

'Me too.' Louisa pressed a kiss to her forehead.

They sat in contented silence for a few moments until a knock on the door interrupted. 'Ma'am? I have Miss Chapman's toast. And some water. I was going to make tea, but Artie said water would help.'

And Ada's stomach remembered it had purged itself of what little she had eaten in the last week. She forced herself to eat the toast Sophie brought slower than the cake, washing it down with plenty of water, though it still left her a little nauseous.

When she turned back to Louisa, she was watching again. She sat ramrod straight, her face neutral and her hands folded into the cat's fur, but only because the cat's presence meant she could not clasp them in her lap. It was what Louisa did when she was uncomfortable in social situations, hiding her discomfort behind good posture and a serene face, but why would she be doing it now?

She has something to say and does not want to say it.

'Whatever it is you need to say, please just say it.'

She relaxed ever so slightly at that. 'How do you always know?'

'I may be the one with the readable face, but you have your own tells. Now, out with whatever bad news you have been holding off on telling me to not spoil my return home. I already threw up on the front lawn. It can't get much more ruined.'

'It is not entirely bad news, per se.'

'We both know I don't know what that means.'

That earnt her a slight smile at least, but Louisa's face turned serious again. 'Whilst you were away, I had an idea.'

'Was it a terrible idea?'

'Maybe. Possibly. But I do not think you will think so. Or at least Mabel did not think you would think so.'

'Mabel?' Ada could do nothing but stare at Louisa in shock for a few moments. 'You spoke to Mabel?' She could not even begin imagining what that conversation had been like or why Louisa had thought it a good idea.

'Your brother was arrested and taken to a borstal, but he has since been released.'

'That bastard!' Ada jumped from her seat and kicked the nearest item, a flamboyant picture hat that skittered across the floor, feathers fluttering. Her aching body protested the action, but she was too angry to care.

Louisa's face scrunched up. 'Your brother?'

'No! I mean... a little bit... but no! The bloody traitorous inspector.'

'Ah,' Louisa said. 'You really will not like this next part, then.'

Ada stared at her. 'Louisa, what did you do?'

Chapter Twenty-Nine

A Plan Enacted

The next day, Ada – against all medical advice to remain at home – sat in her parents' living room and explained the plan to Pete.

'No,' he shouted when she was done. 'Absolutely not!'

'Well, then you can go back to the borstal.' Inspector Lambert was remarkably out of place, sitting in one of her mother's dining chairs.

'Miss Knight bought your freedom at a price, Pete, for your sister's sake and your mother's.' Davey was less out of place. This was far from the first time he had sat here, but he was not his usual relaxed self either.

'I don't remember asking her to do that.' He sneered at Louisa, who stiffened in her seat next to Ada, and once more, she wished to throttle her little brother even as she tried to save him. 'And if I don't choose to pay her price?' he said to Inspector Lambert. 'Take me back t' borstal. See if I care.' The two of them stared each other down.

Ada'd had enough. 'Do you know why I am doing this, Pete?'

He didn't even turn to look at her.

'Shall I tell you? What I thought when you were born?'

That was enough of a non sequitur for him to turn round and peer at her. 'What?'

'I looked at you and wondered 'ow long you would live.

So did John. So did Walter. Though none of us would admit it out loud until you were a lot older and never in front of Mum. What's answer t' that question gonna be, Pete? Fourteen? Sixteen? Eighteen? Are you gonna become another dead brother?'

'I'm not gonna die in a borstal,' he scorned. 'You think I got this far because I can't handle myself?' His hand went to his hip, but there was no gun there now. It sat in an evidence box at Millgarth.

The last remnants of Ada's temper frayed. She jumped from the sofa, arms waving wildly. 'You're gonna handle yourself all the way t' end of a noose and an early grave!'

Louisa also stood, her hand grazing Ada's arm, a gentle, calming touch, but her focus was on Pete. She stared him down; the usual warmth of her hazel eyes turned to sharp ice. 'Perhaps I made a mistake.' She spoke in her haughtiest voice. 'My father said when the Children's Act passed, the borstals would help straighten out young ruffians; that they would be the exact shock to the system that wayward, lower-class boys like you, Peter, need to become upstanding citizens.'

Pete bristled, and Ada fought to keep her face blank. Louisa was attempting to rile her brother up and succeeding, but it hurt no less to have her family so casually dismissed. *This is part of a plan. It has to be part of a plan.*

'Let us hope he was right,' Louisa continued. 'And when I see you next in four years' time, that has turned out to be true. If an extended stay at a borstal can provide you with the discipline needed to prevent your life from ending in an increasingly inevitable execution, then it is for the best.' She turned to the two policemen. 'Do as you will, officers. I am sorry to have wasted your time, but we are done here. And, Inspector, remember exactly who,' she shot a significant glance back over at Pete, 'prevented you from saving your niece from a noose.' She crossed the room to the door.

Inspector Lambert's eyes glinted with steel. 'Oh, I will.'

'Is that supposed to scare me?' But Pete sounded increasingly less cocksure, and Ada did not blame him. She had to fight every sisterly instinct she had to not pull him out of the house and away – from Inspector Lambert and Louisa both.

'Ada,' Louisa called her name from the doorway. She still used her snobbiest voice, like a gentlewoman summoning her lowly companion to her side with little regard, despite everyone in the room knowing that for a fiction. Still, it instinctively set Ada's teeth on edge and made her want to tell Louisa where to shove it.

It's an act. There's a reason for this performance. Louisa has a plan.

So, she followed her across the room and to the door, ignoring Pete's disbelieving stare. 'You really going to leave me here with 'em?'

Louisa opened the door.

If we are going to do this act, I may as well commit.

'Maybe Miss Knight is right,' Ada said. 'Mum and Dad have been too gentle with you, not that I blame them after the years that came before you, but... you need proper discipline and structure and routine. I need you t' live, Pete. This might be your best chance t' be saved from yourself.' The lie came easy. It was possible she even half-believed it, for all she usually eschewed such things as discipline and structure and routine, for what else could be done with Pete?

But her promise remained the same. She could not let her mother lose her youngest son to the high walls of a borstal.

If this doesn't work, at least I can say I tried. I can't save Pete from himself. Mum will understand that.

They were out the door and walking away, her heart sinking with each step, when the shout came. 'Wait! Wait!'

Ada turned around.

Pete stood in the doorway. 'If I agree t' this ridiculous plan, then it's over? I can stay at 'ome?' The last question was the plea of a scared boy, no matter how much he would never admit it.

'Yes.' Ada took a step back inside the house, Louisa close behind. All three of them turned to the inspector for his confirmation, which came as a tight nod.

'Fine,' Pete muttered. He reached over to the table, past Davey and Inspector Lambert, and shoved his hat onto his head. 'Fine. Wait 'ere.' And he stomped out the door, shouldering his way past Louisa and Ada.

'So, what are the odds he doesn't come back?' Davey asked.

'He better,' was all Inspector Lambert said in reply, and Ada couldn't help but agree.

He did, in fact, come back an hour later with Kitty and her mother in tow. Both Jennings gave small, confused frowns at the sight of Ada and Louisa waiting for them on the sofa. Kitty was wearing one of her out-of-date ostentatious second-hand outfits again. The hat – a green floral monstrosity – was clearly at least two sizes too big, its rim resting just above her eyebrows.

'Miss Chapman, Miss Knight, this is a surprise,' Mrs Jennings said. 'Young Peter said it was urgent.'

'Shouldn't you be at home?' Kitty said to Ada. 'You look terrible.'

'Kitty,' her mother scolded as Pete laughed.

'It's fine,' Ada said. 'I do. But it was important we speak with you.'

'We wish to offer our help,' Louisa said.

'You need to leave, Kitty,' Ada added, making her voice as urgent as possible.

'Leave? I just got 'ere?'

'She means leave the country,' Louisa said.

Kitty peered at her and laughed awkwardly. 'Why would I do that?'

It was Ada who answered. 'Adam Richardson was blackmailing you.'

'Blackmail?' Kitty screwed up her face.

'He knew about yours and Pete's counterfeiting scheme,' Ada explained. 'So, the two of you concocted a plan. You even came up with a joint alibi, but you weren't at the picture house, even if Pete was. You were in town, shooting your blackmailer with Pete's gun.'

'What?' she cried. 'This is nonsense.' She laughed again like this was all a merry joke.

No one joined in, and her smile faltered.

'She's right,' Mrs Jennings added. 'This is the most ridiculous notion I've ever heard! Kitty! A killer!'

'Is it?' Louisa replied. 'It makes perfect sense to us.'

'So much less suspicious,' Ada continued, her gaze still intent on Kitty. 'If you go instead of Pete. That way, if anyone hears the gunshot and comes looking for the shooter, you're just a pretty young girl in a crowd, and who would suspect a pretty young girl of murder?' She inclined her head. 'Using their prejudices against them. It was clever, I'll give you that.'

'No!' Kitty shook her head, making her too-large hat twist from side to side. 'No! I don't...' She glanced at Pete, her eyes begging him for help.

'Kitty, drop it,' Pete told her. 'They've figured it out.'

Her mouth dropped open, and she stared at him in silent horror.

'You!' Mrs Jennings pointed at Pete accusingly. 'You did this!'

Pete ignored her. 'It's over.' He took Kitty's hand in his own. 'But my sister and her friend are willing to 'elp us get out of country.'

'Pete? What are you talking about?' Kitty gawked at him like he was bound for the asylum at High Royds. 'It was Miss Franklin who did that. I told you. She's a spy. A peeler's niece and everything.'

'She's even confessed,' her mother added. 'Why are you pointing fingers when the actual killer is already imprisoned? Miss Langwith was right. It would appear you are determined to call every last one of us a murderer.'

Ada nearly laughed out loud at the irony of Mrs Jennings talking about pointing fingers not a minute after she'd literally pointed at Pete and hid her mouth with her hand to contain it.

'Sorry, is something funny?' Mrs Jennings demanded.

'Miss Franklin's confession is false,' Louisa said, ignoring her question. 'And her police uncle will not rest until his niece is freed.'

Having composed herself, Ada added, 'And I won't see my brother in her place, and Kitty matters to Pete. We're offering them the chance t' escape. Go t' America. Start a new life there. We can give them money since all their stolen cash sits in an evidence locker in Millgarth or was returned by you to its rightful place with the suffragettes. We could get you a ticket, too, if you want.'

'I'm not going anywhere!' Kitty howled. 'Pete, let's go.' She tugged at his arm. 'Why are you letting her say these things?'

'Kitty's right,' Mrs Jennings said. 'You aren't shipping my daughter away for a crime she didn't commit.' Her steely voice made it clear this was not a debate.

'Your belief in your daughter is admirable,' Louisa said, 'but...'

'But stupid,' Pete finished for her. He turned back to Kitty and squeezed her hand. 'You don't have to lie anymore. I'm not getting locked up again because your mum won't accept truth. Please, Kitty, we need t' go! We can leave. We can be long gone before that peeler figures it out.'

'But you have to be quick,' Ada said. 'We can get you to Liverpool by evening. They always have ships bound for New York.'

'Here,' Louisa reached into her bag and pulled out a paper envelope, passing it to Pete. 'Take this. It should be enough to get you there and settled.'

Kitty's eyes flickered to the envelope. 'You'd really give us money to go to New York?'

'You're not going to New York, Kitty!' Mrs Jennings shouted. She sighed and said in a calmer voice to Louisa. 'Thank you for your kindness, ma'am, but it is unnecessary. It wasn't Kitty who shot Mr Richardson.' Ada waited for her next words with bated breath, but they never came.

'I am sure you wish to believe that, Mrs Jennings,' Louisa said with faked patience, 'but your belief in your daughter will not matter to a jury.'

'I didn't do it!' Kitty shouted. 'I stole money, yes, alright, I'll admit that. And I took a little extra when I swapped the real money for forgeries—'

'What?' exclaimed Pete.

Kitty continued over him. 'But I don't know owt about any blackmail or murder.'

Pete recovered quickly from his surprise. 'Kitty, let's just go t' New York. Please. We can 'ave a new life there.'

Kitty stared at him for a few seconds, at the envelope still in his other hand. Her thought process was easy to follow. She could go. Why not take the chance to leave, to do something as exciting as cross the Atlantic and move to New York with her sweetheart when the opportunity and money presented themselves? What if Pete had engineered this whole situation to trick his sister and her gullible posh friend, and she was ruining it?

She nodded.

'No!' Mrs Jennings grabbed her daughter's arm. 'No!'

Kitty tried to shake her mother off, but Mrs Jennings' grip only tightened. 'I've made my mind up,' she insisted, with a haughty toss of her head. 'I'm going.'

'We're going,' Pete added with a smirk at Mrs Jennings.

'No, you are not!' Mrs Jennings tried to drag her daughter away, but Kitty dug in her heels, and Pete held tight to her other hand. After a few moments, Mrs Jennings gave up, though she didn't let go of her arm. 'You would really do this to me? After everything I've done t' keep you safe! To keep you here! To save you from trouble this one'—she glared at Pete—'made. I didn't kill that bastard so you could swan off t' America and leave me with no one.'

And there it was.

There was a beat of silence. Mrs Jennings' words echoed around the small living room.

'Huh,' Pete said. 'You really did 'ave it in you. I honestly thought Miss Knight was talking shite.'

'You killed Mr Richardson?' Kitty's voice was quiet, disbelieving. A young girl – lost and scared – in a world flipped upside down.

Mrs Jennings had no answer.

'Because he was intending to blackmail you,' Louisa said. 'Your mother dealt with that problem.'

Kitty's eyes widened as she whispered, 'Is that true?'

Mrs Jennings' reply was just as quiet, a soft admission of guilt. 'Yes.'

It must have been loud enough, though, for the door to the stairs swung open, and Inspector Lambert and Davey stepped out.

Handcuffs dangled from the inspector's fingers. 'Bertha Jennings, you are under arrest for the murder of Adam Richardson.'

Chapter Thirty

A Hollow Victory

T his does not feel much like a victory,' Louisa admitted later that night. They were together in Louisa's study – the one place in their full house where no one would disturb them, except for Galapagos, asleep on her pillow.

It was their first chance to talk alone. The rest of the day had been taken up by going to the police station, talking to Ada's family, and explaining to Mrs Cohen and Miss Langwith what had happened to Mrs Jennings and her daughter. A particularly low point of the latter conversation was having to explain that Miss Jennings broke into the treasurer's safe by guessing the code – Mrs Green's birthday.

Ada sat perched on the edge of Louisa's desk, legs swinging and making her skirts swish, spirals of hair falling from her twists. Her naturally pale skin still had a sickly pallor to it that emphasised the red birthmark on her cheek, and dark circles ringed her eyes. She had turned down the opportunity to go straight to bed, though. If her face said she was ready to collapse at any moment, her swinging legs betrayed the anxious energy still coursing through her. Louisa still hoped to coax her to rest soon. But first, she suspected they both had a lot they needed to say.

'A murderess went to gaol, and an innocent woman walked free,' Ada said. 'A young woman stole from her fellows and will spend a year in a borstal. Even your father would agree that justice was served.'

She was right on that, at least, but he would not have approved of Louisa's actions today. Nor her motive.

Ada's thoughts must have aligned to hers as she sighed and added, 'And it was all to save my brother, who has shown little thanks and who I can't help but fear will squander the opportunity.' She tilted her head. 'Are you having regrets?'

She was about to deny it and stopped herself. She owed Ada honesty. 'I am wondering if we did the right thing. If *I* did the right thing.' This had been her scheme, even if she had done it for Ada's sake. The leaden feeling in her stomach increased at the words. Nothing that had happened since Inspector Lambert and Constable Wilkinson came out of that staircase had felt right.

Even though, as Ada said, Mrs Jennings and Kitty were guilty. Young Miss Richardson was without a father and would grow up an orphan. Mr Taylor grieved for a man who he once loved. The WSPU had still lost money donated by well-intended supporters, including working women who did not have the money to spare and yet had given it nonetheless in the hope of a better future.

But Peter was just as involved with that scheme, and he walks free.

And they had joined the WSPU and betrayed two of its members to the police.

'We did the legal thing to do,' she said to Ada. 'We even, arguably, did the moral thing to do. And yet it does not feel right.'

'But it wouldn't have felt right to let them get away with it, either,' Ada countered. 'Not like Mrs Pearce and Mrs

Parks. Mr Richardson was not like Mr Pearce. He had not hurt them.'

'He intended to blackmail Kitty.'

'Because she was defrauding the suffragettes!' But then all Ada's righteous anger melted, and she sighed again. 'As was Pete.' Her legs swung faster in agitation.

'And we saved him,' Louisa said bitterly. 'Kitty Jennings will lose a year of her life whilst he walks free. If anything, we have let a girl take the fall for a boy.'

Ada snorted. 'You do Miss Jennings a disservice there. Davey said in her anger at Pete's betrayal, she slipped up and admitted the entire scheme was *her* idea. My brother was a willing participant, I won't deny that, but he wasn't the brains of the operation. Miss Jennings was the one who told him to make the suggestion to his new *friends*.'

Hard to imagine Kitty Jennings – with her obstinate outfits and her high-pitched squeal of a laugh – as a criminal mastermind, but perhaps Ada was right. She did the girl a disservice, largely because she was a girl, which was highly hypocritical. How many times had she chafed at being told what women can and cannot do?

Though I cannot see 'women can commit crime, too' becoming a suffragette slogan any time soon. Even if it is a statement they have proven well these last few years.

'It is a fair point,' Louisa conceded. 'Though, she did herself no favours, spreading all those rumours.'

Ada shrugged. 'I guess her logic was that if she sowed chaos elsewhere amongst the suffragettes, it would distract them from her own ill-doing.'

'Well, it backfired quite spectacularly in that case.'

'Indeed. In her defence, whatever else she is, she is still only fourteen. Maybe you were already entirely logical at that age,' she said with a gentle, loving smile that softened any insult, 'but the rest of us still had a lot of learning to do.'

Louisa returned the smile ever so slightly. 'Speaking of adolescents and rumours, did you ever get an explanation for that ridiculous rumour they started?'

'That was just my brother being a little bastard. Kitty might have used it to her advantage once we started investigating, but that was not why they started it to begin with.'

'Do you think he will stop? Peter, that is.'

Ada tilted her head. 'Stop what?'

'Being a little...' Louisa could not bring herself to finish the sentence.

Ada gave a little breathy laugh before throwing her head back with a sigh. 'I want to believe he will. I want to believe he really intends to improve. And he's going t' be working with John. I trust John to keep an eye on him, but...it's not inspiring work at warehouse. Not that there's such a thing as inspiring work for men like my dad and brothers. I can hardly blame Pete for wanting to avoid that, even if I don't approve of his methods. He could have chosen better people t' steal from.'

There was a time when the concept of 'better people to steal from' would have shocked Louisa to her very core, but now she understood. Peter Chapman watched his father and older brothers work hard their entire adult lives for little reward. He viewed Louisa's relationship with Ada as something more akin to Miss Jain and her fancy fellow, that she was buying Ada's time and company and body. Was it so surprising he would not wish to spend his life at the mercy of the rich and powerful? That he would try to – literally – make his own money?

'He could have, yes,' she agreed.

'I am worried this was all for nowt,' Ada admitted. 'That all we've done is delay his, well, "increasingly inevitable execution." I believe those were your worryingly accurate choices of words.'

'I am—'

'Please don't apologise. You weren't wrong, and saying so did its job.'

Louisa swallowed her apology.

'But Pete aside, you can't tell me it would have felt more right to leave Miss Franklin in Armley Gaol when we knew she was innocent, no matter what our personal opinions on her are.'

She was right there. 'What do you think Miss Franklin will do now?'

Ada shrugged. 'She won't be welcomed back to WSPU. She has no home but the one with her aunt and uncle, but for all he has done for her, I can't imagine Inspector will forgive her any time soon. Nor do I think her ire at him has cooled.'

'And us?'

'For all we sided with him today, I don't think we're in Inspector's good books either.'

'I meant the WSPU.'

The news of Mrs and Miss Jennings' arrest, and the part Louisa and Ada played in bringing it about, had shocked Mrs Cohen and Miss Langwith. Whilst both agreed they had done the right thing, it was clear the underhanded way they had done it didn't sit well with either of them. Still, they had promised to keep it to themselves – there was still a future for the pair of them with the suffragettes if they wanted it. Inspector Lambert had similarly promised to keep their name out of any reports, calling them anonymous assets. When the story inevitably hit the headlines – a suffragette and her daughter arrested for murder and defrauding the WSPU might even make the front page – their names would not be attached to it.

Unless someone at Leeds Central Station talks to the press. Bertie Smith was a likely candidate. He had glared daggers at Ada from behind the front desk.

But we will cross that hurdle when and if it arrives.

'We shall see,' Ada said. 'I intend to keep fighting. If I can.' Her fingers tapped an anxious rhythm against the desk.

In the whirlwind of the last two days, they had never properly spoken about her stay in gaol. 'Even though it could mean being imprisoned again? Myself alongside you, possibly. I cannot imagine the mice can tell the cat to leave them alone a second time.' It was the final part of the deal they had made – Ada and her fellow suffragettes released under Cat and Mouse would be found 'unable to be returned to prison because of further health concerns.'

There was grim determination on Ada's face. 'Yes. I won't pretend it was a joyous experience, but I won't back down now. I want t' fight. For all of us, for you and me and Sophie. For Mabel, whether she remains in prison or not. Even for Miss Franklin and Mrs Jennings and Kitty.'

Louisa's hand covered hers, and it stopped moving. She squeezed softly. 'Then we shall.'

The conviction settled over her, reflected in Ada's face. Whatever would happen in the days and weeks and months to come, they intended to fight back.

Author's Note

Deeds and Words is a work of fiction but in writing it I drew from the real history of Leeds' suffrage movement.

Leonora Cohen was the secretary of the Leeds branch of the WSPU, whose best-known act of protest was smashing a cabinet in the Tower of London, as described in Chapter 5. Having given her a brief cameo in *The Murder Next Door*, it made sense for her to return here, and I hope I did her justice.

All the other suffragettes Louisa and Ada meet are fictional, as is the attack on Leeds Town Hall they participate in, but many of the local people and exploits they discuss are based on real people and events – Lillian Lenton and her escape via baker's van; Frank Rutter, art curator and supporter of the WSPU; Mary Gawthorpe and her radical newspaper; Dora Thewlis, Huddersfield's 'baby suffragette'.

The first record I could find for a major bombing incident by the WSPU in Leeds was January 1914. It is from this I drew the idea of the Leeds branch being at a turning point in the summer of 1913, a time when the WSPU's violence was escalating across the country.

And lastly, for any local readers wondering where the Queen Victoria statue is outside Leeds Town Hall, it was moved to Woodhouse Moor in 1937.

Acknowledgements

My thanks firstly to everyone – friends, family, fellow authors, readers, reviewers – who supported *The Murder Next Door* and my first foray into publishing. This sequel wouldn't exist without you.

Second book syndrome hit me hard, so my extended thanks and apologies to everyone who has had to listen to me whine about 'this stupid book' for over two years.

Some particular thanks must go to:

My mum and dad, for their love and support and making me the bookworm I am today.

Nicole, Michael and Paul, for their friendship and advice and always providing a listening ear.

Becky and Iram, for their friendship and encouragement and proudly introducing me to people as their author friend.

My editor, Charlie Knight, for their invaluable advice and helping me get my commas and dashes in the right place.

EM Harding and Katherine Shaw, for volunteering to read the rough draft of the early chapters and offering advice and encouragement that helped me to keep working on this book.

The online writing and book communities, where I've met so many amazing fellow authors and kind and enthusiastic readers and reviewers.

And finally, to you, the readers who have joined me for the second part of Louisa and Ada's story. I hope you enjoyed it!

About the Author

Sarah Bell is a queer indie author from Leeds, England. She has enjoyed reading and writing since she was a child and loves the chance to lose herself in other worlds and times. Outside of fiction, her interests include history and language. Not too surprisingly then, she has a degree in History & English from the University of Huddersfield.

Her debut novel *The Murder Next Door* was published in June 2021 and is the first in the *Louisa and Ada* series of historical murder mysteries.

Stay up to date with her writing news on:

Twitter/X, Blue Sky, Instagram, Tik-Tok (@sarahbellwrites)

And her website (sarahbellwrites.com)

www.ingramcontent.com/pod-product-compliance
Lightning Source LLC
Chambersburg PA
CBHW030924120726
47906CB00002B/468